FLASHING DARK

FLASHING DARK

BOBBIE FALIN

Bobbie J Falin

CONTENTS

To Sam, always

CHAPTER 1

Red-tagged

If I still had hair, I'd be pulling it out right about now. Luckily, it, along with a large portion of my sanity, had been sacrificed to the dark reaches of the vasty a long time ago.

"Recheck your board, Black Rock Seven," I said. "We are priority, docking directly to main station." The tiny dot of light that marked our dock space on the 3-D display in front of me was nowhere near the main shipping ring of Mandragala Station.

"No, ser." The Black Rock Seven Security Officer's expression was bored as he stared out of the comm screen at me. "The docket shows your payload is status: quarantined. You will proceed to Remote Dock D, berth three, as instructed."

"But that's impossible!" We were carrying six skids of apolytosium 17 ingots, an inert alloy used in spaceship hulls! "Check again."

"Look, Captain..." his tone took on the forced patience of someone who dealt with brain-atrophied spacers every day.

"Zant," I said. "Captain Vivi Zant." The name was on the screen right in front of him.

"Captain Vivi Zant. The docket says your payload is red-tagged. If you have a problem with that, take it up with the dockmaster."

I had a major problem with that. There was a ship, crewed by a bunch of card-carrying union bastards, waiting for our cargo. By the time we hit the clamp rings, we'd be an hour late. Now, this guy was telling me there would be an additional holdup while we straightened out this quarantine mess. Small free-haulers like the *Thief's Hand* didn't keep a union ship waiting in dock. It wasn't healthy—economically or physically.

"Why?" I asked.

"What, ser?" His patient tone was wearing thin.

"Why the quarantine?"

"We do not have that information, ser. Please stand by for Mandragala Station docking instruction."

I threw myself back in my pilot couch and scowled at the hologram mock-up of the station as I waited for a green light to signal Mandragala had cleared the *Thief's Hand* for final approach into port. To Remote Dock D, berth three.

Most Black Rock Station staff enjoy their job sitting on the edge of Earth Alliance star systems, swatting at the little spacer mice squeaking to get past their vicious paws.

Does it sound like I hate them? No. As a former Earth Alliance Space Marine, I used to be one of them. Six years ago, spacer time. My ship's time. Because that's all that matters to me on the scale of things. And I was still running errands for the military out on the Rim when they tugged my chain. Still paying for the things they put inside my head and body when I served. Those things let me do their jobs. They are things I really want to keep so I can continue to transport cargo between EA stations and the Outer Rim.

I caught a stealthy movement from the corner of my eye.

Crap! I'd left the vid-link with Black Rock open! I lunged forward to cut the connection as Saurubi landed on the console beside me in a flurry of red, dusky blue and bronze.

She thrust her face at the screen with an angry hiss.

For once, The Mother Universe blessed me with a sliver of luck—the Black Rock officer had turned his attention down to the board in front of him.

I caught my business partner/co-captain by the back of her short vest and jerked down hard. She slid off the console with a screech of claws on metal. Thirty-two kilograms of sinew, bone, and fur hit the deck with a solid thump.

At the same moment, a light on the console bloomed green and a stream of digits scrolled down the in-system nav screen.

Black Rock Seven looked up at me with an expression that asked, "Why are you still here?"

I flashed him a brittle smile. "Remote Dock D it is, ser." I cut the vid link, returning Black Rock and the *Hand* back to their isolated bubbles in space.

Saurubi sprang back to her feet, twitching her ears to shake out any rumples I'd caused to her fur, and leaned on the console to display an intimidating set of canines at the now-dark screen.

"What does he say?"

"He says we've got trouble." I keyed a go code to confirm the co-ordinates, then sat back to rub my fingers over my bare scalp. "What the hell, Saura! Have you lost your fuzzy blue mind? You heard the scuttlebutt at the last drop point!" Rumor was the EA was running security in the Inner Systems so tight that Black Rock personnel were spoiling for any excuse to add some excitement to their day. "Messing with them is dangerous."

"Not as dangerous as me."

I gave her a sidelong look. "That's when you're close enough to hook your nasty little claws into them. Not out here."

That pleased her. It didn't distract her. "What does he say?" she asked again.

"Our cargo is quarantined."

Pointed furry ears bent back, flat to her head, the edges turned outward. "How can quarantine metal?" She made a rude snorting sound. "Tell is wrong."

"Saura—"

"What? You are warrior, Vivi. You must be fierce in the presence of stupidity!"

Fierce, yeah. But I knew the difference between exhibiting 'fierce' and exhibiting 'bad attitude', my past being riddled with incident reports of the latter.

I was trying to do better these days.

Besides, if I pushed this guy too hard, he could send out one of his nasty short-range drones to put a hole in our ship, then bump us into the local star. Security maintained in Black Rock's eyes.

Saura clasped her hands behind her back and began to pace the generous four steps our ship bridge allowed.

I sat in silence, giving her time to regain control over a temper that matched the flaming red pouf of fur she wore in a soft death-hawk cut.

Tabisee are similar in body structure to Humans. They walk upright with forward-bending knees and their facial features are comparable to ours, except for their large, slit-pupil eyes. Their bodies are sinewy, lithe, and covered in fur. They have sharp white teeth and lethal claws, which they considerately keep sheathed most of the time.

And any comparison you might be making to a small earth animal should stop right there. Tabisee are not soft or cuddly—well, their fur is soft—but they are definitely not cuddly. They do not have whiskers. They do not purr. Their tempers are short, and they are brutally honest and pragmatic in nature.

They also hate earth cats, probably because of the parallels Humans ignorantly try to draw from their appearance.

Saura stands one-and-a-half meters tall. The tips of her upright ears barely brush my shoulder, but on a bad day, she can take out a squad of Space Marines in three minutes flat. I've seen her do it, and it wasn't always on a bet for beer money and laughs. Did I mention Tabisee have short tempers? I have a healthy respect for the co-owner of the *Thief's Hand*.

She stopped pacing and looked at me, the bronzy wires intricately tattooed into her skin glinting as if they had a life of their own. "What does quarantine business mean?"

"For us? We can't deliver our cargo until they remove the restrictions."

"Cannot get paid." She summed up the problem precisely.

"Yeah..." I watched her ears shift through a series of positions, open and forward, upright and turned outward, then tilted back and flattened: thought, deeper consideration, then irritation.

"Not good." It was an idiosyncrasy of Saurubi's that she dropped what she considered superfluous words, particularly pronouns. It was something about Tabi Astrogators lack of concern for people and their specifics. Inversely, she said Humans talk too much.

"Worse than not good." I said glumly. "If we can't get our money we can't make our lien payment for the *Hand*. If we can't make our payment..." What that meant sent another wave of panic through me.

Panic was not a useful reaction. I dug down deep, the way I'd learned to dig when we leaped from a dropship into a shitstorm of weapon fire during a Marine raid on a pirate's nest.

That, however, had only been risking death. This could strike to the very heart of our existence with an ugly finality, sending Saura back to the Tabi Empire and me to the life of a scrub, begging on the docks.

"You will fix, Vivi," Saura said brightly. In her logic, the problem was created by Humans, therefore, I should resolve it.

Dutifully I found the bedrock level of confidence—the idiotic Human optimism—that told me I could do anything I had to.

"It's a stupid mistake," I told her. "I can fix it."

***

There was no time to start at the bottom and work my way up, so I bypassed the dockmaster and went directly to the person in charge. We were still two days out from Mandragala when Stationmaster Hu returned my call.

"Captain Zant," he greeted. "I understand your concern, but there are unconfirmed reports of a slagmander nest in one of the ore bins on Galray. We must proceed under the assumption that your cargo is contaminated." His expression did not invite discussion.

I knew about the little red lizards indigenous to Galray's rocky surface. They were merely an annoyance and the harsh climate kept their numbers under control. Their excretions, however, carried a deadly parasitic infection that spread like wildfire in close-packed Human settlements. Over a century ago, when operations first opened on the planet, a contaminated cargo had killed over a thousand settlers at its destination world, as well as wiping out a ship crew and nearly half of Galray Company's production staff.

That's the way things worked in space; you adapted fast or you died. Sometimes you didn't get the chance to adapt.

"Ser, we took on our cargo from a low-orbit foundry, where slagmander contamination is not possible." Galray's mining companies, which produced metals critical to the hardening of ship hulls, now lifted the ore off world by vacuum well and smelted it by concentrating the local star's energy with giant mirrors in a process called sol melt to prevent another infestation and the shutdown of their world's exports. The ingots, strapped to skids, transferred directly from the foundry into a ship's hold. The whole operation took place in a vacuum as another preventative measure against slagmander contamination. Nothing in space touched planetside and no living thing could survive the process. Cargo flowed out of the vast facilities every day without incident.

He shrugged. "Station management has chosen to err on the side of caution. Until the quarantine expires, you can't shift your cargo out of your hold."

"How long is that?"

"The quarantine period is forty-two days."

My heart tried to twist out of my chest. The note on our ship was due thirteen hours after we hit the dock cradle.

"Fourteen standard days have already passed while we were in transit," I pointed out. It was a useless argument; even if we shaved off that time, we couldn't survive the remaining twenty-eight days of quarantine any more than we could survive forty-two days. We had hours to fix this or we would lose our ship.

"We can't take the risk. The full isolation period is in effect. However," he took a deep breath.

"What?" I jumped on the word.

"The medical consensus is that you'd be dead by now if the contamination had breached your ship's life areas. We are willing to attach a decontamination unit to your debarkation tube and allow you access to the station to conduct your business. The ship's hold, however, will remain sealed for the length of the quarantine."

It was the best I was going to get from him.

"Thank you, ser." I thumbed off the connection and sat, staring off into the air.

This was bad.

A stinging pain on the back of my hand snapped me out of my dark thoughts.

"Ow."

Saura lifted her claw. Her ears tipped in question.

"No one is taking the *Thief's Hand*, Saura." I said fiercely as I wiped the back of my hand against my thigh. The blue fabric of my shipskins would absorb the blood droplet and cycle it with my dead skin cells and sweat. "We won't let them."

We couldn't let them.

"Can go to frontier, Vivi," she suggested. "Not put in to port."

Just take the ship and cargo and leave... It took a moment for that to run through my brain. As desperately tempting as it sounded, it was impossible. "No, Saura, we can't." I'd been forced into spacer life on the run once. It was not something I wanted to move back into. "Big H would never stop searching for us if we skipped out on our loan. He has too many connections." His flunkies would climb all over each other to do him a favor, hoping to catch a crumb of his gratitude. "We'll work this out. I refuse to make you a criminal."

She sniffed. "Already criminal."

"Not that way. Not hounded to the edges of charted space."

Her ears tilted forward, twisting. "Then what do?"

"We go in. Scriver can advance us enough money on the cargo to make our lien payment to Big H. Once he's off our backs, I can work on getting this situation cleared up. If we're stuck in port for the whole quarantine period, I'll pick up odd jobs to keep us going." I didn't want to think beyond that to the legal repercussions of our failure to deliver our cargo to the destination ship on time. I sighed. "We may be looking at some tough times."

"Tough times," she echoed acknowledgment. With the high fees on Mandragala Station and our strained budget, we were facing cold, hunger, and thirst.

We'd been through tough times before.

CHAPTER 2

Things to Lose

The magnetic cradle rings of Dock D sent a tremor through the *Hand* as they clanged down on the cylinder of our outer hull.

"Dahphuu!" Saura spat a curse and scrambled to reposition black and white stones on her Go boards.

"Wouldn't it be easier to play on virtual gameboards?" I asked as I scooped a stray white piece off the deck and set it in a free space, bracketed on three sides by black markers.

Pinned in, like us, with options closing, I thought.

"Not same." She plucked up the piece and moved it to another position. "Is physical connection to opponent."

There would be many connections to opponents. I'd never figured out how it worked. Non-Earth Alliance species, outside of military roles, were not allowed inside the EA inner systems, so her presence on Mandragala was breaking the law. Yet, every time we hit the farthest-out stations, a rumor spread through the Go community that Saurubi Cerros Syrhas was back and the calls came flooding in. Everyone wanted to challenge the reigning Interplanetary Agon Cup Champion.

For International Go Federation records, Saura was a retired EA Space Marine; therefore, by reason, she must be Human, right? Her adoring fellow competitors knew better and they guarded their little, not-so-secret secret with zealous enthusiasm.

As long as she kept her furry blue mug off our ship screens and her self inside the ship, the EA ignored her presence, even though they had to know she was Tabisee from her five-year stint in the EA Space Marines. Maybe it was gratitude for our continuing service when they called us up for action on the Outer Rim.

Gratitude? Was I an idiot? There is no gratitude in space.

But they weren't asking questions for whatever reason, so it worked for me.

"I'll check in, so don't get too wrapped up in your games," I warned her.

"You will fix, Vivi." Go boards were rapidly covering every open surface in the control room.

I wished I had the same confidence in me that she had. When those dock rings clamped down on us, the dock fees—thank the gods, stations couldn't charge a breathable air tax anymore—had begun sucking away the last of our limited resources. It gave me a mental image of creds draining from our account the way ice slewed off a comet's tail.

"Shutting down ship grav system." My fingers glided over a console, disabling systems we could do without while docked. My stomach fluttered as our gravity ring began to slow its rotation. The station spin would transfer enough force to keep the Go boards in place and let us move about the ship. We would simply have to exercise caution to prevent bumps and bruises.

Unfortunately, shutting down our grav ring also meant losing our primary source of heat. But we would manage that, too.

"Will have good reason to use workout equipment," Saura said, referring to the chamber full of resistance-based exercise equipment along the inner side of the grav ring. Earth Alliance regulations required spacers to log a certain number of hours to space-time ratio to keep physically fit, and they would ground anyone who didn't log the time. I ranked one percent above the minimum allowable. She used the damn things every day—and she didn't even have to report it!

"That's why we wear shipskins," I sang out defensively. Along with the other functions the fabric in our suits performed, it worked our muscles and circulatory system with our body movements to keep us healthy.

"Not enough." Her ears came forward in exasperation as she looked up at me. "Six weeks watching vids is bad!"

"Ugh." I gave a grunt of disagreement as I finished the last of my java and set the cup on the galley counter before she could cover every surface in there, too. "Old adventure movies are not bad for me." She simply refused to appreciate the Human artform of video entertainment. "You should watch them with me."

Her golden eyes narrowed to slits and her upper lip curled to flash sharp incisors. "Gives you bad ideas."

Was the queen of attitude actually criticizing me? "What? You mean the violence and drama?" I threw my arms out as wide as the passageway allowed and grinned.

She gave me a dark look.

Okay. Being locked up on our ship, freezing our asses off while a station full of activity boomed outside our hatch, inaccessible to her and unaffordable to both of us, was going to be hard on us.

"I know, not a hero." I dropped my arms and sighed. I was Vivi Zant, the whack job space marine who obsessed over weird things. I knew what other corps members had whispered. The sooner I could resolve this and get away from here, the sooner I could exhale the anger and resentment—and fear—twisting up inside of me.

Why the hell was the station taking so long to attach the debark tube to our hatch?

I took a deep breath. "Let's head for the Outer Rim when we're done here. We can pick up a security job or something. Forget about this inner system shit for a while." In the inner systems Saura couldn't step a foot off the ship, but on the frontier she was just another species in the mix.

She didn't look up at me, but I saw her ears perk in silent approval.

The soft chime I was waiting for finally sounded. Our physical connection to the station was up and running, ready to clean away all those dreaded, nonexistent parasites when I opened our hatch.

"Disconnecting from ship system." I pressed a node on the flexible, bio-mechanical circuitry board buried beneath the skin of my left forearm. Felt a flicker of loss as the perivision in my left eye cleared. The implant, known as wetware, was the thing that set a spacer apart from surface-bound population. Coupled with hardware in our heads, it linked us to critical systems inside our ship, enabling us to respond in fractions of a second, and, out on the docks, allowed us to link with equipment and things like bay doors, while most "bounders" had to do their thing with key codes and slide cards. The augmentation was a precious gift, courtesy of the EA Space Marines—a lure to make people enlist. Most spacers, including me, could never have afforded the enhancements on our own.

With most of the console lights on the bridge darkened, and the nerve-vibrating rumble of the grav-ring gone quiet, the *Hand* was snoozing in Saura's capable control.

I moved on to the next step, enabling my station feeds. Hardware in my brain searched out and made a connection with the station systems. Ship feeds always ran in the peripheral vision of the left eye. Now, as they disappeared, I gained another stream of information in the outer corner of my right eye. Station time, maps, FAQ lines. Adverts. All available and eager to respond to the twitch of eye muscle or a querying thought.

I concentrated on the lift location that would carry me up to the main ring, pulling the information out of the Mandragala feed.

I could have made the necessary calls to our lien holder and cargo broker from our ship, but I refused to risk a rejected call. The conversations with Big H and Scriver had to take place face to face as soon as possible.

Saura was watching me now, her golden eyes dark with concern. "Don't have to stay on station ring overnight, Vivi," she said gently.

"It's okay." I swallowed against the tightness in my throat. "It's been two days since I talked to Hu. Scriver should have this mess straightened out by now." Optimism. The stuff dreams—and failure—are made of. We were both familiar with the slow speed of Human bureaucracy. "I'll rack on the ring for the night."

Sleeping in one of the cheap, horizontal pod stacks in a secure area on the dock would be noisy and cold, but, for me, it would be preferable to any flophouse in Spacertown. Just the thought of that place drove a rush of sound and smell through my brain that made me want to retreat to the darkness of my cabin and never come out. "I'll get this fixed before I come back."

Okay. I had twelve hours and a plan of execution. Heading down the passageway past our cabins, I pulled a light jacket from the rack beside the airlock and slipped it over my cobalt blue shipskins so I would meet station 'decency' codes.

They don't call the tight, multi-functional suits spacers wear 'skins' for no reason. Designed to protect from extreme temperature changes, and to control cell-shed while stimulating muscle-tone and blood flow, they fit our bodies like a second skin. Most ringers, or dockworkers, don't give a second thought to them, though there are always a few weirdoes who work dockside for prurient interest. Entering areas where the stationers work and live, however, is a different matter. If we want access to places beyond the docks, rules require a thigh-length loose garment worn over our skins.

All I can say is, if the sight of my skinny, bald, fifty kilogram, hundred seventy-seven millimeter tall body, with the breast bulge of a prepubescent girl, stirs their interest, hooray for them. As long as it keeps their creepy attention focused on me as an adult, and off any kids, I don't care.

"Keep a feed open in case I need to talk to you," I called back to Saura before I hit the hatch release and stepped out into a small, white-walled vestibule. A yellow light blinked insistently above a box stuck on the surface to my right.

'Caution! Entering decontamination chamber', flashed in my perivision. 'Please put on supplied eye protection before activating.'

"Yeah, yeah," I muttered. I pulled the eye coverings out of the box and put them in place while the *Hand's* hatch slid closed behind me. When I touched a red bar that flashed 'activate' on the surface of the enclosure in front of me, blasts of air and light slid over my body. Then the white surface in front of me parted. I returned the eye protection and I stepped out into a long white tunnel on the other side. At the bottom I could see a red glow from the letters of a virtual sign floating outside the sealed opening. It read "Quarantine."

I had another word for Mandragala Station management: discretion. Apparently, it was missing from their vocabulary. Letting a rumor of potential plague spread inside a closed environment like a station could be nearly as deadly as an actual threat. People could panic and panicked people were known to react stupidly. Of course, there was also a certain level of clearance required to access Dock D, so they must have some faith in their workers discretion.

"This is all a crap mistake," I repeated under my breath as I walked the fifteen meters down the debarkation tube.

A station technician dressed in white, accompanied by a dour-faced, blackclad security officer, waited at the bottom. The tech straightened her posture as I came into view. Bracing herself for whatever would happen next?

I understood her reaction. I could even sympathize with it. We spacers are a crazy lot. We come in to civilization trying to lose the phantoms of the lonely deep dark, only to end up frustrated when we can't make the Human connection. Most resort to becoming drunk and angry, which only fires more hostility around us. Fear that some mad hatter might damage the station doesn't help attitudes on either side. It's a self-perpetuating cycle: stationers mistrust spacers and spacers mistrust stationers.

Quarantine could make for an even worse situation. The thought of losing a ship could drive someone to an extreme action—like making a run for it and taking a piece of the station along with them.

Instantaneous vacuum does bad things to the air bubbles that are Human structures in space.

I didn't believe I would ever be crazy enough to rip the maglocks off a station and vac it, but you couldn't let the people in charge know you had limits on what you were willing to do to protect yourself or they'd walk on your back and try to stand on your head.

I took my own deep breath. Easy, Zant, there's no reason to go to war here.

At least, not yet.

"Vivi Zant, owner and captain, *Thief's Hand.*" I forced a smile.

The tech didn't look overwhelmed by the warm and fuzzies, either. "Idents." She held a hand-scanner up to the seal.

I lifted my left arm and she passed it over my wetware.

"You have my ship under quarantine. Who else do you think would bring it in to port under in those conditions?" I growled at her.

Okay, maybe there was a little pent up frustration.

"Can't be too careful, ser," she said in practiced, non-confrontational response. "Please breathe into the respiration tube in front of you."

I pulled the sanitary cover off the little nipple sticking out of the seal and breathed into it.

She studied the small data screen in her hand and I counted off the seconds while the whole interaction transpired. Mother Universe, it was eating precious time!

"Captain Zant is clear," the tech announced to someone at a remote location. I noticed the guard beside her still kept his hand on his weapon as she passed the scanner over a section of the seal. They stepped back as it split apart and I walked through onto Station Dock D.

The tang of metal and oil hit me hard. Gods, I hated that smell! I might have lived out my whole life never knowing it existed, breathing fresh planetary air and feeling the sun on my skin, if the raiders hadn't hit my home on New Bounty.

But they had, and because of it, I knew the stink of station docks far too well. It was the way of the universe.

"Have a good day, ser." The tech and her escort descended the ramp ahead of me and were gone.

I strode for the lifts, to take the long ride up to the main station.

CHAPTER 3

Sidelined by Hope

Mandragala's commercial shipping ring echoed with the slam and bang of giant machines moving cargo from ship to station to vendor, or to ship again. Most of the Human traffic kept to the warmer central area of the ring, safely away from massive machinery and mountains of shipping containers, where thieves, pickpockets, and worse might lurk. The lowlifes hanging out there still found prey in drunken spacers and new meat—the confused and bedazzled newcomers to space that had not yet learned the wariness necessary for survival. At least once every few weeks one of them never got a second chance to learn.

Like I said; you adapt fast...

I stood on the outer border of the main promenade, shivering in the icy, dead air while I searched the pile of rundown prefab buildings stacked high along the wall of the station's central core. The pile, iced with its overlay of lights and adverts, had grown since our last trip in. I could have watched the colors and movement of the ads for hours—my own cheap form of entertainment—but I was on a mission to save our livelihood and they were making it difficult for me to find what I was looking for. I cut back the commercial overlays in my perivision to 'cargo-related only' and studied the quieter business signage that remained after the dancing, blazing carnival of lights faded. High on the pile wall, bilious, blazing green, meter-tall letters declaring "Seven Star Cartage" sizzled over the duller shingles of lawyers, insurers, and expediters.

Scriver once told me spacers were drawn to the color green. He speculated it was some deep, anthropological thing, based on our planetary origins; like an association of safety with the trees we had descended from. I thought it might be because it shared the color with our vacuum food packs.

Whatever.

I worked my way through the press of bodies toward that area of the stack.

Though the crowd was not dense, I occasionally felt the bump of another body. Most of them were accidental: people caught up in conversation or lost in thought. But every once in a while the bump was harder. More purposeful. Like a stationer spotting a bald head and forgetting there wasn't room up here for factories to make their necessities, or fields to grow their food. Forgetting they needed someone to bring in the stuff that kept them alive.

Yeah, assholes. You're welcome.

My resentment faded by the time I climbed the five levels of narrow metal stairs to my destination. Mandragala's gravity had me fervently vowing to work out the next time Saura suggested it. Right now, however, I had to get to the business of saving said exercise equipment.

"Zant, good to see you." The smile on Jakub Scriver's craggy, slightly less than handsome face looked a bit tight around the edges as he beckoned me inside his two-meter square cube of office. "Come in. Sit.

"You look like hell," he added. It was a little, not-funny joke we shared.

"Still adjusting to station environment," I told him as I looked around.

The place was the same old box. Though it was small, I knew, coupled with the blazing green sign, it ranked high on the station's rental scale. Lucky for him, with records stored and accessible on-demand through brain implants and three-dimension personal screens, he had no need for a larger space.

"How's Saurubi?"

The question caught me off guard. Not the mention of my partner's name—he had given us our first job after we bought the *Thief's Hand* and we considered him a friend. It was just that social chatter during work hours in his little, expensive cube was not his style.

A delaying tactic for bad news? My heart rate increased as I slid into one of the two chairs he squeezed in for customers. I decided to play the social game for a little while, though it wasn't my strong point. We needed him as close to one hundred percent on our side as we could get him. "I left her covering every available surface on the *Hand* with Go boards."

"You don't worry all that activity will start the EA asking questions?"

Yeah, I did, but in the years since our discharge, the Tabi Empire must have filed some kind of inquiry with the EA regarding the whereabouts of their expensive little Astrogator and nothing had happened yet.

I shrugged. "The EA knows where she rests her furry ears every night." They sure as hell didn't exhibit any offended sensibilities when they handed us an assignment on the Outer Rim. All we could figure was the personnel exchange with the Tabi Empire must have moved to another level.

A lone picture frame on his desk caught my attention. It displayed a smiling woman holding a little boy. My heart gave a twist. "New?" I gestured toward it.

"Oh." Scriver tried to look casual, like he'd forgotten it was there. "Actually, we formed an official union a few years ago."

In that few seconds pause, I had searched out the station's social announcements: the kid was born right after we left Mandragala last trip. The woman was pretty. She had hair. The kid in her lap partially blocked view of her body, but she probably had tits, which was more than I could claim.

Scriver and I had had a brief brush before our second contract. But the years lived in a grav well for him, as opposed to months spent in fold for me, hadn't played well for partners in a relationship. It was an unhappy detail—or questionable benefit—of life as a spacer.

I asked him about the kid. I like kids, though I have no plans for any of my own. I have my reasons.

The boy was three years old. Scriver showed me another picture. I smiled and told him the kid was damned cute. He was.

Deep down, I fought off a terrible pang of sadness. Three was such an innocent age.

"So, what's the situation down on Dock D?" he asked as he shut down his personal vid feed.

Finally, we were getting to the meat. "They made me blow into a rubber tube, pronounced me 'clean', and left the external cargo doors covered with red tape." I leaned forward, elbows on my knees. "When did they notify you of the quarantine?"

"A few hours before you made Black Rock."

I stared at him. "You were expecting a coffin ship to hit the outer system!"

He grimaced. "Let's just say I was pleasantly surprised when they told me your face showed up on Black Rock's monitors."

Nice he threw the word 'pleasantly' in there. "What have you done since then?"

"What do you think, Zant?" His voice took on an edge of anger. "I have to keep Seven Star afloat. I was looped in when you talked to Stationmaster Hu. I've run through all my contacts since then." The hard veneer of his business armor cracked. "I've tried, Vivi. Station management won't budge on the length of quarantine."

Shit. "Okay. But we still have to collect on our contract."

"Yeah, that's a problem." Light glinted off the fashionably oiled waves of his thick, dark hair as he ran a hand through it. "You know the contract says payment on delivery."

I felt a creeping chill of foreboding. "The cargo is sitting in Dock D, ready for you to take possession."

"In forty-two days! I can't pay you until I take actual possession."

"Jakub! We have to collect at least a partial payment now!"

He shook his head.

"This quarantine is trumped up and you know it!"

"I do. And I would help you if I could. But we have a bigger issue mucking things up, Vivi. A few weeks back a rumor about a scheduled meeting between the EA and the Whooex Union Trade Consortium hit the boards."

Well, shit.

***

When Humans finally met aliens, we didn't encounter just one species. We met a whole Union of fourteen Star Associations. And it wasn't our dazzling charm that drew them to us: it was our mode of space travel.

In the mid-twenty-first century, we found a crashed alien ship on one of Saturn's moons and the real Human push into space began. Within twenty years, we went from sublight speed to a subspace drive that shortened lightyears to years for adventurers willing risk cryo sleep to venture out into the Vasty.

The day after we established our hundredth colonial outpost the Whooex Union of Stars came calling. They did not come bearing an invitation to join in hand, or claw, however; they came with an ultimatum for us to cease the use of our subspace drive. It seemed our method of travel cut across an alternate dimension, threatening the life there. One of the diplomats explained that they, too, had used that method of travel in the early stages of their expansion into space—until the threatened dimension declared war upon them. After a few years of devastating war, they had developed a new method of space travel.

That was fine with us: we were willing to accept a few years slowdown in our colonial expansion in exchange for a better mode of travel.

That was not what the Whooex Union had in mind. Apparently, they simply wanted us to stop using our method of space travel. Otherwise, they explained, our inter-dimensional neighbors would declare inter-dimensional war on us.

No one had come to us threatening retaliation. We weren't the nervous species in the room. "Us, as in Humans?" we asked.

'No," they said. "Us. As in the whole Whooex Union."

Obviously, they had never dealt with Humans before. The now-famous mother of Human advancement into intergalactic space, Chloe Patel made a suggestion to the Whooex diplomats. "Share your system with us. Or," she said, "we must continue to use our destructive drive."

They threatened to destroy us. Our people—as fine a bunch of steady-handed negotiators as ever existed—said maybe so, but we could probably get in a few good licks on one of those other dimensions first. Then the diplomats could try to explain that to their angry, ancient foes.

In the end, they had no choice. It was admit us to the Whooex Union, with access to their drive, or go to war.

Of course, there were stipulations. The Earth Alliance was accepted as junior, secondary member with limited trade benefits. We could handle that, just as long as they gave us full access to the new, for us, drive technology.

It took several decades to master the tech. After that, we gained contact with the several species, including the Tabi Empire, whose spatial territories butted against our own. Frontiers formed and limited trade developed—small time stuff, but good enough for a fledgling alliance. But the crown jewel—admission to the Moneyworld, the Whooex Union Trade Consortium—remained beyond our reach.

Not everyone in the Whooex welcomed us, however. For reasons unknown, the Endar hated us from the moment we sat down to discuss the drive situation with the delegation. They made it abundantly clear they would prefer to send us back to the Stone Age. It seems, however, the Whooex Union has a rule in its charter stating any civilization comprising a hundred worlds or more is an established society and potential membership material.

Lucky Humans? Maybe. We now suspect we know who finessed that perfectly timed bit of legalese, though there's no way to confirm it.

Saurubi once told me the EA should not be too hasty in congratulating itself on its connections, real or imagined. She said some of them could prove more trouble than they were worth. When I asked her to explain, she refused to elaborate.

***

"Jakub," I said. "What has gaining admission to the Whooex Trade Consortium got to do with you advancing us payment for our cargo?"

"Are you from the next galactic arm, Zant? It means we're up for full membership to the Whooex Union! It means an embassy and access to all the markets on the Moneyworld. It means vast commercial potential!"

I didn't know whether to laugh or curse. "The EA has been through this process twice in the last one hundred and sixty years!

Everyone gets their hopes pumped up and the Endarans block us before it comes to vote."

"Vivi! Right now we're collecting paltry crumbs of trade from the few allies willing to do business on the Outer Rim. The Moneyworld is the chance to contact with thousands of worlds! Think of the markets this would open!" He leaned forward, his expression rapt with anticipation. "One hundred and sixty years as a junior member. A hundred and sixty years! They can't keep rejecting us forever. Our charm has got to win them over eventually."

Yeah. I didn't think the Endarans were succumbing to our charm or anything else Human. Saura said they vehemently hated us. She couldn't tell me why, but said their dislike was one of the chief reasons the Tabi Empire chose to ally with us.

"How long is this..." I wanted to say fiasco, but decided it would not be helpful, "vote going to take?"

That sobered him a bit. "Within half a Sol year."

"Can businesses on this station survive a half year of this?" I waved a hand, unable to put a word to the situation. I knew that Saura and I couldn't.

"You can imagine the reaction it's stirred," he said, his expression pleading for me to understand the effect the news had excited on the station—hell, was probably having on every market in the Earth Alliance. "Capital's in short supply on the station right now. It's not just me, Vivi. For the past few weeks, everyone's been sitting tight, waiting for... I don't know what." He sighed. "Anyway, loose funds have dried up all over Mandragala."

"Has the Whooex given the EA the coordinates for the Moneyworld yet?" To this point, they had kept the location of the Trade Consortium World a secret from us. If they had shared that information with our highest levels of bureaucrats, the rumor would be out there, no matter what its level of confidentiality. Then even I would have to concede there was some legitimate basis for this mess.

"They say it's coming." His expression belied his confident tone.

Great. A rumor had preempted our lives. "I don't care about the Moneyworld. I care about keeping my ship. In the next ten hours I have to make at least a partial payment to Big H for the *Hand*."

"I wish I could help you, Vivi, I sincerely do! But if I can't move your cargo, I can't pay you."

I knew Scriver well enough to recognize when he was not going to budge on his position. Getting payment from him before the cargo shifted out of our hold was a dead issue.

But he was also at risk here.

"You know something's not right, Jakub," I said. "If they thought we presented a real threat to this station they wouldn't let us come near it. Why are we sitting in Dock D for forty-two days if they don't believe we're a danger to the station?"

"Because the contagion kills in forty-eight hours. Obviously, you're not infected, but that's not necessarily true for the cargo—"

"It's sol-smelted metal! Everything is done off world. Besides, if the station believes our cargo's a threat, why don't they order us to scuttle it and simply decontaminate the hold?" Not really "simply", but simpler than quarantine.

"Dammit, Vivi!" He hissed as he glanced at the upper right corner of the room, where a station security "eye" monitored all his business transactions. "Don't make the situation worse than it is!"

Make it worse for whom? Delay in delivering the cargo to his customer equaled penalties in his own contract.

Which was exactly the solution I was grasping for. "Look, this has you in a bind, too."

Still irritated with my previous suggestion, he gave a curt nod of agreement.

I continued. "You hold the forwarding contract on our cargo, right? So, let us run out the quarantine by carrying it on the next leg of the haul instead of sitting here, burning through time and money.

Advance us enough credit for supplies and let us have the contract. The quarantine will expire before we reach your end user and it saves you six weeks of penalties. You can pay us for both legs when we deliver it, less the supplies. Neither of us loses." And it legally put us beyond the reach of the repossession process until we had Big H's money. "File the contract and we'll be out of here in hours. You have to pay somebody to haul it, now or later."

"I can't do that, Vivi." His hand flattened on the desktop with a smack. "Hann Brothers holds that transport contract. They delayed their departure time, waiting for it to arrive."

"Why didn't they just pull out when the quarantine came down?"

He gave me a sour smile. "Station management didn't want negative feed on the waves, so they didn't tell the ship captains until after they locked you down. No one is aware of the quarantine except you, your partner, me, station management, a few security, and the 'need to knows' representing Hann Brothers. Now Hann is pissed. They're demanding compensation for the delay from anywhere they think they can get it, including the *Hand* and Seven Star."

"They can't do that!" I stared at him in horror.

"No, they can't. The courts set precedence on that: quarantine is beyond a shipowner or contract's control. But, I'd still have to break the contract with them to switch it over to you. What do you think they'd do to me if I let you slice out their job on top of everything else?"

The Hann Brothers was a huge shipping conglomeration with strong Earth Alliance Space Transport Workers Union, or EASTWU, ties and influence in all the right places. They could, and would, ruin Seven Star Cartage and the *Thief's Hand*.

"Which ship is it?"

"The *Jillie D.*"

I groaned.

"What?"

"The crew of the *Jillie D* and I have history. I was the officer in charge of a Marine detail that hailed them down in deepspace and boarded them looking for contraband. We confiscated somebody's stash of hazeadorn."

"What's hazeadorn?" Scriver frowned.

"A powerful, banned substance deep-sea poachers use to immobilize sea life for quick net catches. A few grams dumped in an ocean can cause a huge amount of destruction. Poachers drop it, move in, grab everything that surfaces, then leave while the stuff continues to spread, suffocating water life and causing massive marine kills. We never discovered the identity of the smuggler, but the kind of money hazeadorn brings would have spread around to several people."

"Ship crews are too damn tight to let a thing like that pass," he observed.

Ship crew had to be tight. Those bonds with your crewmates might be the only thing that kept you alive if disaster struck out in the Vasty. Unfortunately, sometimes those bonds transferred to an ugly, arrogant attitude toward anyone outside their circle. Someone on the *Jillie D* had a grudge against me. It meant a significant number of the crew were out to beat the hell out of me—or worse—in revenge for a fellow crewmember's loss.

It was a message they wanted to send to all the indies: Don't mess with an EASTWU crew.

"Hann won't wait six weeks for this load."

"Of course not. Crew has recall at zero hour, tonight. Hann has demanded compensation for the load shortage and the delay. The station is giving them free dock time back to your original put in."

No doubt, Mandragala would figure out a way to recoup that loss from Seven Star and the *Thief's Hand*.

Things were looking desperate for us. "Let us take the next leg of the haul," I urged again. "We can save you the late penalties!"

"Can't do, Zant. It's the principle of the thing with them. You know that."

The principle being the opportunity to eliminate another small contractor from the competition.

"If they agreed, would you do it?"

He shook his head. "I can't ask. I can't jeopardize my connections with the Hann Brothers. I need them. But I have—"

"What about us, Jakub?" I interrupted. "I'm asking you to throw us a lifeline here." I broke off to draw a deep breath, knowing station security was closely monitoring our exchange, including our vitals.

With good reason. After several successful litigations for negligence or failure to provide reasonable protection from unstable individuals, star station owners lived in a state of constant terror. Lawsuits had forced a complete handover of one massive facility and a change in ownership dynamics on another. People with things to lose recorded everything for legal protection against people without anything left to lose.

Saura and I were rapidly falling into the last category. "Jakub, I can't go to Big H empty-handed. Give us something—"

"I can't, Vivi. I don't have it!" His expression looked strained. "Maybe you can get something short term...from one of the banks."

"For a spacer who's only collateral is already tied up? Not likely!"

His mouth tightened. "Look. There is something. I don't know anything about it, so I was reluctant to mention it..."

"What?" I snapped.

"Damn it Zant! I'm trying to tell you! Someone contacted me right after the *Hand* began station fall. They said they want to talk to you."

Was he sweating?

"Who?"

"I don't know. He left an address in Spacertown—"

"You know I don't do Spacertown!"

"I don't know what your problem with Spacertown is, Zant, and I don't care. All I have is the address he gave me."

Damn the reaction Spacertown evoked in me! I clenched my hands to my sides to hide their sudden shaking. "What does he want?"

"Didn't tell me." He was sweating!

"Well, tell him to meet me here."

"I don't have a way to contact him. Just an address. It's in your feed. You know you don't have a lot of time."

What the hell? Why was he suddenly acting like a spacer going through station customs with a kilo of space dust shoved up his ass?

Maybe because he thought it was some kind of illegal transaction. Like I didn't have enough trouble already.

"You're right. I don't have much time." I needed to keep this association, but I had to move on. Try to work a deal with Big H. "I'll be in touch." Scriver wasn't a bad man; he was only caught up in a bad situation, the same as we were. "Thank you for your time, ser." I nodded and left his office.

***

"Captain Zant! I heard you were a plague ship." The chair creaked ponderously as Big H leaned back and regarded me through narrowed eyes.

"Not a plague ship." Mother Universe! I should have known word would have already reached him. "The quarantine is on the cargo."

"So, you got my money?" That was Harry Grantham: neither dainty in appearance or demeanor.

"Not yet."

"Payment's due in nine hours." He cocked his head, a humorless smile splitting his heavy lips and pushing up ridges of salt and pepper bristles on his heavy jowls.

"The quarantine's for six weeks."

"Hunh."

I got directly to the point. "Scriver can't advance payment on the cargo. I came over to work out terms with you."

"Vivi. Captain. You know I don't want your soup-can of a ship." He straightened in his chair and braced his elbows on the desk, his plump hands flat on the surface in front of him. "Hell, I'm perfectly happy to let somebody else deal with the logistics of the crew, ship, and space. But I do want my money when it's due." He smiled again. "Lady Business is a cold, hard bitch."

And Big H worshipped at the Bitch Goddess' feet.

She seemed pleased enough with him. Harry Gratham was the one Human in Earth Alliance space with a remote link to the Moneyworld.

Several years ago he had managed a tenuous link with a financial institution close to the massive coalition of worlds and their markets—sort of like knowing a guy who knows a guy. It was the nearest the EA had come to the sacred cash cow of the Moneyworld. It didn't make Harry any money, but he became a celebrity in the eyes of EA financial markets that were desperate to worm their way into the heart of Whooex commerce. Years later, we still hadn't made any inroads into those coveted markets and the shine on Harry Gratham had dulled; but influential people still considered him one of our best hopes to crack the shell around the Moneyworld.

He leaned back in his chair again and crossed his arms. "No. I can't help you, Captain. If word got out I went soft on you, I'd have every piker I held a note on coming in here with a sob story about their cargo."

"But this one is true. You know it!"

He stared at me impassively.

I didn't particularly like the man who held the note on our ship, but he ran a successful business based on reason and fair risk. "If I can pay the interest—"

"Payment's due in nine hours. No exceptions. Some exciting opportunities are opening up and I need all the capital I can get my hands on."

Damn the Moneyworld! "Even if you take the *Hand*, the cargo remains under quarantine. You can't take actual possession for six weeks!"

"Maybe," Big H nodded. "But tell me, how're you and catgirl"—as lien holder on the *Hand* he was also aware of Saurubi's presence in EA space—"gonna come up with the money to cover the loss of the cargo?"

I thought the top of my head would come off with the rush of my fury. "The cargo doesn't come with the ship! It belongs to Scriver! What are you trying to do, get us killed?" No investor could let a debt like that slide.

Big H chuckled. "Relax, Zant. Scriver won't kill you; not when he can pass the debt on to you. Catgirl will go back to the Tabi Empire, to face charges for not returning at the end of her service in the Marines, and you'll pay the debt. You know the law."

A black cloud of horror threatened to engulf me. Yeah, I knew the law. According to the EA, personal belongings and cargo must be removed from a repossessed ship within twenty-four hours, or it became default property of the new shipowner. I just hadn't thought about it before. Scriver probably hadn't, either.

Big H was right: I would have to assume the loss and become indentured into service to Mandragala Station. I'd become a scrub, rented out as crew to whatever ship would bid for my service to pay off an impossible debt.

I felt as if he had kicked me in the gut.

"Believe me, Zant, I don't want your damned ship; it's not ready cash. But, if it's the only way to get my money, I'll take it." The chair creaked again as he clasped his hands.

For the first time I noticed that the heavy rings, intimidatingly crusted with blazing jewels, that usually decorated his fingers were gone.

Liquidated for capital?

Images of ragged refugees, huddling together on the outer dock for warmth, flitted through my mind. I saw my face among them.

"Figure out a way to get my money, Vivi."

No matter what it cost us, I had to do that. We could not lose the *Hand*.

***

Five hours and eight small lenders later, I was frantic. After hitting the legit sources, my last three stops had been to the most reputable loan sharks. All to the same response: no one had money to loan, regardless of the interest rate I offered to pay. With the deadline to pay Big H four hours away and the station's twenty-four-hour clock moving toward night cycle, I wasn't any closer to solving our problem.

My next stop would have to be the lenders in Spacertown. With the sum we needed, we'd never get out from under that.

Scriver had to help us.

"What is it now, Zant?" The man who stared out at me from my personal comm screen looked wearier than when I'd sat in front of him six hours ago.

"Scriver, if I don't get paid for our run we lose the ship and Big H takes the cargo with it. Neither of us can recover from that. Give us the next leg of the carry. Please! We'll do it for half the rate." It was a bad deal, but it would buy us some time.

Harry would be pissed to the max. He would penalize us. He would make us renegotiate our rate. He would have his henchmen beat me to within an inch of my life. But a big pile of creds sitting in front of him—eventually—would have a magical way of smoothing over the rough spots in our business transactions.

Scriver shook his head. "I can't, Vivi. I gave you what I had."

Did I see that glint of sweat back on his forehead?

"Damn the union, Scriver! We're both going to lose!"

"It's not the union, Vivi." He leaned in toward the screen, his voice low and urgent. "It's—" He straightened back up. "I can't pay you: that's all I can say." He shook his head. "My advice, friend, is go to the address I gave you."

Friend? "Jakub! We—"

"Vivi! For once in your life, stop fighting a losing battle! Shut your whining and go to the address I gave you!" The image blanked, leaving me staring at the address hanging before me.

CHAPTER 4

Sideways

Every planet, station, platform, or flotsam island in EA space has a Spacertown. That's all they're ever called. The management wants to ensure that when we skinny, gravity-sensitive, hairless—from the depilatories we use to keep our hair from clogging our ship filters—Human misfits swarm out of our ships, we can find the place as quickly as possible. It's always on the worst piece of property available, usually along the edge of the station ring out near where the ships nose in and the racket of loading and unloading never stops, or, onworld, where ships landing and taking off roar endlessly and their drives light up everything day and night. The places are crime riddled, rundown, cold or boiling hot, with the utilities—and the security—intermittent to non-existent.

In the locations where the law does get actively involved, Spacertowns get an additional name added to the front for clarity in the court system. They become Mandragala Spacertown, or Pele' Spacertown. They are no different from Zephyr Isles Spacertown or Vacca Spacertown except, maybe, for size. The nightlife, bars, sex trade, drugs, crime, and general lowlifes are conveniently located near their patrons, and the patrons are conveniently isolated from the decent citizens who have permanent addresses, though sometimes those decent folks want to cross over the line—get a little dirty for the thrill of it—before they slip back inside their secured zones. There's a lot of dirty in Spacertown. It makes money.

You would never know that from the appearance of the place.

I hate Spacertown. It twines through my dreams. The memory of it grips me with cold, creeping panic. It's a personal thing; something I don't choose to discuss. Saura knows why. So do my foster parents and my superiors in the EA Space Marines. It's need-to-know only.

Now desperation drove me to its outer edge.

Nausea tugged my guts as I checked the address Scriver had dropped in my personal feed. The storefront looked as if the only things holding it up were the spacer bar leaning into it on one side and the tattoo parlor on the other. Sort of like they were putting the squeeze on it.

The place was a quaffa bar. In military terms, an EYOR, or "enter at your own risk."

The EA military has a zero tolerance policy on the quaffa; its use is grounds for immediate dismissal from service. Stations also ban their personnel from frequenting the joints. But there's always a quaffa bar somewhere in Spacertown, and it always has plenty of glassy-eyed, blissful patrons.

The bar's door, a cloth banner painted with the Whooex Basic symbol for Elegant Air, rippled in the breeze from two fans strategically positioned to keep the fumes of the place from escaping into the concourse. It wasn't that the owner felt any concern over the danger addictive smoke presented to passersby; he simply wanted to make sure every bit of the stuff recirculated back to the people who were paying for it. No free sniffs here.

Thank the stars for the owner's greed.

Desperate as things were, Saura and I did not need a connection to anyone hanging out in this place. I turned away.

"Zant?"

I glanced around. None of the people moving past reacted with any interest toward me, and the buildings were too tightly squeezed together to allow a shady figure to beckon from a dark alleyway.

"Zant." Something brushed my wrist.

I looked down and a flash of white fury rushed over me. What was a kid doing on the concourse in this hellhole?

"Are you Zant or not?" The question carried a gravelly, sardonic tone I'd missed before. The image of the child-face resolved into a porcine snout, small, beady eyes, and heavy jowls. A hand with short, stubby fingers lifted a cigar to a toothy mouth.

The Frairy stared up at me impatiently.

"I'm Zant," I growled, fighting back the adrenalin charge of horror that had slammed me when I thought a kid had approached me in this goddess-forsaken area of the station. "What do you want?"

The short, stocky alien grunted, causing a large puff of blue smoke to float up from the cigar. It caught in my throat.

"His Frilliness wants to speak to you." He jerked his head toward the Elegant Air.

One of the few things I knew about Frairies, other than their bad attitude and notoriously awful taste in clothing, was that they were frequently found doing business in and around quaffa bars out on the rim. Rumor said the fumes did not affect them.

What was one doing standing in the middle of an inner system station, where EA law supposedly banned aliens? And why wasn't anyone reacting to his presence? The crowd moved around us without even a downward glance at what I could only describe as an upright pig dressed in a purple suit, orange plaid shirt, green bowler hat, and tiny silver ankle boots.

His Frilliness? "What?" I asked brilliantly.

"You want somethin'. He wants somethin'. Unless your wealthy uncle died and left you a fortune in the last few seconds."

So, it was about money.

Yeah. It was about saving the *Thief's Hand*. And me. And Saurubi.

In spite of my better instincts, I nodded. "All right."

"This way." The creature struck off through the milling press of Human bodies towering around it. It moved fast. The only way I kept up was by watching for the bouncing curve of the bowler hat, an effect caused by a gait reminiscent of an upright, walking mouse.

It passed under the banner of the Elegant Air and disappeared inside.

Swearing, I paused outside the range of the fans. Despite the stringent position of the military and stations against the drug, people did not necessarily become addicted to quaffa the first time they experienced it, or, for that matter, ever. However, a wise Human did not enter a quaffa den without the companionship of several close friends who could be depended upon to make sure everyone in their group also left the premises, no matter how resistant one of their number became.

Note that I said wise, not desperate. Besides, you can go in without indulging; but you pay, either way.

"Give me a mask," I told the skinny, unkempt girl at the door.

"One federal." She pulled a packet from beneath the counter but did not offer it to me.

"That's more than the cost of going in bare," I protested. "Shouldn't I get a discount for not indulging?"

She shrugged. "Quaffa costs money whether you breathe it or not."

"Oh, right," I snapped as I passed my wrist over her payment reader. Chalk up another expense to this quarantine business. I could have used the filter stowed in the cuff of my shipskins, but the elaborate, compression-packaged item would cost a lot more than a federal to replace.

She slid the packet across the grubby surface to me.

I tore off the protective cover and fitted the square of blue filter material over my nose and mouth, pressing the edges securely to my skin before I brushed aside the painted banner and stepped inside.

Apparently, this bar believed in giving its patrons their money's worth: the air was murky with brown smoke. I'd be really pissed if I lost the damn Frairy in all the gloom. I'd be doubly pissed if breathing this air rendered it beyond communicating with me. I'd be triply pissed if the mask I had just paid a small fortune for was made of cheap paper and I ended up lying on the floor of this dump until someone dragged me out.

Which reminded me, belatedly, that Saura had no idea what foolishness I was engaged in.

I spotted the Frairy headed deeper into the bar toward some high-backed booths individually isolated by heavy privacy curtains. He stopped at the rearmost one to wait for me.

"We want to do this sometime today if you don't mind," he growled when I got within hearing distance.

Oh, I had a sarcastic, illegal alien on my hands. I glared down at him. "How the hell are you even on this station?"

Ignoring me, he whisked the drapery aside with his stubby hand. "Sit down and mind your manners, Flygirl."

I took a step forward and stopped, too stunned to move. The Frairy gave me a shove and I plunked down in the booth to keep from falling across the table.

Stepping in behind me, he dropped the drape.

***

The alien sitting—or, rather, floating—across the table from me looked similar to a fancy Earth jellyfish, with multiple tendrils, some wide and ruffled, some nearly as fine as hair, trailing from a meter-wide, semi-transparent, pinkish dome.

It was an Oulunsk.

Rumor had it most members of the Whooex Union view the Oulunsk—or MoMo, as the creatures prefer to call themselves—as brilliant but lawless pests. The EA takes a more circumspect approach to the one-meter tall levitating jellyfish who are one of the three founding members of the Whooex Union and supposedly the oldest civilized species in our known galactic space.

MoMo are acknowledged geniuses in the field of invention. They created and own sole rights to the language translation hardware and chips in my, and everyone else in the Whooex Union's, head. They also created the fold drive that most Whooex members use for space travel. They know what the rest of us want or need, which is no surprise, since the little buggers seem to show up, uninvited, everywhere. Not just in Human space, but across the entire expanse of Union member Star Associations. While the Whooex Union Charter clearly states that no member species can enter another Star Association's recognized space without mutual agreement, the MoMo do not honor boundaries, real or imagined, in their insatiable curiosity about their fellow members.

No doubt, there are many things we do not know about this most ancient of races. There is probably very little they do not know about us. And, whatever they don't know, they are actively intent on discovering, right down to military and political secrets. The Earth Alliance has diplomatically followed the lead of other Union members and classified them as active historians—since no one is capable of keeping them out of any place they want to be anyway. They sort of show up and float around without bothering anyone or anything, then mysteriously disappear. They never reveal what they learn.

I once heard a story about one of Earth Alliance's planetary banks opening its vault to discover several of the creatures floating around inside. The owners didn't find anything missing, but, supposedly, even items inside the lock boxes had MoMo mitochondria on them.

The incident inspired an interesting question that made some people very nervous. Every species has a few skeletons they want left in the back of their closet. Are the little buggers capable of accessing those skeletons and using them against us?

We do know they list their planet of origin as a place called Rhom, which does not show up on any star map, but they now claim another world, unnamed and also hidden, as home. And we know that the Endarans hate them, which isn't a big surprise since they hate Humans and Tabisee, too. The Endar Primacy is the main obstacle to the Earth Alliance's full membership in the Whooex Union and our access to the Moneyworld. They're the guys that advocated for our complete annihilation on first Whooex contact. Such a disagreeable, confrontational species certainly would not appreciate anyone who had the ability to get inside its most secure areas.

At least Endarans stay in their own space.

The MoMo across the table floated a few centimeters upward, rippled a frilly blue bit of its trailing under-section, and settled back in position above the bench.

"You guys aren't allowed this deep in EA space!" I exclaimed when I finally found my voice. "Is security aware you're here?" Space Marine security training does not vanish with decommissioning.

The Frairy gave me a 'yeah, right' look. "This is a quaffa bar. Nobody's payin' attention to the other patrons. Now, shut up and settle in for a listen. His Frilliness wants to talk to you."

"I have enough trouble without getting picked up for associating with illegal aliens. Let me out of here." The Frairy standing at the end of the bench firmly blocked my way unless I wanted to go under the table. I looked down at the nasty carpet and debated whether I wanted to make my exit that way. "Can't these people see you?"

"Of course they see us." The Frairy shrugged.

"You paid them off!"

"We improved the economic status of a few. Others, no. Your race has a marked predilection for curiosity, but some of your species are willing to overlook anything that doesn't relate to them personally."

I felt icy tingles run down the back of my neck. "That's how sabotage and invasions happen."

The MoMo's uppermost frills ruffled with pink.

"What?" I glared between the MoMo and the Frairy. Diplomacy was one thing; these two were violating EA law by being here!

"We do not seek to invade Earth Alliance space," the Frairy said with icy formality.

Some people obviously wouldn't stop them if they did.

Another part of my marine training finally kicked in. I didn't want to start a diplomatic incident in a Spacertown dump. "I didn't mean you were intent on invasion," I said stiffly. "It was an observation on how things happen if people turn their backs and let it."

"Oh," the Frairy gave me a mocking look of relief. "Thank goodness we're not suspects. Meanwhile, His Frilliness wants a word with you."

"I don't think my translator covers Oulunsk." Some language packages were unavailable in Marine software, mostly for species on the far side of the Union, where we had never made contact—and, of course, Arpi, the Endaran language.

When the EA military first began to implant Whooex language chips in Human personnel, it wanted the option to remove all the enhanced parts at termination of service. That policy quickly changed. Space is vast, and sometimes the government must rely on the assets it has in place. The Space Force came to the realization that leaving language translation hardware active in exiting personnel gave it the advantage of having trained, security-minded individuals available for immediate recall throughout Earth Alliance space, especially on the Outer Rim. The benefit of better communications skills when we interacted with our fellow aliens enhanced security.

Space Marines were never considered completely decommissioned for that reason.

"There is no MoMo to Human translation." He twitched the end of his flat, pink nose and made several chuffing sounds I took as laughter.

"So, how do I know he's saying anything? How do I know you're not making things up?"

"You'll have to trust me."

Not likely. "He signs you with his tentacles?"

"No." The chuffing came again.

"It's telepathy."

The chuffing ended abruptly. "Enough socializing. We'll proceed with the discussion now."

Had I hit a sensitive spot? Did Frairies and MoMo share a mind link? Was it natural or mechanical? It could make for some interesting security discussions in the future.

"Look, you have a problem," the Frairy began. "Your cargo is red-tagged. We have a solution. We can arrange for you to move it forward, bypassing the quarantine."

What? A miracle from out of the deep dark? I didn't think so. "Sounds great, except I've already asked the man who holds the contract on the load and he said no."

"As the owner of your cargo, His Frilliness can contract out its transportation to whomever he chooses. Hann Brothers refused to transport the shipment to the destination he requested, nullifying their contract."

"Wait! You own our cargo?" I twisted to stare at the MoMo, unsure whether to react with relief or fury. "Since when?"

In an amazing display, the MoMo slowly blushed a stunning hue of rose from the top of the dome to tentacle tip.

"Since before you took possession at Galray." Waving his cigar airily, the Frairy added the ash off the end to the crust on the floor.

I pulled my attention away from the MoMo to glare at him. "You can prove that?"

"The Haruth Conglomerates. Check with Jakub Scriver."

As if Scriver actually knew who backed any company he dealt with. Yet, he had been sweating heavily when he steered me to this joint. Maybe a conversation with these two had worked him up. To me, the pair looked more a comedic team than a threat, yet here they sat, in the heart of EA space, trying to strike a deal with me. I wasn't laughing. Who knew what power over Human trade and transportation they wielded? "He'd say anything you two told him to say."

"He told you to come here."

Exactly. I glared at him. "Who's the consignee?"

"All you need to know is where it's going." The Frairy clamped his teeth around his cigar and dug into a thick pack belted halfway down his cylindrical torso. He drew out a flat black box seven centimeters on each side.

My breath caught in my throat when I saw the elaborate symbol etched into the top. It was a 3-D star chart. EA ships used them—unless they happen to be lucky enough to have a Tabisee astrogator serving onboard—but ours took up an area on the ship bridge the size of a large travel trunk. The technology he held would be worth the price of a settled world to the EA.

He set the box in the center of the table and the MoMo extended a tentacle tip to brush across the symbol.

A starmap bloomed in the air between us, hundreds of tiny lights pricking the smoky air.

Several fist-sized smudges of colored light—nebulae, I recognized them by their distinct shapes—told me the map was set on a vast scale. An intense pinpoint of red light five centimeters off the surface of the table on my right indicated the location of Mandragala Station. I had to search a few moments before I found the tiny bright blue dot marking the cargo destination. It was far across the tabletop and up in the air to my left. It looked a long way from home.

In truth, it looked a long way from anything.

"Where is that?" I asked cautiously.

"It's a raw-material processing facility in the Scylla Quadrant."

The nonexistent hair on the back of my neck stirred. "That's not EA territory."

"It sits on the Proambu frontier near the outer edge of the galactic arm." He stared me straight in the eyes, as if daring me to react.

I dared. "Are you crazy? There's a territorial boundary between the Proambu and the Endarans out there!"

"Endar," he corrected me. "For them, all things are Endar. One, twelve, twelve thousand, they are Endar. There is only the Endar Primacy. And that is Proambu space. A decommissioned facility. We have their permission to use it for this cargo exchange."

"What about the Endar? Do you have permission from any of their war-class ships patrolling the area?" One thing I did know: Endarans—or Endar—had a reputation for pushing into systems bordering their own to intimidate and harass their neighbors.

The area of space we were discussing happened to be a widely known point of aggression.

Did these two even care?

"Don't need it. It's Proambu space."

The Endar obviously didn't consider that detail important. "We're done here. Find yourselves another sucker." I had wasted fifteen valuable minutes with these clowns.

"You'd rather lose your ship?"

"I'd rather be alive." I said, my resolve weakening.

"Alive and station-bound."

Shit. He'd hit on my greatest personal fear, being station-bound, my labor rented out to pay for the expenses I incurred. The bastard!

Big H's threat flashed fresh in my mind. It ground my outright rejection of his offer to a halt. "You're not on this station legally. How can you make a deal happen?"

"Good question. Not important." He waved his cigar dismissively.

"So, what are my papers going to say: a Frairy and a MoMo contracted me for this job? And then EA Security picks me up?"

"Nah. They wouldn't believe that."

"Exactly."

"Just make the deal, Flygirl. Say yes and leave it to us to work out the details. And stop worrying. You know the EA's hands are plenty dirty when it comes to getting things done, right?"

Yeah, I did. That argument wouldn't help me if I came down on the wrong side of things.

If I let us lose the *Hand*, however, I'd open the door for the Tabisee to take Saurubi back home to whatever punishment they decided to mete out. The Tabi Empire took great pride in their space fleet; they would not deal kindly with a deserter.

We didn't have any options left, but taking the *Thief's Hand* into a distant area of disputed space was insanely reckless.

"Look," the Frairy said, "We don't take risks with our cargo, either. This is a simple exchange. A drop-off and pick-up, then back into EA space to deliver the new load. Fast in; fast out. The Proambu shut Idwal Platform down because the system was mined out, not because of problems with the neighbors."

"I can verify that information."

He shrugged. "Check it out. We're not asking you to put you or your partner's fuzzy blue skin at risk."

A chill ran over me. The *Hand's* registry listed two names: Vivi Zant and Saura Cerros, with Saurubi's name chopped to disguise her identity and her race not checked—a legal option left over from early Earth history.

Was he making a subtle move toward blackmail? I decided to ignore it, hoping he missed the slight hesitation in my response. "What's the new cargo?"

"Nothing you can't handle. The paperwork and destination information for bringing the cargo back into EA space will come with the material when you pick it up. This is all legal, I assure you. When you see the return destination you'll be fine with it."

"And you won't give us the details now."

"Nope."

"Why didn't you do this through Scriver?"

"What? You think he'd officially make a deal with a Frairy and MoMo?" He chuffed.

Bastard.

"No, seriously. He insisted we transfer the cargo manifest so he could keep his association with the Hanns clean."

That rang true.

I stared at the blue dot of light. Although everything sounded borderline legit, I wasn't jumping into this deal without consulting Saura first.

It wouldn't hurt to hear the details, though. For Saurubi. "What's the pay?"

He settled on the end of the bench beside me. "The amount currently owed you by Scriver, the same for delivery of the ingots to Idwal. The same again for delivery of the new cargo, destination to be disclosed upon your taking possession of said cargo. We'll take care of supplies and fuel required for both legs of the trip, loading here on Mandragala since there'll be no source on the Proambu facility."

Desperate as we were, the offer was too low for the risk the operation entailed. I let it hang for the moment.

"How do you know what supplies I need?" Saura had some particular tastes.

"We accessed records of your past purchases."

Much as that annoyed me, anyone with enough curiosity and the perseverance to search could find that information. The food preferences had probably betrayed Saura's presence on the *Hand*.

"You're asking me," I stayed with the singular, "to risk my life and ship to enter disputed territory inside another Whooex member's space." I emphasized every word that could be associated with danger. "That's hazard pay. Quadruple the offer and we'll talk."

No one ever approached the bargaining table with their best offer on the first pass.

The Frairy looked properly outraged and offended. "Impossible."

"Then let me out of here." I moved to push him off the end of the bench but his fanny stayed firmly in place. We both looked at the MoMo.

No lovely blush color this time. The jellyfish's under-frills rippled white and blue with more activity than at any time since I'd been there. Agitation? Anger? Telepathic communication?

If His Frilliness didn't act fast, I was climbing over the glammed-up runt blocking my way out of here.

"One and a half times the first offer. It's the best we'll do," the runt said.

"Double the original offer for every leg."

The Frairy puffed on his cigar, making the air of the booth even hazier. "If it were my decision, Flygirl, I'd let you walk, but His Frilliness agrees: two times the original offer on both legs of the new contract. We hold with the original agreed on payment for your initial delivery to Mandragala, however."

Not a bad deal.

"I want to think it over." I planted my feet on the floor and shoved sideways, forcing him off the bench this time.

The Frairy stood up and glared at me. He thumped his cigar ashes on the floor, just missing my foot. "You don't have a lot of time left, Flygirl."

True, but I wasn't taking this sort of risk without consulting my partner first. "How do I contact you?" I asked him

"The name's Thok. It's in your contact list."

Of course. Why wouldn't it be?

Fighting down an abject fear that I was making a disastrous mistake by walking away without sealing the deal, I nodded. "I'll let you know." I wanted to talk to Scriver, to corroborate their story before I took it to Saura. "Soon," I added before he asked.

"Ya got two hours. We don't hear a no from you, we'll figure you accept the deal."

What? Default agreement must be a Frairy thing. "I'll let you know." Two hours. Shit! I was wasting precious time.

"When?"

"I'll let you know," I repeated. "Soon."

CHAPTER 5

The Inglorious Path

Scriver wasn't answering my calls.

I dodged into a bar a few doors down from the Elegant Air and persuaded a young lady to attempt contact with him on her personal comm module in exchange for a drink. He didn't answer her, either.

I pictured him hunkered at his desk, seeing the blinking light in the corner of his feeds, seeing the area of the station where the calls originated and not making a twitch of response.

My new acquaintance fluttered two-inch, luminous blue eyelashes at me. I lined her up with two more drinks to divert her ambitions and slipped back out on the concourse to call Saurubi.

No response there either. My message was probably lost in a multitude of game communiqués. Damn her fuzzy blue hide!

The time I used in discussion with the clown posse—my brain wouldn't let go of the image of the Frairy's clothing—left me with two hours to reach the *Thief's Hand* and talk over the deal to Saura. I could make it in sixty minutes if I cut straight across Spacertown. That left me a margin of one hour...

Desperate times call for desperate measures, I told myself to shore up my determination. There was one more loan shark in Spacertown, who also happened to be right on the route I needed to take. It would be painful for us if she agreed to help; Miss Patricia took her pound of flesh in a deal. But she had a reputation to maintain—that spacers could count on her. If she said yes to a loan, it gave me a second option to present to Saura. I might live to regret it, but we would have a better chance at survival with Miss Pat than with the job the MoMo and Frairy offered.

I looked at the bustling crowd, swallowed hard against fluttering panic and the knot in my throat, and headed deeper into Spacertown.

The places grow to fit what need requires and real estate allows. Downside Spacertowns are larger than ones on stations. Rim settlements might be just one shanty. No matter the size, they're all havens for everything illegal. Of course, you have to go to the Outer Rim for alien sex, but you can get what you want as long as the participants are all consenting. And there's a line between legal and illegal. Sex slaves and children fall on the illegal side. That doesn't stop some people. Sex trafficing is widespread, even though the EA tries to police it.

It isn't aliens who run those illegal operations, though they occasionally participate on the Rim as paying customers. It's Humans preying on Humans, like it's always been, though some of those traffickers barely qualify as part of our species. They prowl the deep dark, preying on low-defense ships, or striking settlements named New Bounty, or somewhere else innocently hopeful, for their flesh.

Vivi! Stop! My thoughts had me trembling so hard I could barely walk.

The sound of a station chime and the background on the digital clock in my perivision switching from light to dark didn't help my mental state. The lighting overhead dimmed sharply and my stomach lurched with conditioned horror. The Station was moving to night cycle.

Immediately the pulse of Spacertown quickened. Neon blazed brighter in the lowered light, its glow washing over dingy prefab walls. The sound of bar bands rose, their thump driving into the floor of the ring, sending vibration into the soles of my feet. Colors flashed as scantily clad stationers, thrill slumming, mixed with the bright shipskins of spacers on the midway as they moved in and out of doors and alleyways. Whoops of laughter and shouts burst like bubbles on the surface of low growls of lust, greed, and anger that eddied beneath.

God, I knew this scene too well!

I froze, suddenly seeing everything from the perspective of an eight-year-old child, with adults towering around me, their faces twisted and leering with false smiles.

"Move, you idiot!" Someone jostled my shoulder and I realized I had stopped in the middle of the concourse.

Taking a deep breath, I pulled my mind back from the abyss of memory. I had two choices here: I could let the past wrench the future out of my hands, or I could find Miss Patricia and work a deal.

The crowd from the bar on my left spilled out onto the walkway in a wave of laughter, shouts, alcohol and perfume. I moved through them carefully—getting into an altercation with a drunk would waste precious time.

"Plague ship." I heard a mutter behind me.

Icy tingles ran across my shoulders. Someone must have recognized me. But Scriver said only a few of the officers on the *Jillie D* knew of the *Hand's* status.

Don't be a fool, Vivi, I scolded. Lower rank crew had the noses to root out anything in their ship's business. And it had to be low-rank crew. The ship's officers wouldn't want to claim responsibility for the panic a leak like that could stir on a station.

Refusing to react, I kept walking.

Passed another bar.

"Hey, you. Zant!"

Damn! I recognized the loud, cocky voice behind me.

I did not have time for this.

Heads around me were turning in curiosity, people sensing trouble. There was a nervous female giggle behind me.

"Hey, Zant," the voice rang out again.

The crowd went so quiet I could hear chairs sliding and footsteps inside the bar beside me. I could envision the frozen poses, the uneasy, hungry expressions. I could imagine the furtive movements in the doorways calling out more observers with the mouthed word 'fight'. It was always the same, everywhere.

Conceding the inevitable, I turned.

Three people dressed in the red and yellow shipskins of the *Jillie D* stood at the front of the gawking crowd facing me. Two more red and yellows stumbled out of a bar and pushed forward through the crowd to join them, but the tallest of the first three, Dallas Ellerby, stopped them with a movement of his hand.

Oh good, we were having a fair fight of three on one.

The crowd around me, realizing that I must be "Zant", shrank back, leaving me in my own cleared zone. I could feel the tingle of their anticipation: they wanted to see a fight.

I really wished I had tried to contact Saura one more time as I flexed my muscles and balanced on my feet, feeling the drag of the station's gravity on my body. One important thing a spacer had to remember: the bigger the structure you're in, the stronger and more efficient the gravity field it generated. If I worked out diligently in the grav ring of the *Thief's Hand*, where the ship's gravitational effect exerted the strongest, I would still be at a disadvantage against a crewmember from a massive ship like the *Jillie D*. I might have something over a sedentary slob from the larger vessel—I was definitely more agile—but I was never going to beat down someone from a bigger ship by sheer strength.

There were, however, ways to gain advantage.

If you fought dirty.

"Let this go, Ellerby," I said quietly.

His mouth quirked in a cold smile. "Can't. You cost me and my friends money, Zant. We don't forget. Now we're gonna piss on you and your plague ship."

Scattered gasps went up among the crowd as they sank their teeth into the word "plague." Heads tilted together, lips moved. The fool! You didn't yell fire in crowded, confined spaces, and you sure as hell didn't say the word plague in a space facility.

Station security was not going to be in a good mood when they got here.

"Let this go for now," I said. For now: the words were a promise, on spacer's honor, that we would address this at a later time. He had a hundred witnesses.

"No. I think I want to take the inconvenience you've caused me out of your hide right now—and for as many more times in the future as I think it'll take to make up for it." He started forward, the other two following a step behind him.

The onlookers had formed a wide circle around us, the itinerant crowd pushing the stationers to the back as they leaned forward in hungry anticipation of the promised show. A figure at the back turned and ran down the concourse, probably going to recruit additional crew from the *Jillie D*. More people poured out of nearby joints to watch. The band in the nearest bar fell silent.

"Damn you, Ellerby," I said. "You're creating a station problem."

"Only for you."

He'd gotten close enough to take a swing at my head. His fist brushed the side of my jaw as I ducked and thrust my body forward, dropping my left shoulder and planting it in his gut. Despite the defensive hardening of his shipskins I heard a satisfying grunt of pain.

Shipskins are designed for hazardous conditions where unexpected acceleration can turn objects around you into sudden airborne missiles, or when gravity failure bumps you off fixtures. They hardened to distribute the impact of a localized blow and to protect the tissue beneath them from penetration. It doesn't prevent bruises, and it still hurts like hell.

They can't stop momentum, either.

Ellerby had three inches in height on me, but we were both spacer-thin. I drove him backward until he collided with one of his boys.

All three of us went down on the deck and the punch fest began. He got me on the side of the head a couple more times while I worked on his ribs, but the fighting was close and ineffective. We were a bunch of wet space noodles slapping at each other. Then someone kicked me in the back at just the right angle. That hurt. Before I could recover, hands dragged me up and held my arms. The preliminaries were over, and I was about to get hurt badly. It fired me to flick my fist up and back, into someone's face, loosening their grip on my right arm. I followed it by planting my elbow into their midriff, then bent my knees and spun left, dragging the other guy off balance. He stumbled into Ellerby, pulling me along with him. This time the hands that pulled me up grappled my forearms, pinning them as they turned me to face Ellerby.

Blood trickled from the corner of his mouth and he panted, though I wasn't sure whether it was from pain, fury, or anticipation. Hopefully, the first two figured in there strongly. He punched me in the stomach, this time making a solid connection, and my knees buckled.

"You space-junk bitch," he hissed, his breath hot across my scalp.

He should never have moved in that close. I slammed my head up into his chin, sending him staggering backward. He paused, shook his head, then stepped forward and went to work on my gut with a couple of solid punches before I collapsed and he didn't have a clear shot anymore. His henchmen were trying to wrestle me back to my feet when the station security sirens went off. I took the opportunity the distraction offered and aimed a knee in his crotch. The skins would protect you from a frontal kick, but if someone angled their knee just right...

He folded like an Origami Drive engaging. The two crewmembers holding me swore and tried to twist me toward them. I took one down with a back sweep of my foot to his ankles, which pulled us all sideways and onto the station deck again.

By then I was hoping security got to us before the two fresh crewmembers did.

The guy on my left had me pinned and was flailing at me. I felt his weight suddenly lift away. A hand caught my upper arm and dragged me to my feet. I caught a glimpse of gleaming dark hair.

"Zant, you stupid idiot," a familiar voice snarled.

***

"How could get in fight without me?"

I caught flashes of Saurubi as she stalked the passageway outside my cabin. Her ears were pinned back so tight against her head they nearly disappeared.

I shifted the ice pack from my right eye to my jaw. "I didn't plan it. Ellerby and his gang jumped me."

"Could call me." She stopped long enough to glare.

"I did!" I gave her the best dirty look I could muster through my half-swollen-closed right eye. "You weren't picking up."

"Oh." She drew a breath. "Must have been during playoff." She resumed pacing without the slightest twitch of contrition. "Look like not fight as well as expected."

I didn't do as well as she expected? We were damn lucky someone had pulled me out of the fight before station security arrived. Speaking of which...

I delicately shifted position on my bunk. "How did I get back here?"

Saura stalked past. "Scriver dumped at base of umbilical and left."

"Scriver!" An image of dark hair flashed in my memory. Of course. He was up to his neck in this. If the station locked me in a cell, we couldn't save his cargo from Big H. "That bastard! Well, at least you didn't have to post bail," I said grudgingly.

Saura stopped to stare at me again. "Why would post bail if have warm place to eat and sleep?"

That was the kind of practical thinking that made me respect my co-captain so much.

"Oh, shit! Speaking of saving money, how much time has passed?" It couldn't be long, or we'd be talking about something totally different—like how to keep in touch from different prisons in the Whooex Union—as station security escorted us off the *Hand*.

I struggled to my feet. "Saura! What time is it?"

"Use feed," she answered unsympathetically.

I tried to pull up the time in my perivision, but my feeds had deactivated while I was unconscious and were slow resurrecting.

A lilting series of musical notes announced someone at our stationside hatch.

Whoever stood out there, it couldn't be good for us. "Saura, ignore that!" I called after her. "Ouch." My head throbbed. "We need to talk! Now!"

There was a drone of conversation at the hatch.

Damn it.

"Saurubi! Don't—" I stumbled into the corridor in time to see several carrier bots, loaded with cartons, stomp onto the *Thief's Hand* and take a right, headed toward our third cabin.

"Stop," I told the scraggly dockhand that stood in the passageway. It took me three meters and two more orders to "stop" before I got his attention.

He gave me an irritated glare. "I'm warning you right now; I'm filing a complaint on this job. No one should have to transfer this much cargo up the debark umbilical of a ship and store it in a cabin. They make these cans with cargo bays and big doors."

I glared at him through my one good eye. "What the hell are you doing?"

"You said to put this stuff in the third compartment on the left."

"My partner said that." Apparently, Saura had given directions over the comm, unlocked the hatch, and disappeared into her cabin. "I'm telling you to take it all back."

His face had the same crusty sheen of dirt as his overalls. It gleamed with a guilty sweat. "This is a flash job." Meaning he'd squeeze it in between his legit work for some extra cash. "It's paid for and your partner," he gave me a skeptical look, "said to put it in the third compartment. That's it. I got another job waiting for this bot herd. It goes in the compartment and out here in the passage if you refuse to open the cargo bay. I move on. End of story. You want to send it back, the contact info is on the receipt. I give reasonable rates."

I took a step away from the pungent body odor filling the corridor: the guy obviously didn't waste his pay on a bath ration.

"I didn't order this." But I suspected I knew who had. Ice clamped my spine. What the hell? I never agreed to take the Frairy's job! I hadn't even discussed it with Saura yet.

Meanwhile, bots continued to thump past, carrying cartons into the guest cabin we seldom used for anything beyond light storage. Watching the supplies pour in, I felt the rising edge of panic. They were piling stuff in the passageway, blocking the hatch to the cargo bay, before they finally stopped.

"You should leave before a safety inspector gets a chance to see this mess." The dockworker thrust a grubby personal comm at me, and I numbly thumbed my signature.

Returning the stuff was going to be almost impossible. The cost of a bot crew to transport it back and the restocking charge would be huge. Damn that Frairy and MoMo!

Cursing me under his breath, Mr. Personality left, taking his bot herd and leaving his pungent aroma to linger. I waited until the outer hatch closed behind him.

"Saurubi!"

She slid out of her cabin before I finished saying her name. "Vivi, what goes on here?"

"I don't know!"

She regarded me steadily. "What you do?"

"Nothing, Saura, I swear!"

"Someone did—can see in expression. You did not want to happen. Did you marry someone?"

I laughed in spite of the situation. That was one solution to our lien problem I hadn't considered. "No! I didn't do anything."

"Well, someone did. Supply invoice is marked paid, but nothing came out of *Hand* account. Checked from cabin. Found message Big H left earlier. Said knew you could do it. Said not cut so close next time."

"I told them I wouldn't accept the job until I talked to you first." I hadn't counted on getting the crap beat out of me...

Her ears eased upright and turned outward, signaling that she was listening. "Tell."

"There's a Frairy and a MoMo working out of this quaffa bar—"

"Is joke, Vivi? Because right now not good time for jokes."

"No, really! They're there! Don't ask me how they're on the station, but they paid off people down in Spacertown, and the rest are ignoring them."

"Damn cloudheads!"

Cloudheads? She had to mean the MoMo. "Yeah, I know. Anyway, after Scriver refused to help us he sent me to an address that ended up being a quaffa bar called the Elegant Air. This Frairy hailed me by name right in the middle of the concourse with no reaction from anyone around us. His name is Thok. We went inside to talk to someone he called "His Frilliness." It was a MoMo. I tried to walk away right then, but I couldn't get past the Frairy." She gave me a dubious look. "It sounds stupid, but trust me, I said no to what they were offering until I could talk to you. It was crazy."

Her eyes narrowed and a growl rumbled in her throat. "What was offering?"

I told her.

Her eyes went even narrower. "Where is cargo destination?"

"Scylla Quadrant, at a decommissioned Proambu facility called Idwal."

Her ears shot straight up and her eyes widened.

I'd never seen her react so strongly before. "Mother Universe!" I exclaimed. "How bad is this? Do we need to report it?"

"No." Her body lost some of its edginess. "But is dangerous area."

"I didn't accept the job yet. I told them I'd get back with them after I talked to you and I left. I guess I've cut it close—"

"Close? Vivi, is past close! Have been out four hours."

Our deadline with Big H was long past!

His message...

"But," I stammered, "I didn't accept..." I stood there, staring at her, my mind churning. Then it locked on one person. Scriver. He sent me to the quaffa bar. He'd been in contact with the clown posse. And Hann Brothers couldn't retaliate against him if the cargo owners took arrangements into their own hands, or tentacles. I ground my teeth in fury. He knew I was too stubborn to accept it without seeking one last alternative and had followed me into Spacertown to make sure I got back to the *Hand* in time to seal the deal. It wouldn't surprise me to find out he tipped off Ellerby just to stop me.

His butt must have puckered when he had to drag me out of a fight to save me from station lock up.

The bastard had made the decision for us. A mixture of outrage and treacherous relief flooded me, making my head throb worse. The *Hand* was safe. For the moment.

I wasn't ready to thank him.

"Saura, I did not agree to this job! I cut across Spacertown to talk to Miss P so I could have something else to offer when I discussed this with you. I had time! Then Ellerby caught me out."

"Went to Spacertown to talk with ruthless loan shark?" Her eyes were unreadable.

"Yes." It sounded bad. We had discussed Miss Patricia in the past, shaking our heads at the tough terms the woman put on other spacers.

"If Vivi Zant enter Spacertown, then must trust feelings on offer," she said.

We looked at each other, the truth of our situation striking us at the same moment. It didn't matter what either of us thought about the job. We couldn't recall the lien payment from Big H anymore than we could afford a bot herd and the restocking charge necessary to send the supplies back.

"Is too late," Saura put thought into words. "We must do job."

"Damn Scriver! He finagled us into this!" I flung myself up the passageway to the bridge and hit a call key to the station.

His jaw was set, his eyes hard when he appeared on screen. "What?"

"Scriver! You bastard! You set me up."

"You think I'm gonna sit here and let Big H destroy my business? I have a family to think of."

Tiny arrows of jealousy that had no right to be there shot through my heart. I struggled for a response.

"You're welcome, Vivi."

"No! You don't get that. We're the ones who have to go to the edge of nowhere and put our asses on the line!"

"I know your life goes so perfectly," he said sarcastically. "But when I'm on the event horizon of a black hole and somebody offers to tow me back, I'm not turning it down. You weren't going to either, so climb down off your pretentious perch. As much as you hate it, you owe me a thank you. I saved all our asses."

"I was working on fixing things," I huffed, trying to hold on to some dignity.

"Nobody has the time for that, Vivi," he said. He glared, eyes narrow with anger, then the fire was suddenly gone. "You can take the deal or not. If you're too stubborn to accept the opportunity, I'll sue you for damages and loss of property. Nothing personal. I'll walk by the outer dock every day to check on you, all wrapped up in your rags and stubborn pride, waiting for the next junker out to work off your debt. Tell Saura I said goodbye."

"You bastard!" I screamed, chills of rage and terror running down the backs of my arms.

Too late. He was gone. I slammed a hand to cut the link anyway. "Son of a bitch!"

Saura was standing behind me when I spun around.

My anger flowed to frustration. "We're stuck."

She shrugged. "Will not be anything Tabisee or Humans cannot handle."

"Humans are capable of handling poison snakes, Saura. It doesn't mean I'm willing to do it. This may be something illegal."

"Vivi," she said gently, "MoMo do not do illegal."

I had to take her word on that; the Tabisee had dealt with the Oulunsk several hundred years longer than Humans had.

A twisted sense of relief tried to flow into me. I pushed it away, refusing to let it override my anger. There was something very wrong with this whole situation. "Saura, are you saying this just to save the *Hand*?"

"Of course saying to save *Hand*. We can do job."

"I don't want to end up in some Endar prison."

"Vivi, Endar not take prisoners. Endar annihilate."

"You're okay with that?" I asked, aghast.

Everything in her posture seemed to tighten with resolve. "Is no glory in walking safe path of old age." Her ears turned forward and tipped with anticipation. "Must check weapon systems. If trouble, we will leave scars before overcome."

Our weapons systems consisted of a pulse cannon, used for breaking up space junk in our path, a medium range laser for defense against small boarding craft, and a few handhelds we'd brought with us out of the service. None of that would win a battle against a deep-space cruiser of the type we would encounter that far out in the Vasty.

I'd heard Saurubi speak of Tabi warrior ethic before, but never encountered it firsthand in a situation involving me. "I—"

She gave another rumble in her throat I recognized as laughter. "Relax, Vivi. Ship is ours and now have job." She gave me a pat on the arm. "Am sure cloudhead sent course plan to file with Mandra-gala. Is false, of course, but will be flawlessly legal. Now must ready for breakaway." Humming brightly, she settled into her chair at the control boards.

I stared at her with a deepening sense of foreboding.

Saura only hummed when she pushed away from the bar at the start of a fight.

CHAPTER 6

Idwal

"Vivi, I'm afraid." The whisper is close to my ear.

"Go back to sleep, Anthy." I push at him, but my brother only buries his skinny three-year-old body deeper into my chest and stomach.

"Vivi. Please."

It's always the same for me coming out of hyper-sleep; in that few seconds of waking, before consciousness takes firm hold, flash memory kicks in. Others wake from deep sleep with pleasant dreams or cramped limbs and pain, but I flash dark, waking to nightmares.

I don't want to remember what that waking brings, but I can never stop the rush of memory—the dogs barking in the yard, the creak of the backdoor as our father slips out into the darkness to investigate the disturbance. How the burst of light from the raider ship flares and blinds me, even with my eyelids closed. It's so bright I could swear it makes a sound as it throws everything in our small house to stark brilliance or shadow.

Our father and mother die in silence, the same as all the other adults in our small colony, but I remember the sound of smashing wood as a metal giant—a man in a heavy combat suit—crashes into our home and rakes our bed with more light. A Human form steps from behind the sheltering bulk and crosses to grasp our arms and drag us out into the glaring light in the street.

I recognize him. He's one of three strangers who came into our town for the harvest festival earlier in the day. They moved among the adults, talking, sampling foods, laughing. Papa told us they brought the prospect of trade for our excess grain harvest. That possibly New Bounty would get the trade we needed to become a recognized, settled planet in the Earth Alliance. The news excited the adults, making them indulgent. They smiled when we took extra candy or cake instead of scolding us.

Now I hear soft sobs as the raiders thrust more colony children into the dirt around me.

Five-year-old Mandy begins to scream for her momma. The man goes over and drags her to the front, where we can all see. The energy lash sizzles blue when it touches her back, and her screams rise to mind-tearing pitch. Three lashes. When he throws her back into the dirt, she is limp and silent.

"You and you." He jabs a finger at Jonathon and me. We are the oldest of the twelve children. "Each of you is in charge of five younger. They are your group. You make sure they eat, sleep, and stay quiet. Any trouble and you get the same as they get." He flicks the energy lash in the air and I stare as it sizzles with blue light. "Now, pick her up." He points at me. "And all of you get moving."

***

A pattern of taps penetrated my nightmare. It was a programmed signal, telling me there was something outside my dream-horror; that my "dewdrop" was beckoning me. I surged for the lifeline that careful conditioning had taught me the sound offered.

"Gaughh!" I opened my eyes to see Saurubi perched on the transparent dome of my suspended animation cylinder, or SAC. She rapped the plasglass bubble one more time, then retracted her claws and rolled off as I hit the internal release.

The dome slid down into the side of the cylinder.

"Was bad?" she asked as I sat up.

"Always is." She already knew the answer. It was why the Corp had partnered us after our first deep sleep. She always woke quick and clean; I always flashed dark, trapped in the horrors of my past.

Flashing dark was both a blessing and a curse for me. It kept the memory of Anthy fresh in my mind, and it had gotten me paired with the alien astrogator who became my business partner. On the other end of the spectrum, I could never escape the trauma of my past. No matter how much therapy I underwent—and I'd had plenty—it continued to haunt me whenever I awoke from deep sleep.

I snatched the monitor patches off my skin and flung them away. "Wish could help."

I forced a smile. "I appreciate what you already do."

The EA Space Marine Corps—the biggest mover of Humans in hyper, or deep sleep—had recognized the problem of flashing dark in a small percentage of its personnel a long time ago. The countermeasure they settled on was simple: pair the marine with someone who didn't have the problem during the buddy assignment. Saura was my "dewdrop," a term some goof had coined from an ancient song about pretty sleepers or something. The pairing had molded our friendship. She knew my story, along with my foster parents Admiral and Liz Maxte, and a long chain of psych-doctor types who had tried to smooth out all the dents and dings—hell, more like all the open, jagged gashes—in my mental state and reset me to something close to normal. It had worked for the most part, but I still had a bad time with Spacertown, especially during station night-cycle. Shadows filled with skulking deviants, real or imagined, waiting for the sex-slavers to bring out their wares, loomed in the dark. While I was in that zone an unpredictable word or movement could throw me into a dangerous rage that led to fights, injuries, and confinement.

I refused to feel ashamed of the anger, and that was part of the problem. Those darkest moments put me in a state where, unchecked, I would have gone into those dives and killed all the perverts skulking inside.

It wouldn't bring Anthy back...

Saurubi pushed at my shoulder. "Come. Have arrived at edge of system. Time to eat while ship completes scans." She bound out of my cabin and took a right toward the galley.

She was working her way through a third rip-and-run redi-meal while I poked a mess of beans, rice, and cheese and debated whether to take a fourth bite. She paused to eye me critically. "Bruises from fight healed in cryo. Expect to carry share of workload or will make new bruises to replace old."

I laughed. The hundred and fifty centimeter-tall Tabi could do worse than bruise me if she had a mind to do it. "You're no bigger threat than a kitten," I scoffed.

The comment sent her furry, upright ears back in irritation. She despised the nonsensical way Human media tried to draw comparisons between her people and cats.

Reaching across our small galley table, she flicked the edge of my plate with a claw, setting the container spinning. "Eat. No shirking."

She finished the last of her food in one gulp, dumped the containers in the recycle slot, and exited the galley with a dusky blue strut any cat in the universe would envy.

I shoved down a few more bites and followed her forward to the bridge, where she had a 3-D display of the system pulled up at her station. The light from it glinted off the intricate, wire-thin copper tracings of tattoos imbedded beneath her fur as she moved to check the *Hand's* stats on our boards.

The Tabi Empire had certainly intended Saurubi Cerros Syrhas, Astrogator Class Superior, for more complicated tasks than tweaking navigation settings on a tiny cargo hauler in EA space.

She had come to the Space Fleet in an officer exchange program. The agreement with the Tabi Empire—our first and still closest ally after Humans gained admission as associate members of the Whooex Union of Stars—had called for the exchange of some of their valuable astrogators for our cooks.

Tabisee love to eat, but they're not much on cooking. A joke circulating in the EA claims they moved out into space to find a decent meal. Bad cooks aside, the Tabi Empire produces astounding deepspace navigators. It's as if they have 3-D star maps inside their heads, even for places they've never been before, which enables the Tabi Empire to use a different ship drive than other Whooex Star Associations. They recently came to recognize the value of learning the more dominant system, however, and because the EA was relatively new to the Origami Fold, our collaboration came naturally.

And that was how Saura and I were paired as battle buddies. We worked well together and when our time in the EA Space Marines was up, we slapped down equal money for down payment on the *Thief's Hand,* a cylindrical soup can of a cargo ship with a rotating gravity ring midway down its length, and happily moved into the civilian sector.

There was just one tiny problem. When Tabisee finished their five-year term of service with the Earth Alliance, they were supposed to return to their own corner of the galactic spur.

Saurubi sort of overlooked that small detail.

Earth Alliance declared her persona non grata and banned her presence in the Inner Systems. The Tabi Empire declared her a rogue and a deserter. Oddly, however, neither Star Association attempted to detain and return her to her people. EA Space Fleet knew where she was; they occasionally pressed us into service on the Outer Rim. It appeared that as long as we kept a low profile and focused most of our business activity out there, with only short returns to the

Hand's port of registry, Mandragala Station—where Saura stayed aboard ship—neither power seemed particularly interested in us.

I suspected the Tabisee were not happy with her failure to return home. When I expressed my concern, she simply shrugged and said she wanted to own and work the *Thief's Hand* with me.

Our friends and acquaintances sometimes mistook our relationship for lovers, believing she stayed because of me. They were wrong.

There's a saying on the frontier, 'we'll find a way.' As inspirational as it sounds, it does not refer to positive attitudes and collaborative thinking, the way administrators want to believe. It relates to sexual relations between species. They get creative. We did try it once, when we found ourselves forced to share a room on Vacca. It turned out that's just not what we're about. Now we get our kicks separately out on the Rim. Jointly, we're friends and business partners who know we can trust each other with our lives: our history has proven that many times. But Saura stays in the EA, on the *Thief's Hand*, because she wants to.

Don't misunderstand. I'm not naïve. We're all aware she's observing the common ins and outs of life in Human space. If that doesn't bother the EA, it sure doesn't bother me. Besides, I learn from her, too. The real question that gnaws at me in the dark hours when sleep eludes me is how long we have before the inevitable catches up with us and she's forced to return to Tabi space and possible punishment for her independence. She'd cuff me severely if she knew, and say "stupid, search for trouble." She would be right. It didn't mean I was wrong.

I peered over her shoulder at the 3-D map, then glanced at the monitors to confirm what I was—or wasn't—seeing. "Is this right?"

The monitors should have reflected gravitational fluctuations all over the scale from local planets and system debris. Instead, they were nearly flatlined. The only objects showing in the three-D map were the star, a blip for the station, which was too small to register mass at this distance, and a gas giant with a single moon and a fuel platform revolving around it. It looked as if something had almost swept the entire inner system clean.

"Proambu must have used system material for ringworld project." Her fingers stroked the right side of her display, pulling up additional information.

"Someone has actually done that?" The concept of a ringworld, its massive band encircling a star, its habitable surface turned inward and the night and day cycle controlled by giant, circling plates was not new. Earth writers had postulated the constructs' existence more than two centuries ago. But the amount of technology and material, not to mention the expense required to create the vast things, had made them only objects of speculation in the EA.

"Proambu have. Twice. Are working on third construct." Her ears tilted back.

"What?"

"Picking up trace residue from weapon discharge closer in to star."

That set the back of my bare scalp crawling. The gas giants that dotted Whooex Union space were free fuel for any ship that had the equipment to convert their substance. Unfortunately, their isolation often lured pirates, who preyed on the smaller ships dropping out of fold to harvest their fuel. "How recent?"

"Dispersion pattern indicates is recent."

"Debris?"

"None."

No one had been hit, then. "Was it pirates?"

"Would be stupid pirates. No good ships for profit out here."

Stupid, indeed, to set up operations in an area contested by two Star Associations as powerful as the Proambu and the Endar. Only idiots would come out here. "Maybe someone test-fired a weapon on their way out after they fueled."

"Possible." She looked over at me. "Go in?"

"I don't think we have a choice." Damned MoMo and Frairy.

"With much empty space, will be hard for pirates to sneak up. Idwal will also have defenses." She set the *Hand* on course to station fall the facility. "Will run long-range monitors."

I watched the display image flicker out of focus and back in as our scanners took over. It looked the same. "I understand why they left the gas ball, but if they took the rest of their equipment, why did they leave Idwal behind? It must be an expensive piece of property." Then again, expense might not be an issue for beings who made ringworlds.

"Whooex files say Proambu moved some equipment into next star system to begin new deconstruction. Is where they encountered hostility from Endar."

The tingle in my scalp slid all the way down my spine. "We're that close to Endar space?"

"System past next is Endar Primacy."

I drew a deep breath. Okay. Endar, two systems over. "Is it possible a Proambu crew might have accidentally wandered into their system and set off this little feud they've had going on for what, two hundred years?"

"With such high tech is hard to imagine Proambu make mistake. Is most ancient of the Whooex civilizations, though not founding member. Also, least interactive. Have trade presence on Moneyworld for past several hundred years, but mostly stay in own space."

I didn't want to think of the Moneyworld or its role in putting us out here at the edge of nowhere with a recent weapon's discharge right now. Still, with time progressing at a faster rate on stations and worlds while ships slipped through the bends of folded space, by the time we delivered whatever cargo we picked up here, our next job could actually be a contract to the Moneyworld.

"Something upset Endar two hundred years ago," my partner continued. "Became extremely hostile toward Proambu. Now contesting Proambu claim over next system."

From EA perspective, the Endar didn't seem to require a reason to be hostile. They hated us even before we had any recorded interactions with them. One thing was for certain: there was one direction we were not carrying any new cargo, no matter what the MoMo paid us.

Saura dismissed the data and refocused on the shipfeeds flowing on her screen and perivision, while I watched the tiny light that represented the *Thief's Hand* on the 3-D display. At the pace we were falling, it would take us several days to reach our destination.

Saura's ears snapped up.

Shit! "What?" My heart raced as she leaned forward, fingers adjusting our sensors.

"Flicker of something on far side of system in heliopause." She magnified an area approximately a hundred and eighty degrees around the rocky ring.

The readouts remained steady.

"A ghost?" Another chill drove down my back. There was speculation that ghosts were the shadows of ships using Origami Drive, that sensors picked up on their lower ranges as they folded through a region of shared space. A more realistic, ominous explanation was that they were traces of real ships under stealth or camouflage mode, lurking at the edge of sensor range. "Is it Endaran—Endar?"

"No trace of heat or conversion debris, but is long distance for *Hand's* sensors to reach. May be tumbling trash. Oh!"

The 3-D display in front of us disappeared as the bridge went dark.

I snatched her left hand, driving my thumb into the location at the base of her wrist where her data feeds were located, to shut them down.

"Vivi!" She jerked her arm back and glared at me in the red glow of our emergency backup system. "By Holy Plinth, what doing?"

"I was disconnecting you from the ship," I stammered, caught between confusion and relief. "I thought something was attacking our system." We were slowly blinking back to life. The red light gave over to normal lighting. "What happened?"

"Idwal responded to arrival ping. Ship systems rebooted to adjust to Proambu data feeds." She gave me a measuring look, then grinned, her incisors glinting in the light as the rest of our systems resurrected. "Is good to know you care, but have safeguards in place to protect against feed anomalies. Tabi realize must be wary of Human hackers."

I blushed, unable to defend my species.

"Also received Proambu language package." Saura's ears twisted with interest as she appeared to examine some new information inside her head.

"What? An upgrade out of the cold?" I was right to have reacted with concern.

"MoMo supplied," she said calmly, as if someone remotely dropped information into her brain every day.

"You have to accept that kind of upgrade through a legal process," I protested. "How the hell did they obtain access to your hardware?"

"Placed at Mandragala, with trigger to allow access here." She shrugged. "Required to do job."

"Yeah, but..." The thought of some random being having access to my brain horrified me. "They can't just do..."

"Vivi." When she said my name in that firm tone, I had learned I better focus and listen. "Know who designed language hardware, right?"

"Yeah," I said slowly. "The MoMo. Why?"

"MoMo created. Own exclusive rights."

I knew they had designed the translation system implanted inside my brain. I hadn't realized they retained some kind of backdoor access to it. "But, altering without user permission? That's tantamount to hijacking a brain! Does everyone know?"

"MoMo reserve right to modify only translation device in Whooex Union. Even Endar must agree."

I bet that galled those bastards. "But," I protested, "our brains contain highly secured information."

"Vivi, is MoMo. Little is protected from. Besides, Proambu facilities not open to other species. No alternative language posts to read. Must communicate in native language with Idwal to board and move around inside."

Okay. I still didn't have to feel comfortable with how the critical information had arrived. "I'm liking this less and less," I muttered.

"Facility sent *Hand* approach path," she announced.

I checked my own translation software. Thankfully, no files to help me read or understand Proambu had invaded my brain. "I'm chip mute," I told her. I had to stick close to Saura when we got there. "What's our approach?"

Her nose wrinkled as her brain made the necessary translation. "Straight into primary cargo bay xittikp," she made a choking, spitting sound for that last word, then smiled at my dismayed expression. "Not worry, can read and pronounce."

Pronounce. Really?

"Do you think we should make a subspace jump to the facility? Fast in, fast out."

She stood. "Think should not make risky move to save few days inconvenience. Hot jump could draw attention if another ship in area." So that flash in the far reaches of the system was still on her mind, too.

"Someone like the Endar?" We were not in their territory, but who, other than the MoMo and Frairy—and Scriver—would ask 'whatever happened to Vivi and Saurubi' if we failed to show back up in EA space?

Agreeing to the longer timetable, we set the ships monitors and moved on to mundane maintenance tasks to kill the several days until we arrived at Idwal.

Routine chores eventually brought us to the hatch of our cargo hold.

Saura pressed the switch on the panel and we gassed the chamber for a third time. Any threat of infection from slagmanders was long gone—if it had even existed in the first place—but the thought of the nasty little creatures crawling around inside the *Hand* had made pressing the switch once more feel necessary. Since it took several hours for the process to complete and recycle the air inside the hold, we settled down to inventory the supplies in the spare cabin that the MoMo had dumped on us at Mandragala.

"Is lot of Human food," Saura observed.

"I think so, too. It looks four to one Human to Tabi. Could their calculations be that far off?"

She cut me a sidelong look. "Is MoMo, Vivi."

"Right: they're never wrong. Do you really believe that?"

The position of her ears said yes.

I sighed. "So, what are they trying to tell us? Is there somewhere we would go that might require you to deep sleep the next leg while I stay awake?"

She tilted her head, thinking. "Not send into Tabi territory."

"We're not going anywhere that puts you at risk."

"Only area doesn't allow Tabisee is Mu Juad."

"I've never heard of the Mu Juad."

She shrugged. "Very aggressive, difficult beings beyond Endar space. Likelihood of Human encounter is nil."

"Does the EA know they exist?"

"Cannot say. Many things EA does not know."

Great. There were unfriendlies in the deep dark that Humans did not know anything about.

I gave myself a mental shake. Of course there were. There were things in the Vasty that would blindside the whole Whooex Union.

"Who are these Mu Juad guys?"

"Savages." Her lower lip curled in scorn. "Mu Ju want nothing more than battle. EA not worry. Have to pass through Xix and Tabi space to contact. If see, best to avoid. Mu Ju are scum with no social grace."

Strong words from my generally gracious partner. I nodded. "What do they look like?"

"Green biped less than one EA meters tall. Have large, multifaceted eyes." She glared at me. "Give wide berth. Is all need to know."

This from the girl with four-centimeter retractable claws on her hands and feet. "Got it."

A series of beeps announced the decontamination cycle had finished. I keyed the sequence to open the hatch and we walked into our cargo hold to inspect the six skids of processed metal bars that had forced us to the far reaches of charted space to save ourselves.

CHAPTER 7

Step Three System Disassembly Unit

Our six skids of troublesome ingots looked lonely sitting in Idwal's vast hangar. I stood looking around the bay while Saura secured our mechanical loader suit back inside the *Hand's* hold. I stood because walking to anything involved at least a two-kilometer hike. The far wall wasn't even visible.

Dock number xittikp nestled below a bundle of massive dock bumpers and between a pair of struts that supported a collection dish that would dwarf Mandragala Station. It was the ideal location to protect a valuable ship and cargo from the stray debris that must have crashed around the system when Idwal was active.

Our first view of the platform on approach had revealed a dark, tapering stub with reinforcement ribs running down its sides. A transparent ring circled the lower, smaller end and a massive bowl sat atop the wider one. It looked strange, but not impressive. Then Saura pulled a station video showing the disassembly unit in operation, and it was almost beyond comprehension. A grid of blue energy strands had once extended out beyond the mouth of the bowl to a width that would hold ten Earths. The operators were able to turn that bowl's blue mouth in the direction of their destructive activity to catch the shattered debris of a planet as it fell inward, propelled in a stream by the deconstruction machinery that crushed and shot it sunward. Idwal captured and processed the raw material, then shot it into folded space through an immense slot beneath the dish to another Proambu worksite, where it became part of their next ring project.

Then Endar aggression in the next system stopped the project cold and left the place abandoned.

Saura said that for all their technology, the Proambu were not a violent species and mostly ignored the Endar. I wondered if they ever considered setting Idwal down in the heart of the Endar Primacy and breaking up the homeworld the Endar called the Hive.

I chuckled at the thought. "So, what do we call a thing that breaks down planets into their constituent particles and shoots them across space and time?" I asked Saura on my comm.

"Proambu call Step Three System Disassembly Unit," she replied. The station lighting glinted off the reflective material of her light excursion suit as she stepped off the *Hand's* cargo ramp.

Time to make a choice whether to leave the 'shine' on our awaysuits for its higher protection against sunlight and flash weapons, or to dull it and lose some of its protective qualities in exchange for stealth. I stroked a control embedded in the sleeve of my awaysuit, and it dulled to a shadow-hugging gray. When I looked back, she had done the same.

The suits were Marine planetary surface garb, designed to protect the wearer from hostile environments and to enhance concealment. The light, flexible material allowed for ease of movement, but, if subjected to pressure beyond the defined safety range of our shipskins, reacted, becoming instantly rigid, capable of absorbing an impact force to prevent tissue damage. It could bounce and transfer the energy of a projectile from an earth weapon without the wearer feeling it—I knew that from multiple experiences boarding hostile vessels—and it prevented physical damage from explosive impact or sudden decompression while snatching and converting that energy to power for its own use. It could absorb tazer fire and short laser bursts while making the wearer nearly invisible.

Anyone who thought the suit made them invincible, however, was a fool. New and different weapons constantly showed up around the Outer Rim. In fact, as part of the deal to keep the suits, hardware in our bodies, and software in our heads, we were committed to seeking out and filing reports on any new tech we came across. Confiscating the stuff was recommended, but optional.

"I'll take the ship feeds, since Idwal is talking to you," I told her. She usually preferred to monitor the *Hand*, but today she was the only one who understood what was going on inside this place.

I ran a fingertip lightly over the controls embedded in my forearm beneath the dulled material and the *Hand's* feeds bloomed in my perivision.

I closed the ramp. The massive bolts slid into place with a solid boom and home was secure.

"Now go lower ring, locate new payload." Saura made an experimental leap in the light gravity of the station and sailed toward me.

"Seems like those clowns could have arranged for things to be on this level," I complained. The instructions that dropped for Saura while we docked said we would find our new load on the lower terminal ring. That area, with its public dock and debarkation umbilici, was the little glass ball on the far end of the platform, one hundred and sixty levels below us. In a place a lot less sheltered from the threat of open space than this area. It appeared the Proambu felt more concern for their expensive ships and cargo than they did for guests.

"No whine!" Saura thumped me in the back with her foot as she made another leap and sailed past. "Keep up!"

My suit stiffened from the blow, causing me to stumble forward. "This place is too damn big," I grumbled to annoy her.

Ignoring me, she gestured at a massive airlock in the wall ahead of us. "Instructions say take gravity tube down and proceed Section Ten."

"I sure hope everything here is in working order." One hundred and sixty levels on this station's scale was a long walk.

"Yes." Saurubi completed the distance to the lift and paced impatiently while I caught up.

"Damn," I exclaimed, staring up at the towering doors. They were big enough for a small ship to pass through. "How long will we have to wait for those things to open?"

"This for staff." She pressed a bar next to a smaller portal at the outer edge of the nearest door. It was a mere three times as large as a Human doorway.

The door slid open.

"Whoa!" I took a step back, suddenly appreciating the firm sensation of the deck beneath my boots.

We stood on the lip of a transparent cylinder approximately five meters in diameter, staring across the open space at the stars.

Or down a plasglass tube, depending on where your eyes drifted.

"Is okay. Is gravity tube."

"No. Not okay." Even with the descriptive name, I hadn't expected a big, long, vertical tube full of nothing but air! Cautiously I leaned forward to peer downward. No bottom in sight. "Saura, have you ever used one of these things?"

"No. Are common in some Union cultures. Step inside, same as elevator. Fall will detect weight and form resistance to suspend. User controls acceptable rate of descent."

'Fall' and 'acceptable rate' did not work together in my vocabulary. I could speed vertically or horizontally in vacuum tubes, hauled along by a towline, but not vertically, in gravity, with no floor beneath my feet. "I'll walk. I need the exercise."

"Vivi," she said in her best put-upon tone. "Is one hundred sixty levels. Can control speed by brushing fingertip down side of cylinder. If wish to ascend, brush fingertip up strip. Movement will reverse and go up at chosen rate of speed."

"What if it fails?"

"In two thousand years of operation, is no history of gravity tube fail."

"Is that true?"

"Don't know. But information supplied says no accidents in last two hundred years."

"How do the Tabisee know all this stuff and Humans don't?"

"Because Tabi Empire is full member of Whooex Union over four hundred of EA years; EA has barely established diplomatic relations with quarter of members."

True. We constantly scrambled to update our education system to incorporate all the new information we encountered.

"A quarter you say. Who have we missed?" I stalled, building up the fortitude I needed to step out into the air.

"Gave research material. Read! If Humans ever allowed on Moneyworld, must know information."

"Yeah." I mentally vowed to do a better job of keeping up with the stuff she shared. Meanwhile, here was new technology and a chance to discover something about another species. I sighed. "How do I get inside?"

"Step forward." She bounced past me, out into the cylinder.

When I recovered from my shock, I saw that she had not plummeted to her death, but stood calmly in the air, looking at me. "Fall will not operate until you tell it which direction to move." She gestured at the wall nearest her. "Is individual. If want stop movement, press finger." She demonstrated by stroking downward and sinking a meter. She pressed again and stopped in sheer space, staring up at me.

I thought I was going to lose my most recent meal.

"Don't dare," she warned fiercely. "Now stop being infant."

"How do you know it will recognize a Human? Our contact with these creatures is minimal—if any."

"Don't call creatures. Is offensive. Fall will recognize you. Stop stalling."

"You'll miss me if I plummet to my death." I held my breath and stepped out into the air.

It felt as if I had stepped onto a firm surface.

Great. The thing worked and I remained alive. I avoided looking down into the void beneath my feet as I reached over and tentatively stroked my finger downward. If Saurubi heard my stifled gasp at my sense of movement, she mercifully refrained from comment.

After a few moments of steady downward movement, I grew confident enough to turn and look at the universe outside the plas-glass outer wall. It was intimidating, staring out into space without the frame of an obvious barrier separating me from quadrillions of lightyears of airless vacuum. It also grew quickly boring. I turned back and stroked the black strip to speed up my descent.

"How far down this thing are we going?"

"Station ring is bottom level."

A long way to go. I stroked the strip again, and Saura made an impatient sound as I dropped past her.

She knew what was coming.

Before I reached the bottom I'd become a real pro at using a gravity fall. I had danced around the perimeter of the tube, jumped and done a forward roll with only a mild shock to my forehead when I struck the invisible floor, experienced a fast fall just for fun, and floated face down, staring fearlessly into the depths beneath me.

I stuck the landing on the elaborate mosaic floor of the public ring. "Whoo-ho!" Grav tube was the way to travel.

Saura gave a sniff of irritation as she reached out and moved her glove in a horizontal gesture across the wall. The exit door slid open to reveal a spacious vestibule. Paintings on the walls detailed a landscape full of odd, exotic plants and trees that probably reminded a station crew of what they were missing while they worked out here on the edge of nowhere. I didn't see how anyone could miss a coarse vine with finger-long thorns, but I guess everyone thinks there's no place like home.

Saura and I simultaneously drew our tazers and set them to stun—never assume you're safe, even in the heart of civilization, and especially on the edge of it—then crept the vestibule's short length to peer out into the ring.

The space the Proambu had designated for travelers and station personnel stretched approximately a half-kilometer across and high, and was a lot less chaotic than Human dock rings. I could see a few freestanding kiosks and shops and some brightly painted blocks of color with stenciled glyphs, similar to shipping containers. There were also a few huge machines and loaders, but most of the heavy stuff appeared relegated to the massive area at the top of the facility.

Lights, situated below the support beams high above, gleamed on the metal surfaces of the floor and machinery. The lower ring had appeared dark from space. I wondered if the MoMo had arranged for internal illumination to activate with our use of entry codes, or if the glass shielded the light from the outside.

At least I would be able to see whatever suddenly tried to kill me out here on the edge of nowhere if something attacked.

"Looks quiet enough." That didn't mean someone hadn't gotten here before us and found a place to lie in wait. I picked up a small vase of withered plants off a nearby table and pitched the thing out into the ring. It hit the surface with a horrendous clatter that echoed in the vastness.

There were no answering flashes of hostile fire.

CHAPTER 8

Incoming

"What think?" Saura asked after several seconds passed and nothing moved or shot back at us. "Good to go?"

I nodded.

She tipped a gloved forefinger forward and with thoughts of the flitting ghost from the outer system on both our minds we advanced outward to take shelter behind one of the shipping containers, our weapons raised and ready.

When I looked back toward the vestibule, I saw a gigantic symbol painted on the wall of Idwal's inner core.

"What's that say?" I asked.

"Is Proambu equivalent for number five."

"Do they use the same number system as everyone else?" Everyone else, for me, being Human and Tabi.

"Yes."

"Crap. This must be Section Five." The message she had received gave our new cargo location as Section Ten, halfway around the enormous ring.

"Is no way to get there without walking distance." Saura shrugged. "Only two falls from upper level. Since top bay much larger, would require longer walk to cross over to fall in Section One."

"Maybe we can cut through the core," I suggested hopefully. Security in Human and Tabi space severely restricted access to their stations' central cores, which held administrative centers, critical mechanicals, and residential living facilities. No one wanted scumbag spacers prowling the housing blocks, and even scumbag spacers didn't want crazies accessing air and water processing facilities. Station residents had chip implants and passed eye scans to enter the core. Security escorted non-residents with business inside. Who knew what Proambu protocols were, however? "Did they supply you with a key code?"

"No."

Sometimes valuable intelligence only emerges in a need-to-know situation, so we located the nearest corridor and followed it inward to Idwal's core, to an imposing doorway with all sorts of Proambu glyphs posted on the walls surrounding it and a keypad located slightly above what I would consider a normally comfortable height.

Saura shook her head. "No code comes and cannot read these."

That ended our shortcut. I sighed. "I hope this doesn't involve carrying heavy objects back to the ship."

"Can take cargo up fall in Section One and find loader to move across upper bay. Can read enough basic symbols on panels to get that far."

That would take more time than I was comfortable with out here. "I wonder why they sent us down here to pick up something they could have left in the cargo area."

"Perhaps thought easily missed there."

Perhaps. There was a lot of stuff in the vast upper area. But there were also ways to tag even the smallest item for the intended recipient to find. The jellyfish and the Frairy were putting us through extra work and I appreciated Saurubi's calm acceptance of the situation. Despite their fiery nature, Tabisee could be remarkably calm, patient creatures—until they decided it was time to act on something. Then they became a ruthless and deadly force that was nearly impossible to stop. I, on the other hand, was merely Human: curious, impatient, suspicious by nature, grumpy, unreasonable, and headstrong. I was damned lucky my partner possessed the more stellar traits.

I shifted my attention to the readouts from my suit's environmental sensors that ran in my perivision and my disposition improved a few shades. "Hey, air down here is acceptable for Human/Tabisee consumption." I shut down the commlink before she had time to protest and pulled the press seals on my suit.

Her chest rose and fell in an exaggerated sigh of despair when I removed my headgear.

I sniffed. "The air has a metallic stink."

When I did not turn purple and fall to the floor, gasping, she removed hers. "No one make you remove physio-vital part of suit," she said tartly as she flicked her ears to fluff helmet-flattened fur.

"It's a long walk. We may as well be comfortable."

We struck out again, staying close to the inside curve of the core to shave distance. Occasionally we moved through an obstacle course of odd fixtures that must have been necessary to Proambu life.

During one clear stretch, I glanced across the ring at the massive bank of pressure glass curving up and over our heads to the outer wall of the core.

That was some impressive engineering.

On Human stations, the outer ring walls are solid material. The best viewport I've ever seen on an EA station was a series of three windows six meters in height and maybe a meter-and-a-half in width sitting side by side. The vista they offered made them a big attraction to people on that station, including spacers.

We spacers are familiar with the view outside our ships—sometimes we work in space for hours—but to see it through something larger than the faceplate of a spacesuit is still enticing.

The sight of the Vasty and the stars around Idwal's system, however, made my gut twist. What sorts of thoughts ran through the minds of beings who crushed planets and who stared out with bold eyes into the vastness of the stars for leisure?

Refocusing back on my immediate surroundings, I threaded my way through another cluster of tables and chairs that might have been part of a café or bar. It seemed the former residents actually gathered for social activities, though the chairs, doors and all the equipment were larger than Human-scale.

Nothing eased my tension about being out here, seeing these things firsthand. "We must have been out of our minds accepting this job."

"Did not have choice," Saura reminded me.

"I should never have gone with that Frairy."

She frowned. "Then where would be? Stranded on Mandragala Station, struggling to survive? *Thief's Hand* is ours, and we are getting paid."

"True," I acknowledged. "But, the way we got to that isn't right, Saura."

She smiled, her sharp incisors glinting in the low light, but her eyes were hard. I suspected she felt the same way as me. "Too late back out now."

"Yeah." It had been too late to back out by the time I regained my senses after the *Jillie D* crew's beating. My gaze drifted to the outer wall again. The gas giant was creeping into view on the left from behind the massive strip of reinforced wall that set this section off from the next one. The small moon would soon follow it. Horizontal moonrise here would be interesting.

"Odd they left that little moon," I commented.

"*Hand's* sensors picked up presence of small structures out there. Maybe left additional support base for refueling ships," she told me.

"I wonder if the Endar use the platform."

Her ears suddenly went up.

"What?" My heart thumped. Damn, I hated being out here!

"Activity," she said. "Station sensors show small ship has emerged from behind moon. Must have hidden in clutter."

My mind flashed to the trace of weapon fire the *Hand* had picked up as we came in. "Unfriendly?" Pirates hanging around to pick off ships that dropped in to harvest fuel would be stupid to hazard entry into this platform's defense field. We'd required pass codes to avoid destruction.

"Station defense is not arming," she observed.

That made things even more confusing. "The *Hand's* not picking up anything unusu—oh shit! The ship's sensors just twitched to some activity on the system rim." A trap? "Saura, the ghost you thought you saw..."

"Perhaps not glitch, Vivi. Station sees, too." She pulled a 3-D display of Idwal's system up in the air in front of us, her fingers flicking as lines flowed outward across it. One stopped short, beside a red dot, flagging the location of the newly emerged ship out at the gas giant's moon. The other continued in an agonizingly slow arc, marking the distance to the edge of the system, to what might be our ghost. It finally stopped in the heliosphere and held a steady glow.

"It's not going away this time," I said tightly.

"No," she agreed. "Vivi, bad situation may be developing. Should get to Section Ten very fast. Must retrieve what is there and leave."

The lighter gravity made the run easy, but we were both breathing hard when we plunged across the three-meter wide tracks of the massive security doors that separated Section Nine from Section Ten. We stopped just inside to catch our breath and scope the area.

There were a few flat carts scattered around and rows of seating out near the edge, similar to the boarding areas in a Human spaceport.

A sound that I had taken for a local background noise in this new section finally drew my attention. The series of hisses, clicks, and musical notes seemed to repeat in a pattern.

"Proambu," Saurubi said. "Is countdown for arriving ship."

"Are you serious?" A countdown meant the ship had approach codes. Could it be our cargo, arriving late? Or was the ship returning to Idwal for some other reason? Did they think to reclaim their cargo and take ours, too? "How long until it gets here?"

"Approximate one hour EA time."

Long enough to find our stuff, haul it to the ship, and get out. Barely.

"What are we looking for, Saura?" I asked, hoping this time the answer would be different.

"Pick up cargo in Section Ten. Further instructions await on return to ship."

The same. "This pretense to a scavenger hunt is wearing thin." I glanced around the huge, sparsely furnished area. "It can't be a hold-filling cargo if we need to move it from down here. Let's find it and go."

We searched the area around the airlock first, looking for a crate or box. Something out of place, clearly left for us. When we failed to turn up anything, we moved inward, Saurubi checking closer to the core while I examined the outer area.

"Nothing," I called out. "You?"

"No. Appears incoming ship may contain cargo."

I knew neither of us were comfortable with that.

Should we stay and meet our possible connection, or retreat to the *Thief's Hand* and wait until they finished their business and left Idwal? The deep dark brought out a dangerous crazy in some people and we had no idea what crewed the approaching vessel. Thoughts of an encounter with reivers or pirates sent chill running over me.

I'd learned a long time ago that it was better to err on the side of caution.

Saura's eyes drifted left, toward Section One and I knew she was thinking the same thing.

"Let's go." I started back across toward her.

Before I'd taken three steps, the tone of the Proambu message changed.

Urgency has a universal tone.

Through the glass around the airlock, I saw a movement. The mechanical umbilical for passenger debarkation had started a slow extension out into space. It telescoped, pushing out segments behind a chunky cup-shape on its far end that housed magnets to clamp on and seal it to a ship. Inside the transparent tube I could see red lights coruscating outward along its length.

"Did that ship activate it?" I yelled.

"Must assume has access code, same as *Hand*."

Which meant they actually could be our contact.

And they were hiding behind the moon, with a ghost in the outer system and traces of weapon fire in between, raising the odds they were in trouble. I swore. How much were we obligated to help them? EA law was all over the board on that. We had not signed up for a fight.

The lights at the corners of the airlock blazed white and a square of green light pulsed on a panel to the right of it. The umbilical had fully extended. The red lights outside changed to yellow and switched direction, flowing back toward the airlock.

The tone of the Proambu message changed again.

"Is safety warning," Saura called. "Ship is coming in too fast."

I finally made my way back across the ring to her. "It's almost here?" I panted. Nowhere near an hour had passed. Someone was rushing to get here. "What's the status of the ghost?"

She frowned as she tried to make sense of the alien communications that must be bombarding her.

Her eyes widened.

Only something extreme could put a stricken expression like that on my partner's face.

CHAPTER 9

Ghosted

"It jumped? Are they crazy?" I shouted. That was the only way the ghost ship could cover the distance to Idwal and arrive in time to interfere with the tiny speck speeding toward us. If the ghost dropped back into real space close to the platform, their sudden mass would distort the gravity well around the station, sucking parts off the structure like syrup, deforming and even devouring chunks of it. It might even breach an outer wall.

With no way to predict where that might happen, we had no safe place to run.

A sudden sensation, as if something pulled at the very center of me, seized me. The pressure behind my eyes and in my ears rose, drawing back toward the direction from which we'd come until it felt as if everything was pulling out the back of my head. Far around the ring metal squealed in a slowly rising pitch, followed by several loud pops that sounded similar to a projectile gun firing—or station supports cracking.

Abruptly everything snapped back to normal, and station sirens began to shrill.

The *Hand's* status scrolled at the corner of my left eye, flashing urgent yellow warnings, and a vibration in the wetware under my gloved wrist buzzed warning. The ship was telling me there were dangerous changes in local space—that something large had emerged in precarious proximity to the local gravity sink.

"Shit, they're here!"

A distant boom sounded, and a shudder ran through Idwal. Machinery rattled in the high reaches above our heads, sending down a mist of dust. Another siren, rising and falling in tone, joined the continuous shrill of the first one. Lights all over the section began flashing red.

The lights on the inner chamber of the airlock went yellow.

Further back around the ring a klaxon started blaring harshly. A deep rumble every stationer and spacer knows and fears penetrated above all the other noise. It drove a new and steady vibration through the floor plates.

Somewhere behind us, the massive section walls, designed to isolate a damaged area of the ring from the rest of the station, were closing.

"Vivi—" The same thought struck us simultaneously: one of us had to get back topside and make sure our ride out of here stayed safe and viable.

Saura was the only one who could work with Idwal's systems.

"Go! Secure the *Hand*!" I said. "I'll do what I can here." If the approaching vessel was our connection and it was in trouble, I had to help.

I shifted the *Hand's* feeds back to her. "If you need to take the ship and fold, do it." I had my suit. I'd survive until she dared to come back for me.

"Put damned helmet on," she fired back as she sprinted toward Section One and its fall. The echoing boom of the section door sealing drowned out anything else she might have said.

I dutifully pulled on and secured my headgear while I watched her leap across the tracks between Sections Ten and One. Those gargantuan doors remained fixed, so the station had successfully isolated the damaged area. The sirens and lights continued, but the klaxon silenced with the wall closure.

It didn't mean we were safe. The ghost was still out there, and it obviously did not have good intentions.

The pattern of the Proambu message changed again, this time becoming a regular series of loud sounds that, amazingly, managed to penetrate above the rest of the clamor. No doubt it was giving instructions for ring evacuation. Unhappily, it was not meant for me on several levels.

I stared out toward the moon, its right side limned by the glowing greenish giant it circled, and spotted a flicker of blue flame from the small ship's forward thrusters as it tried to brake its headlong rush. Saura was right; it was coming in too fast.

I wondered what happened to the ghost. Maybe it had to cope with the material it pulled off the station on its arrival. We couldn't be lucky enough for it to have destroyed itself with its insane move.

I jogged to the ring's outer wall to watch the approaching vessel. For the first time, I could pick out some details. What I saw left my mouth dry. The damned thing was an in-system shuttle, designed for runs between deepspace ships, insystem, and stationary structures! It was impossible for such a vessel to make it out here to the far reaches of Idwal on its own.

Was the ghost its parent ship, lurking on the outer rim, waiting for it to emerge from hiding and head for the station? Or was the small vessel's parent out there hiding among the structures of the moon?

The shuttle racing toward Idwal was too small to support life for more than a few days. Whatever was going down out here, the timing of the *Hand's* presence was too coincidental for us not to be involved, courtesy of our alien friends back at Mandragala.

I glanced at the airlock. The lights remained yellow as it transitioned to vacuum. Whoever was coming in would not gain access to the station until the air purge completed.

The blue flare of deceleration jets blazed against the stars. I didn't recognize the shuttle design, but the pilot exhibited skill as they glided up to the magnetic lock, retro-thrusters blazing, and settled snugly to the seals. The lights on the umbilical turned into a steady green line.

It was ready for passenger transfer from ship to station airlock.

For the first time it occurred to me the Proambu must have a great deal of confidence in the pressure glass walls of their public ring, not to have dropped blast shields over them with the shuttle at such close proximity. Meanwhile, the hatch on the ship glided open and a small figure emerged. It took a few hesitant steps forward, past the docking cuff, and stopped to look back.

Saura's description of the Mu Juad as bipedal and one meter tall struck me. I hoped we weren't caught up in some elaborate scheme to ignite war on the Whooex Union or the EA.

There was shadowed movement inside the ship's hatch. A space-gloved hand gestured for the smaller figure to keep moving.

I stared, transfixed, my heart pounding. Was that a kid? Nausea and rage hit me simultaneously—if those two clowns thought I would run kids—

A figure, adult-sized and in unfamiliar spacer garb, followed by another, emerged from the hatch. The first tall figure gestured the little one forward and grasped the arm of the one behind it. The two stumbled along the umbilical, following the little one, while the hatch to the shuttle closed behind them. None of them carried anything in their hands.

Realization shook me. They moved as if they were a family unit.

What the hell was going on here?

The light in Section Ten dimmed. I turned to see the black silhouette of a massive deepspace ship sweep between the glow of the gas planet and the ring.

The larger figures on the umbilical saw it too. Their gestures became frantic.

The ghost was a threat to them.

Did it want them alive? Staring at the umbilical and the attached ship, I realized how fragile Idwal's structural setup was on this level.

When the platform had been active, its creators' biggest worry had probably been tracking stray debris that approached the station. A serious problem, for sure, but one they could easily handle. They had—still did have—some type of automatic zap system to take care of extra-station threats. That would have to shut down temporarily on the approach of a permitted ship. Saurubi had keyed a code before we came in. The little transport shuttle would have done that, too.

The ghost had timed its jump to that opening, and the station be damned. The realization made my skin prickle.

I lost sight of the ghost. Once it cleared the planet glow, the thing disappeared in a ripple of darkness, as if the stars had swallowed it. What the hell kind of effect was that?

But it was still out there, and it had a target in its sights. Did it want the target alive or dead, and if dead, how seriously dead? The resulting debris from a direct hit on the shuttle could rip Section Ten apart. It would certainly destroy the umbilical and throw anything inside it into space.

If it wanted them alive, it had to wait until the passengers boarded Idwal, then come in after them. Since the defenses on the upper dock where *Thief's Hand* sat had reactivated by now, it would force them to come in through the public ring.

I had a bad feeling a ship that wasn't concerned with the damage a jump into Idwal's gravity well would cause, wasn't particularly concerned with taking prisoners alive. That meant if magnetic locks to the shuttle were slow to detach, the pilot would be forced to rip free to escape.

The three people on the umbilical appeared to be dressed in insulated pressure suits designed for making a quick pass between a station and ship—like they were doing. Those suits lacked any reinforcing material to protect from debris or prolonged exposure to the Vasty. They had to get inside the safety of the station's reinforced airlock. If they didn't move fast, they would die.

I ran my gloves over the seals in my suit and headgear to make sure everything was secure while I studied the control pad on the airlock. Everything on this side remained yellow while it worked toward vacuum to allow entry from space side.

The lights around the external side of the lock abruptly flashed green twice then changed to a steady red, signaling the chamber was in a vacuum state. If the kid hit the right button, the external doors would open and let them inside.

I pressed against the plasglass beside of the airlock to watch the kid, the shuttle and ghost momentarily forgotten. The lights on the umbilical coruscated red, and the outer doors began to separate. At the same moment, out in the darkness of space to my right, I saw a tiny pulse of light.

The next second everything blazed white.

CHAPTER 10

The Immediate Problem

It took fifteen seconds for my flash shields to readjust and restore vision. That was fifteen seconds of eternity while debris rattled off the station's outer shell less than a meter in front of my nose. The sound of those muted strikes was horrifying.

The shields cleared onto a scene of devastation. The shattered remains of the umbilical swung by a single top support cable amid a wildly spinning, expanding field of debris. The shuttle was gone. The passengers were gone. All blasted into oblivion by the ghost.

I hadn't thought the inside of the ring could get noisier, but the Proambu message system added another layer of stridency, probably calling for an emergency crew that would never come.

I peered into the airlock. The outer doors were sealed and the environment status lights inside the chamber and out, were red, telling me it was in vacuum state.

Getting down on my hands and knees, I looked through the lower section.

My chest tightened. Lying hauntingly beyond my grasp through at least twenty centimeters of pressure glass lay a small booted foot. The kid must have gotten the doors open just before the blast struck. I didn't want to think on how hard that small body would have hit the stationside wall, but I didn't see any blood, in floating droplets or pooling on the floor. Of course, with a suit, that didn't mean much.

The only way I could open the chamber was by restoring atmospheric balance with the station interior.

Scrambling to my feet, I went to the control panel.

There were parts of a ship my chips let me repair because they gave me access to technology Whooex members shared. It did not include Idwal. These controls were exclusively alien technology and beyond me.

Saura and her limited Proambu might have helped, but I rejected the idea of using my comm. We had a freaking aggressive ship outside the station. If they observed our earlier activity, they knew where the *Hand* was nestled. If not, I didn't want to draw attention there with a detectable signal.

I could go up, make sure everything was all right with the *Hand*, and bring Saurubi back to help me, but the little form in the airlock held me back. The transition suit the kid wore was little more than a precaution in the event something minor went wrong between the ship and station. It didn't have a large air reserve. No more than an hour. Possibly less. A trip up the fall, across the gigantic bay, and back would take too long—if the fall was even working now.

The thought nearly squeezed the air out of me.

If these people were our cargo, I had to salvage what remained.

Was the reeling devastation outside enough to satisfy the ghost's murderous intent, or did it want to wipe out any witnesses to its crime, too? We might be facing a seek-and-destroy excursion inside the lower ring. Or—my heart tripped in dismay—they might take a more direct approach by putting a plasma blast into the dock area around the *Thief's Hand* and another one into Section Ten. That was the quickest, most efficient way to end things.

It was also extremely destructive.

Tactics came down to how worried the ghost was about offending the Proambu with more property damage.

Obviously, it hadn't been a big concern so far.

Who the heck were the people in the shuttle? Why would a MoMo and Frairy arrange their transportation at this remote point in space? And why would someone want to kill them? I knew it was wrong to transfer anthropomorphic behaviors onto them, but they had appeared to be a family unit to me.

I had to get the kid out and keep it alive if I wanted answers.

I punched every lighted button on the panel. The airlock refused to cycle out of vacuum state. Either something was broken or it required action from inside the lock, which wasn't going to happen anytime soon. I pressed my forehead against the door, staring into the chamber beyond. Small bits of trash were starting to float into my field of vision. None of it was blood droplets. I'd seen enough of those rounded, dark globules in zero gravity to recognize them.

Jacking one of the most critically sensitive mechanical systems in a space facility was not going to be easy. By its nature, an airlock is a big, controlled hole in a structural wall with endless vacuum on the other side. Nothing that breathed anything or depended on equalized internal/external pressure wanted to meet vacuum unprepared. I had some experience forcing airlocks during boarding missions in the Marines, but only as an observer while one of the specialists in my squad did his or her magic. Watching is not the same as doing.

Pulling a multi-tool from my suit's kit, I pried the cover off the control panel. Great. No wires. Just a thin, concentrated stream of blue light with little runnels branching off to the sides, some lit up blue, some white, to feed the currently inoperative buttons.

Reason told me if the stream broke, the doors had to do something.

I searched the section for an object I could use to hold them open. The Proambu had shut the place down clean and tight. I finally resorted to prying a tabletop loose from its base with another tool from my kit. Then I half-dragged, half-shoved the thing over to the hatch and propped it at an angle, with one corner resting on the seam of the doors. If they sprang open, the top would fall inward and block them from closing. Then I could force the opening wide enough to pull the body out. The dangerous part would be how the station systems reacted to the inner doors opening onto a vac'd airlock. Hopefully, it would recognize the scale of the event as minor and not trigger the closing of the massive section walls. If that happened, I would have no way to reset them to open: stations always secured those controls safely away, with access restricted to maintenance and management. I—we—would be trapped in Section Ten with the damaged airlock as our only escape route.

Of course, it was also possible a safety mechanism on the lock doors might trigger enough force to shear the tabletop—and me—in half.

Positive thoughts, Vivi. I needed to find something to interrupt the blue stream without frying myself in the process. Experimenting with my multi-tool was not a preferred option; shoving non-conductive ceramic material into an unknown power source might make the tool explode.

A second search of the area turned up a small lid that I wrenched off a trash chute and some metal tags I pried off several storage crates stacked along the inside wall. I had just finished peeling off the third one when I glimpsed a vanishing patch of stars outside the plasglass wall.

The ghost was circling again, likely scanning for signs of life in the debris of their handiwork.

The distance to either of the section doors, to put a massive bulk between me and the ship's sensors was too far to cross. Besides, my movement might trip any sensors directed this way. So I did the only thing possible: I dropped right where I stood, sprawled loosely, my face shield turned away from the glass and the ship. The awaysuit should block my body heat from scans, but who knew what type of life sensors the murderers had. If they noted my presence the first time, they might see I had moved. Maybe they'd attribute that to the explosion.

Or, maybe they weren't looking for me at all. There was that little body lying inside the airlock. I had a gut feeling if they detected it was alive, whatever crewed the ghost would try to change that.

Frustration gripped me. With the debris of their handiwork spreading outside the station, the ghost's path would swing farther out this time, taking longer for it to move past.

It would also take longer for it to return a third time. If it returned that third time, most likely its occupants were planning some action.

I finally gave up and turned my head just in time to see the jagged tail of darkness pass beyond the section wall and the stars ripple back into view.

Swiftly I climbed to my feet and stared at the blue light in the open panel beside the lock. Since I didn't know how anything worked, it hardly mattered that it was also alien tech. I was floundering in the dark already.

The stream cut through my plastic piece without a puff of smoke. Pitching it away, I took up one of the metal tags. It was smaller than the opening, so no need to fold or break the material. I only hoped it didn't explode and destroy the door system, and me, when it contacted the power flow.

Another clean slice.

I folded one of the strips into four layers. Same result. Cursing, I flung it aside and stared at the blue stream. I needed something special. Something built to block and reflect an energy stream more powerful than forces normally found on a station.

Something similar to the material in my awaysuit.

Something like...my glove.

I had the left one off before I even thought things through. I folded the forefinger into a compressed length. The gloves were made of the same material as my awaysuit, but they were more flexible. In an overall assessment of the suit, they were the weakest point. They had to be if you wanted to crook a finger around a firing mechanism or press a button.

The bare fingers of my left hand felt stiff without my glove. I hadn't noticed the temperature in the ring earlier when I took my helmet off, but the place was chilly. The air wasn't freezing, but I hoped the glove stayed intact so I could put it back on.

There was no point in overthinking things. Any delay only brought the ghost closer in its next circle to Section Ten. I wanted the kid out and us both up the fall before that happened.

Grasping the glove in my right hand, I turned the thickest edge of the material to the blue stream and slid it in.

The flow erupted outward. Blue fire danced over the surface of my suit and a searing pain engulfed my bare left hand. The power lanced off my fingertips, striking the floor with a blast that threw me back into a row of stationary chairs. The airlock slammed open. The blast of station air that rushed to fill the vacuum blew the tabletop inward, while all the debris inside blasted outward into the station. The doors rammed closed against the plate and stopped. Lights on the lock flashed red.

My suit protected me from broken bones. I stumbled back to the airlock.

The rush of air had moved the body. The boot I'd seen in the glass was attached to a little, limp form lying facedown on the lock plate. I bent to inspect the gray, nondescript suit for tears. The material was old, similar to early, primitive stuff we often saw on the frontier, but it was intact, and that was what mattered. I reached out to turn the body.

Saw my left hand was a charred, cracked mess leaking blood and plasma, the ends of my fingers split and shattered where the energy from the lock had blasted out through them.

Shit! I was hurt bad.

With the sight of the damage, pain struck. I fell back to sit on the airlock floor while nausea and agony rolled over me. I nearly blacked out, but a strange vibration at the base of my spine forced into my attention. The station floor was shaking.

Idwal was isolating Section Ten!

I grabbed the back of the kid's suit with my right hand—a spinal injury, like the damage to my hand, was repairable, but first we had to survive this—and tried to lunge back inside the station.

My grip slipped and darkness closed in on me.

CHAPTER 11

Bloody Angel

The energy lash is agony across my back. One of the older boys who was on the ship when we arrived told me screaming makes it hurt less and satisfies the sadistic streak of the crewmember wielding the whip; to make the punishment shorter. Maybe it is true. I'm too young to know anything about psychology, or what the word "sadistic" means. I scream because of the pain.

It feels as if it's searing the flesh off my bones, but I know it's not. There won't be any marks on me after this punishment. That's why the slavers use the energy lash on us. Human trafficking does not offend their clientele, but they don't want to see any signs of abuse on the merchandise—or at least not that kind.

Mandy got me into this trouble. She's never resolved herself to our fate. She cries at night and calls for her momma. She wandered off a few hours ago, looking for her parents again—walked out of the small bunkroom assigned to me and the five other kids from our settlement that I'm in charge of. She got back into engineering and almost lost a finger in a locker door. It's badly bruised, and she hasn't stopped crying since they brought her back.

It's not the first time she's gotten me whipped. I try to tell myself it's because she's so young, but my brother Anthy is even younger, and he's no trouble. Of course, Anthy is always smiling and sweet, in spite of our misery. He doesn't really know what has happened to us. He laughs and plays, and the crew likes him. Mandy just cries and has a snotty nose all the time. She's still one of the five kids I have to protect from the lash. They're little. They don't understand.

The energy from the lash sizzles over my nerve endings one last time and I scream.

***

Something patted my cheek.

I opened my eyes.

A tiny angel with solemn features stared down at me, its hair the color of watery bloodstains on white cloth.

"Saura," I croaked. This wasn't my dewdrop.

A quizzical expression came over the angel's face. After a moment, the expression deepened to a puzzled frown.

There were things beyond the angel's head: beams, ducts, vents. Station things.

I shuddered. Moved my hand.

Memory came back in a blaze of agony. My hand was a charred wreck. I—we—were under attack. Idwal had sealed me in, and there was a kid... I reached out and grasped the angel by the arm with my good hand. Felt the rough surface of a transition suit beneath my own glove.

This kid.

Apparently, enough time had passed for it to recover consciousness and remove its headgear. I couldn't tell whether it was a boy or a girl, but it was a beautiful human child. The kind people exclaim over and instantly adore.

Like my little brother Anthy.

Not the sort of child one expects to find on a retired matter processing facility on the edge of nowhere.

Was this our cargo? The question flashed in my head. Were the larger beings who accompanied it part of the deal?

There was all that extra Human food in our third cabin...

What had those two clown-idiots back at Mandragala gotten us into?

I was still functioning. The software in my head and the nanites the corps put in my body were working to contain pain and repair tissue, but nothing inside me could fix that much charred skin, and the pain-drain wasn't going to work for long. I had to get additional relief into my system if I wanted to get us out of here.

I released the kid's arm and fumbled with the tool pack on my hip. After a few seconds of watching, she—for some reason I thought it looked like a she—pushed the pack's cover back and looked at me.

It contained several items, and she didn't know which one I wanted.

"At the top, in the fold," I whispered. Ragged pain tore at my brain. If I didn't secure relief soon, I'd slip into shock.

The kid frowned, expression sad, and shook its head.

"Talk!" I barked in frustration. The expensive language software buried in my head couldn't do anything until I had a few sounds to work with. "Dammit, say something. Anything!"

She flinched at the anger my voice but stayed beside me.

This was not the time for a language lesson. I plucked at the flap with my good hand, trying to get at the tiny, precious cylinder nestled there. She watched for a moment, then lightly pushed my hand away and tugged at the fold. The tape securing it separated and the ampoule rolled out.

Mother Universe, it was intact! I closed my eyes for a second in gratitude. When I opened them, the kid had it in her hand.

She held it out to me.

I reached, positioning it carefully in my fingers. My hand shook with pain and the anticipation of relief, but the kid held rock steady, allowing me to grasp it firmly between my thumb and two fingers before letting go. As long as I held one of the ends pressed against my skin and put pressure on the opposite one, the precious painkiller would inject.

The thing was illegal as hell, but all spacers carried one. Security everywhere knew and ignored it—unless you were unlucky enough to encounter the one dirty bastard who would confiscate it to resell. Those guys didn't last long on the job. Word got out, and they met a knife to the ribs in a dark corner somewhere. Spacers watching out for fellow spacers. Sometimes that it was all the justice we had. Carrying the little ampoule was that important. It meant the difference between life and death at times like this.

I fumbled, desperately afraid of dropping the thing before I could inject its contents. I could crush the shell in my teeth and swallow the stuff, but the effects took longer that way. If I passed out from pain before it started to work and my body chose shock over waking, we were probably going to die.

I got the ampoule positioned against my charred skin so my thumb could press the end. It was designed for a gloved spacer hand to use—the accidents in space that made its possession a necessity frequently happened outside a ship during repair—but my hand shook too hard. I dropped my head back onto the deck plate in frustration.

Tried to rally my strength again.

The pain suddenly subsided.

The kid held up the empty injection cylinder with a questioning look.

Even if she didn't speak, at least she had good sense.

She placed the empty ampoule back in the hidden fold while I took a deep breath and waited for the painkiller to spread its effect. The stuff bought a spacer time to return to their ship after an injury. It would keep me clearheaded and pain-free for an hour at best. It wouldn't cure anything and it sure as hell wouldn't rescue us.

When the shakiness cleared my body, I sat up and looked around. We were in the airlock, with the tabletop jammed widthwise and slanted upward in the opening. With the restoration of air, the gravity field inside the lock had restored.

I was in serious trouble. Pushing down panic, I positioned my left arm in my lap and rolled my forearm upward. Ignoring the blackened, oozing thing beyond the cuff of my suit, I mentally ran through the Spacer Prayer—meant to cover every entity in the known universe—then pressed the commlink buried in the skin of my inner forearm. The sleeve might have protected those controls.

Or the energy blast that cooked my hand might have traveled up the nerves and bone to destroy the circuitry. Hence the prayer.

A vibration of response sent a rush of dizzying relief through me. I had contact with the world outside my body. I keyed the sequence to buzz Saura.

No response. I tried the ship. Nothing. Either Saura was lying low, or she and the *Hand* were gone. Temporarily, I hoped.

I tugged off my headgear. The smell of burned flesh and dust hung in the air.

The kid watched me warily, ready to spring away if I reached out again. A strange woman on an alien station; yeah, I understood her reaction. For kids, most adults were bad news. I counted myself lucky she was willing to get near enough to help me at all.

I took the opportunity to look at her.

She looked Human. She had pale skin, the kind of porcelain that went with white hair. I checked her eyes—usually that's a giveaway for another specie-origin. Human-normal brown irises regarded me with steady intelligence. She had two arms and two legs, two nostrils and two ears—the right number for any features that counted. I guessed her age at six years.

Had she realized the fate of the people who had traveled with her yet? I'd seen tears and sorrow on more small faces than I cared to remember, but hers was not one. Either she didn't know, or she'd exhausted her reactions while I was out. If I could persuade her to speak, my translation software could cue in on whatever language she spoke and tell me where she and the dead spacers came from.

"Who are you?" I gestured with my good hand, fingers fluttering at my mouth to indicate words coming out, and pointed at her.

When she shook her head, dismay washed over me. The movement did not indicate confusion at my question. It said she did not speak.

But she could hear.

"Freedom? Amaterasu? New Palestine, Beijing, New Chai?" I named some of the worlds that distinct Human languages dominated.

She squeezed her face in a funny expression then frowned at me again.

If she were mute, she would have used her hands. If her people communicated by expression—something I'd never heard off—it would take more time than we currently had to understand each other.

"We have to find a way into the next section and up to my ship." I got to my feet, paused until a swirl of dizziness passed, then clambered over the plate and out into the ring. The lights had dropped several levels in brightness while we were in the airlock. As I stood there, they dropped again and the red lights around the lock hatch shut off with a loud mechanical clack. The warning sounds that had clamored relentlessly over the past hours were dropping off in noticeable stages.

Section Ten was shutting down.

When the power cut off, the air pumps and temperature controls would go. We'd have the section's oxygen—until it got too cold for our lungs. Then we had our suits to protect us until their power reserves ran out. I would be dead from shock long before that happened, but the kid...

She followed me across to the gigantic doors that sealed us away from Section One. The Proambu announcements stopped abruptly and another level of lighting shut down. In the dimness, I searched for an override switch to open a way between the sections, though I didn't expect to find one. The hard truth of survival in space is that a few beings trapped on the wrong side of a decompressing section are not worth risking the integrity of a whole facility. Still, I walked the length of the door in case the Proambu did supply an access hatch. If they did, I missed it. Section Nine's wall would be the same.

The pumps stopped, and a vast silence settled over the place. We had a big problem if the *Thief's Hand* didn't appear outside Section Ten to rescue us soon and that couldn't happen because of the threat lurking outside.

A twitch on my right sleeve drew my attention. The kid was staring out past the airlock.

A wave of dismay washed over me. The light-eating blotch against the starlight had returned, only this time it was smaller. The ghost had sent in a shuttle.

The kid tugged for me to retreat toward the core. Whoever was on the shuttle terrified her.

They terrified me, too. "You stay here," I told her.

I went to the airlock to snatch up our headgear. For a brief moment, as I stood there watching the star-devouring smudge thread its way nearer, I felt a surge of hope. The station's security system would surely sense its presence and strike in defense. Then I realized, with all the scattered debris swirling outside, Idwal had probably shut down the local defense array.

The kid put her headgear on when I handed it to her. I secured mine, then, catching the material of her suit between two fingers, I drew her back to the structures fronting the inner core. They were plain, solid constructions and I knew from my earlier search that the door on the third one would open.

Putting my right hand on her back, I pushed her inside. "Wait here," I said.

The look in her eyes said she wanted to protest; she didn't know how.

I closed the door.

The people on the shuttle would see that the airlock stood open stationside and was empty. If they wanted the kid, they were going to have to come inside and I didn't want her in my way if I had to defend our position.

If things went really bad, I just hoped she had the sense to stay hidden and, conversely, to come out in time to make contact with Saurubi.

Yeah, that might be a bit much to ask of anyone. It wouldn't fall on her if I could prevent it.

I walked back to the outer glass.

The shuttle had activated bright external lights and was nudging aside the debris its mothership had created to make its way closer to the station wall. The death-black hull, with its outline of spiny edges, created an odd effect. It sucked away any light that fell on it like the event horizon of a black hole, an effect I'd never seen before.

This shuttle was larger than a Human one, marking the inhabitants as larger, too. Several species in the Whooex met that description. Outside the Whooex Union, who knew how many species existed?

Whoever they were, they weren't coming inside while the plate held the doors to the airlock open. Even if they activated the outer controls, Idwal would never let them override that obstacle. They didn't realize it yet, but we were at an impasse. Getting inside would demand a really aggressive action on their part. My instincts told me they would try.

An attack would delay Saura's arrival, which squeezed the window tighter on the time the kid and I had.

Damn that Frairy and MoMo!

I drew my tazer and dropped down between some chairs back toward the wall of Section Nine. They were bolted to the floor, with little risk of them rushing out the airlock if whoever was out there managed to breach the ring. I breathed in slowly to sharpen focus and prepared to pick off boarders as they came inside. There would be flying debris. Some of the overhead fixtures could wrench out of their settings. But the invaders would have combat gear similar to mine. I slid the setting on the tazer to its highest level, to kill, and buzzed Saura one more time while I waited.

No response.

Heart pounding, I gave in and queried the *Hand* directly.

On the third try, I got a low-level, double pulse in my wrist. It was the signal the ship was shutting down.

Mother Universe! Had I missed a response from Saura during all the craziness, warning me the *Hand* was under attack? I tried to run a quick back search, but the program didn't respond. Shit! What had I missed? What had happened to make Saura put herself into a SAC and place the ship's power on reserve? It didn't tell me if she was injured or if the *Hand* had sustained damage.

There was no rescue coming anytime soon.

I wanted to roar in frustration. What had I been thinking, talking to a Frairy and a MoMo? I'd gotten us shanghaied into this job, and now everything was falling apart.

No. Training and rational thought pushed through. The *Hand* had responded to me. The ship was functional. Saura was safe. All I had to do was take care of these bastards, then I could leave the kid here, go outside and up the wall of the facility to the *Hand*. Secure more painkillers, check on Saura, and bring the *Hand* down to the kid—who appeared to be part of our intended cargo. We had a third

SAC to go with the third cabin. I could set our destination back to Mandragala and we'd work out a strategy for the rest after we got home.

I had a plan.

Can you do that, Zant?

Ser, yes ser!

The shuttle came to a stop several meters outside the airlock. I settled lower to the floor to watch the hatch slide open and three long, thin, bipedal figures in black suits emerge. Two arms, two legs, and a head. I ran through the catalog of Whooex specie-members in my software. They could be any of several.

One of the crew moved across the gap to peer inside the airlock, then motioned at the other two. Someone inside the shuttle bay shoved a bulky item out. They wrestled with the thing and it blossomed outward.

A net. The bastards had a freaking net! My heart plummeted. They were going to blow the lock and catch whatever rushed out with the air.

They were after the kid, and they wanted her alive. Otherwise, they would have just blown this section and left. I was merely an inconvenient witness. They would bundle her aboard their ship and shove me toward the sun, with an additional slice to my suit material.

I looked around, searching for something to give me an edge—as if things had magically changed in the last couple of minutes.

Nothing.

Meanwhile, the first guy was attaching some large, round objects to the outside of station. Magnets with lockdowns. I heard the solid thud of their contact and a secondary "thup" as they secured onto the plasglass surface. The other two blacksuits began securing corners of the net to the anchored magnets.

A long mechanical item emerged from the hatch. As they passed it forward my heart sank even lower. Mechanical jaws. Standard gear for military assault on a station airlock.

Section Ten would soon be open to the universe.

I got up and stumbled over to the doors. Kicked tentatively at the plate wedged between them. With a little work and careful timing, I might have one defensive weapon against the murdering bastards outside—if I could manage the task with one hand and a rapidly diminishing painkiller.

The blacksuit closest to the airlock finally saw me. It paused. Across a gap of several meters we stared at each other, though neither of us could see the other's features through our headgear.

Word of my presence traveled back to command inside the shuttle. I saw activity at their hatch. Someone peered out then disappeared again. The blacksuit resumed its work.

They had dismissed me as a low-level threat.

Big mistake!

I climbed inside the airlock. The inner doors had slammed closed on the tabletop so fast they caught it mid-fall, angling the lockside end upward a half of a meter. I put the fingers of my right hand under its edge and lifted.

The plate slipped up a fraction.

The door actuators whined.

I lifted again, being careful not to flip the thing out of the grip of the doors. There was little chance of that happening, however: it took every gram of strength I had to move the plate.

The guy working the jaws finally realized what I was up to and redoubled his efforts to pry the spaceside doors open.

He'd be at that awhile. Grimly I yanked up one more time, maximizing the angle to catch as much of the air blast exiting the station as possible. When those outer doors opened, the plate was going out into space. It wouldn't stop the inevitable, but it might punch a hole in the net and do some damage. And, as it blew outward the inner doors would slam closed again, causing the boarders to force them open, too. It would only inconvenience them, but it would give me a chance to take out one or two with my tazer as they came inside.

If the painkiller lasted.

I set aside my weapon and activated the beacon in my suit. That would allow Saura to recover my body if they threw me into the Vasty. Then I climbed back inside the ring.

The last of the section lights had shut down while I repositioned the plate, so the only light now came from the gas giant slowly moving past Section Nine's wall, and the shuttle's external lamps. That actually worked for me. I walked toward the core, making sure the blacksuit with the hatch-buster observed me. It was the logical place to retreat. When I got into the shadows, however, I cut over along Section Nine's wall, back through the seats to settle in position across from the airlock. When I was satisfied I had a clear, unobstructed line of fire, I situated the base of a seat between my thighs, locked my ankles and rolled left then right, making the chair base strike my thighs. The suit material turned rigid, locking me in place.

I wasn't going anywhere.

Too bad the pain relief meds were seriously beginning to wear off.

CHAPTER 12

Everything Goes to Pieces

It was the blacksuits' bad luck the Proambu airlock surrendered its resistance all at one time. The outer lock doors simply sprang open. The station air gushed out, catching the plate and shooting it outward, straight into the mechanical jaws positioned outside the hatch. They both crashed into the blacksuit operator caught behind them, hurling everything back into the net. Glimmers of metal shards spun outward, slicing the rigging lines.

The inner doors, freed of their obstacle, slammed shut, creating a swirling backrush of air inside the ring. Things creaked and rattled ominously in the darkness above me.

The damage inflicted by the hurtling plate gave the boarders a quick change of focus. The two uninjured ones freed the webbing on one side of the lock to tow the injured jaw operator and his tool back to their shuttle. Runnels of sweat crept down my body as I watched their retreat and wondered how much pain he felt compared to mine.

A dull sound drew me back from the edge of darkness. Shivering violently, I lifted my head and stared through bleary eyes. The blacksuits had removed the net and were wrestling it and the magnets back inside their shuttle.

It surprised me they were giving up that easily after taking what we Humans considered minor peripheral damage.

That was fine by me.

The problem was, I'd forgotten about the kid. I should have known that when everything erupted it would frighten her and she would come out to check on things. By the time I realized that, she was a stark silhouette in the light shining through the glass.

She had her back to it, looking inward, trying to locate me.

Mother—! "No!" If the blacksuits saw her, they would resume their effort to breach the ring. Frantically I ran my hand down the inside of my thighs to relax my awaysuit's grip on the chair base.

The movement sent a wave of dizziness rolling over me.

My painkiller had run its course.

I tried to reach the left sleeve of my awaysuit. In the cuff of my shipskins I had a stash of stim packs. I had avoided the thought of using one until now because a stim would blast my system with energy and counter the anesthetic.

Now I needed a final bit of edge to work through this.

I took two steps and fell on my left side. My right arm refused to push me up. Trembling uncontrollably, I watched the blacksuits bundle their equipment into their shuttle.

Their hatch remained open on what seemed a long period of inactivity...

The dull thud of something striking the plasglass of the inner airlock doors pulled me back to reality. A blacksuit stood inside the chamber, staring directly at me. When he saw he had my attention he made a gesture, a flippant motion of the hand with the first two fingers extended, the way spacers signed goodbye. Then he kicked out of the opening, pausing long enough to slam a hand on the external controls and close the outer doors before he pushed off and retreated to his shuttle. This time the hatch closed behind him. The light cut off and the shuttle became a black blotch rippling over the stars as it slid away.

I stared, confused at what had just taken place. They had gotten inside the airlock while I was out, then they just waved and left? Nothing was that easy.

And why had he bothered to close the outer doors after fighting so hard to open them?

What did it matter? They were gone. I needed to get the kid and get us the hell out of here—

The airlock erupted into the station with a spray of plasglass and construction material. Instantly, the air in the section, rushing outward, swept the ball of destruction backward, out into space.

The effect of the two forces clashing ripped a massive hole in the station's outer wall and Section Ten opened onto the universe.

***

Damned Frairy! I shrugged to shake it off and the small form spun away into free space.

Mother Universe! That was the kid! I made a frantic grab for her foot, caught and pulled her back before she flew through the gaping hole in Idwal, out into oblivion. Instinct made me pull her tighter against me before I had time to collect my memory on what had happened.

Objects in the area were moving fast, spinning out into the Vasty, so I hadn't been unconscious for long. Still, the kid couldn't have much air left in her suit.

The ghost shuttle had vanished. Whatever was going on here, they'd apparently thought it was worth three acts of war against the Proambu and one unofficial act against the Earth Alliance.

At least they had given us a way out of Section Ten.

Pressing the kid to my chest, I tried to reach the controls on my left arm again. The sight of my hand nearly caused me to pass out. Frozen droplets of blood and plasma clung to blackened flesh and frost-rimed cracks that were deep and red. A chunk of exposed bone gleamed at the base of my forefinger where the frozen flesh had struck something and broken away. I had to stop and force control over panic. The cold had frozen my wound and dulled the pain, allowing me a few seconds of clarity. It wouldn't last. I had to stay calm and get to Idwal's upper hold, to the *Hand*. A med facility could always regrow damaged parts of my body. The MoMo and Thok would pay for that and any other damage we or the *Thief's Hand* sustained. I would make damned sure of it.

I needed a stim pack now for sure. I forced up the sleeve of my awaysuit and discovered, to my horror, that without the glove, my shipskins had not been able to protect my arm. The cold of space had moved up beneath the cuff, locking everything in a block of ice. The reality of my situation was even worse: the cold would swiftly continue up my arm, into my shoulder and up to my brain. It was only a matter of which killed me first, but I was going to be dead very soon.

If Saura was gone, so were the kid and I.

The little form I held pressed to my chest had stopped moving, whether from weariness, resignation, or lack of air, I didn't know. I tightened my arm and bitterly apologized to her for my failure.

I should have been smarter, better prepared for the unexpected. I should have insisted on more information from the cursed clown-duo on Mandragala.

Once again, Vivi Zant had failed to protect the young and helpless.

I howled in pain deeper than anything physical as Idwal slowly rotated, the gap in its side filling with the starry vastness that surrounded its remote bit of space.

Amid the debris there was a purposeful movement of something making its way toward us.

No sharp, starlight-eating edges on this one, I noted as my mind shut down.

***

Saura? But she wasn't white...

I blinked.

My angel was back, her hand poised above my face. It confused me until I realized she was staring down from outside a med unit, with her hand resting on the curve of the glass. Her transition suit was gone, replaced by something white that draped small shoulders and made her appear even more delicate.

I tried to smile, to ease the concerned expression in her dark eyes, but the effort was exhausting.

Her mouth tightened, but the tension in her face eased.

A gnarl-knuckled pale hand with three long, spatulate fingers and an equally long thumb settled on her shoulder and gently nudged her away.

My memory twitched.

Ritto-ssa. The EA did not have official relations with them, but they had a presence on the Outer Rim.

I could not form words.

A memory flashed: the maw of deepspace, with debris floating between it and me. A sense of the cold sinking in, the thinning air. The fear and outrage of knowing I was dying in the Vasty.

We had been rescued. I lay in an auto-doc of some type, inside a ship, and the kid was with me.

Where was Saura? Had our rescuers found her? Did they even know she was out there? The kid didn't know—maybe couldn't have told them even if she did.

I tried to move my head, to look upward, but my neck refused to respond. I tried to speak...

Barely forced a grunt.

I had no way to let our rescuers know there was another person on Idwal and that every passing second was taking us lightyears away from her.

A wild animal wail filled my ears and a warm sensation ran down my cheek. I was making the noise. I was crying.

There was a flicker of movement outside the glass and quiet peace flooded me, pushing my distress aside. Someone tranquilized me into darkness.

I woke several times. Probably there were many more I didn't remember. Sometimes I could see a blur of movement at the edge of my vision, but every time, my angel was there, watching me. Each time I attempted to tell our rescuers they had left someone back at Idwal.

Each time, I fell back into oblivion.

I was growing weaker. Moving closer to death. The Ritto-ssa had rescued me, but they did not know Human physiology. They could not fix me.

Worse, they had left Saurubi behind.

***

Nothing stirs the Human spirit like the touch of sunlight. Maybe it's something left over from our primordial days, when its glow told us it was a good day to hunt and forage as we climbed out of our tree or cave. I don't know. To me, it feels like...life.

I opened my eyes to blue sky and the face of my angel centered in a halo of sunlight. I was still in the auto-doc, with her hand perched in its place on the glass above my cheek. This time, however, her eyes looked sadder than usual as she stared in at me.

I sensed movement nearby. Activity flickered in my peripheral vision. The auto-doc had moved off the ship and into a place that at least mimicked a planet sky.

Perhaps a Human planet.

I wanted to know if a twin of my auto-doc stood nearby; one containing a splash of red and dusky blue, but I wasn't able to turn my head. I looked up at my angel.

She had an expression of regret on her face.

No! Wherever this place, who, or whatever was here, she was too young to cope with it on her own. If she stayed with me, I could help her.

Her brown eyes told me she recognized my concern. Her hand lifted from the glass. With a smile, a wave, and a flit of white, she was gone.

Our rescuers must have noticed the spike of distress in my vitals because peaceful darkness folded in around me again.

CHAPTER 13

Facing Down Memories

"Where's Anthy?" My heart pounds.

I left my five charges safe in our bunkroom when a crewmember called me out to move boxes in one of the holds. Now I am staring at only four children.

"Where's Anthy?" I repeat. I catch Jun by his straight, black hair and slam him against the bulkhead. He is seven and old enough to understand the rules.

His eyes widen with fear. "I didn't see."

"See what?" My panic rises. Anthy is three and capable of getting into lots of trouble.

"I didn't see him leave," Jun stammers.

"He left with the shiplady," Appa pipes up behind me. I swing about to look at the five-year-old. Her eyes are large and innocent. "The sad one. Anthy went with her."

I release Jun and put my hands to my sides to keep the others from seeing how much they shake. Why? What did that woman want with him? Crew contact with us is strictly limited. The first night, when they herded us out of the shuttle and into the ship, they gathered us in the hangar, a small knot of weeping, terrified children, and the Captain told us: no one spoke, touched, or interacted with us unless it was ship business. He brought Old Pieter to the front and told us the short, grizzled old man was in charge of us—that he knew how to take care of us. Old Pieter nodded and said we must listen to him, do what he said, and tell him if anyone in the crew bothered us. If we did not tell, terrible things would happen to us when he found out. Old Pieter always found out, the Captain warned. He squeezed his eyes narrow when he looked at us to let us know he meant it. We moved closer together and believed him.

Old Pieter told us he was not our Momma or Papa. He was better. He knew how to take care of children because he was special-trained. There was no sense of kindness to him, only a sense of responsibility. He was an old man who walked with a heavy limp. He did not smile, but he did not get angry and yell at us, either. He firmly repeated what he wanted done until we did it.

Or he punished us terribly if he thought we deserved it.

"You stay here!" I tell the four youngers. I am beginning to sweat as I turn and run back up the dim passageway. The metal grid under my feet rings softly with the impact of my weight.

Where is Anthy?

They tell us not to trust the adults around us, which is not difficult after what they did to our families. The distrust has grown even deeper since I talked to children from other groups who have been here longer. They tell me stories about what happens when they are taken out on the docks at night when the ship puts into a port. I am horrified. I am afraid for me, yes, but for the younger children more. I and the others from New Bounty are farm children; we understand some of what the others tell us better than they do. It is wrong. We know that. We are only children, however. We cling to what we know, and what we know now is this ship and its crew. They hold us prisoner, but they also feed and care for us. Old Pieter tries to make us feel a part of the ship. He slips us small, secretive kindnesses, rebuffs us with harsh words, then pulls us back with a rare, crooked smile. One of the older boys, Jon, has warned me: it is all cleverly meant to draw us in. We will learn to do what we are told to do, or we will die.

My heart races with fear for my little brother.

I turn down an intersecting corridor and run through pools of light and shadow, past dark metal walls until I come to the children's showers. My heart pounds as I step inside the humid room. Bad things have happened here: the older kids have told me. Once, a crewman cornered a kid... They said the Captain put the man into an airlock without a suit and opened the outer doors. They forced the children to watch so they would understand that no one except the "clients" could touch them. It does not stop an angry older kid from attacking a younger occasionally. When that happens, the older kid disappears. I hear whispers they go to lower levels of the ship. That below our deck they keep adult Humans to sell for labor. Sometimes the victim is put back in with the other children; sometimes the victim disappears, too.

Anthy is not in the shower room.

I step back out, frantic, and look up and down the passageway. As I turn to run further in my search, I see movement at the lighted intersection far up the way.

***

I woke to the sound of crickets.

Crickets.

In all my years in the Vasty, I had forgotten the sound of insects chirping on a warm planet night. Someone had delved deep into my subconscious to find I would respond positively to that sound.

The realization that someone was rummaging in my brain sent a shot of adrenalin through me. I lifted my head to look around.

A white-walled room the size of the total living quarters on the *Hand* told me I was planetside. Room on stations was too valuable to give over to more than function required. I rested in a gravity sling, a device used in medical facilities to aid healing, and there was no chrono or calendar in sight to add the pressure of passing time.

I tried to connect with the world system, to discover where I was, but the chips inside my head did not pull any information back to me. The walls shifted to a darker shade of gray, a color intended to sooth, and I realized I had been down this path before, after things went bad off Vacca. I was in a rehab facility. All the effects, including tech connections, or the lack thereof, were meant to calm me.

Because discovering the extent of my injuries and their long term effects would distress me.

An image of yawning space flashed before my eyes and the machines monitoring my vitals took over, pumping stuff into my body to force calm. The flood of chemical oblivion could not stop the images of Idwal, Saurubi, the ghost ship, the kid, the pain, or the emptiness of the Vasty this time. It all needed to come out sooner or later, and someone had determined the medical diagnosis for me was the old EA combat treatment philosophy of "sooner."

Get it out; get it over with. Move on to solutions. Ooh-rah.

I had been through this before; I knew the logic, and I knew how it must resolve.

I fell into a dark time, second only to watching a ship explode off the Zephyr Isles, as I faced down my memories, sorted things out, and healed.

The walls of the room slid with kaleidoscoping color.

***

I blinked and the walls shaded a dark, stormy gray.

There was movement at my left shoulder. Twisting my head, I discovered a large mudslide covered in medical whites tweaking the settings on my monitors.

I breathed out a sigh of relief.

Everyone knows that the Xix, or Zeeks, as we Humans call them, run the best medical facilities in the Whooex Union. The lumpy, brown, two-and-a-half meter tall creatures look similar to big piles of dirt and gravel, but their understanding of life and what makes it work is unsurpassed. Their expertise in the physiology of Humans is legendary.

Which is a supreme irony, since the Xix were once a conquering terror. They spread out across star systems, decimating countless populations and worlds. Then they discovered how other lifeforms functioned.

Zeeks have only two states of being: living or dead. They can overcome minor damage to their bodies, but there is no healing their heavy, soil-like forms if they experience extensive damage. Discovering that other creatures' bodies could mend and heal was a transformative event in their social evolution. They began a fervent study of biology and science and, over several hundred of our years, became the most competent doctors in the Whooex Union. Now they nurture their fragile fellow unionists with the gentle care of a gardener tending precious plants.

The creature beside me reached over a brown hand five times the size of my own and patted my left shoulder reassuringly.

My left shoulder.

That snapped me to another level of reality. I lifted my arm, twisting it to stare at my left palm. The flesh was as smooth and pink as baby skin. The Xix had put me through regeneration! It would take a lot of wear and tear to acquire my arm's original state of aged toughness, but, by the Mother Universe, it was there! I rolled my shoulder to feel the movement, then laid my head back in the gravity sling so I could put some order to the emotions that flooded me.

The Zeek made a soft trilling sound I recognized as laughter.

"Thank you." I turned my head to look up at it. "Thank you."

The creature blinked its three brown eyes and gave a slight downward gesture of its brown, lumpy head in acknowledgment. It was like watching a bank of earth fall toward me.

The Zeek resumed fiddling with a bit of handheld tech while I took some time to compose my thoughts. With so many questions burning in my brain, I found it hard to focus. I could see my personal feeds in my left side peri-vision—they read normal—but my ship feeds were missing. The one in my right eye, which gave me information on the external world, was dead. I tried to make a connection with the world system. Failed.

The attendant stopped its work and stood watching me, anticipating my need.

"Can you tell me where—" I rasped. My throat felt scaly from disuse.

Before I could finish my question a commotion in the hallway outside the room pulled the Zeek's attention away from me.

No. No interruptions! I needed to find out where I was. And Saura! How long had I been here? A regen this major generally took ninety days. Ninety days! I needed to find Saura, then locate the kid.

I tried to raise my voice, to reclaim my attendant's attention. "Where—?"

The Zeek swung toward the door. I heard a rumbling sound of protest from another Zeek—too low for my translator to interpret—then a hissed snarl of response.

My translator picked out the word "illegal."

My attendant emitted an unhappy sound and took a step toward the hall. He stopped short as the door flung open and a tall, dark form swept into the room.

Any mental comfort I had gained from my present environment fell to zero.

CHAPTER 14

Doubling the Paragraph

I'd never seen one in the flesh, but I knew what I was looking at, the same way I knew fire burned flesh and poison killed.

The Endar ignored the bulky medical attendant standing in front of him with a dismissive air that said no other being in the universe would dare lay a hand on its person. The red eyes swept imperiously over the room and locked on me. "I ordered your administrator to report to me the moment it woke up," it snarled at the Zeek.

The Marines played a recording of the Endar language, or Arpi, for us once. It sounded like a series of creaks, snarls, snaps, and clicks. Rumor said they considered their native tongue sacred and did not speak it to the rest of us other, lowly species. Arrogant bastards. All I knew was my EA language pack never received software to interpret it, leaving me chip mute to Arpi.

This one had its translator set to convert its audible speech to Xix. The sounds came out with a harsh, snarling undertone my attendant did not effect. It was disturbing, but my software translated XIX.

The Endar had referred to me as 'it'. Looked as if we shared the same level of regard for each other.

The Zeek gave another rumble, which my language chip interpreted as "just woke."

"And yet you have not reported. I am forced to rely on the security monitors to receive my information."

The white-coated mountain made a slight bow. "Patient able have visitor two minutes."

The Endar cut the attendant a dismissive glance. "I will take all the time I require."

The Zeek made a distinct sound of displeasure and took a slow step toward the door.

"You will remain," the Endar ordered.

The attendant stopped, then shuffled around to face into the room. He locked his eyes on the monitors above and behind me.

"It is well enough to travel?" the Endar asked, its red-irised eyes locking back on me.

"Human recovers."

"Not here. Not any longer."

It would be nice if someone told me where 'here' was. "Can someone tell me where I am, please?" I asked.

The Zeek started a rumbling response.

"Be silent!" The Endar snapped. "Human, you do not belong here."

Left up to the Endar, I doubted I would belong anywhere in the universe.

"I am the High Jerak Seok, Faiya of the Endar Primacy," he continued. "Your presence on this world is a violation of Whooex Union law. You will be removed immediately."

How does one respond to such a gracious greeting? Not in the manner of my first instinct.

At least he hadn't announced my arrest. Yet. "I want to talk to the Earth Alliance Ambassador." I croaked. One of the few things we'd gotten right on Earth, all on our own, was the Whooex Union setup for diplomatically relating with fellow member Star Associations—at least in the formal arena.

"Humans have no representation here."

The Ritto-ssa had brought me to a Whooex world that did not have diplomatic ties with the Earth Alliance? Great. That meant I must tread carefully to minimize political ramifications.

Serious as the situation appeared, there could be a reasonable explanation for it.

"High Jerak Seok," I gave him a polite nod while my mind struggled to come up to speed. "I assure you, there is no intentional violation of law here. I was injured in a deepspace accident. My rescuers did not have the skills to heal me. I'm sure they brought me to the closest medical facility they found. You are aware I have recently awakened and I am not currently linked into the world system." If this world banned Humans that made sense. "Please tell me the name of the world on which I trespass."

The Endar stared at me as if he didn't comprehend my words, though I had the distinct impression he simply didn't consider them worth a response.

I took advantage of the pause to absorb the details of his appearance. My information might never get to the right people, but, once an EA-trained observer, always an EA-trained observer.

I had heard Endar were tall and thin to the point of near-stick-figure caricatures. Check that off as accurate. The High Jerak's face had Humanoid features—meaning a discernable set of eyes, a nose, and mouth—but its head was longer and thinner, and its face flatter, so the eyes and lips sat almost flush to the smooth gray surface. Between, there was a faintly raised, corrugated ridge running down the center between a pair of long, diagonal, fleshy slits.

A thin neck with ridges of smooth, rounded material that reminded me of tubes supported the head. Those cartilage strips supposedly enabled his people to turn their heads over one hundred and eighty degrees. His eyes were rounded, similar to a bird's, with blood red irises and a shiny dot of black pupil. The skin on his hands was gray and tight, accentuating tendons and bone. Though most of his body was covered, I knew it was gaunt, the long, flexible sinews sharply revealed over his bones. His long, triple jointed fingers sported scythe-like black nails. More striking than all that, however, was his garb. His outermost robe was an open, floor-length black leather coat, stark, expensive, and authoritarian. Beneath it, he was drowning in more layers of leather, from short jerkins to long vests, to coats in varying lengths. They were all thin, black leather, with simple lines, and heavily worked with intricate detail. A thin strip of red satin tucked at the neckline of his top layer jarred the senses against all that black.

The parts of the High Jerak's skin not covered with leather were smooth and grey, shading darker along the sides of the hands and face, and his thick black hair flowed from a sharp widow's peak on the forehead, straight down his back.

Straight. Rigid. The same as him. No doubt, High Jerak Seok was an important being in the Primacy.

The sight of all that leather sent wavelets of uneasiness lapping over my own skin. Humans possessed the technology to manufacture something far superior to tanned animal skin, but there were still people willing to lay down huge sums of money to own bits of clothing made with the real thing. It was an effete symbol of prestige.

I was willing to bet his leather was real.

The EA didn't know enough about the Endar to put up a paragraph in a textbook. When I got off this world, that information would double. I didn't want to prolong my contact enough to contribute more.

In contrast to our ignorance, the Endar knew a lot about us. As prospective members, we had opened our greedy, grasping souls to the Whooex Union. Now, after one hundred and sixty years as junior members, the Whooex Union of Stars had yet to hand us the full manual on itself. There were twelve inviolate zones, full of other, sentient peoples, many of whom we knew little to nothing about. Maybe we should have been a bit more circumspect. A little less aspiring.

Too late now.

The High Jerak continued to stare at me with its unblinking red eyes.

Someone once told me that when Endar got extremely agitated they emitted a pungent, unpleasant odor. I felt pretty sure their best politicians, diplomats, and especially a High Jerak, had figured a way to overcome any "stink" handicap. Still, the juvenile entertainment in the thought helped ease the intimidation factor for me.

"The Ritto-ssa report they found you floating in space outside an abandoned mining facility in the Scylla Quadrant. Why were you there?"

We both knew it would take more than an exchange in a medical facility to produce the kind of details he wanted.

"I was not in Primacy space," I said.

"You are on a world where we are responsible for security. Humans do not have an alliance with the Proambu. Why were you there?"

"Fulfilling a contract. With proper clearance," I added. Mother Universe, let that be the truth! I clenched my fists beneath the coverlet, suddenly fearing the Frairy-MoMo trickster team could be entirely capable of pulling off the operation at Idwal without proper authorization from the owners. The High Jerak would have to contact the Proambu to confirm it, however, which, considering their situation, didn't seem likely to happen. But still... "I was injured in an accident at the facility."

Those blood-red eyes were unsettling as they stared at me. I hoped he didn't know enough about Human physiology to recognize the thin film of sweat on my face as burgeoning unease.

"What sort of accident?"

"A section blowout." Anyone who ever thought of going into space knew the terror that kind of event caused.

"How did it happen?"

"I don't know."

"You were there! What caused it?"

"I said I don't know. The station is in Proambu territory. That's not Endar jurisdiction," I said.

"Sabotage?" He continued as if I'd never spoken.

Did he mean by me, or someone else? "Not that I'm aware." My instincts told me being near this creature was bad for my health. I wanted him to leave so I could focus on the things I had to do. Things to which I suspected he would strongly object.

"Did you have companions?"

Did I have companions where? "No." I didn't know where Saura was at the moment, but I suspected Idwal's proximity to Endar space made this character a greater threat to her than anything in the deep dark. No way was I letting his people get their hands on her.

"The Idwal Facility. It is an isolated area of space. Curious, how the Ritto-ssa managed to rescue you so quickly."

Yeah, I silently agreed with him on that: the system seemed strangely active for its remote location. "You'd have to ask them." It made me feel a little treacherous to direct his attention back on my rescuers—it sounded as if their report might have been a bit spare on the details, too—but I did not intend to help expand his information.

The dusky areas at the edges of the High Jerak's face darkened. "Do not insult me with your transparent attempt at deflection, Human. What were you doing at the Idwal Facility?"

CHAPTER 15

Making the Right Choice

The gloves were off.

"Picking up a contracted cargo." Whooex law said I didn't have to divulge any details of a private legal transaction to him.

The High Jerak went still as stone.

"What cargo?" he asked after a moment.

Well, crap. "I don't know. I didn't find it." Which was true. I wasn't sure if the kid and the people that died out there were our intended cargo or not.

"You lie." A dark flush traveled up the sides of the High Jerak's face. "Who contracted you to go there?"

"That is Human business."

"Who—"

"No." I shook my head, not caring if he recognized the action as a refusal to answer. "I want to invoke my right to legal representation."

"Who—" he reached for me, claws extended.

"Not touch patient!" It felt as if a wave of sound pushed through my flesh as the Zeek's warning thrummed deep and loud.

Apparently, the attendant's warning carried some meaningful force. The High Jerak drew back his hand and glared at me. "You are an illegal, undocumented presence on this world."

A chill of panic tore through me. Security declaring me "undocumented" put me in the ranks of homeless, jobless drifters that appeared and disappeared all over inhabited space. The High Jerak was telling me I, too, could disappear—possibly into his personal torture chamber—without anyone ever noticing.

It also told me the Endar did not exclusively control this world. If he arrested me, I went on his books, where some non-Endar might ask questions. Classifying me as undocumented made me invisible.

Fear twisted my stomach. I looked at the Zeek, hoping it would detect my distress and cut the interview short.

The High Jerak saved him the effort. "Turn over everything related to this thing and have it ready for transportation off-world at once," he snarled.

"Rehabilitation not complete," the Zeek objected.

"It can rehabilitate in its own filthy space. Your creed prohibits discussion of anything that transpired in this room if I, as one of the participants, forbid it. I forbid you to speak of this encounter with anyone. Prepare this creature for immediate removal. It leaves aboard the cruiser, *Obega*, or we will file charges against this facility for collaboration with an illegal species." He looked at me. "We could not prevent your arrival here, but we can make the stay as short and nondescript as possible."

The brown mound bowed slightly as the High Jerak swept out the door.

I searched my memory chips for a registry on the ship, *Obega*. Nothing came up.

The High Jerak's threat seemed to make some impact on the Zeek. It lumbered over and began to remove my monitor patches.

"What is the *Obega*?" I asked.

It paused, no doubt doing its own form of search.

"Tabi ship," it rumbled.

Tabi. I could work with that. "Thank you," I said. Next question. "Where am—"

The Zeek cut me short with a soft grunt. It gently closed a hand around my left forearm and rolled it to face upward. Between its brown fingers the new skin above my wrist showed pink and smooth, the blue veins delicate beneath the surface.

Blue veins I should not be seeing...

Realization slammed me. The silvery, tattoo-like symbols that normally etched my flesh were missing. The flexible surface of the wetware control grid that should sit beneath my skin was gone.

Rehabilitation not complete. The statement slammed me with its terrible significance.

My brain sent an automatic, panicked signal to the nerve endings in my wrist.

Nothing. All my interfaces with the *Thief's Hand*, all the hardware I needed to interact with nodes on EA stations and facilities, all the enhancements accumulated in the Marines, were gone.

How—? How could this happen? Without my wetware, I could not communicate with any system outside my body, including the ones on this world.

It was my greatest fear realized: I had truly joined the ranks of the scrubs.

My mind blanked with horror.

The pressure of Zeek fingers on my now-trembling wrist pulled me back to the present. I looked up into the three horizontal eyes in the great, pebbly face. With a comforting rumble, it spread its fingers to hold my forearm in its palm and lowered the piece of tech it was fiddling with earlier toward my skin.

Before the mechanism could touch my flesh the door chime sounded and two Endar wearing security-black burst into the room. They looked half-naked compared to the High Jerak's layers of leather, but they had a decent start on their own odd accumulation.

The Zeek released me and stepped away from the sling with startling swiftness as they moved toward me.

"No! Wait—"

One of the Endar pulled a short black rod out of his layers and raised it toward my temple.

The Zeek made a loud, urgent sound of protest.

The threat of getting my brain scrambled by some alien tech shut me up and cleared my head. I didn't have my wetware right now, but I was alive and able to fight another day.

They ordered me out of the med sling and into my shipskins. Then, with my backpack containing my awaysuit in my hand, marched me swiftly down several empty levels to the most elegant, and, again, empty, aircar lobby I had ever seen. The only thing that sullied the beauty of the aqua, green and silver décor was my leather-clad escort.

Separated from the watchful eyes of the Zeek attendant, I was at their mercy, so I kept my mouth shut when they shoved me into the sleek, black, unmarked transport module waiting at the curb. The High Jerak said I was going to this *Obega*. That did not guarantee I would get there. We had passed no other living on the way down to the aircar, so there were no witnesses to my presence here if I disappeared.

My escort did not enter the vehicle with me. Once the door closed, I spoke, trying to gain control of it. I ran through every language in my translation package. Nothing. The vehicle's windows remained opaque and the passenger interface refused to respond to my questions.

The transport accelerated, pushing me gently back into the seat, carrying me toward the *Obega*.

The silence gave me a moment to recover. I gave two quick blinks to activate my perivision and tried to establish a link with the world system again. The side screens flickered acknowledgment of the request but remained blank.

What the hell? My wetware had nothing to do with the hardware in my brain. I should be able to link to the world system the same as every other citizen of the Whooex Union.

I sent another request.

Nothing.

Now cold panic really tightened inside me. Were the chips inside my head damaged? Had the Xix—?

A request for information on Mandragala Station, on Idwal, on EA launch protocol, all pulled up reference accesses in my left perivision, and information scrolled from memory storage. I nearly cried. All my brainware was safe.

Yet, the feeds for this world remained mysteriously blank in my right perivision.

Maybe the aircar was shielded.

Endar bastards.

The solitude allowed me to focus and go over everything that had happened to me. First, I checked out my rejuvenated limb. I flexed my fingers, closed my hand. Punched the transport seat several times in frustration. It hurt. It felt normal. The skin of my arm was baby new, but the muscles and nerves felt adequately developed. I would have to work at regaining full strength, but, heck, I was a spacer: I didn't have a lot of strength to begin with. I rolled my left shoulder and my neck. Everything appeared to be in working order. I only had one massive problem with it: the Zeeks had not restored my wetware.

I should be happy to be alive. I should be grateful to be physically complete. The Ritto-ssa and the Xix had saved my life. And simultaneously destroyed it. Without the augmentations in my wetware, I joined the lowest rank of dockworkers. Capable of only performing manual tasks. I was basic gravity muscle—and I didn't have much muscle.

The aircar would reach the Tabi ship, *Obega*, soon. Odds on, it was a tramp spacer and my fare off-world included a commitment to work off my passage. With wetware, I could have bargained myself a better situation, started working my way back to the EA and reclaiming the things I had lost.

Tracking down a certain MoMo and Frairy...

Now, however, the *Obega* would probably occupy the rest of my short, miserable life.

At least it took me away from the High Jerak Seok and a small step toward recovering my partner and my ship—which I was no longer capable of co-captaining.

EA Space Fleet would not be happy with me over the loss of my wetware. It wasn't that Human technology was so advanced we had to fear exposing our secrets. Hell, the EA was so far behind everyone else their trash was our treasure. The problem centered around our habit of taking that trash and re-engineering it to do new things its creators had not intended it to do. That re-purposing made some members of the Union uneasy with us.

I didn't know if the military had enhanced my wetware, but I did know I could never afford a refit without the Corp paying for it, and they didn't like me that much. Even if I could reclaim my original rig from the Xix, I couldn't afford the reinstall.

At least I had the tech buried in my brain, including my language chips and translator. Without them, I would be dead meat for certain.

I turned my thoughts outward to Saura. The *Hand* had never signaled me it was under direct attack. Had the Ritto-ssa located it, docked so innocuously on the upper hangar, and pulled my partner out? Had they brought her here, too?

Maybe—my heart gave a twist of hope—maybe, somehow, she'd gotten the *Hand* out. Folded before the ghost found her. Maybe she was searching for me.

Maybe. But if I didn't make the right choices here, it wouldn't matter. The first thing I had to do was get back into EA-friendly space.

No, it wasn't: the words blazed like meter-high letters in my head.

I press my body deeper into the seat, my heartbeat rising with realization. The kid! She was on the shuttle that had brought all this down on us. She must know something about what had caused it. With her to corroborate my story, I had a chance of getting an investigation. I could get help recovering Saura and the *Hand*. Demand compensation for the loss of my wetware or even get it back...

In my mind, I saw the kid happily waving as she bound away from my med unit and disappeared beneath the blue sky. She was on this world.

I had to find her.

The Ritto-ssa ship had brought us to a spaceport on this world. Logic said they would take me to the nearest medical facility, so the nearest port was the place to begin my search. The High Jerak said he was putting me on a Tabi ship off this world. It most likely sat in that same port.

He was sending me exactly where I needed to be.

I felt bad for the Xix facility, getting an accusation of collaboration with Humans filed against it, but I was not going to be on the *Obega*.

I was not leaving this world yet.

CHAPTER 16

Cryo Chamber

There's something about the smell of a planetside spaceport. There's a tang of space—an oily scent you don't find anywhere else on a planet, or even in the closed confines of a station ring. The ships on the enormous pad have been out in the Vasty. We used to discuss it in the Marines; what it brought to mind when we smelled it. For me, it evoked a sense of impending freedom.

But not today.

Spidery, triple-jointed fingers cut shadows across the sudden flood of sunlight inside the aircar. I ducked beneath them and slid out. The Endar guard hissed, seized my upper right arm, and jerked me upright in a grip meant to make me pay for my slippery maneuver.

We stood at the base of a boarding ramp that led to the open hatch in the side of a ship. It was an immense, deepspace jobber, the towering curve of its bulk blocking my view of everything to the left, right, and ahead of me.

A flashback of memory, of ripples distorting the stars of the Vasty, flooded through my brain. Panic that I had controlled thus far despite the situation threatened to break through my composure. I had only seen a black hull like this in one place and it had done its best to kill a child and me.

But the Zeek had identified the *Obega* as Tabi.

What did I actually know of the Tabi Empire and its politics? I considered Saurubi my best friend as well as my business partner. That didn't mean I knew anything about the billions of her fellow beings and their relationship with the rest of the Whooex Union. We assumed we had a solid alliance against those species we considered a mutual enemy.

Yet, two Endar were freely walking me onto a Tabi ship.

To hell with this! The *Obega* was not taking me off this world.

But I couldn't make my escape yet. With the open area of the spaceport around us, there was no place for me to hide. My escort would simply kill or maim me, then carry out their orders. I had to wait until they deposited me inside the ship.

I tried to connect with the world link again now that I was out of the aircar. Nothing.

Inconvenient, but that wouldn't stop me.

I submitted, docilely allowing one of the Endar to pull me along for several meters before I twisted in his grip to look out over the port behind us.

A wave of vertigo rolled over me.

No fabricated structure in space can mimic a planetside horizon, no matter how large it is. That perspective is always enclosed or curving out of sight, which limits the range of view. A planetary horizon, with its unlimited expanse, sickens most spacers into immobility. Space Corp training and my early origins on a ball of dirt helped me manage my reaction, keeping it to a momentary disorienting rush.

Everything popped back into balance and I could see this was a massive spaceport. A major planetside spaceport. Hulks of ships, many of them bigger than the *Obega*, studded its vast, flat surface. Some of the smaller ones were luxury yachts, the caliber of which I'd only heard in rumors. I saw ships of a hundred colors and worlds, from shiny new to ancient, battered hulks squatted on a dark surface that stretched off into the hazy distance. And that was only what I could see on this side of the ship's towering hull.

Beyond the port's edge, I saw a further, hazy horizon with the darker jag of city-shapes against the sky. A glimmer of blue caught my eye. A faceted jewel of pure blue sat face-upward inside a filigreed setting like a rare gemstone in a ring. Considering the distance, the thing had to be immense. Immense and breathtaking.

The second Endar guard moved to block my view. If he was concerned I would recognize the place, he needn't have bothered: it didn't resemble anywhere I'd ever seen.

But I'd be able to find out where I was now, after seeing that blue jewel.

I had no doubt of my immediate destination, however, and the lack of port facilities on this side of the ship told me there were no witnesses to observe this passenger transfer.

The Endar hauled me into the dimly lit passageway. They moved quickly now, as if maybe this ship was ready to launch and they wanted off before that happened. Despite their rush, I began to feel a burn of confidence. I'd spent two of my young years on a ship similar to this. Disregarding the flat black hull, it was like a million other tubs moving through the depths of the Whooex Union, and I was familiar with the basic layout.

I could escape this thing.

But I was on a timer, dependent on how long it took these two to march me to my destination, settle me in, and exit. That was how long I had to get back off.

Helped along by a shove, I stumbled through a side hatch and into a long, narrow chamber. We'd reached our destination.

Towering walls rose to shadowy heights on both sides of us. The place was a cryo, or life storage, chamber. Racks of horizontal containers extended upward, row upon row, penetrating several decks. In space, where the loss of crew could mean no one to hit a button at a critical moment to save an expensive ship, life got stowed in the safest area possible. We had reached the guts of the ship.

The absence of green lights on the sides of the suspended animation containers, or SACs, caught my attention as I scanned the racks high and deep down the aisle. No green outside meant no life inside. There was no crew cryoed here.

This ship was highly automated.

As if to confirm that, a bot attendant glided forward to greet us. The meter-and-a-half tall mech had black, hard-edged facets covering most of its shape. Four multi-jointed arms extended up and out toward us as it floated up. I'd seen images of cryo attendants from other Whooex members, but nothing as streamlined and stark as this. The thing resembled the two black-clad creatures grasping my arms more than it did a Tabisee.

Despite its strange appearance, the sight of the bot eased some of my apprehensions: at least my escort couldn't slip it a few creds to set my life monitors wrong.

"I am held against my will," I told it in Union Basic, the patois of ships and spacers across the Whooex. A Tabisee attendant should understand and respond to help me.

I don't know if my captors understood what I said, but one jabbed me hard in the gut with the back of a bony fist.

The autobot did not react to my statement or his action.

While I gasped in pain, the two Endar wrestled to get past the bot in the narrow passage, their plan, apparently, to put me into cryo themselves. Obviously they were not familiar with deepspace ship protocol. The mechanical attendant could not concede its role to them: its programming in such a life-critical process did not allow that. Nevertheless, they persisted in their efforts.

I watched as they snarled, shoved at the bot, and tried to feint their way past. It stayed stubbornly in place at the mouth of its domain, blocking their every attempt to maneuver into the passage beyond.

Meanwhile, unsure of its intended subject, the bot tried to prep the Endar on my left for a SAC. Precious time passed while the Endar spat back and forth in their hissing, hacking language in what must be rising frustration, until they finally realized they had the means to redirect the bot's activity.

They pushed me forward.

The bot attendant instantly refocused attention. It whirred and extended some sensors to scan me, then flashed a few lights.

"Help me," I said in a low voice, hoping its programming would respond to the universal plea.

That earned me another hard blow, this time to the back of the head and the autobot still did not respond.

It continued to fuss over me for another minute, then abruptly paused its activity.

I'd been cryoed many times during my service in the Marines, so I was aware the Endar had not yet completed one last crucial action in the process. The attendant and I both waited.

There was a lot more spitting and snapping from my black-clad escort before the solution occurred to them.

The sides of its face darkening with what I hoped was fury and embarrassment, my left-side friend searched his leather pockets, withdrew a data chip containing my travel clearance, and extended it to the bot. It whisked the thing away with one of its appendages and sprang into action again. Snatching the bag containing my away-suit from my grasp, it sped several meters down the chamber aisle to where a long, coffin-like box rolled out of the rack lengthwise, foot end toward us. The transparent lid rolled open.

The mech shoved the chip into a slot on the SAC, dropped my pack into a compartment on the end, then whizzed back to stop in front of me. It dispensed a small packet of sensor pads from a slot in its front and began to place them at critical points on my body.

The placement of the pads went awkwardly, as if it had never encountered Human anatomy before. It finally paused, servos whirring quietly, readjusted its position, and raised another appendage to the level of my eye. It blinded me with a quick flash of light, then clicked and whirred some more. The lights flickered on the end of the SAC.

The bot resumed placing pads, this time more accurately. If it remained in control of the situation, I might survive this cryo experience.

I didn't intend to bet my life on that.

CHAPTER 17

Vertical Exit

Though most of my attention was devoted to the accuracy of monitor pad placement, I kept an eye on my escort. They were shifting uneasily, and it wasn't from concern over whether I survived the next step of transport off this world. Their window to get off the ship was closing.

If they were present when I went into the cryo chamber, they still might try to disable the bot and change the settings. If I stalled the process, they would have to give up and leave before I went inside.

I needed to find the kid. She was my only hope—the one person who would know what had happened out at Idwal. With that information, I could get help rescuing my partner and our ship.

The Endar on my left shifted and spat a few words at the bot.

It continued its work in the dogged, methodical way of mechanical units.

I gave a fake sneeze and brushed the monitor pad on the right side of my neck out of place as I wiped my nose with my wrist. The bot finished the task of attaching a last soft disc to my ankle before returning attention upward. It replaced the pad on my neck then gently but firmly clasped my forearm and tugged me toward the cryo drawer. I followed quietly, knowing at this point the Endar would have no problem killing a despised, troublesome Human for resisting its fate.

I twisted around to keep an eye on them, only to see the last flick of black leather disappear past the edge of the door back into the ship corridor.

"Ow!" I stared at the empty injector attached to one of the bot's appendages.

Crap!

This first shot was meant to calm me; the second would knock me out.

I could not win a physical struggle with a mechanical attendant of this size. I had to create a situation and hope no one had programmed the bot to counter it. And I had to do it fast, before I was hooked into the SAC systems with additional sedatives flowing into me.

I let the thing settle me into the drawer, my heart pounding hard despite the injection. When it straightened away to prepare for the next step in the process I tugged the sensors off my wrists and hid them beneath me. That would force it to pause and open a new packet to replace them, drawing its focus away from me.

The bot stopped what it was doing and dipped closer, as if confused by the missing pads. When it withdrew, I pulled the sensor pads off my forehead.

The bot up came with a syringe.

My panic surged. If it injected me, I was out for the duration. Maybe permanently.

I twisted up out of the drawer, evading the thrust of the needle by millimeters. I ended up on the inner side of the chamber with the bot between me and the exit. I got my rapidly numbing hands on its back and pushed down, shoving it into the SAC as I awkwardly catapulted over it.

Gravity and drugs exerted their control and my graceful jump became a clumsy flop. My feet skidded on the decking, and I fell back against the autobot, driving it further into the drawer. I shoved away, put my back against the opposite rack and kicked with a foot, jamming the bot firmly between the front edge of the SAC and the rack above it. Servos clacked and whirred as it struggled to lift free.

Some people would have busted the thing right then, but, heck, the little guy was only doing his job. Besides, I'd heard some species had semi-sentient bots. I'd feel bad if I thought this one ended up sad and alone on a junk pile somewhere for failing this task.

But I didn't want it following me, either.

I fleetingly considered locking the bot in the SAC, but this was an automated ship and it would pause the launch cycle and sound a warning if it failed to locate a signal from a critical part of its system, drawing unwanted attention.

I spotted the bot's power pack. A dislodged energy supply would be a reasonable excuse for its absence that the ship could accept. By the time a swarm of the little auto-wrenches made their way down here to diagnose and fix the attendant, I would be long gone.

Reaching down, I fumbled back the tab that fastened the battery. The block popped free into my hand. The bot gave a peep and sagged, the extension with the hypo barely missing my leg.

I dropped the battery and snatched up my awaypack.

The clock was ticking. The Endar had left the chamber minutes ahead of me, but I knew which way they had gone in their rush to exit the ship. Shrugging into the straps of my pack, I took a right out of the life chamber after them.

Overrunning them was not a risk. They were moving quickly, while I was stumbling and pushing off the walls of the corridor to keep moving forward. Besides, I wasn't following them. I knew that as soon as they exited the main hatch it would lock. I had to find another way off.

Following a lengthways passage on a deepspacer will eventually lead to a cargo hold or an engine room. I figured this one was cargo-forward so it could nose into a station and unload. If it was as close to launch as I feared, all the outer hatches were already dogged. That left a cargo bay as my only way out. The ship klaxons that would sound the all-clear before launch sequence had not gone off yet, telling me the cargo loading tubes had not withdrawn. There was a chance I could escape through one of them. Everything hinged on finding a bay without a sentient guard monitoring things.

My legs were rubbery and my vision blurred by the time I located a directional board posted in the passage. I squinted at the lighted symbols, hoping my translation software would kick in and send a scroll of interpreted text running at the corner of my eyes.

It didn't happen, either because it was beyond my software or because the tranquilizer was affecting those critical connections in my brain. If someone, namely the Zeeks, had thought to reinstall my wetware, I could have communicated with the ship's layout map directly. Instead, all I could do was stand there, weaving, with darkness pushing into the edges of my vision.

I jerked when a warning klaxon blared. That was the first sign the ship was preparing for launch. The spur of adrenalin got me moving forward again.

The corridor ended in a closed hatch with dead silence behind it.

Loading cargo is a noisy business.

My options were to move up or down a deck. With the tranq in my blood, I would not handle upward very well. Besides, cheap cargo usually stowed in lower external holds where the risk of damage during transport was higher—and it loaded last.

I got most of the way down the ladder before my legs gave out. I fell the rest of the way.

With my back against the deck plates, I felt the vibration of heavy machinery. Cargo was still shifting somewhere.

Pushing to my feet, I stumbled over to a pressure plate on the bulkhead beside a bay door and slammed it with a shaking hand.

The hatch slid open onto a glorious display of activity.

Named for an alien creature capable of grappling and carrying off livestock and large children, the levitating freight movers known throughout the Whooex Union as whizbats, did not require sentient supervision.

Desperate as I was, I did not charge out into the bay. I stopped two steps inside the hatch and blearily watched the cargo lifters, with their four massive, three-meter long dangling legs. They whipped about the chamber, grabbing containers off a conveyor belt that lifted them out of vast storage areas beneath the spaceport and whisked them into place inside the hold. The outer areas were already stacked high and the whizbats were dropping containers in neat rows, building walls that moved steadily inward toward the conveyor.

Despite the noise of the activity around me, darkness nudged my vision. I'd been running on adrenalin up to this point. Now, seeing a way out, I was starting to lose my edge.

I thought about Saura and our ship out in the cold darkness and dug down for the fire of anger. No one was taking away anything else I valued.

The fog in my brain thinned and I realized I had to move to the far end of the conveyor, where the umbilical latched to the external hold doors. Fighting to stay out of the flight path of dangling containers, I staggered along the nearest stack of boxes to where the arriving cargo released from the rows of vacuum holes that held it on the belt during the vertical lift out of storage. Climbing on the metal maintenance walk, I edged past the moving boxes to stare down the throat of the huge tube. Crossing the belt to climb down the ladder inside the tube was impossible. The belt was moving too fast and in the wrong direction. Even if I got over there, the climb down was too long. I could end up falling or the umbilical might retract and crush me. I checked the area beside me, where it connected to the ship's hull. The seal was tight, offering no chance to wiggle between it and the ship to the outside. Besides, the fall to the spaceport surface, if I got through, would probably kill me.

The *Thief's Hand* was a chow box compared to this vessel. The comparison brought a pang of sadness, and the sadness brought renewed resolution.

The klaxon sounded again.

Lights along the conveyor rippled warning yellow. Within seconds, the flow of containers ended, the lift shut down and the belt came to a halt. The sudden silence was nearly overwhelming.

The whizbats began to form up in a line down the center of the hold, preparing to exit. I'd found my ride out—if I could catch one.

I had no idea how a whizbat would react to the sudden addition of my weight to its hanging grapples, but I was about to find out. As soon as the last container dropped into place, the things streamed toward the mouth of the umbilical. They flew fast and hard, with little space between them. If I didn't time things just right, the blow from three meters of hard metal grapple would crush me.

I let the first one zip past to see how high the grapple tips ran above the belt. They cleared by a good ten centimeters.

A loud crash and a crack of light bloomed between the umbilical seal and the ship's hull. The damned tube was retracting to base storage even as the whizbats flew into its gaping gullet.

Left with no choice, I made a flying leap for the fourth whizbat and got my arms and legs wrapped around one of the steel grapple legs. The sudden addition of my weight threw the thing off kilter. It tilted and my hands slipped on the smooth metal. I lost grip with one leg and my foot dragged on the rough surface of the conveyor belt. The resistance nearly jerked me off my precarious perch. I scrambled, my arms struggling to pull my body upward on the grapple, only to slip lower. The whizbat slowed with the inertia and the one behind slammed into it, causing my whizbat to slowly rotate, putting me directly between the two. I closed my eyes, unable to watch the slabs of metal swinging toward each other. If I fell off now, the metal legs of all the whizbats behind mine would smear my body across the cover of the belt.

The cobwebs in my brain vaporized and my heart squeezed as my whizbat struggled to reposition its place in line. It gave a soft mechanical "squee" and slewed toward the widening gap between the ship hull and the umbilical. Daylight blazed in front of me. The whizbat headed for the open air of the spaceport. At the last moment, however, it righted itself and slid into the umbilical opening. As we passed into the yawning maw, I caught a glimpse of the spaceport surface far below me. I would not have survived that method of exit.

The whizbat, still struggling to regain its balance under my added weight, tapped the back wall of the umbilical before dropping. The slight delay caused a grapple arm on the unit behind me to strike the upper crossbeam of mine with a teeth-rattling clang, sending us into a dizzying spin. I shut my eyes and held on with everything I had.

The whizbat's controls made a clicking sound above my head. It leveled out, the spin stopped, and the air felt abruptly cooler. I gave a whoop of terror as it accelerated its drop down the vertical shaft into the blackness beneath the port.

CHAPTER 18

In the Dark

A crewmember turns into the shadowy section of the corridor. A small figure walks beside it, holding the larger one's hand. It's Anthy.

Feeling a rush of relief and outrage, I run toward them. I'm angry, not with my brother, but with this adult. I want to report them to get revenge for the panic they've caused me, but I also sense it might be a dangerous thing to do. I don't recognize this person from a distance, which means I must be careful. A crewmember can assign a kid difficult tasks. They cannot cause us harm, but they can make things hard on us.

They are walking slowly toward me. I can hear a voice now. The sound is pleasant and female. It reminds me of my Mama. Does it remind Anthy of Mama, too? Of course it does. I know it, and I feel a wash of resentment. These people had no right to do what they did to our families—what they're doing to us. They are almost to me now. I stop and draw deep breaths, trying to calm myself. This person is only walking with Anthy, and he doesn't know he should not have gone with her. He is talking to her happily. I must be careful what I say and do for both our sakes.

They stop before me. Anthy drops her hand and comes over to hug me. I smile and rub his head, and look at the woman. She's smiling at me.

"You're his sister, Vivi. He told me about you."

She is pretty. That does not mean anything.

"I was worried," I say angrily.

"I understand." She nods and looks serious as if she truly does. "He looked a bit pale, so I took him to the infirmary to have him checked. He's all right now." She gives Anthy a fond look. "I know you do your best to take care of the ones in your charge. The light down here is not good, however, and I feared you might not see how pale he is. Also, you might not be comfortable asking for help." She studies me.

"Pieter takes care of us," I say stiffly.

"Yes, he knows how. There are some things you can do, though, if you know about them. There is a solarium on deck ten. You can go up and get some natural light," she explains when I look puzzled. "You are from a planet. You need sunlight. Stars are suns. Their light will make you healthier. I will suggest it to Pieter for you. And him." She looks down at Anthy and smiles.

Another twinge of anger and jealousy runs through me. Who is this person, thinking she can seek a place in Anthy's life? We do not need her. "I have to take him back," I say.

I wonder if I will tell Pieter about her. Despite my anger, I think her smile is nice. She seems kind, but that will not help me if I am punished for this. I cannot let Anthy undergo the lash. I will not. It would kill him.

"Don't worry," she says. "I will tell Pieter I took him to the infirmary. There will be vitamins for all of you children from now on. Everything will be fine." She takes a step backward. "Go back now."

I take Anthy's hand and start back down the corridor. He walks beside me silently without looking back and a rush of relief floods me. Perhaps this was nothing more than what the woman says and there will be no trouble. I do not need trouble. My charges do not need trouble.

"I see doctor, Vivi," Anthy announces suddenly.

"You be quiet," I order, jerking lightly on his arm. "You be quiet and stay with the others from now on when I'm out." I'm mad again. Tears sting my eyes. I think things will be okay this time, but this can't happen again. I grip his hand tighter and feel fear.

***

Mother Universe, I was flashing dark outside of deep sleep! Why—?

The damned kid! The doctors would say she triggered something in my brain—a need in me to protect her—when she romped off on this strange world, all alone. That I was still trying to compensate for my failure to save Anthy.

Angrily I shoved the dregs of the dream out of my mind and blinked in the pitch-black silence. Something hard pressed my ribs and the straps of my pack were cutting into my shoulders. And it was damn cold.

Oh, yeah. Whizbat. I must be in the belly of their storage area under the spaceport.

I moved my body carefully. No parts pinned under anything, but the curved foot of the grapple lay under my ribs, with the awaypack twisted up the side of its leg. Now that I was aware, the stone surface beneath me felt as if it was doing its best to suck my body heat out through my shipskins.

I sat up cautiously and wondered what had jerked me awake.

A metallic clack sounded in the distance. I heard a corresponding whisper of movement in the darkness.

Fear shot through me. The Mother Universe only knew what dwelled in this pit of darkness.

Whizbats needed maintenance the same as every other piece of machinery, but if their technicians wore black leather, I didn't want them to catch me lying here. Besides, my body was a bit insistent on getting some water.

Wondering how long I'd been out, I climbed to my feet and stretched.

My world feeds remained dead. They were the most basic codes possible, simply giving one access to free information such as the time, news, global positioning, maps, etc, supposedly available to all citizens on any world, whether through chips or an external device. If mine weren't working, it meant one of three things: my tech was damaged; it required a system reboot; or the world system did not recognize the Human codes—and that the High Jerak had told the truth when he said I was here illegally. A reboot was my preferred solution, though that might be difficult to achieve on my own. Actually being illegal was bad, but one I could maybe work around. Damage was the scariest diagnosis; I couldn't pay the Zeeks for my regenerated arm, much less additional repairs, unless I reclaimed the *Thief's Hand*, saved Saura, and got back to work for the next several hundred years.

Again, the sharp clack sounded in the distance. This time a series of echoing clicks and ticks followed, running toward, around, and past me. Then a series of booms rolled forward and over me. The whizbats performed the mechanical version of coming to attention. Beneath my hand, the metal vibrated gently with power, ready and waiting. They were either preparing to move to maintenance or a new job. Wherever they went, there must light. And water.

***

The loss of my world feeds was a major inconvenience, but I had other things to distract me as I rode the whizbat up out of the dark pit, into the upper storage levels. When I finally spotted a well-lit opening, I made a daring leap off into a massive warehouse.

After hours of wandering between endless stacks of goods, I should have encountered some sign of life. I hadn't. Which meant I had to decide whether I wanted to continue wandering the floor maze until I died from thirst or move up to the transport system whipping along above my head in hope of finding a way out.

Moving walkways that transport cargo and people on flat surfaces are a great idea. Handgrips on cables that tow beings through weightless environments are a great idea. Moving walkways, or flyways, mounted high in the air above stockpiles of goods, with gravity and a hard surface twenty meters below them and no handgrips, are insanity.

The flyway was nothing more than a meter-wide belt gliding along through the open air. I only managed to stay on the damned thing by getting down on my hands and knees.

After traveling it for over an hour without seeing any indication of life, a wall or exit, I was hungry, thirsty, and my knees were sore despite the protection of my shipskins. I sure as hell hadn't made any headway toward finding the kid.

Occasionally another flyway would intersect the one I clung to. At those junctures a small, stationary platform with a control stand to one side anchored the connections. It offered me the opportunity to get to my feet and stand for a while before resuming my painful, headlong hurtle forward.

The small platforms also had the additional stability of a support post that extended down to floor. I grasped the one beside me gratefully while I looked out over endless rows of containers. A movement caught my attention. In the distance, two figures were walking along an aisle. The tall, thin one dressed in black definitely looked Endar. The other was much shorter and wore a light, neutral color. They were moving away from me.

Instinctively, I drew back behind the support, though the sixty-millimeter diameter pole would hardly shield me from view if they looked my direction. They were the first sign of life I'd seen in my hours of travel through the immense place, but my instincts warned me against calling out for help.

Whatever they were, wherever they were going, however, there had to be water. I hadn't had any fluid intake since leaving the Zeek facility, and I was feeling the effects. If I went down to the floor and followed them, they might lead me out of this place.

But I had to move fast.

The pole I gripped extended down to the warehouse floor. A collar and stub shaft linked it to a round metal plate cut into the decking beneath my feet. It was a primitive setup: the two buttons on the control panel in front of me were self-explanatory. One had an arrow pointing up beside a line meant to represent the pole; the other had an arrow pointing down.

I reached for the down button.

Something struck me hard across the back, snagging my away-pack straps and jerking me backward. One of my feet touched the moving track and shot out from under me as I snatched out for something to break my fall, but the pole was beyond my reach and I tumbled off the slideway.

Instead of falling, however, I was whipped sideways as whatever held the straps of my pack whisked me out through the air.

My heart surged toward exploding. I twisted to look up and saw the flat metal bottom of an air bike. The dull gray paint bore no registration marks, stickers, or manufacturers' symbols to give me a hint of it, or the rider's, origin.

"Son of a bitch!" In Human warehouses workers sometimes played a game. Riding mechanical fliers, they grappled a co-worker by the safety harness and hauled them off to some distant spot. Then the victim had to make their way back to the job site without drawing the attention of a supervisor.

It was too much to hope this was a game.

So, it was time to complicate things in the way Humans did it best—by doing something stupid. Grasping my right shoulder strap with my stronger hand, I hit the chest release on my pack with the left. It snapped opened, and my body dropped a half meter as I slid out of the straps.

My hold on the right strap kept me from plummeting to the floor, but the additional length I had just added to the flier's load threw it off balance. The rider glanced down and I stared into a startled Tabisee face.

The fur was gray and missing the shock of red hair. The ruff around the face was longer and thicker than Saura's, signifying it was probably a male. He thrust out a hand, his fingers splayed in a signal: wait. I looked up at the grapple, now barely caught in one of my pack's straps, and held on.

The air bike was fast approaching what had been, for me, an aggravatingly elusive wall. The rider slowed and the bike dropped height until my feet skimmed the warehouse floor. I shrugged free of the pack straps, stumbled and regained my footing. The Tabisee set down a few meters ahead of me, my pack skittering along the floor behind him.

I ran toward him.

"You bastard son of a mother--!" I leaped, catching him from behind as he swung his leg off the flier, sending us both sprawling to the floor.

Sad fact: a spacer hitting a planet born is an invitation for broken bones. Still, I got in one good punch to his head without hearing the crunch of finger bones before hands were dragging me off him.

"What in the name of the Holy Plinth—" a female voice exclaimed in Tabi. Fingers pressed into my shoulder flesh, holding me firmly. "We do not need this!"

"Best to kill it and dump the body," the rider said as he got to his feet.

"No," the female said. "Not yet. We don't want to create an incident. It could make things difficult for us all!"

Tabisee that spoke in full sentences. That meant they were part of a downside force, where diplomacy required a full clarification of intent when one spoke.

The male Tabi looked at me in irritation. "Dahzi zhu ha," he muttered.

Oh, still with the attitude!

Interfering insect scum: I'd learned my street Tabi from Saura. "Pok kai," I snarled back, daring to tell a planetside being at least fifty centimeters taller and packing twenty kilos more solid muscle than me to go die in ignominy in the street.

I wasn't thinking at my clearest right then.

He lunged for me. The female, however, anticipated his reaction. She planted a hand in his chest and shoved him back. Then she glared at me. "Keep that up and we will kill you and endure the repercussions."

The male gave an exaggerated shrug, as if putting his muscles and bones back into physical order, and glowered at me.

I felt a secret rush of gratitude for her interference. These Tabisee were much larger than my partner, the female standing shoulder to shoulder with me. Their gravity-honed muscles bulged in sharp contrast to my skinny spacer body.

They were dressed in plain black clothing, without rank or identifying markings, but their movements and manner set off a tiny self-survival alarm inside my head. They were not ordinary laborers.

Undercover or stealth ops, then. And they were not pleased at having a Human stumble into their zone of operations, potentially draw attention to their activity.

Before I could say anything, a thick, stuffy bag slammed over my head and one of them lashed my wrists together in front of me.

"Hey," I yelped in protest. These people were supposed to be our closest allies.

"Shut it or we tranq you," the female snapped.

Tabisee tranquilizers do not work well with Human physiology, so I shut it.

"Mathet will not be happy about this," the female muttered as she forced me into a shuffling walk.

I didn't know who Mathet was, but I sure wasn't getting any happier, either.

CHAPTER 19

Shouting At the Universe

The Tabisee secured the air bike in a container, then pulled me inside the space with them and closed it up.

We shifted.

Humans don't use teleportation much; the tech is expensive and requires a huge investment in infrastructure. But even with my head in a sack, I recognized the twitch in my gut when I stepped through a fold in space. It was a flicker, meaning the shift was brief. We were still planetside, in the same general area. The air remained bone-cold and dead.

We walked on a surface that muffled our footsteps, then passed through a door into an enclosed space and I felt the stomach-churning drop of an elevator. We followed a short hallway to a small room, where they left me sitting on a hard chair at a table. During the whole time, my escort stayed silent.

They also forgot to remove the hood and cuffs.

I was angry and confused. The Tabisee were supposed to be Earth Alliance's closest allies. They claimed to have nearly as many diplomatic problems with the Endar as we did—yet they were apparently giving them direct access to their ships!

And why were they treating me as if I was some lowlife slinker?

Despite all the tension, the burst of activity in planetary gravity after my time in a medical recovery tube was taking its toll. I drifted off into exhausted sleep until the hood was whisked away.

My escorts moved past me to take up positions behind my chair, while a third, new Tabi paused just inside the doorway. He wore the requisite black leather that seemed to universally scream security. Three thin, blue enameled rings piercing the lower lobe of his right ear identified him as a captain in the Tabisee Planetary Force.

Right now those ears were turned out and flat, pressing back as close to his head as they could fit.

Not happy.

"Human." The High Jerak had radiated less hostility than this Tabisee captain as he walked over to lean on the table. I didn't bother to look down when I heard metal click on metal. Who was going to tell the man in charge his claw caps were illegal? Instead, I glanced at the nametag on his chest. It was in Tabisee, but my software told me this was indeed Mathet.

Unhappy Captain Mathet Waa Silvec.

"Why are you here?"

"Can I have some water?" I croaked. Some forms of self-preservation took precedence over others.

His eyes flicked past me and a bottle of clear fluid thumped on the table beside me. He watched silently while I struggled to open the container with my tightly lashed wrists. When I finally wrangled the cap off, I chugged half the water. It was as warm as spit, but it kick-started my brain.

I set the bottle down and held up my cuffed hands. "The last I heard, our people were allies." I felt a sudden twinge of wariness: on the frontier "allies" sometimes only counted for as long as someone was useful and whether the current location was isolated enough to dump a body without detection.

"Allies?" His hand lashed out. The bottle bounced off the wall, spraying water from the gashes where his claws caps ripped it.

Okay, that got my attention. I carefully took my arms off the tabletop and put them in my lap.

"The EA can't go through the process like everyone else? You people always have to get ahead of things—try to get some advantage!" He leaned forward again, putting his hands in the place where my elbows had previously rested. "Well, the EA has miscalculated this time. We will not put our empire at risk because you are impatient."

"Whoa." Things were getting way out of hand when people started talking at the level of empires. "The EA's got nothing to do with me being here," I said. "And I didn't ask your people to yank me out of the air, or to cuff and drag me here. I was doing fine on my own."

"You were wandering in a secured Endar warehouse." I recognized the ear position from Saura as he settled into a chair across from me. It said 'Vivi, can you really be that stupid?'

Endar warehouse? Okay. Maybe I was not doing as well as I thought. But his people had been there, too. Which, if that was true, gave me another reason to distrust these Tabi. The EA sure as hell didn't let other species wander around our secured warehouses.

Between Endar access to Tabisee ships, Tabisee access to Endar warehouses, and my cuffed wrists, my best action was to break off this contact fast. Unfortunately, sitting at a table in cuffs and surrounded by bad attitude limited my options.

"I assure you, any trespass was unintentional. If you point me toward a door, no one will ever know our paths crossed. There are things I need to attend to."

He stared at me as if some strange creature had crawled up from the primordial muck into the chair across from him. "Who are you?"

At last, a question, under Whooex conventions of a hostile situation, I could answer. "Vivi Zant, captain of the *Thief's Hand*, deepspace commercial cargo freighter light class, port of registry Mandra—-"

"A commercial ship captain without wetware," he said flatly. Apparently, somewhere along the way someone had scanned my left arm and noticed my lack of critical tech. "Does the Earth Alliance think we are stupid?"

I was having a hard time with the missing wetware, too. "If the EA sent me I would have wetware. But, no; a Ritto-ssa ship pulled me out of a deepspace accident and brought me here. The Xix kindly put my body through rejuv to recover my left arm. They didn't restore my wetware."

Yeah, I sounded bitter. It didn't matter. I could sit and argue with Captain Mathet Waa Silvec or move on to other things I needed to do. "You've got my permission to do a retinal scan if you want to confirm my identity."

He nodded, and the male guard stepped up to brace my head while the female passed a scanner over my eye. They held their positions as the information transferred from the scanner to the peripheral feed in the corner of their captain's eyes.

I was not worried about the bounce telling him I was ex-military and that I had some heavy-duty hardware inside my head. I was concerned with it linking my idents with their wayward little astrogator.

My shipskins worked efficiently to pull the sweat off my body as I waited.

"Captain Zant, or whoever you are," the ears had risen a little, but they remained in the danger zone. The guards released me and stepped back. "Why are you here?"

Not for whatever reason he suspected, for sure.

Should I tell him about Saura? No. Not if I had an ounce of hope that I could get someone else to help me. If I told the Tabi and they even believed me, they would recover her back and punish her for her failure to return home, ending our partnership. "I'm looking for someone." And, while I sat here arguing with a supposed ally, the kid was out there somewhere, moving ever further out of my reach.

"Are you insane?"

"No." Odd question. "Why?"

"Your people could have asked us to do a search." He leaned forward, his copper eyes narrowing. "Unless the EA is working behind our back. Which we would consider a serious breach of trust."

"No!" I didn't want to create an incident with our closest ally. "I swear. I woke up here after a station accident!" I softened my tone, to reduce the level of stress in the room. "My internal feeds aren't working. I have no idea where I am."

"You don't know where you are, but you claim to be looking for someone?"

Put that way, it did sound questionable.

He leaned back without breaking his stare and a chill of foreboding crept over me. Of course, there was an array of instruments beyond this room trained on me, trying to interpret every flicker of my responses, down to the cellular level.

"Earth Alliance would never jeopardize their current opportunity by sending someone as incompetent as you to the Moneyworld," he said.

"The what?" My brain did a stumble. Not good. Not good. There were two things forbidden on the Moneyworld: telepaths and Humans. Unless we had gained membership while the *Hand* carried us to Idwal...?

But, no. The High Jerak said I was an illegal presence, and Mathet had just said 'current opportunity', so the EA had not achieved membership yet.

And here I was...

Shit! "That's not possible." Why in the hell would the Ritto-ssa bring me to the Moneyworld? Anger, born of panic, warmed me. "Is this some elaborate joke? Fool the Human? What? Are you studying my reactions?"

Mathet cut me off with the flick of a finger. "Who knows you are here?"

"The Zeeks," I said. "The Ritto-ssa crew who brought me here. Some Endar—"

I could have bounced a meteorite off his ears they went so rigid. "The Endar are aware you are here?"

"I talked to them—though the word 'talked' hardly applies. They put me on a ship to send me off world. I escaped."

He blinked. "You escaped?"

"Some guy calling himself High Jerak Seok tried to question me, then he ordered two of his people to stick me in a cryo unit on an outbound freighter. I got off."

"You—" His whole posture said he was having trouble with my story. At least he didn't shut me down. "How?

"I pulled the power pack on the auto-attendant before it sealed me in a SAC and dropped down a cargo loading chute as it detached from the ship."

He looked past me at the guards. "Find out what ships left the Endar pad in the past two days."

Endar? Nice try. "I can save you the trouble. The High Jerak called it the *Obega*."

"Impossible!" Captain Mathet Waa Silvec's irises actually blazed brighter gold, a reaction I had only seen once with Saurubi, when some pirates ambushed us on what we mistakenly thought was an abandoned space junk. Several of them had died seconds later. "If EA intelligence is that poor, we should rethink our alliance with you."

Back to that again. "He said—"

"The *Obega* is a Tabisee ship!"

"Yeah, I know." Which begged the question: if the Endar and Tabisee had access to each other's ships and warehouses what else did they share? As he said, maybe we should rethink our alliance. "And you picked me up in a Tabisee warehouse."

"We picked you up in an Endar warehouse," he snapped. "Access to storage beneath the spaceport is exclusive to assigned Star Association field areas. It's impossible for you to access an Endar warehouse from a Tabisee ship."

"Your people were there—"

"We were running a stealth operation. Which you compromised."

I hoped he didn't expect me to apologize for that. As for the exclusive access to warehouse thing, I only had his word on it. "This High Jerak told my Zeek attendant he was putting me on the Tabi ship, *Obega*."

"Check on the status of the *Obega*," he ordered the guards.

He was making the argument that I had not been on a Tabi ship sound pretty damn convincing.

A Human on an Endar Primacy ship. The thought left me chilled and nauseous. Had I been destined for some Endar lab, for dissection or experimentation if I hadn't escaped down the loading tube?

"It left yesterday, ser," the female reported.

There was a long moment of silence.

"If you came here injured," Mathet was not done with my story yet, "and you don't know where you are, how can you be looking for someone?"

Good question. "There was a Human child on the Ritto-ssa ship. I saw her slip off when they carried me out. She's very young—"

"There is no Human child on this world," he interrupted.

"There was no Human child," I corrected. "There is now. I saw her leave. I need to find her."

"Humans are forbidden on Moneyworld. Do you think the Endar would waste any time blowing it into a major incident if they found one here? They would instantly try to link the Tabi Empire into a conspiracy with the Earth Alliance. In fact, I find it strange they did not use you to do that very thing. But then," cold amusement pulled up a corner of his lip, "it sounds as if they had other plans for you."

Bastard.

I forced myself to focus on the brighter side of the discussion. "If no one has reported seeing her, she's out there."

"Or she is dead."

"No!"

"How long were you at the Xix medical facility?"

"Regen for a Human arm takes ninety days." Said aloud, it did sound like a long time for a small child to survive on its own.

"Well, then." He shrugged.

He could be right; she might not have survived. Or she could be out there right now, wandering, cold, hungry, and scared. That was a problem for me. 'Dead' I could accept. I could walk away, sad but intent on finding another way to save Saurubi. 'Might be alive', I could not walk away from. I had lived inside the slave trade. I knew about the lowlifes lurking out there, waiting to prey on the helpless. Besides, I had to talk to her. She knew who had attacked her ship and tried to kill us—who had ripped my partner, my ship, and my way of life away from me.

The water and the information were finally working to engage my brain. I realized I had a bigger problem now than when I walked into this room with a bag over my head. These Tabisee were not my allies. On this world, they couldn't afford to be. By Whooex Union law, I was an illegal presence in the heart of the Whooex economy. These three put their Empire at risk of trade sanctions by even talking to me.

And I was putting the future of EA membership at risk by being here. Everyone knew the Endar had an iron grip on security on the Moneyworld. It was one of the ways they had blocked our admission to its commercial markets for one hundred and sixty years. They held power, and they used it to exert their agenda.

Rumors abounded in the bars on our Outer Rim—how members either went with the Endar way of thinking or suffered the consequences. I'd asked a Ritto once over a drink: With more than twenty species in the Whooex Union, why didn't they join together against the Endar? Had they never heard of safety in numbers?

He had quivered with amusement. "That is what we like about Humans. You stand alone and shout at the universe. You give us hope. The Endar hate you for that same reason. We fear you will lose because of it; the rest of us are unable to cross the line to stand with you."

Unable or unwilling?

So many innocent people would suffer if the Tabi Empire turned me over to the powers controlling security on this world.

There comes a point when you smack up hard against the wall of reality. I'd had plenty of time to consider my personal situation while I wandered the warehouse. Without my wetware, I was a waste of air, a scrub doomed to a life of indentured servitude when I got back to EA space. I could curse the MoMo and the Frairy every day for the rest of my miserable life, but the odds of recovering my tech were stacked against me. It meant the odds were stacked against Saura, too. If I didn't get back to Idwal, she would die. We had not linked the *Hand* into Idwal's massive power grid. Knowing nothing of their alien system had made it too risky. Now, when the batteries on our ship went dead, the power to the SAC would die. That alone would not have been bad, but the *Hand*, attached to the station, would pass through the blaze of Idwal's sun with every rotation, raising the ambient temperature inside the ship too high to protect life inside an unpowered SAC.

"I want to talk to someone in your diplomatic service. Someone in charge."

Mathet leaned back and crossed his arms again.

"All right. Let me talk to the Ritto-ssa. I have to find out what happened—" I tried again.

"Impossible."

"Then you talk to them. There's—"

"Are you stupid? We can't talk to the Ritto-ssa about a Human we cannot even know exists! The Endar already accuse Tabisee of collaborating with you because our governments are allics. Now they'll be watching our activities twice as close as before."

"This is important."

"So important the Earth Alliance is willing to jeopardize every-thing, including the relationship with its closest ally—would risk even destroying its closest ally—for it?"

"No! But it's not—"

He looked as if he wanted to gut me.

I wasn't giving up on finding the kid, but I sure as hell wasn't go-ing to let it kill Saurubi. I couldn't get back to Idwal, but her people could. They might punish her for not returning home after her ter-mination of duty with the EA, but at least she would be alive.

"There's more to this situation." I took a deep breath and plunged into my story, referring to Saurubi only as my partner. I wanted them to realize someone needed rescuing before I told them who it was. I also left out any details on the MoMo and the Frairy. The clown-duo was my problem—to be resolved personally.

"You abandoned your partner. How does this concern the Tabi Empire?"

"I didn't abandon her! She was on an upper level of the facility with our ship when the ring section blew. She made it to a SAC. I know she did! The blast threw the kid and me out into open space, where the Ritto-ssa found us and pulled us out of the dark. But she's still out there and she needs help!"

"Spacers attacked in a disputed area of space where they had no legal right to be." He shrugged again. "It sounds as if it's an issue for the power in charge of that sector."

His callous attitude twisted my insides. "My partner is Tabisee," I said.

"No!" He grabbed me by the throat and slammed me against the wall. The cold metal of his claw tips bit into my flesh. "You blunder into a bad situation and now you want us to clean up your mess! You think you can manipulate us?"

"Ser," the female guard spoke up softly. "You may not want to kill her yet."

I made a choking sound of agreement.

The captain's grip on my throat tightened. "Why, Shoff? Tell me why, and it had better be good."

"There may be some truth in what she says."

Darkness crept into the edges of my vision.

"For reasons of deniability, I cannot forward this to you. You understand," she added.

Ears tilting out in disgust, Mathet flung me back into the chair and went to join his people in staring at the female's feed while I took the time to catch up on my oxygen intake.

Mathet came back and settled into the chair across from me. Everything about him had gone unreadable. "What do you want from us, Human?"

"Just save my partner," I rasped. "Tell me you'll do it and show me a door. I'll be gone and you'll never hear from me again."

"No," he said. "I don't think so."

The bag slammed back over my head.

CHAPTER 20

Two Raids and a Rescue

Three sleep cycles ago, one of the older kids told Kamen his parents were on the ship, on a deck below us. He may have done it to cause us trouble—if a group causes a problem, they are publicly punished—or he may have done it merely to upset Kamen. He's big for his age, but he is weak and whines a lot. The kids from other groups, especially the older ones, pick on him.

I don't think he told Kamen because he wanted to be nice.

Now Kamen is obsessed with finding his mom and dad. He thinks they don't know he is on the ship and if he gets to them, they will be a family again. I don't believe it. If it is true, I wish it could be for Anthy and me, but I know it can't; I saw our Mama and Papa lying in the yard. I saw the wet, dark ground beneath them.

I hear the older kids talk while they clean the showers. They say the decks below us are slave pens. I don't understand it, but I know it's not good. I know the older kids slip around the ship using the maintenance tunnels behind the walls. They laugh about having to move quickly to keep from freezing.

Now Kamen is missing. I have looked for him everywhere...

***

"Wake up, Zant." Light blazed overhead and something heavy thumped down on my shins.

I sat up and squinted. The male half of my recent security escort, who had dumped me in this hole carved into the bedrock, stood at the foot of my cot.

The cell was barely large enough to hold a narrow bed and my awaypack. There was a hole in the door for food to drop through and a hole in the floor for my waste to drop down. I suspected the cell was located somewhere far away from the Tabi embassy, in a place where no one would find me if the security team conveniently chose to forget my existence.

If they expected to see me break down in frustration and fear, or to plot my next move in EA espionage after they had locked me in, they were doomed to disappointment. Exhaustion had claimed me almost immediately. Judging from the number of food bars and water bottles someone had shoved through the door slot, more than a day had passed.

"Get dressed," he ordered.

Plates of body armor enhanced his black leather security uniform today.

Tactical body armor. What the hell?

"Get dressed," he repeated.

"Yeah, yeah." I rolled to my feet and reached for my awaysuit.

"No." He pointed at the black bundle he'd pitched on the cot. I could see curved pads of stiff, synthetic material in it.

Tabisee and Human anatomy are similar, but we are not interchangeable shapes. "Look, uh..."

"Meeroush," he said. "My partner is Shoff. Get moving!"

Giving me their names meant he had no worries about me sharing the information with anyone. Smug bastard planetsider. I hated when someone underestimated me—even when the odds were so obviously piled against me.

I managed to suck up my wounded pride with a defiant thought: if they took me out of this cell, I could escape.

"I don't think this armor will fi—"

"No talk," he snapped. "Get dressed."

I tugged the black uniform over my shipskins and started attaching the plates. I'd seen Tabisee armor before. Saura's was spotlessly shiny. This stuff, like his, was dull. I ran a finger over a pad. It felt as if someone had sanded the finish off with an abrasive. Lacquer darkened anything on it that would gleam, but all the joints were well oiled and flexible.

It looked as if someone liked to sneak around in other people's shadows.

"The knee joints won't line up," I told him.

"Deal with it."

As predicted, the molded forms fit me badly. We did not have the same amount of muscle in the same places. My lower legs, being longer and thinner, let the shin guards twist, while the padding inside the knee covers restricted the bend in my legs. The finger joints in the gloves fit wrongly on my hands. Overall, the legs and shoulders hung loose, while the buttocks and lower abdomen clamped tight.

I was trying to twist everything into a more comfortable fit when Meeroush grasped my arm. I barely had time to snatch up my awaypack as he pulled me out the door into the hall.

Two Tabi waited in the corridor; the other half of the security detail, now tagged as Shoff and Captain Mathet Waa Silvec.

I nodded at him. "You checked my story."

"The Ritto have indirectly confirmed they picked you out of the debris at Idwal Station. However," he added when I opened my mouth, "they have no record of a second lifeform recovered with you."

"That's wrong," I said. "She was on their ship. I saw her." Why would the Ritto-ssa deny rescuing her?

He ignored my comment. "Get headgear on her."

"Down and dark." Meeroush slapped a helmet over my head. It, too, was Tabi.

It wobbled due to my lack of upright ears. I found the chinstrap and tried to limit the movement. "Where are we going?"

"Human." The captain had a way of saying the word that made it sound as if he addressed the lowest form of space spack. "This is a stealth op. Stay silent, keep up, and do what you're told."

What the hell? "Yes, ser," I said.

It appeared that was all the information he intended to share. Mathet and Shoff turned and started down the hall.

"Set audio channel to twenty-two." Meeroush's voice sounded muffled outside the headgear.

Visuals streamed at the right corner of the helmet's eye-dat field, but I had no idea how to set the audio channel. When I didn't respond, he reached over. The helmet rocked as he keyed a sequence on the left, external side of the headgear. The Tabisee equivalent of the number twenty-two came up in the feed and his voice bloomed inside the helmet.

"You carry your stuff." He pointed at my awaysuit pack.

"Testing suit audio," Shoff's voice said in a background feed.

"What's going on?" I asked him, taking advantage of the audio check to ask a question.

"A recovery operation,"

The speakers in the helmet were too high for my ears and chatter from a second channel bled in. I found the volume control and turned it up.

"Records show the Ritto-ssa put something in one of their storage facilities at the same time the Xix medical facility received you."

I drew a sharp breath. "What is it?"

"We don't know. The message came to us through a third party. With the risk of the Endar monitoring our activity, anything relating to you is dangerous to us."

True. There was no way the Tabi could know to inquire about an incident at Idwal unless an escaped, illegal Human named Zant told them.

"What about the kid?"

"That is not our concern." Meeroush shifted back to guarded responses.

I bit back frustration. They didn't want an association with one Human here on the Moneyworld much less two. Finding the kid was going to be up to me.

Getting out of the Tabi cell was the first step toward that. "Is this a space op?" I lifted my shoulder to indicate my awaysuit strap.

"No. There is always a chance the Sat Quar might raid our compound. We can't leave that thing for them to find."

"Sat Quar?"

"The name for Endar security on the Moneyworld."

"They can violate the sanctity of your embassy?" An embassy was...inviolate. Wasn't it?

He shrugged. "Who can we complain to?"

Did Humans, with their clamor to acquire a commercial presence on the Moneyworld, have any idea what they would encounter here, with the species who hated us in control of security? The place seemed more a police state than a bastion of intergalactic commerce.

"They have not taken such drastic action yet, but they want to discourage our alliance with Humans. They try to make things as uncomfortable for us as they can."

As in accessing their ships? Hunh. I walked in silence, unsure of the political situation on this world. I had no proof the place where they captured me was a Primacy warehouse. I didn't have any proof it wasn't, either.

"Hey, I'm sorry," I said, in case they were telling the truth. "I didn't set out to cause you a problem."

He shrugged. "It's only one of the newest in a long list of issues between Tabisee and Endar. You say you met with the High Jerak Seok?" he continued.

"Yeah. In all his ugly layers of leather."

"How many layers?" He sounded intrigued.

"Thirty, maybe more."

"They say the leathers are the skins of their vanquished enemies."

Considering the boney limbs of the Endar, I found that hard to accept. "That's a lot of dead Endar."

"Not nearly enough," Shoff hissed as we came to a stop beside her at the end of the corridor.

So, we shared the feed. Maybe looking for me to make a slip while Meeroush chatted me up?

"Enough talk," Mathet said as Shoff swiped a panel beside a set of doors.

I could hear faint background chatter from their operations base inside my helmet. The tone of the feed intensified as we stepped inside an elevator.

"Captain Mathet." I heard the Tabisee equivalent of "Endar" and "arriving."

"Proceed with your orders," he responded.

"What—?" I started to ask.

Shoff reached over and pressed on the side of my headgear hard enough to push my head sideways. The background feed went silent.

With the distraction of the extra feed gone, I took the time to check out my companions from behind my darkened face shield. They all had the well-muscled, flexible bodies of the physically active planet-bound. If they had half the speed and agility I'd seen in Saurubi, they would be awesome fighters. Which meant I should move my skinny spacer body out of the way quickly if we encountered conflict.

Fine by me.

The Tabisee stood motionless as the elevator dropped. I tried to mimic them, but the armor was pressing hard on a patch of my ship-skins under my awaypack strap. I finally gave in and rolled my left shoulder to reposition it.

Three heads snapped to look at me.

"Sorry," I muttered.

The doors slid open on what appeared to be a laundry facility. A lone, black-clad Tabisee stood waiting for us. My three companions surged out of the lift, moved swiftly past a row of laundry carts into the mouth of a large storage cabinet, and out through the back of it into another elevator car. The lone Tabisee began heaving folded towels into the cabinet behind us as the back panel slid closed. Meanwhile, Shoff pressed a sequence of keys on the new control panel. Instead of the car dropping, its back section slid open to reveal a third chamber. We stepped in and Shoff directed her attention to another panel. This time we dropped.

Meeroush gave me a sidelong glance, and I nodded my admiration. A triple blind. Nice.

"Switch to closed com system," Mathet ordered. "I'll monitor feed for the south tier raid."

My head bobbed sideways again as someone made an external adjustment.

South tier raid? I looked over at Meeroush. "Are we meeting up with another team?"

"Distraction," he said shortly.

They had another operation running to draw attention away from our activity. It was not difficult to guess who they were trying to distract.

After an extended drop, the elevator opened on a long passage that was padded with soft material on the walls, floor, and ceiling. I recognized the setup. Someone had cut a tunnel in bedrock and lined the thing with sound-dampening materials to elude someone else's sensitive monitoring equipment. A single strand of lightwire, overhead, illuminated the way. I felt sure we passed through a similar passage on the way out of the warehouse. It appeared the Tabisee liked to go out walking, unobserved by their fellow Union members. What the heck kind of place was this Moneyworld?

Tugging at the hard, molded plates that clamped my buttocks, I followed Mathet and Shoff out of the lift while Meeroush brought up the rear.

"Keep moving." He gave me a light shove.

It was a long, silent walk to the tunnel end, where Shoff keyed a code into a panel mounted on the sound-dampening surface. A section of padded wall swung open on darkness. Following the others, I stepped from padding to a metal plate that vibrated through my footwear with the thrum of heavy machinery. Meeroush closed the opening behind us while Shoff pulled a lumi-stick and gave it a good shake. Light flooded from it to reveal the deck and handrails of a small platform. We moved down a short series of steps and past several huge, droning mechanical shapes, then ducked through a break in another stone wall, into a larger mechanical chamber. We walked past more droning machines for what must have been a kilometer.

At one point, we stepped over a strip of mossy plant growing along a seam in the floor.

Plants in this darkness? "Tough stuff," I said gesturing at it.

Meeroush grunted.

We climbed a short metal stairs to another platform. This time Mathet opened the door at the end and peered out. When no weapon fire took off his head or sliced away body parts, he motioned us forward and we stepped out into a long, narrow space backed on one side by a tall, featureless wall and on the other by a huge rack stuffed with boxes and containers.

The three Tabisee paused.

"The Endar have contacted the embassy. They are making inquiries on the raid," Mathet told my companions.

"Have they asked for you?" Shoff asked.

"They are demanding to speak with me. My presence at the south tier makes it difficult. We must finish this before they send a squad over there. Shoff, you have the location. Lead."

We moved quickly down the wall and out into the silent darkness of a massive warehouse. In the light of Shoff's lumi-stick I could see that an automated sweeper occasionally made a run over the floor, but a heavy layer of dust covered everything on the towering racks around us. This was not a living facility with flyways zooming overhead and cargo transferring in and out. It was a dry, ancient skeleton.

We followed a wide, central avenue with symbols painted on the ends of the racks we passed, but my translation software didn't throw anything up in the corner of my right eye.

"Are these trade goods?" I asked Meeroush. Business must be slow, judging from the amount of dust blanketing everything.

"Just accumulated stuff," he replied.

"From...?"

"The Ritto-ssa Trade Compound. They've been a presence here for a long time."

We were in a Ritto-ssa warehouse? My brain lit with cautious hope.

Shoff turned right between two of the towering racks. Several long strides in, she stopped beside a large crate that jutted out into the aisle and motioned us past it.

On the other side, in a gap beneath the shoulder-high rack, three small green points of light burned in the darkness. She moved forward and passed the lumi-stick over the side of the box to reveal a battered stencil. "*Thief's Hand* EADSCLCV 42101," Earth Alliance Deep Space Commercial Light Cargo Vessel, showed on the end plate of the suspended animation container shoved lengthways into the space.

"Holy sh—" It couldn't be. My knees would have buckled if the stiff Tabisee armor hadn't clamped my kneecaps so rigidly. "The Ritto-ssa got her out?"

Shoff and Meeroush caught the side of the SAC and dragged it out into the aisle. Unlike the rest of the stuff in this place, its surface showed clean and white.

"Open it, Human," Mathet ordered.

Well, that explained why they brought me along. They didn't know how to open the SAC. I grinned with joy inside the helmet as I shrugged the awaypack off my shoulder.

Saura was here! Safe. Alive.

Then reality thumped my brain. These Tabisee were not my allies. They just needed me to help them retrieve their precious astrogator. After that, I became a liability.

Instead of squatting in front of the SAC with my back to them, I settled on the lid, putting the control box between my legs and my companions in front of me.

The process was quick and simple. I keyed a sequence of numbers, flicked a latch, and lifted a protective cover to deactivate the container's life suspension process.

I looked up.

My escort had shifted their positions while I focused on the switch. Mathet stood several steps to my right, his back against the parallel rack, while Shoff and Meeroush had moved closer in front of me. With the big crate on my left and the racking at my back, they had me effectively penned in.

They wouldn't be thinking about putting me in the SAC and walking away with Saura, would they?

"What happens now?" Mathet asked. Even if they were ill-intentioned, they wouldn't do anything to endanger Saurubi.

Neither would I. "We wait until it turns steady white." I stood.

My instincts screamed for me to make a lunge for freedom—to charge out into the darkness while these three were focused on safely retrieving their fellow citizen from the SAC—but I had to know if Saura was inside the container. If she was safe.

Besides, they needed to get her out before they could put me inside.

Thinking I could move faster than the Tabisee was pure idiocy. I knew from experience that they were twice as fast as Humans; plus I had to cope with the pinching, clamping confines of the armor they'd stuffed me into. But, I swore to myself, if they did act against me they better make sure they put me down for good. Because if I survived, I would make sure everyone in the Whooex Union knew what had gone down here. This whole situation, from Mandragala forward, stank to the stars and there were limits to what I was willing to pay for someone else's games of intrigue.

The SAC beeped three times, and everyone looked at the lights as they turned a steady white.

I reached down and touched the locks along the front of the SAC. The containment field shut off with a soft hiss as air inside the SAC equalized with the air in the warehouse.

Heart pounding, I stood and rolled the opaque cover up and over.

Saurubi, dressed in her blue shipskins, lay inside. She hated the things because they squashed her fur against her wiry body, leaving the exposed fluff at her cuffs and neck poofed in an outrageously funny effect. She always wore them under her awaysuit, however. That told me she had not had time to strip and don her Tabi uniform of gold vest and red shorts, which she favored for deep sleep.

I looked for dirt or smudges of blood on her flesh that would indicate injury. Everything appeared clean. Then I checked the interior life readouts to make sure her heart rate and brain function showed normal levels.

Sensing there was no time or patience for an electrochemical stimulus to ease her transition out of hibernation, I pulled the monitor tabs off her neck and forehead and silently started to count.

At twenty-five, she gave a sharp gasp and opened her eyes.

CHAPTER 21

Boldface Treachery

"Do you require medical aid?" Mathet asked coldly.

"Give her a min—"

"Be silent, Human!" he snapped.

Ally or not, I shut up.

"Do you require—?"

"No," Saura cut him short. Her voice sounded raspy and weak from her time in suspension. She looked around blearily, then put shaking hands on the side of the SAC and tried to sit up. "I do not require medical aid, ser."

From my own time spent in the damn things, I knew she really did require another few minutes for her body to adjust to the physical changes it was going through. I twitched with the need to reach over and help her, but Mathet's glare held me silent and immobile.

"On your feet, First Astrogator."

She did not move.

Any other time she would be marshaling her strength in preparation for a lunge at her tormentor, but right now, I knew her heart was racing and she was nauseous.

"On your feet—"

"Let me help her," I said.

Mathet ignored me. "Meeroush, get her up. Shoff, take her out of the arm—"

I did not have to hear the rest. They planned to strip me out of the armor, put Saura in it, stuff me in the SAC and walk away.

It was the smart solution to their Human problem.

Their plan didn't account for Anthy—the kid—I corrected. Their plan didn't account for a Human kid wandering around on this world.

The low mechanical rumble and thud of a heavy door sliding open somewhere in the distance froze us all. Getting caught in this warehouse probably wasn't a good thing for them. Getting caught in here with a Human was a potential disaster.

Shoff looked down to extinguish the lumi-stick and I snatched the moment of distraction. I ran, straight-arming her into Mathet as I dove past.

Bad move—left arm.

"Get her!" Mathet hissed.

Biting back a cry of pain, I skidded past the end of the rack into the next row, into darkness, and fumbled along the crates on the far side until I found a gap wide enough to fit inside. I scurried in and crawled. The opening angled off to one side and I followed it, squirming between cartons until I came out in the next aisle over.

The Tabisee helmet had night vision, but I didn't know how to activate it. I scurried down the next aisle, half running, half limping in my ill-fitting armor while chills rolled down my back with the expectation of a clawed hand on my shoulder at any moment.

If the Tabisee wanted to avoid detection by whoever had entered the warehouse, they would have to be cautious in their pursuit. I, however, had to avoid both encounters and dodging down random aisles in the dark was not a good strategy. I needed to find a place to hide.

Life in space had taught me, when in doubt, move to high ground. Turning to the storage rack closest to me, I began to climb.

That spacer logic would have worked out great if I hadn't been coping with both gravity and the armor. The suit did not bend in the places I needed it to bend and the gloves were too short for my fingers to fully flex. Plus, the heavy dust that covered everything caused my hands to slip precariously every time I put my weight on them.

I had worked my way two meters up the face of the rack when the overhead lights blazed on.

At that moment I was glad I didn't have enhanced night vision. I looked over to see a Tabi standing at the mouth of the aisle fifteen meters away. Shoff. She stood, frozen, possibly trying to adjust to the sudden illumination.

The light also revealed a cross support right above me. I grabbed for it, got a tentative hold, and tried to pull myself out of her reach.

It took her a single jump. She snagged one of my feet and hung on, adding her weigh to mine.

The tender new muscles of my left arm shrieked in protest.

I kicked, trying to dislodge her, throwing more weight onto my left side. My new hand slid off the support beam. Desperately, I flailed to reestablish my hold.

The twisting and tugging on the armor took its inevitable toll. I gasped in pain, my right hand lost its grip, and I crashed down on the Tabisee below. We sprawled on the floor.

"You stupid—!" Clambering on top of me, Shoff grabbed me by the shoulders and slammed my head against the floor until I stopped squirming. The helmet protected me from the worst damage, but my head, rattling inside the loose shell, left me too stunned to resist as she hauled me to my feet.

She gave me another hard shake then dragged me back to rejoin the others.

Mathet and Meeroush had moved out into the center aisle and several rows farther down than we'd previously been. It seemed a confusing tactic for a stealth operation until Shoff pulled me to a stop and I realized there were a lot more black-clad figures standing around in the warehouse light. I blinked, trying to clear my vision and my heart froze.

Five tall, thin figures dressed in varying lengths of black leather coats stood blocking the aisle in front of us. The four with the shortest coats held long, ugly, sticks with glowing purple tips.

Tanglers: given the name because of the way your feet tangled up if you tried to run after one zapped you. They were a nasty weapon that messed with their target's nervous system. They did serious damage if their controls were set for a species different than the one their blast struck. The EA had banned them, declaring the risk of harm in mixed species confrontations too high. They did not want a diplomatic incident.

It figured they would be the weapon of choice for the Endar.

My attention shifted to the leather-plumped outline of the fifth figure, who stood facing Mathet and Meeroush. The Tabi captain had removed his helmet. Meeroush, with the limp form of Saurubi draped over his arms, had not. Shoff and I followed his lead as we came up beside him.

"...fled into the warehouse through the side entrance. It was open and did not show signs of forced entry, so we followed in pursuit. We saw one individual, High Jerak, but I suspect there are more," Mathet said

High Jerak! My blurry eyesight finally picked out the thin strip of crimson rimming the collar and a shot of ice ran down my spine.

Shoff readjusted her grip from my shoulder to my arm. Her hand tightened as Mathet continued to spin an elaborate tale. "Someone attacked one of my rookies and stole her armor. The two officers in pursuit also fell under attack. Then the lights came on. I fear we've lost the offender in the distraction." He made the last bit sound slightly reproachful.

Looking at us, his story seemed entirely plausible. Saura, in her skins, was unconscious, while dust coated Shoff and me from head to toe. Meanwhile, her grip on my arm served to hold me upright after she'd rattled my brain. If I had entered this place with Tabisee pursuit, I might have struck at them in exactly the manner Mathet described.

Except I was not on the loose. I was standing in the middle of a cluster of hostile aliens, praying one side liked Humans a little more than they liked the other side.

The High Jerak's red eyes swept over us. "Describe the intruder."

"Bipedal. Two arms. Not too tall." Mathet gestured lower than my height. "It ran when it saw us. It carried this." He kicked my awaypack forward into the space between the Endar and us. "We found it wedged between some crates near my rookie's unconscious body. Maybe they thought to come back for it later. It appears to be some sort of tool bag..."

"We will investigate it." The High Jerak motioned one of his men forward to pick up my awaysuit. "This raid you are running outside, Captain Silvec—were we made aware of the initial problem?"

"A security monitor noted a tripped sensor in a section of our local warehouse. We had to move swiftly to catch the perpetrators in the act."

The edges of the Endar leader's face darkened. "Captain, we've been over this before. You are required to file a report of unlawful or suspicious activity to the Sat Quar, so we can determine the appropriate action to take. As appointed security for the Whooex Union Trade Consortium, we strive to implement a cohesive overall response for its members. We cannot tolerate individual security details running around, taking arbitrary, independent actions. It undermines our role in the minds of these," he rotated his long hand in an encompassing gesture, "people. Some of them already resent our presence. There are elements out on the streets stirring up protests against the approaching assembly. They do not want Humans added to the population. Some beings do not harbor warm feelings for anyone who supports their admission. The Tabi Empire's position places your people in a dangerous situation. There may be a time we are unable to come to your assistance."

I didn't know enough about the politics of this world to be sure, but it sounded as if he had just threatened the Tabisee.

Mathet nodded, his ears in the most rigidly fixed, neutral position I had ever seen.

The High Jerak's eyes slid to Saura and I felt a twist of panic. Her shipskins covered most of her tattoos, but the dim light picked up glints of copper pattern on her face and hands. Not to mention her being around half the height of her planet dwelling brethren and dusky blue instead of gray.

"Is that one of your much-lauded astrogators?" He sounded far too interested for my comfort.

Shoff's grip tightened the armor pads down on my arm until my fingers felt numb.

"A request from an admiral, to let one of his favorites experience planetside operations. I do not think he will request again."

"You should be more careful with your treasures," the High Jerak said. His attention shifted over to me and Shoff and his intrigue slid to distaste. "Your injured—do they require medical attention?"

"We have a med-evac inbound. With your permission, we will relinquish this scene to you and rejoin our taskforce. Our operation is wrapping up."

The Endar's red eyes regarded Mathet. "It is surprising to find you taking an active role in a simple street operation, Captain. You seem to have sunken into the shadows of late."

"As you say." Mathet nodded stiffly. "One welcomes an opportunity to get out into the open air."

The two eyed each other. I held my breath as each seemed to dare the other to take a step further in their word exchange.

"Your stolen armor has a tracker?". The Endar returned his attention to the current situation.

"If it has not been disabled. This being, whatever it is, appears quite adept at moving about..." Mathet let the sentence hang, as if inviting him to share any additional intelligence he had.

The High Jerak ignored him. "You will file a report on this incident through your embassy office. We will keep you apprised of our progress in recovering your stolen property. Our people will have additional questions for you. My officers will escort you back to your operation." A slight gesture of his thin hand brought two of his force forward, one from each side, to bracket us. "It will allow them to investigate this curiously unlocked door. And, Captain," he added, "the next time you conduct a raid on a suspected theft ring, you will notify us in advance and we will assist you. The Primacy bears responsibility for crimes committed against Trade Members on this world."

"Of course." Mathet nodded.

We made our way back down the main aisle accompanied by a pair of Endar security officers. With a lighted warehouse and no need for stealth, we moved briskly to the back wall, where we turned smoothly in the direction opposite our original point of entry, toward a heavy security door.

Leaving the Endar to inspect the lock, we stepped out into the open air of the Moneyworld.

CHAPTER 22

Surface Tension

Shoff's grasp on my arm retightened. If she thought I was going to make a break for it with the change of scenery, however, she was mistaken. The towering walls of the alley threw the narrow slit into heavy shadow, triggering a flashback of childhood terror in me. Back to Spacertown. To places I never wanted to step foot inside again.

It took me several breaths to fight down the panic, clear my thoughts, and come up with a reason for stepping into that murky nightmare.

The High Jerak had, oddly enough, saved me from a Tabisee attempt at betrayal, Mathet had not turned me over to him, and—most important—Saura was safe. Of course, our partnership was over. I would never get her back from her people now. Which was for the best, since, without my wetware, I was useless to her.

My thoughts left me hollow. And angry. Which was not constructive. I had heard that from so many doctors and analysts: redirect your energy. Find a way to channel it positively.

Okay. A little kid was wandering this world, alone and in danger. If I found her, she might point me in the right direction so I could exact a little vengeance—justice—from someone.

Was it possible to claim any justice for the three of us, or for those dead people on the shuttle? Nothing could give back the things we had lost.

I had to try.

I was not helpless.

I was—out on the surface of the world! Now I had to lose the Tabisee, find some other disguise—I refused to wear the Tabisee torture device one moment longer than I had to—and find the kid. I would figure out the next step after that when the time came.

People were moving in the distant, brighter light at the mouth of the alley. It was a colorful mix of species. Some were walking, some were running. The runners were all going one direction.

I suspected we were going that way, too.

The street was a wide, deep groove, lined on one side by massive, blank-walled warehouses and on the other by what looked to be multi-storied housing units. It sliced off in a straight line in both directions to a distant haze. The structures could have used a coat of paint, but I had seen dingier streets in glitzier neighborhoods on other worlds.

There was a cluster of activity and a growing crowd up the street to our right, but that wasn't what snared my attention. In the distance, beyond all the commotion, rose an enormous, dark arch.

I was used to seeing massive structures and towering walls on space stations. Unrestrained by planetary gravity, architecture sometimes extended for kilometers inside or outside rings or platforms. This was different. This thing sat on the surface of a world, subject to gravity. It was immense, its crest arching into the sky, and it was threatening.

"Whoa!" I stopped walking. "What the hell is that?"

Shoff jerked me back to movement. "If you want to know something, check your world feed!"

"Apparently there is no feed compatible for an illegal Human." I snapped back.

"Be silent and keep moving," she hissed as she pulled me to the right, into the flow of the crowd.

I glimpsed black shapes in the alley behind us as we turned. They were closer than I expected. "The Endar are following us."

"Of course they are, idiot. If you screw this up for us, I will personally gut you."

If I screwed this up, she'd have to get at the back of a long line to gut me.

Ahead of us, through the throng of onlookers, black-armored Tabisee security troops were moving around a line of bedraggled alien beings. Judging from the range of body postures, from slumped to rigidly upright, I was seeing the unfortunate remnants of the Tabisee raid.

A troop transport sat on the street in front of an apartment building while a crowd was forming on the warehouse side, opposite it. For now, the observers were giving the troops a wide margin on the street, but the numbers were growing rapidly, pushing the front edge out toward them.

Most of the prisoners in the queue looked like short tree trunks with several long, thin, branchy arms and a mass of short, bare roots on which they motivated.

"What are they?"

"Carquetchians," she said. "The thieving underbelly of the universe."

It was a new species for me. "So the raid is for real."

"Of course it is. No one makes a move on this world they can't back up with reason and evidence."

"Is this a police state?" This was the Moneyworld, the commercial and marketing jewel in the crown of the Whooex Union of Stars. An iron glove clenching its throat did not fit the image I—or anyone else in the EA—had formed about it.

"The Endar aspire to make it so."

Damn. But that problem belonged to EA. I had other concerns, like staying viable and mobile. "You planned to shove me into the SAC. Why?"

"Humans," she said bitterly. "You have no clue of the problems you create."

"I'm listening. Enlighten me."

She made a sound of disgust and increased our pace.

Meanwhile, the number of onlookers opposite the carrier continued to grow. As we passed through them, they merely gave us a glance and moved aside, but ahead, along the front edge of the crowd, I could see scatterings of more excited behavior.

It seems there are a few members of every species, anywhere in the universe, who behave the same way in a volatile situation. They move in an agitated manner, mutter to anyone who will listen, wave their appendages, and raise the general stress level of everyone around them. They are the fans that fire the embers of riot.

It appeared they were doing their best to work this crowd into an explosion of flame.

One of the Carquetchians in the Tabisee prisoner line made a break for freedom, moving surprisingly fast on those little roots. It made it halfway across the open zone between the Tabi and the crowd before a trooper got a manacle clamped on its middle and stopped its flight.

A cheer went up around us.

Despite the valiant scurry of its little multi-feet, a tazer brought it down.

A groan of disapproval rose from the observers.

'Can't fight the taze, my brotha', my fellow marines always joked as we rounded up perpetrators on the Outer Rim. I would wager Tabi armor could negate the nerve-scrambling blast if I found an opportunity to run.

The Endar likely had a weapon to take down anything that moved, armored or not.

A couple of black-clad troopers dragged the tree-creature back and manacled it at the end of the line.

During the brief excitement, a small med-evac ship had appeared overhead. It dropped between the buildings and settled in the cleared space the Tabisee claimed at the center of the street. A side panel on the unit slid open and more gray-furred Tabisee, this time dressed in white, hopped out pulling a stretcher behind them. Mathet split off from us, striding toward the troop carrier, while Meeroush hurried to the med-evac team with Saura.

A medic was shoving needles into her neck and hands before they even put her on the stretcher. My partner was safely in her peoples' hands.

I had a grasp on how things worked here: the Endar controlled the show, and the Tabisee had to look out for their people's interests. They were already on bad footing because of their ties with the EA, and they didn't need me to make things worse.

I felt like I was betraying Saura when I glanced around, looking for a way to slip away from the churn of activity. But the only allies I expected to find on this world had already locked me in a stone cell, and, even with proof to back my story, had planned to shut me away in the SAC. I had no reason to believe they would change their tactics when we returned to their compound.

They might cuff Saura's furry little ears, but she was no longer at the mercy of a failing ship system and the deep dark. Almost certainly, as one of their cherished astrogators, she would find her way back into their system quickly enough.

She could back up parts of my story. But not about the kid. She hadn't witnessed that.

It was time to cut ties with my reluctant allies and find the kid. I flexed muscles in preparation for action.

"Ow!" The armor plates bunched, pinching my buttock so hard I stumbled sideways into Shoff.

"Idiot!" She shoved me upright.

I think we both saw the black leather and red silk hovering over our shoulders at the same time. The High Jerak was following only a few steps behind us.

"Perhaps I can be of assistance," he said lifting a long-fingered hand toward me.

If he got his bony fingers on my arm, he would not feel hard, coiled Tabisee muscle.

Shoff thrust me forward, out of his reach. "No need to trouble, ser. She's going out on the med-evac." Managing a sort of half-bow to the Endar, she increased her pace, shoving me, stumbling, toward the med-evac.

Seok stared after us.

"Take it easy! You're making the situation look worse," I said as I half-limped, half-ran beside her.

"You will destroy all of us with your behavior—"

"This damned armor doesn't fit!"

As if in retaliation for the complaint, it pinched my butt again.

"Son of a—!"

"Stop it! This is not a game."

No, it wasn't. I blinked back tears of pain. "They can't arrest someone for reacting to an injury!"

"They are Sat Quar. Whooex Union Trade Consortium Security. They can arrest any of us for any reason, or for no reason. Now, get in the evac, sit down, and be silent. And keep the helmet on!" She hoisted me up the two steps into the med-evac with the strength of one arm and slammed the door closed behind me.

Gentler hands inside caught and guided me across to a seat.

I had just lost all chance for escape.

Activity buzzed around me. I watched the medics working on Saura. "Is she all right?"

"She's good," one of the techs said over his shoulder.

The evac door beside me on the opposite side of the air ship suddenly slid open. Meeroush caught me by the back of the neck and yanked me off the med-evac while Shoff clambered up past me. The door slammed behind her.

"What are you doing? I need to—"

"Shut up and walk normally. Your life depends upon it," Meeroush ordered.

Several black-clad Tabisee moved up to fence me from the view of the crowd on the far side of the med-evac as it ramped its engines to lift away. The Tabisee and the people gathered to our right side ignored what had just happened.

As the medical transport slowly began to rise, a Frairy dressed in a ground-dragging red coat, with a silky green scarf wrapped around its head, suddenly burst out of the crowd. It raised a heavy club and slammed it against the side of the evac, bashing the metal surface beneath the cockpit. He hit it several times, making a deep dent before it rose beyond his reach. He waved the club above his head, let out a furious whoop, and dived back into the crowd. The bystanders on our side screamed with what sounded like delight.

"What—?"

"Keep moving."

The craft lifted away to reveal a different situation on the far side of the street. The crowd there was now focused on the four rod-carrying Endar standing along their front edge. The High Jerak stood in the open area, talking fast to someone somewhere else while he watched the med-evac speed away.

I locked my eyes forward, onto the prisoner chain.

"You have Frairies here?" I growled in an aside to Meeroush.

"So?"

"They're telepaths!"

"No, they're not. Shut up and get on the troop carrier."

At that moment, a fight broke out between two Carquetchians in the line and the effort to break it up stopped our forward progress. We took a step back, away from the tussle.

"Where are they taking Saurubi?"

"They have orders to take First Astrogator Syrhas to our embassy for medical care. The Endar will attempt to divert the ship to a hospital, where they can take custody of any patients who are on board. Which is why we pulled you off. Shoff is nearly as dusty as you, so they won't be aware we made a switch unless you mess things up. Satisfied? Now move!" The Tabisee troops had sorted out the fight and were dragging two limp bodies to the transport.

Was I satisfied? No. There was a Frairy on this world, and I was pretty sure one of them was telepathic no matter what Meeroush said.

Meanwhile, hoots of support and derision rolled through the crowd. Curiously, the scattered bits my translation software picked up told me most of it was targeted at the five Endar and not the Tabisee.

As the multiple, rooty feet of the last Carquetchians slid into the Tabi carrier, a fist-sized piece of crumpled scrap metal whirled over the heads of the crowd and landed in the street.

I was sure no one heard it strike the surface, but the sight of it hitting the pavement sent a shockwave of silence through the throng. I counted two breaths before the noise rose again, louder. If this mob had access to rocks or other dense debris, someone was in real trouble.

A little chaos right about right now worked for me. Once the Tabisee took me back inside their compound, I was destined to disappear into a stone cell forever. Or worse.

Now, however, because of Mathet's story in the warehouse, the Endar were looking for a criminal in Tabisee armor out on the street.

I looked at all the shouting, squeaking, appendage-waving bipedals on my right. Some were shorter or taller than me. Some were rotund, others, skinny. A scattering wore some type of head-gear. I could find a disguise somewhere in that mix.

Meeroush planted his hand on my back and shoved me the last few steps to the carrier hatch.

Across the space, the Endar had spread out along the front of the mob, obviously confident in their presence to intimidate and sub-due them. The High Jerak stopped talking, his eyes locked on our group.

As he took a step toward us, drawing one of his troops with him, a piercing howl rose above the clamor.

The street noise abruptly silenced as all heads turned, almost as one, to look behind the mob. The howl sounded again, this time closer. Cries of pain, protest, and outrage tracked its approach.

Damn! I recognize that howl. Someone had pumped up on adrenalin or drugs and released their state of red rage on the gather-ing. Humans called them berserkers. A lot of people were going to feel some real pain unless someone brought the thing down fast.

The Tabisee and Endar were also reacting. Troops stationed at the hatch hastily grasped the arm of the guy ahead of me and hauled him on the ship while the Endar lining the street took a step away from the crowd and leveled their purpled-tipped weapons in the di-rection of the sound.

In that frozen heartbeat of a second the mob to our right, where the Frairy had disappeared, broke under the pressure of the panicked beings at their backs and surged into the open space around us.

It was not the distraction I would have ordered up, but it was the distraction I needed. I twisted out of Meeroush's grip and dived to-ward the wall of alien flesh rushing toward us.

I made it twenty steps into the onrush before a charge of energy rattled through my body and I collapsed into oblivion.

Meet the Natives

We aren't supposed to know the name of the ship. If something goes wrong and we are ignorant, the law cannot trace us back to it. It doesn't stop us from knowing. The older kids always know when its name and registration change. They say they can tell by the physical condition of the port we are in: those registration forgeries take place on the most remote outposts in Human space, in places outside space fleet control where things are the most rundown.

Meanwhile, our pirate captors make sure business goes on. The quality of the patron goes from rough-edged to jagged, and only the most experienced kids go out, accompanied by a personal handler. Sometimes neither of them comes back. It makes the captain and crew furious.

We are the money. Our physical appearance matters. We are well cared for, if underfed. The slaves in the holds below us need the food more than we do. Their treatment, however, is brutal and harsh. As long as they have arms and legs to perform a required task, the scars and bruises, even a missing eye or ear, does not matter. They only have to be capable of working when they leave.

***

"—sure is an ugly son of a bitch."

Yeah. I had listened to the Frairy expound on my natural good looks for a while.

The time had come to engage with my surroundings again, so I groaned and rubbed at my nose.

The Tabisee glove took off some of the skin.

Shit! Someone had removed my headgear. The armor, however, still lovingly clenched my body in all the most awkward places.

I opened my eyes to a low-ceilinged, plascrete-lined bunker with heavy shadows along the lower sloping walls. It smelled faintly musky. In the center of the room, a Frairy, a Carquetchian, and two transparent pinkish beings who looked like sacks of water sat around a sturdy metal table playing cards. Memory told me the pink blobs were Brktar, but my chips contained no details on them, and I didn't have a language pack for Brkt or Carquet. The only other objects in the room were two vertical-barred cages. I was in one. Meeroush lay in the other one. He seemed to be unconscious. Or sleeping.

I decided to jump into the fire. "I didn't arrest your people," I said to the Carquetchian as I sat up.

"He knows that." The Frairy glanced over at me. The Carquetchian and the Brktar continued playing their game as if I had never spoken. "If you speak Basic you can get your message across to them." He grinned at me, exposing even rows of sharp little teeth. "Don't expect to develop any detailed plans, though."

I stayed with Frairen for now. "I have to get out on the streets. There's someone I have to find."

"Not happening."

"We can make a deal."

"With what? You don't even have salvageable wetware."

Was that the first thing people checked for here? "We can work out something."

He turned his attention to the activity at the table without answering.

I glanced at Meeroush's outstretched form. "What's wrong with him?"

"He's fine."

"I need to get out of here before he wakes up."

"Why? He's your ally."

"Not on this world, he's not!"

"Yeah." The Frairy looked at me, his small, round eyes bright and critical. "Maybe being illegal makes you an unwelcome guest to your allies. Anyone who ever favored Earth Alliance's membership in the Whooex Union is already under pressure from the Endar Primacy for just acknowledging you even exist."

"I didn't plan to come here. I was injured—"

"You realize your timing is really bad, right? The Earth Alliance is up for admission to the Trade Consortium again and everyone has an opinion on it."

"Is it true? Is everyone protesting EA membership?"

"Nope."

"But the Endar said—"

"The Endar think your membership is an extremely bad idea." He paused to watch the Carquetchian lay a card on the table with one of its lower branch-like extremities, then continued. "You guys stir some bad blood with them."

"I got nothing to do with that."

"Want to tell them?"

"No."

He threw two cards on the table and one of the pink beings gave a sad, haunting shriek. The Frairy cursed it soundly when it extended a pink pseudopod and absorbed the pile of plastic and metal shapes at the center of the table into its body. The stuff moved slowly to clump in its abdomen.

I wondered fleetingly how one went about robbing such a creature. The possibilities were not pretty.

Still cursing, the Frairy tossed more coins on the table while the Carquetchian shuffled the cards with three of its appendages.

"What's a Frairy doing on the Moneyworld?"

"What are you and the rest of you bastards doing on a Frairy world?"

"What?"

"This is my homeworld, lady. The rest of you people are here at our tolerance and because of a stupid pact made several thousand years ago. You're an infestation that has commandeered the host."

"Wait." I had to put that one into words. "You're saying Frairies are native to the Moneyworld?"

"Where do you think we're from?"

"The darkest pits of hell" didn't seem to be a diplomatic response from someone locked in a metal cage, so I shrugged. "I don't know. Not here." This Frairy seemed angrier than Thok. Maybe not having a sidekick to transport you through the walls of the highest-security vaults in the Whooex Union or hitch rides on the outside of starships lowered your social skills a notch.

A familiar-looking green scarf lay on the floor next to the reinforced door across the room.

"You clubbed the Tabi ship! Why?"

"To help them out."

"By damaging their ship?"

"I damaged a comm node so the pilot couldn't receive a command from the Sat Quar diverting him away from the Tabi compound to an Endar-specified med center. He can't receive the order, there is no charge of flagrant disregard."

"Oh." He had saved Saurubi from an encounter with the leather-layered High Jerak. Meeroush and Shoff had anticipated the Endar diversion. "Why do you care what happens to a Tabi med-evac? Unless you're working with them."

"Aw, you found us out," he said sarcastically.

"Look, I think that's great. You're an ally. I'm an ally. Right now, I need to get out on the street."

"Hey!" He lifted his little hands to stop me. "Not working with you. Don't want to know the invasion plans."

"Invas— I'm not a spy!"

The other players put down their cards and focused various forms of ocular sensors upon me.

How much should I say? Shit! I had no idea whose side these beings were on.

I shifted my feet and metal rattled.

"Chains?" I snatched the diversion, half in relief, and half in outrage. "You didn't put him in chains." There were no restraints on Meeroush.

"We didn't lock his cell door, either. Be grateful we're trying to be friendly here. Some of the places we could put you would leave you too traumatized to work with afterward."

Considering some of the terrible things I had seen one species do to another, or even to their own, I decided to accept the current situation as it stood. "Okay. What do you want from me?"

"We don't want anything from you. And we don't want to know what the EA's up to, either."

"The EA's not up to anything! There was an accident. I was dying in the Vasty and my rescuers didn't have the resources to save me. They brought me here in error." How many more times did I have to tell this story?

"Right. And the Zeeks upgraded you for free."

Oh, sarcasm. I should have known the civility wouldn't last. "They grew me an arm. And I'm grateful," I added.

He shrugged. "Why'd you run from the Tabisee? They're the closest thing to an ally you have on this world."

"Because I need to find someone."

The Frairy cocked his head to one side and studied me critically. "Really? Because I thought you said you came here in error. The EA needs to work on its deception skills. You guys are awful liars—or is it just you?"

"There's this kid," I tried to keep the frustration out of my voice. "She left the rescue ship when they carried me off."

"Kid? Young offspring? As in Human?"

"Yes."

"You a slaver? We don't like slavers." Surly sounds rippled around the table.

"God, no! She was rescued from the accident with me."

"Who is she?"

"I don't know."

"Man, you are losing credibility fast."

"She survived the accident with me. I saw her leave the ship when they carried me off. She waved at me—"

"She in the company of others?"

"Others? No." I anticipated the next question. "She's young. A fledgling Human."

"How long ago?"

"Ninety days," I said glumly.

"Street rats got her." He turned back to the game.

The swift ease with which he dismissed the kid's chances of survival made the skin of my scalp crawl. "You mean rats rats, or street gang rats?"

"What? You think we're not civilized? The vermin is manageable. It's the dregs of civilization I'm talkin'. The kind of filth that steals and kills and crushes hope. The kind who will cut your throat 'cause they want your blood to clean their dirty blade."

"She's Human. Maybe this tall." I gestured her approximate height with my hand. My original right hand. "In ninety days someone has to have seen her."

"Local 100866," the Frairy said in Basic. The Brkt with the visible winnings wobbled. "What is talk on streets?"

"No two-leg, Human-like." Local's voice was an amplified sound of bubbles breaking on the surface of water, but it ran through Basic.

The Frairy looked at me as if that settled the issue.

"Excuse, please," the other pink guy burbled timidly. "Cluster merchants, not ours, water market level report theft food recent past. Owner notes small loss but not incident. We thought internal incompetence, but many reports. Perhaps wrong?"

"Yes! No!" I was up with a rattle of chain, gripping the bars of the cell. "Is still happen?"

The one the Frairy had addressed as Local 100866 drew a card. "Possible. Curious. Think is youngling?"

"Yes! Where thefts? Can take me?"

The game at the table continued without a response.

Ninety days. Was I crazy? I was so swept up in my own problems I had never fully thought through the logistics of this situation. Could a Human child her age survive on an alien world, unnoticed, for three earth months?

Meeroush shifted position in the cell beside mine.

Getting out of here would sever my connection to the Tabisee—to their benefit as well as mine.

"Please let me out of here." Meeroush didn't intimidate me nearly as much as Shoff; I had the impression she would take my ass apart and enjoy every drop of blood she spilled, but the big male could put a severe hurt on me, too.

"You'll be okay. We won't let him kill you."

Very funny. I clung tighter to the bars, intent on making Meeroush pry me off if he came after me.

The mixed lot of beings at the table played several hands in silence.

There was something I had to ask. "Excuse me. Are you guys... Frairies...uh, telepathic?"

The card game stopped. Four sets of eyes locked on me again.

"Can't people play a game of cards around here?" The Frairy laid his cards face down on the table and glared at me.

"I'm not trying to offend anyone. It's just...I'm pretty sure the other Frairy I met was telepathic."

He relaxed into wariness. "Who did you meet and where?"

"He called himself Thok. He..."

"Where?" he barked.

"Not here. Inside the EA. He was traveling with a MoMo."

"Then he's a traitor to his people and the lowest form of filth." He turned his attention back to their game.

Because he was a telepath, or because he traveled with a MoMo?

Maybe it was because of the way he dressed, I thought sarcastically, but the Frairy before me hardly qualified as stylish in his batik sarong and scuffed half-laced, untied work boots.

"Why is he a traitor?" Linking myself to Thok was not the most strategic move to make, but if I kept the conversation going, I might pull some useful information out of it. "He's the only other one of your people I've ever encountered."

He slapped cards on the table and one of the pink guys wailed again. "How did you come across that despicable piece of offal?"

"I had a brushing encounter with him on an EA station."

"What? Were you both in the same jail cell?" Snorts and ringing tinkles that I took as amusement rippled around the table.

"Something like that." I really didn't care what his problem with Thok was. He hadn't answered my question. "Are you telepathic?"

He kicked the chair back and walked over to stand in front of me. Despite the fact the top of his head met me at mid-chest, his movements emanated a dangerous level of bad attitude. A heavy-nailed forefinger poked me in the chest armor through the bars. "No one on this world is telepathic. Insinuating anyone on this world is telepathic is an accusation. An ugly accusation. It gets people killed. Got that, Flygirl?" He turned away.

Flygirl? The Frairy on Mandragala had called me that. "Hey! What's your name?" I demanded.

"Duff," he snapped as he settled back into his chair and resumed play without a backward glance at me. "Not that it will help you."

I looked over to find Meeroush sitting with his back propped against the far corner of the cell, watching me.

"What did you do to me?" I asked him.

His hand, casually resting on his thigh, rolled to reveal a silver rod about fifteen centimeters long. He flicked his thumb against it and a ripple of white energy crackled across one end.

Okay. I moved further down the front of the cell bars and turned eyes forward again.

The game continued across the room in a mix of Frairy curses and squeals while I internally squirmed under the burn of Tabisee eyes. I knew from experience with Saura, the only way to reduce the hostility level was to open a cautious discussion on the errors I had made and let the anger vent.

I looked back over at him. "You okay?"

The ears moved forward and down and his eyes smoldered golden fury.

A loud click-click sound cut through the noise of the card game.

Duff instantly sprang up and across the room. With a rattle of keys, he threw open my cell door and scurried in to unlock the shackle around my ankle. "We got trouble," he snapped in Meeroush's direction.

The security officer was out of his cell and into mine before Duff freed my ankle. "Who?" he shot at the Frairy.

"No idea," the Frairy replied. "We have a cheap-ass warning system with no video because our allies won't share their tech."

"It would expose our alliance," Meeroush said. "Is it the Sat Quar?"

"We know they are out on the street, headed this direction." He gestured impatiently with a hand. "There are only two exits out of this place. You can wiggle out of this by claiming we took you in during the riot, but Flygirl has to go into the drain."

"They would never believe a Tabi—"

"Fine. You tracked the saboteur here and caught me. Whatever. But you have to claim your right to take me in for questioning over the damage to your med-evac. You can't let them take me into custody. Your med-evac, your jurisdiction."

The Carquetchian was pulling the metal grate off a large, round floor drain with its little squiggly finger-roots. One of the Brkts slithered past him and down the opening.

Meeroush grasped me by the back of the suit and dragged me out of the cell and over to the edge of the hole.

I'd just seen what the pink guys at the card table could do. "No! Wait!"

"It's the only way out for you," the Frairy said. "The Brktar will mask your presence until we can get you back."

Get me back? "No—"

"Shut up, Zant." Meeroush slapped the helmet down over my head. The self-situational cams inside it flickered on to show thick green moss lining the gaping circle at my feet.

"How deep?" he asked Duff.

"Enough. They won't see she's down there. The moss will counter any heat signature."

Crap!

"Can we retrieve her without a problem?"

"Don't worry, our friend will stay with her. It's easier than getting her back from the Sat Quar."

"Keep your mouth shut, Zant," Meeroush hissed at me. He lifted me out over the floor drain with one arm.

"Wait!" Duff and I exclaimed simultaneously.

And I thought he didn't like me.

"Shut off her comm. Otherwise, you'll have to listen to her squeal the whole way down."

Meeroush gave me a broad grin. Then he dropped me.

CHAPTER 24

Alternate Route

I fell straight down three meters and stuck in soft green.

A moment later the light dimmed and I thought I saw the shadowy outline of coins through a tint of pink as something settled on the top of my helmet and shoulders, jamming me deeper. The confines of the pipe became fixed as pink ooze filled the spaces around my upper body.

Things got even darker when someone replaced the drain cover.

I didn't know if Meeroush had turned off my comm, but I was receiving enough audio to hear the rattle of something opening and the Frairy protest.

"Damn it! We had a code worked out! Can't you people—"

"Where is Vivi?"

Saura?

"Slow down, short stuff," Duff snapped. "Jeez, you two look like crap. What the hell happ—"

The comm picked up a choking sound.

"Tell us where she is." It was Shoff's dulcet growl.

"Gaugh!" the Frairy gasped. "You don't have to be so violent. We didn't know who tripped the prox sensors, so we dropped her down the drain."

Again Saura sounded in my audio. "Where is?"

"She's fine. The Tabi want her kept out of Endar claws, I do what I have to do."

Really?

"Tell where—"

"Hey," I called from inside the pipe.

Something nudged the bottom of my boot and cold panic rolled through me. My arms, extended above my head, were gripped by pink Brktar ectoplasm. I tried to plant my elbows into the sides of the pipe and worm my body upward.

I was pinned tight.

Duff, Meeroush, and I were going to have a long talk when Saura pulled me out of here...

I felt my body rotate a fraction to the right.

Holy Mother Universe! The exclamation froze in my throat as my body moved back to the left a few millimeters past my original position—as if something was trying to break me loose from the lining of the pipe. For the first time, I noticed the pressure of the Tabisee armor was tighter than its normal, torturous clamp on my legs. I slipped downward a fraction.

"Hey," I shouted again.

There was a scrape of metal above me and the grate lifted away. The weight on my upper half disappeared as the Brkt on top lifted to glide back up into the room. I tilted my head back enough to see Saura's relieved expression.

"Vivi! Meeroush will pull out now." Did she sound slightly panicked?

I dropped a little lower in the pipe.

"Tell the Brkt to stop pulling me down!" I yelped.

Meeroush snarled a curse. The opening darkened as he leaned in, reaching down.

I dropped again.

Shoff growled something.

"What?" I heard Duff exclaim. "How should I know? If it wants her, you can't stop it."

I wondered if anyone else heard the click-click of the Frairy's warning system above the ruckus they were making.

"Damn it!" the Frairy exclaimed. "The Endar followed you in. Now we're schamoofed!"

I missed any responses as something tugged at my foot and images of ravenous pink ecto-blobs shot through my brain.

"...three of you? How am I supposed to explain it without ending up in a cell inside the Grip?"

The armor on my legs clamped tighter and I shot downward.

***

The thin light of the drain disappeared as I bumped around a ninety-degree curve in the pipe and clattered sideways. My brain quickly stopped its silent scream and shifted to swearing as my helmet banged along the curves. It was worse than my struggle in the Ritto warehouse with Shoff and seemed to go on forever. Then I had the sudden sensation of shooting out into the air. The pressure gripping my legs snapped me like the loose end of a cable and I sailed sideways, into another horizontal tube. I yelped in terror as my headgear slammed the edge of the opening and that was the last I remembered.

The sudden stop probably popped me back to conscious thought. I lay there, reality shifting between the cold, dim corridors of a slaver ship and the plascrete walls of a drainage tunnel.

Reality finally settled on a drainage tunnel.

Water and green stuff oozed from every joint in the Tabi armor when I rolled onto my side. My whole body throbbed in one big network of hurt.

I was lying at the bottom of a plascrete tunnel several meters in height and width, that stretched off into the shadowy distance in both directions. Scattered, shallow puddles of water dotted the floor, their smooth surfaces reflecting the dim light radiating from the walls. The Brkt sat at the base of one wall in a pool of liquid. It appeared smaller than I remembered.

Seeing the hole in the ceiling was well over three meters above me, I guessed it must have broken the shock of my fall. I wondered if it felt as bruised and ill-used as I did.

"Hey, you okay?" I asked as I climbed to my feet.

It sat in the puddle and did not move.

This place had to be a part of the city's drainage system. Not good. I had helped clean out some of the things that took up residence in the sewers on one Human station. It had involved a minor strategic battle and powerful, low energy weapons. The Brkt and I would not be the only things in this place.

The bigger concern was, did the Endar monitor activity down here.

They were on alert for a skinny, awkward Tabisee security trooper inside the city, but I doubted they would search at street level in a city the size of the one above me. They would rely on informants.

I needed to lose the armor, but I had to find a place to hide it, then get a message back to its treacherous owners so they could retrieve it. Even if I did not count them as allies, I had a bigger diplomatic picture to consider.

First, I had to find a way out of this tunnel, figure out a new disguise, and start searching the streets.

I felt a sting of regret over the loss of my awaysuit—I could have used it right now—but I figured Mathet really had spun the best story possible to escape the Endar in the warehouse.

I looked at the Brkt. "Which way out?"

It sat still as stone. No light rippled in its depths.

Had I killed it when I landed on it? That made me feel bad. If it was injured I had no idea how to help it. My only recourse would be to carry it until I found some of its kind.

The tunnel sloped slightly downward on my left. In a place like this, down usually led to maintenance and mechanical levels while up led to... more physical effort.

Down it was.

I turned back to the Brkt.

Something dropped out of the pipe, hit me square in the back, and knocked me flat.

Reconnecting

A short, black-clad Tabisee was standing over me. "Vivi. We have problem."

"Saura?" I stared in dazed disbelief.

"You should get up."

Yeah, I should. "How did you get down here?"

"Followed you."

There was a second Brkt in the tunnel now. I could see the shadow of coin shapes in its depths. It was bigger than the first one and did not appear to be leaking. "You let that Brkt pull you down?"

"Gave no choice."

She'd probably threatened to punch it full of holes. "This is insane! Why are you here? The med-evac was taking you to the Tabi embassy. You were safe!"

"Vivi. Not safe. Med-evac crashed. Shoff pulled out before Endar Sat Quar arrive."

"Are you all right? If that Frairy caused the crash— He said he only damaged the comm equipment."

"Endar caused. Sure will claim others did. Pursued us from wreck," she continued. "Frairy had to balance retreat. Two into room, must be two out. Had to go down pipe."

Two in, two out. "You think the Endar will notice the difference in height between you and Meeroush?" It seemed impossible to miss.

"Difference between Meeroush and Shoff is comparable to difference between Shoff and me."

Not quite, but if Duff created enough distraction—which he seemed thoroughly capable of doing—he might slide the discrepancy past their attention. "What about the others?"

"Carquetchian is Tabisee prisoner. Frairy will claim city law applies."

I bet that would be a tough sell. Damn the MoMo and the Frairy on Mandragala for getting us into this. Damn them all.

I pulled a strand of green moss off my shoulder and tossed it aside. "Are you okay?"

"Effects of deep sleep have worn off."

"I'm sorry you woke to such disaster."

"Better than not waking. Feared you lost when felt vibration run through Idwal."

Idwal. "Yeah," I winced. "Things have really gone sideways, Saura."

She gave a sniff of dismissal. "Will manage. Are partners."

Yeah. Partners without a ship. "You may want to rethink that." I motioned her to step back while I climbed to my feet again.

She put out a hand to pull me up. "Explain."

She was my partner, and I owed her an explanation. But she was also Tabisee. How much should I involve her, especially with the economy of the Tabi Empire at risk?

It tore at my heart, knowing I shouldn't do it. But, as she said, we were partners. I just had to be careful what I got her involved in now.

I gave her a brief rundown on everything that had happened since our parting on the lower ring at Idwal: the destruction of the shuttle, the kid in the airlock, my injury, and the resulting destruction of Section Ten. The Ritto rescue, waking here on the Moneyworld in recovery, to the High Jerak's interrogation, my escape, and the Tabisee on this world—everything except how the Zeeks had not restored my wetware. I couldn't drop that on her now.

Then I stood there, plucking strands of green from the armor plates while she considered it all.

"Vivi, are Endar aware of child?" she asked.

"I think High Jerak Seok knows more about Idwal than he's admitting."

"Where is child now?"

"Somewhere here onworld."

Her ears went rigidly upright. "By Holy Plinth, Vivi, say not true!"

"Why?"

"Vivi, child is telepath! Powerful telepath. Heard cry for help when you injured."

A wave of shock ran through me. "No way! I didn't hear her."

"No surprise. You are thick in head." My partner thumped the side of my helmet with her palm. "Child call for help."

"But—I don't understand. Tabisee aren't telepaths."

"Are not. Came through anyway. Painful loud."

"Are you sure?"

"Very sure! You bring most forbidden thing to Moneyworld."

"I didn't do it intentionally!" Holy crap! The impact of this on the EA... I was on a path to single-handedly set Human commerce back to the Stone Age. "I only rescued her!"

"Not blame Ritto crew. Logic says came with you."

A Human telepath on the Moneyworld! The Endar would use that to destroy Earth Alliance's chances of ever gaining access to Whooex trade markets.

I wanted to sink to the floor in despair. The armor wouldn't bend.

"Sure is a child?" she asked.

"Not completely. But mostly. This is the first chance I've had to search for her."

"Say ninety days since Ritto bring here."

"Ninety-two now, I think," I said glumly.

"Many people on this world."

Many dangerous people. We'd be better off cutting our losses and running. She and I, heading for the spaceport and hustling a ride off this dirtball before things got worse for everyone.

No. "It doesn't matter, Saura. She's a kid. I can't walk away and leave her as prey for every lowlife here! I have to find her." A chain of young faces, long left behind, swam across my vision. They were victims I had not been able to save. I was responsible for this one being in this situation.

I had made so many bad decisions...

"We will find child, Vivi." Saura's statement was firm and absolute, the way it should not be.

"No, not we." Two days ago I'd cried inside for her help. Things had changed. "The High Jerak was too intrigued with you back in the Ritto warehouse. He'll check Mathet's story out. If they can't make things match up, he'll come after you. Hell, he's already given orders to shoot you out of the sky! You have to go back to the embassy, where he can't get to you." I had always feared her people would take her away from me. Now I was urging her to go to them.

"Pftt," she made a dismissive sound. "Vivi Zant thinks can stop me helping?"

No way was I taking that wrath on, especially when I couldn't bend at the knees. Dammit!

Whatever the future brought, now was the time for us to act.

Then I remembered the Brktar. Damn. Double damn. I'd forgotten they were down here with us. That showed how off-keel I was. They'd overheard everything Saurubi and I had discussed.

The one who had pulled me down the tube looked even smaller now. "Is he okay?" I asked Local 100866.

I thought he wobbled, but the dim light emanating from the walls made it difficult to tell for sure. Considering what I had seen of their reactions thus far, it could mean anything up to and including a death threat. I looked at Saura. "We have to move, but first, can you shut down the tracker tags in these suits?"

"Know little about clunky planetforce suit Officer Shoff demanded put on before crash," she sniffed in irritation. "But will try."

Shoff had probably saved her life.

"If you can close down the commlink in the helmets that would be good." At least we could eliminate that bit of spying.

"Vivi, understand cannot move freely on world without suit?" she asked.

"Yes. I also understand my presence here puts your people at risk of huge repercussions. But I won't let them put me back in a stone cell beneath the Tabi compound. As soon as I find a place to safely stash this suit I plan to sever all ties with your people."

One of the Brktar emitted a loud hum and I looked over at them, relieved to change the topic of discussion before it expanded into an argument. The puddle the two sat in was spreading and they both appeared considerably smaller in size.

Maybe we could reduce the damage by taking them with us. Besides, if they were injured, it was bad form to leave them behind.

"What about the two of you?" I asked. Carrying sacks of fluid in this gravity was a logistics problem. "Can we—"

"No, Vivi," Saura said firmly, anticipating my thought.

I heard a scuffing sound behind me. This time I did see Local 100866 quiver.

"Lift hands and turn. Slow," a voice said.

I didn't need to see a language tag in the corner of my eye to recognize Frairen now. Maybe Duff was telling the truth and we really were in Frairyland.

Saura and I turned to face six white, rag-covered mounds of varying heights. Dirty squares of cloth with holes cut for their eyes draped their heads.

The image was not particularly intimidating. The long black sticks with shimmering purple tips they held, however, were.

"Vivi, careful," Saura's tone said the suits wouldn't protect us from a nasty zap.

Yeah, mine hadn't protected me from whatever Meeroush had used on me.

"Shift speak this ball, Shorty, and take off lids. Now!" The speaker and leader of this motley bunch of rags was also the shortest. It had to be a Frairy, of course.

I suspected he was not on the Tabi payroll.

"Slow," Saura told me as she undid the seals on her headgear and lifted it off.

There were a few jerks, twitches, and mutters when I removed mine.

"What hell it be from?" the biggest ragpile grunted.

"Proambu," Saura answered. "Separated from diplomatic envoy—"

"You liar, bitch." The leader cut her off. "Ain't no Proambu comin' low on this ball. Try twistin' words again and you feel heat." A tangler swung precariously close to her shoulder.

Saura's ears flicked outward and dipped, but she didn't flinch.

"Turn off track tech and power down."

"She can't," Saura said.

"Do for. Then hold them lids pressed to front with arms wrapped around, fingers laced."

I turned my helmet up and watched the places her fingers touched. Her finger slid back to one and she touched it again.

Was she taking a risk these ragpiles didn't have the means to detect some tracking signals?

"Suits, too," the leader said.

She pressed two places on my collar. The suit relaxed its clamp on my legs.

She gave me a sidelong glance.

"Scan 'em," he ordered.

One of his men swept a handheld device over our bodies. I held my breath, but no shriek of betrayal warned of something she had neglected to deactivate.

I wondered if this ragged leader had any idea of the numerous tracking and security devices spacers had implanted in their bodies. Even I had no idea what a precious Tabisee astrogator had hidden inside her.

Oh, wait, Vivi. Saura deactivated her stuff years ago to stay off EA security scans, and mine didn't work because the Zeeks had failed to put critical parts back into my forearm.

We were on our own here.

"We aren't here to invade anyone's turf or to interfere with anything." I said as I positioned my helmet against my chest. Of the five hostiles I could see, two were taller than me, but not particularly heavy. The third was a hulk. Those white rags covered a lot of flesh. I doubted any of those three were Frairy. But the speaker and the one beside him were. My impression of the last one, standing behind us, was somewhere between the tall and short. It could be anything on this world, even a stunted Endar—if the Endar ever took off their black leather and slipped into casual rags. Cruising drainage tunnels probably didn't fit their style of undercover work, though.

Regardless, I did not want to take on any of these dirt-bounds while wearing Tabi armor, loosened or not. Saura, on the other hand, would enjoy going a round or two with them.

The ragpile behind us made a hooting sound of triumph from the area where the Brktar huddled.

"Don't—" I started to protest.

A tangler swung dangerously close to my face.

"What find?" The leader asked his compadre.

As the ragpile came into view, my heart sank. It carried the soggy winnings from Duff's card game.

"Thought to hide under trash," it crowed, waving a thin, dripping, transparent membrane at me.

"I..." I managed to steal a glance over to the spot where the Brktar had sat. There was nothing there except wet surface and another bit of membrane. "You didn't have to kill them!"

The ragpile stopped waving the skin. Its eyeholes peered at me. "What, what, kill?" It looked at the wet concrete and back at me.

"Nothing," I muttered. "Just let us go about our business."

The leader confiscated the bounty and shoved it into his robes. "Why?" He asked, focusing his eyeholes on me as the last coin disappeared into his filthy rags. "It your birthday or somethin'?" Chuckles sounded around me.

I was beginning to understand why Frairies were not welcome inside the EA. They would need too many ass-whippins.

"Move out." He gestured. "Step fast."

Great. We were headed the upward-slanted direction.

One of the taller guys jogged on ahead while the rest of us fell into a brisk walk. The other tall one and the spare Frairy took the lead; the leader, the tank, and the Brktar-killer brought up the rear. The formation told me we were not in friendly territory.

I glanced over my shoulder at where the Brktar had been. The puddle had nearly disappeared.

"Move." A tangler swung close to my cheek, giving me a close look at the layers of grunge built up along its end bracket and the tatters of old rags wrapping the shaft.

Saura's ears turned down and back. Our captors, however, did not seem overly concerned with the sight of a clearly irritated Tabisee.

"What we do with?" the tank asked his leader.

"Check, see. Get jing for them sure," came the reply.

"That one look 'spensive happy-time girl. All shiny."

He thought Saurubi was a prostitute because of the starmap tattoos on her face? I choked back a laugh and waited for the goddess of fury to rain hellfire upon them.

The goddess did not erupt.

It couldn't be because she failed to understand what he'd said; if I did, she did. So, she either judged it was not the right time for a lesson in respect, or she actually thought the numbers were against us. I doubted that last one. I kept my eyes forward and off my partner lest she take out her displeasure on me later for witnessing the comment.

The leader continued, "There be someone wants 'em. If not, we eats 'em."

The tank gave a low, hollow laugh. "No much meat." Something prodded the armor plates on my buttocks.

"We get somethin'. Ugly one has somethin' can sell, sure."

The joke was on him. Thanks to the Zeeks, the ugly one didn't have anything to sell, sure.

For a while, the area of drain we walked had smooth, unbroken walls. Then heavy, solid doors began to show up with increasing regularity. Their chipped and patched edges bulged with sealing material around openings cut into the plascrete. They looked grungy, with scrapes and scars on the surfaces as if they had been in place for years. Many had faded symbols painted on them. There was no visible method to open them on the outside.

I had a bad feeling our destination lay behind one of them, probably in an even worse neighborhood.

Garbage clustered in mounds beside the doors, most stuffed into dark, opaque bags, but the larger debris varied from scrap metal to old shelving and broken furniture. It all looked recently discarded, though we occasionally passed a soggy item lodged against the base of the wall. It took a moment for me to figure out what I was seeing: the residents of this area used the drain tunnel for an alley.

I hated alleys. They were dangerous places, anywhere in the universe.

The painted symbols on the walls were similar to those in Spacertown, identifying the back exits of shops for deliveries—and other shady business. It appeared the businesses here simply dumped their garbage out the backdoor and let a gush of water carry it away. Considering the size of the trash, the force required to sweep the tunnel clear must be immense. I wondered if the flood came through at a set time and if a warning sounded. Our captors didn't act as if they felt a need to rush, so there must not have been an imminent threat.

Or they were too stupid to recognize it.

After a while, I unlaced the fingers of my left hand and signed Saura: 'make a break'.

She swiftly responded 'no'.

That was okay for now. We only had two directions to run. We sure weren't getting inside the doors we passed.

I suddenly realized I'd lost the hydra-filtration system in my away-suit to the Endar thanks to Mathet's inventiveness. Now I had no way to filter the water on this world to ensure it was safe for me to drink. I hadn't considered that when I drank from the water bottles in the Tabisee compound, but those were from a civilization I semi-trusted. I had no idea where tangler-toting, scavenger Frairies who patrolled sewer tunnels got their water. The thought dulled my thirst.

At least Saura had done something to relax the armor. I plodded along, trying to conserve energy while watching for an opportunity to slip our captors.

Eventually, we moved out of the alley area into another stretch of solid walls. The air slowly grew colder. We came to an intersection where our tunnel, along with five more, opened onto a domed chamber. There was a huge hole with finished edges in the floor at the center and a matching one where the ceiling arched overhead. We'd found the source of the temperature drop; our breath steamed from the cold air rising out of the pit. A steady moan from its chilled depths filled the chamber.

Saura shot me an uneasy glance. Her ears perched upright now, the tips turned inward in silent signal: prepare. If our escort thought they could dump us down this hole they were in for a fight. The two lead guys continued around the hole, taking up positions on the far wall next to the second tunnel on our left.

A sudden movement in the mouth of the tunnel caught my attention. Their scout reappeared, moving fast enough to label a full-on retreat. He stopped when he saw us, gestured toward the first opening to our left and dived inside. The guards followed him.

"Move," the Frairy behind us grunted.

Seeing as being eaten, skinned, or sold into whatever did not advance my search for the kid, this seemed like the perfect time for us to part ways with our escort. Someone else, however, had a vote in this. I flashed Saura a questioning look: our current companions or the unknown? The tunnel the scout had exited definitely was not an option, but we had three more perfectly good openings to our right, and I didn't think the ragpiles would risk firing a blast across the mouth of the tunnel their scout had fled.

Fingers flashed caution.

I dived between the tank, who had moved up to flank us, and the edge of the pit, heading toward the tunnels to the right.

The shaft of a tangler struck me across the shoulder. It was not the business end, but the impact was hard enough to knock me off balance.

I felt cold air graze the side of my face.

Shit! I twisted, trying to throw my body back toward the chamber wall as the pit loomed, but the darkness beaconed like a magnetic attraction; I kept falling toward it. My brain shrieked terror and my muscles strained against weariness and gravity.

An armored hand clamped my right wrist and snapped me forward. I half-flew, half-stumbled a few steps and slammed against the chamber wall.

"Idiot," Saura snarled. She shifted her grip to my shoulder and pulled me scrambling and limping toward the mouth of the new tunnel. After a few steps, I got my feet back under me and we ran.

Purple light bloomed across the walls, and a hand of air struck our backs, throwing us to the floor.

"Sorry folks, change of plans," a familiar voice boomed cheerfully. A flurry of sound filled the space as a new group of figures streamed in from the mouths of all the tunnels.

Duff.

"Great," I muttered.

The tunnel was so close...

"Get up."

I got to my feet and turned to face a Frairy with a hand-weapon leveled at me. Duff sauntered over and cocked a wrinkle of skin above his left eye. All his elaborate clothing was gone, exchanged for a plain, olive one-piece jumpsuit. It actually gave him an official look.

"You don't mind changing dates to the dance, do you?" he asked.

"I thought you and the Tabisee were allies." I gestured at the gun trained on Saurubi.

"Unofficially." He didn't wave the weapon away. "Meanwhile, day-to-day business goes on."

"What is day-to-day business?"

"The official business of a Frairy world."

"Oh. Is that what the—" I made a gesture at the plain jumpsuit.

"Smart Human. Now, hands up."

I sighed and raised my hands. Saura did the same. "You a cop?"

"A neighborhood enforcer of sorts." He twisted to watch his men at work behind him.

That explanation could mean anything. "We're not looking for trouble. I already told you—"

"I know, illegal Human lookin' for illegal Human kid. Super violation of this world's laws." He twitched a finger and another Frairy came over to pull our hands down and secure them behind our backs.

At least a dozen green-clad, armed Frairies swarmed about the chamber. Our recent captors lay in unmoving white mounds scattered across the floor.

"Who are they?" I asked Duff.

"The ragpiles? Bunch of skinners. Won't be happy bout this change in their plans." His eyes flicked over me critically. "Don't think they could do much with you. But that," he gave Saura's blue fur an admiring look, "that would sell for some good money."

Frairy guts spilled all over the floor was the last thing we needed right now. "They wanted to eat us," I said before Saura could react.

"Guess times are harder than I thought."

"You think this is a joke?"

"Am I laughing, Flygirl? Besides, I didn't create this situation. You did."

Thanks to one of his people.

"Their leader has the winnings from your poker game on him," I said.

"Is that so?" Duff called out something to one of his men. The other walked over and rummaged through filthy robes. He brought Duff a handful of damp coins and chips.

The Frairy leader shoved the mass into his pocket. "I suppose the bastard will want this back."

"Local 100866? He's dead," I said angrily. "Him and the other one."

"Did you see him die?" The Frairy's expression was entirely unsympathetic.

"No. One of those bigger guys brought his money and a—" What? A skin? "A transparent membrane. There was a lot of water and another, smaller membrane along the wall..."

Duff chuckled. "I'll have this spent before he comes looking for it." He took in my appalled expression. "They ain't dead. That's their defense mechanism. It will take him time to pull his stuff back together and grow a new containment skin, but he'll be back squeaking for his stuff. At least he and Dart 770 had the sense to escape. Better than I can say for you two."

Well...shit. I watched his men drag the limp ragpiles to one spot. "What did you do to them?"

"Percussion grenade. Had to cut them out of the picture. Skinners are hard-takers. They don't ransom back their finds."

"Someone needs to teach them economics," I muttered.

"What? The economics of being flayed alive if they're caught? Kidnapping is not tolerated here."

"But murder is?"

"What's one less air-breather? Not near as much loss as a pile of coins." He turned to the Frairies working in the chamber. "Wrap things up, folks. No traces."

Several were running horizontal light bars mounted on long poles over the surface of the walls.

"What are they doing?" I asked.

"Drawing away energy left from the grenade. It reduces the blast residue so scans will miss or mistake it for an old hit."

A chill ran over me. Could someone apply tech like that on a scale like, say, a settlement, to destroy evidence of a recent attack? Did the EA know of its existence? "Whose tech?" I asked.

Duff's small teeth flashed with humor. "Not yours, Flygirl."

Several other members of his crew were unfolding a two-meter metal disk on the floor.

Saura's ears perked in alarm. "Not take Human through transport ring," she snapped. "Endar will pick up DNA signature."

"Not off this one, they won't. The Whooex Union doesn't have this tech."

Her ears twisted warily. "Whose tech?"

"Proambu."

"How does Frairy have?"

"We have well-placed friends."

Well-placed friends, like, perhaps the MoMo? Much as I wanted to ask, I kept silent.

"How know Endar not monitor?" Saura persisted.

"Because it was designed to protect Proambu worlds from Endar incursion."

"Are sure will take Tabisee or Human?" She voiced my question.

"You're not at war with the Proambu, are you?"

"No."

"Well then." Duff shrugged.

As soon as the Frairies stepped away from the transporter, Duff grasped my arm and hauled me forward onto the thin plates.

"You're sure this is safe?" I asked.

"No," he answered cheerily. "But anyone who can master the tech required to build a ringworld can handle a simple differentiation of chromosomal materials in a matter shift."

Simple? "That is—" abruptly I found myself standing in a dim stone niche. "—not simple."

CHAPTER 26

The Bad News

Across from us stood a row of cells.

"Aw, come on," I protested as Duff's people freed my hands and shoved me into one.

Saura made a similar sound of displeasure as they pushed her into the one next to me.

"This is a freakin' dungeon!" I exclaimed.

"You're prisoners," Duff replied.

They all returned to the niche and disappeared.

"Dammit!" I slammed my palm against a bar.

Saura stood in silence while I walked off the pain.

In the middle of that, a Frairy appeared bearing water bottles and sandwiches. He shoved the containers through the bars and left without a word.

Which led to more silence as the food and water was gratefully consumed.

"Okay," I said at last. I walked over to the shared wall of bars between our cells to face Saura, who was now sitting stiffly against the far wall. "We're not in a good situation." Understatement. "And I'm sorry for all this. I know how it affects you. It wrecks our partnership. But I'm glad you're here. When I first woke up, I didn't know what happened to you. I was afraid you were at Idwal, and I had no idea how to get back out there to rescue you. Finding the kid and discovering what she knew about what went down out there, then getting someone's official attention was my only hope. And, yeah, I know how bad my presence on this world is for the EA and for the Tabi Empire. I sure as hell don't expect your people to put themselves at risk for me."

Ears snapped out and forward. Amber eyes regarded me even harder than before. She was listening.

"I swear I did not know she was anything special." Someone had to be monitoring our exchange, and I didn't want to pile fuel on the fire by saying the t-word. The Brktar might still be a threat but, apparently, they would have to recover their forms enough to tell someone what they overheard—if they'd understood us. "She's little," I gestured her height, "and white-haired." Like an angel? No. I would end up having to explain the concept to her, and I didn't know how much time we had. "I lost my left arm and my wetware getting her out of the airlock. I tried to get through to you, but the *Hand* signaled it was shutting down. All I know is whoever destroyed the shuttle wanted the kid dead badly enough to blow Section Ten wide open. They spaced us, Saura!" It was the first time I actually allowed myself to confront the incident since it happened. Outrage and shock choked me into silence.

I forced myself to move on, explaining how I woke up in an autodoc on a Ritto-ssa ship with the kid hovering over me. How they brought me to the Xix and the kid left the ship while they carried me off. "The Zeeks rejuved my arm. But no wetware." I ruefully lifted my left arm, as if she could see the flesh beneath the layers of armor and shipskins.

She considered me for a long moment. "Is problem," she agreed quietly.

I could not speak.

"But do not have ship, either. So must focus on current problems."

She was right: the loss did not effect the current situation. My heart ached: I would be so much less without her.

"Idwal sent out distress signal when ghost jumped into gravity well." Saura got up and came over to lean into the bars next to me. We stood side-by-side facing each other. It allowed us to talk in lowered voices. "Twisted station face. Dock bumpers stored above *Hand* came loose and drifted down to block ship."

Drifted. A welcome word for our ship. I remembered those massive cylinders, bigger than the *Thief's Hand*, that hung above the dock where we put in. One of them, with any gravity, could have shorn our ship right off the station port.

"Bumpers masked *Hand*, but ghost must have seen put into station. Fired into area and clipped lower hull. Damaged life support. Watched ghost on station sensors leave and return. Saw shuttle drop. Then more alarms. Station cut contact and reactivated defenses. Could not detach from Idwal. Air was going. Had to shut down, seal *Hand*. Set timer and went into SAC with plan to wake when clear and Idwal would accept codes again. Next thing, wake here."

Things had been as harrowing for her as it had been for me. "Mathet didn't tell me if the Ritto-ssa pulled your SAC from the Vasty or the *Hand*." I hadn't inspected the unit that closely. I was too elated with the discovery it was here on this world, with her safe inside it.

As for the *Thief's Hand*, we might never know its fate.

All because of a deal I struck with a Frairy and MoMo while trying to keep our ship. Bitterness rose inside me.

"Maybe Ritto made attack," Saura suggested.

"Ritto ships are big-bellied and round. The ghost and the shuttle that attacked Section Ten were sleek, black, and had spiny profiles." An image of stars rippling out of sight as the ship cruised over them made me shudder. "And the crew was slim, bipedal, and wore black suits." Rittos were big and bulky.

"As soon as I woke in the hospital an Endar calling himself High Jerak Seok came busting in. He wanted to know what I had seen out at Idwal, but he never asked me anything directly. I think he knew more than he let on. Saura, someone destroyed a shuttle full of Humans and massively damaged a Proambu facility to finish the job. There could be a record somewhere that puts us at the scene as witnesses. Someone might still want us dead."

Her ears drifted forward and inclined in what I recognized as intense thought. "Why High Jerak put on ship off the world? Would work best have live Human here. Say you spy, yes?"

Her reasoning made bone-chilling sense. "I thought he was just doing his job, asking questions and getting me off a world where Humans are banned. But now my gut says no. He wanted to know what I saw." The blacksuits at Idwal could have been Endar—among a number of other beings, known or unknown to the Union. We—I—really need to find the kid.

"Could destroyed shuttle come from ghost?" Saura asked. "Maybe defectors?"

"No. That pudgy, soft-curved thing could not come from those jagged, light-sucking black hulls."

"Come from Ritto-ssa ship?" Her ears gave an annoyed flick, "Tabi security thinks you pulled out of Vasty incredibly fast."

Shoff must have grabbed some time to question her while they were running from Endar pursuit after the crash.

"If Idwal sent a distress call when the ghost first jumped and damaged it, it's not unreasonable the Ritto got there quickly. With the fuel platform, the area is not completely isolated." I shook my head. "Here's the thing: a shuttle like that could not get out to a remote area of space on its own. Its systems couldn't sustain life for more than a few days. It came from the direction of the gas giant. I think a parent ship was hidden out there and we missed it."

"Maybe ghost stalking parent ship from edge of system when we drop in." Saura looked thoughtful. "Possibly fired at it."

A ship, hiding from the ghost, its tiny shuttle making a mad dash for the station and the *Hand*. "You think our cargo was on that shuttle, and the ghost destroyed it."

"Three living beings. Received information while going up fall."

"Why in the hell would they set up a rendezvous in that area of space?"

"Convenience, or hiding activity," Saura said.

"Gods, Saura. We've been seriously played."

"MoMo do not play, Vivi." Her amber eyes narrowed with annoyance. Tabisee were straightforward and humorless in their business dealings with other species. Being the targets of manipulation did not sit well with them.

"The quarantine was a setup," I said bitterly. "Those two clowns wanted us desperate enough to take the job. I walked right into it."

"MoMo did not intend ghost to kill cargo," Saura pointed out.

True. I sighed. "I wonder where the people on the shuttle came from."

She looked at me.

I had seen them. She hadn't. "It can't be a lost Human colony, Saura. Our old subspace tech could never get us that far out, and under Whooex Charter Law, we can't establish a settlement anywhere near Scylla Quadrant. Besides, no one would kill over that. They'd take it to the Union Council and force our colonist out of the area. Then there's our destination after Idwal. I guess we'll never know—"

"Was Jian Jian," she said.

"That's an EA military research base! Why in the hell would we take Humans there?"

"Child is special," Saura reminded me softly.

"I swear I never sensed anything." I hastily took a step sideways, in case she tried to give me a slap to the head.

"And now is on Moneyworld," Saura said. "Endar have used argument of telepathy in Humans against membership since EA first joined Whooex Union."

"And this happens right when the EA is up for consideration for admission. Saura, my planet feeds are dead. I have no idea how much real time has passed since we left Mandragala, but in the warehouse the Endar said a Human delegation is coming. I have to find the kid and get her off this world."

"Is good plan." Her ear position said sarcasm. "How we do?"

"We don't," I said. "I do."

Dusky blue fur started to puff up around her neck and jawline.

"Saura," I hastened to explain, "you are in more danger than the kid and me right now. The High Jerak thinks I'm gone and he doesn't know the kid is here, but he expressed a strong fascination with you in the Ritto warehouse." It had made me uneasy then. Now it sent a flutter of panic through me. "Mathet was fast on his feet with his explanation, but the High Jerak will investigate deeper with Tabi Space Fleet." I didn't even want to consider what would happen if the Endar found the SAC she'd arrived in. "You have to get off this world before the High Jerak comes looking for you."

"I. Help. Find." She clicked the tips of her claws on the bars with each word.

"Okay." Obviously, I wasn't going to be the one to dissuade her. "But we rest first."

She was fresh out of stasis, and I wasn't in much better condition. By silent agreement, we retreated to our bunks and fell asleep.

Two trays of food and several bottles of water sat inside my cell when I next awoke. Saura was working on her second tray when I looked over at her.

"Eat all," she said. "Put extra water here." She showed me the loops on the armor to attach any bottles I didn't drink. It was the old spacer maxim: Take in all the food and water you can, when you can. You never knew when you might get more.

"Yes, ser."

Shortly after we demolished the food, Duff and his crew re-appeared.

CHAPTER 27

Many Eyes on the Prize

Returning our headgear, Duff ordered us to "cover our ugly-ass faces", then the Frairies marched us out of the cellblock and through an arch to the top of a broad stone stairway. The air flowing up past us so cold I could see my breath in puffs of vapor.

We descended maybe forty steps before my spacer muscles rebelled against gravity and the repetitious movement. After the third stumble, the Frairy on my left, who kept catching me, gave me his shoulder for support. Saura didn't seem any better off, though she continued under her own power. Her ears were turned down and out in a nearly horizontal line, letting me know my display of weakness did not please her. I didn't care as long as someone got me off those freaking, seemingly endless stairs.

When we finally reached a broad, flat area with multiple passages branching off, my aide unceremoniously abandoned me to cope with gravity on my own. After a short rest and water break, we continued through a large stone archway into a vast chamber buzzing with the activity. My Human height gave me the advantage of seeing over most of the heads around me. Frairies, Carquetchians, Brktar, and even the hulking profiles of a few Xix moved through the mix of people pushing carts, carrying sacks of food, talking, strolling, or walking with purposeful intention. Children ran, laughing, shrieking, and dodging through the organized jumble of what I imagined was pleasantly typical of daily downsider life here.

Bright, consistent light emanated from somewhere above, and the air was pleasantly cool. Far across the chamber, in narrow gashes of brightness, I saw faint movement, as if a street or walkway lay beyond the arched wall of the place. The space was vast.

"What is this?" I asked Duff.

"A market. A community center. Whatever is taking place at the moment."

I glanced up at the massive pipes channeling through the heights above us. A familiar-looking shaggy, dense green moss swathed them, only now reversed to the outside surface of the pipes. In fact, the moss grew on a lot of the surfaces around us—almost everything above three meters from the floor, and right down to the floor in some obscure areas.

"What's the green stuff?"

"The green stuff," he said, "is one of the inhabitants of this world, Human." He sounded as if I should know something I clearly did not.

"A plant—"

"A being," he corrected sharply. "It is the Cheel."

I exchanged a look with Saura. She shrugged.

As we walked deeper into the space, Duff's men on our left pressed closer. We moved over a few steps to go around a large block jutting up out of the floor. Rows of uniform holes perforated its sides.

Holy crap! I recognize that setup! There must be more of them out there, hidden by the flow of bodies. Someone had isolated and cut a massive water storage cistern out of the city's system. We should have been swimming right now and the pipes gushing outward with liquid.

"How did you bypass a pump station this huge?" I asked Duff.

He shrugged. "It is not cut out. It is contained, sort of like a false bottom. Happened when the Endar first began working their way into the role of security over the Trade Consortium. While they were too busy to notice, the residents of Rhom rearranged a few pieces of infrastructure..."

"Whoa," I said. "Whoa, stop!"

Our whole group stopped. Duff stared up at me.

"You said Rhom. The real Rhom?" The MoMo were rumored to be from Rhom. If this was their original homeworld, someone could tell me where they had gone after leaving here.

"Keep your freaking voice down!" he ordered.

His men closed in tighter as we began to walk again.

"Yeah, but, I mean, the original Rhom?" I dropped my voice to a whisper.

"What do you know about Rhom?" he demanded.

"It is the original homeworld of the Oulunsk, or MoMo. It is not on any star map the EA has, and the MoMo abandoned it for another world."

"Well, they aren't the only original residents." He poked me in the armor covering my solar plexus with his finger. "The rest of us are still here!" He sighed. "And the MoMo didn't abandon this world. They were forced out. They were the ones who decided this world would be the perfect place to establish the Whooex Trade Consortium with the Endar Primacy and the Jhampoon Coalition, damn their stupid jelly asses! They didn't see what was coming until everything spiraled out of control and the Endar forced them out because they were telepathic, and then Rhom got devoured by their creation."

"But—"

"But what? Let me give you a little sitrep, Flygirl." That tag was beginning to wear on my nerves. "You Humans think this is a happy place where everyone shares in the bounty of Whooex Union Trade.

The Moneyworld! All razzle-dazzle! Fortunes to be made! Well, that may be true in the big chunk of real estate at the center of our city called the Trade Consortium, but not for the rest of our world. This is a city-world of losers. The non-native population outnumbers the natives two-to-one. Our resources are strained to breaking, and the Consortium members don't want to contribute any of their profits to help fix the problems—which is one of the main reasons they caved to Endar control of their security. Let the Sat Quar police their Zones and keep them safe. Let them ruthlessly enforce the law, allowing trade members to continue the business of making money. Unfortunately, not all the bright-eyed entrepreneurs flocking here end up inside the Zones. Who's in charge of the failed, destitute, get-rich-quick-schemers that end up in our city? They came here with a focus on making money. Do you think they give up that dream when their schemes fall through? Hell no! They spend all their time trying to make an easy buck. Crime is rampant, and we don't have the resources to fight it. Sometimes the Endar herd up the ones loitering around the Zone and send them off-world, to auction their services out. We don't like the solution, but they're not from our world, and our share of that money helps our strained resources. It also creates a huge problem with people hiding out in the city."

Yeah, without my wetware to ensure a useful position on a ship, I faced that same fate when I got back into EA space.

"We thought the MoMo wanted to keep the location of Rhom hidden," I said.

"The Whooex Union Trade Consortium keeps the location hidden from non-members. But they like the name Humans have given the place. It eclipses an ugly bit of history they want to forget," Duff said bitterly. "You'd be wise to forget, too. The MoMo have found their own way over the past two thousand years. They use Frairies and other members to represent their interests here, and, yeah, they keep the location of their new homeworld hidden from everyone, including us.

"Meanwhile, we cope with the fallout here. Especially after the Endar took over Whooex Trade Consortium security two hundred years ago. To us, it seems common sense that no one group should have that much control over a multispecies assemblage like the Whooex Union Trade Consortium. But," he shrugged, "we are only one member among many. This is, however, our world. We occasionally have to remind others of that. The Endar want to extend their authority beyond the Zones, out into the surrounding city, T'lek T'la. We are determined that will not happen."

I had already sensed that peeling back the clawed fingers of the Primacy, once they locked their grasping intent on something, would be nearly impossible. That's what scared me about Saura being here.

"It's an ongoing battle," Duff said. "The Endar hate to be thwarted or embarrassed. They aspire, always, to become more powerful."

"So, this thing with them not having jurisdiction outside the Trade Consortium, does that cover me?"

"No. Although we constantly have to remind them there are lines they can't cross, we cannot, in turn, give them a reason to think they should. Illegal is illegal."

We resumed walking in our loose formation, with Saura and me at the center.

"So, how did cutting this place out of the city's water supply change things?" I asked.

"It cut down on noise transmission," he said.

"Hunh?" This place was an echoing chamber of noise.

"You'll see." He nodded at a massive green column that dominated the center of the space.

We walked for several more minutes before we arrived at its base.

The lush green cylinder sat atop a circular, elevated platform of mottled, pale yellow stone. The growth stopped at the bulging base of the column, leaving the richly carved yellow platform clear. The floor beneath our feet was a finely finished mosaic pattern of gray and white stone. It was old, worn, and beautiful.

A cadre of spiny, blue, red-robed beings kneeling at the base of the platform discreetly moved away at our approach so we could take their place.

Saurubi's ears twisted with uncertainty as we exchanged looks.

Above the clamor of activity around us, I heard the sound of giggling children. It grew closer. Several young Frairies and Carquetchians ran past. One, a small Frairy dressed in what appeared to be children's play clothes, stopped. She turned, then wove between us to climb the steps. Her playmates paused for a second to watch, then ran on as if their friend's behavior was not unusual.

The child walked to the column and put her hand in the moss up to her shoulder. She stood there, her head tilted. After a long moment, she turned and came back to the edge of the platform in front of us.

Her eyes locked on me. "The Cheel asks why you are here," she said.

"Don't play, Piika," one of the nearby Frairy guards scolded.

The child drew herself up in tiny, indignant composure. "I do not play, Papa. This is my day to speak for the Cheel."

"Speaker," the Frairies around me said with uncharacteristic respect. They dipped their heads to her.

She nodded acknowledgment to them. Then she looked at me again. Did she have any idea what hid inside the Tabi armor and headgear? Did she sense a difference in me? "The Cheel asks why you are here."

I had expected the Frairies to drag me before their leader and throw me at his or her feet. Instead, I found myself speaking with a child.

I didn't want to complain when things were simple, but maybe this was a bit oversimplified. "I do not mean to disturb you," I started.

The child smiled widely. "I am not the Cheel."

"So, it's not speaking to me now?" The idea of a creature hijacking a child at play and channeling through them disturbed me. It felt wrong.

"It speaks to me. I speak to you. You speak to me and the Cheel hears what you say. It asks why you are here."

Okay... "There is a child on this world. She doesn't belong here. She's alone and in danger. I want to find her and take her to a safe place."

She tilted her head and considered me. I had a sense there was a far greater presence behind her action.

"Is she telepathic?' I asked Duff.

"Don't be an idiot!" he snapped. "There are no telepaths on this world. Young children simply happen to be able to speak with the Cheel."

"Sorry." What the heck was this Cheel, to put small children forward to communicate for it?

Piika studied me. "You fear for her safety. Why?"

"Because she is alone. I fear someone will harm her." Apprehension twisted hard inside me. I stopped talking.

"Why do you care?"

"I—" I turned to Duff. "This is wrong. I don't want to go into all this with another kid."

"Life is painful," the Frairy child declared solemnly from the platform.

Jeez! She was a little kid! "Yes, but—"

"People die," she continued.

Yeah. Sometimes horribly, like the people who had traveled with the kid. This little one didn't— I finally found my voice. "This child does not need to hear this."

The Frairy girl glanced at the column, then back at me. She shifted her attention to Duff. "The Cheel wishes to meet with her."

"Well, Flygirl, looks as if you've earned some sort of a dispensation." Duff grasped my arm and pulled me away from the platform, into the bustling crowd. "Don't get excited. It could just be a quick death," he added.

The child descended the three steps to follow us.

Duff looked down at her. "Now?"

"We will wait for the others," she answered. She did not elaborate.

Duff turned to his squad. "Form a loose perimeter. You," he growled at Saurubi, "stay with us."

The guards melted into the crowd.

The child, Piika, moved to stand silently beside me. She was a painful reminder of what I should be doing instead of idly standing around this place. At least she and the Cheel-thing had not denied the kid existed.

I tried to ignore the thorny little bit of reproof at my side by looking closer at our surroundings. High above us huge pipes divided off from the massive green column, similar to branches of a tree. They ran in every direction out into the shadows of an unseen ceiling. I had a sudden flash of insight: every one of those tubes had the same moss lining as the drainpipe that had dropped me into this underworld. There were probably pipes all over this city filled with the stuff. And, if this chamber was any indicator, it covered homes, alleys, and pavers, too.

I gave in and looked at Piika. "May I ask: what is the Cheel?"

"Life." A small hand gestured at the column, though she was too short to see it from her place in the crowd.

"I saw a similar plant growing somewhere else."

She nodded. "Cheel."

"In the pipes?"

She nodded. "Cheel."

"So it grows everywhere?"

"It is one. It is the Cheel."

One? I studied the moss, rising green, serene, and immense in this place. I remembered the plants growing in the darkness of the mechanical spaces we'd pass through to release Saura from the SAC. "One type. Grows everywhere?"

"One."

Oh, come on! Did they all have a twisted sense of humor that made the Human the butt of every joke? I took a deep breath and cautiously made a circular motion with my hand to encompass the area around us. "One?"

"One." It was in the way she said it. She wasn't joking.

An image of earth ants and certain fish schools flashed in my mind. One: as if the Cheel were a colony of individuals?

I pulled free another bit of the moss caught on the wrist of my armor and stood with it pinched between my fingers, not sure what to do with it.

"It grows everywhere, except," she frowned, "in the Consortium."

Did her expression indicate stress? I reminded myself not to equate Human emotions with alien ones. Most times, they did not correlate.

"Why not there?"

"The Endar destroy it."

Oh. Defoliation. "That upsets—angers—you?"

"It does not anger you?" Her little mouth tightened, thrusting her lower jaw forward and I was pretty sure I wasn't violating any protocols by interpreting that as anger.

"I'm trying to understand. Why do the Endar want to keep the Cheel out of the Trade and Diplomatic zones? Is there a—guest—who is allergic to it?" Sometimes the simplest explanation was the right one.

"No. They want to limit what it can see."

"The Cheel sees?" I said after a pause.

"The Cheel sees everything." The glare turned defensive. "It does not interfere."

Yeah. It sounded dangerously close to a word Humans had. Omniscience. We had fought wars over that kind of thing. "You worship it?" I hoped with my whole being the word translated correctly. If this was some type of religion, I should shut up and sit down before I started a holy war.

"No." The forward thrust of the jaw came back, along with a crease between the little brows. "Cheel is Cheel. Frairy is Frairy. Frairy is many. Cheel is one."

"It—" I stopped. Closed my eyes. What I thought she was saying...

After a long moment, I opened my eyes. "Cheel is one? Many parts? Parts all see as one?" That was—

"You got it all figured out now, Flygirl?" Duff asked.

"She says the Cheel is one being—"

"All the parts are linked into a shared intelligence. It sees what they all see. Yep."

A being who saw nearly an entire world? It made my knees feel a little weak.

Duff glanced down at my gloves. "Every strand is a part of the whole," he said.

I looked at the moss gripped between my fingertips. "What about if it's not attached to anything?"

"If it establishes contact with a viable surface it will live and share its presence with the whole."

"Oh." Now what the heck was I supposed to do with it? I couldn't simply drop it.

I definitely had to go through full decontamination before I stepped back on a Human ship.

"Put in pocket," Saura hissed. "Fix later."

I stowed it in an empty pouch. "Sorry," I mumbled, half to it, half to Saura.

I leaned closer to her. "Are you hearing the same thing I'm hearing; that this Cheel thing is a hive organism? That it knows everything its parts see."

"Heard," she nodded. "But only sees; does not share thought."

"Does your embassy know about it?"

"Do not know what embassy knows. Host world not astrogator business. But would be very effective policing mechanism."

I felt pretty sure the Frairy had that one down.

"You could have told me all this and made it simple," I told Duff.

"And let you miss the chance to interact with the locals? Believe me, you Humans need to up your social experiences. If the Earth Alliance gets through their admission vote unscathed by your actions, your people will have opened the floodgate on complicated interactions with other species."

And if I blew it, the whole Human race would be left sitting in our little, isolated area of space all by ourselves for another hundred years or more.

That was too much to think about. "How much does this Cheel interact with the other peoples of this world?"

"You mean, is it a dominant force? No, it doesn't command Frairy armies. Is it influential? For us, very. Why shouldn't we use every resource we have? It watches, and it knows. The trick is to ask it the right question."

"It knows everything that is going on?"

"The Cheel sees everything within its range. Knowing is a different thing altogether. It sees you. It doesn't know why you are here. It wants to find out. I bring you in for it to ask. Simple, yes? Should be, but it's not. There's a big hole in the Cheel's overall vision. You see, the Endar know what the Cheel is, too. They have been here since the unfortunate day the newly formed Whooex Trade Consortium decided to make our world its cozy economic center. After they succeeded in pushing the MoMo out, they went after the Cheel. By that time, we were a bit smarter. They claimed it uses telepathy. It doesn't. It's indigenous to our world. It's a citizen. We gave them one concession for their crap argument: permission to defoliate the Zones. Now they keep the Diplomatic and Trade Zones swept clear of all plant life. No one can bring a plant into the area. The bastards would eliminate the Cheel altogether, but they can't." He gave me a slightly amused look. "You could say they've kept the Zones swept clean of Humans, too."

The kid and I were the means to continue that policy if the Endar found us here. Which led to the question. "What happens next?"

"The Cheel will decide." He turned attention to the Frairy girl. "Why are we still standing here, Speaker?"

His tone seemed a bit rough for addressing a child. "That's—"

"Shut it, Zant!" he snapped.

Piika smiled up at him despite his scowl. "They are here," she said serenely.

"Who?" Duff twisted to look out across the crowd toward the sunlit openings. He swore. "Are you kidding me? The assassins?"

"The who?" I strained to see where he was looking. Deep in the chamber, amid the mix of bright colors and bustling activity, I saw familiar black. My heart skipped a beat when I realized the garb was similar to what Saura and I wore.

Two Tabisee in full body armor plowed their way toward us.

"As-sas-sins. As in 'you're dead'," Duff growled. "This could get ugly."

"Tabisee assassins?" I looked over at Saura. "Is he right?"

"It is possible," she said.

"Who uses assassins on a diplomatic world?" I heard my voice raise a pitch in panic.

"Do not know." She watched the two weave through the crowd toward us. "But are definitely working."

To me, the words 'assassin' and 'working' did not safely belong together. "Saura, you are my dear friend and partner, but I can't go back inside a Tabisee cell." I took a step back, away from her.

"Am good friend," she agreed. "And you should not try to leave. Frairy escort has hard eyes and hands on weapons."

I saw two of Duff's green-overhauled crew regarding me from the crowd. They did not look friendly.

And now there was this being who could watch me wherever I went—except the Zones, where the Endar seemed to call all the shots.

"All right," I stepped back to her side. "Let's find out what the as-sassins want." From the variation in their height, I was willing to bet it was Shoff and Meeroush.

They didn't waste time on stealth; they sliced straight toward us, coming to a stop in front of Duff. The shorter one brushed at a patch of dust on its upper arm.

"Excellent timing," Duff greeted them affably.

"We will take them from here."

Yup. Meeroush.

"The game is bigger than that," Duff replied.

"This is Tabi business," Shoff hissed. She moved a hand toward her hip.

There was a subtle but distinct stir in the crowd around us. The press of everyday Frairy bodies oozed back a bit.

The green-clad Frairies appeared more numerous than I had first thought.

I could visualize Shoff's ears, rigid with irritation inside her head-gear.

"You should come with us," Duff told them.

"We do not—"

"Yeah, I kinda think you do. Take a breath and relax. You'll get her back. But the Cheel wants to speak with her first. Besides, it would be good for you to come along." He stared up at the two of them steadily. "We insist."

"It is time," the child, Piika, announced cheerily.

CHAPTER 28

The Cheel Plain

I managed to remain silent while we wove through a series of empty stone passages to another massive, moss-covered pipe. Piika located an opening in the green mat and we pushed inside, onto a metal platform. The rusty plate was the only thing between our feet and the cold vertical darkness of the open pipe. Beside the platform was a metal lift basket sided with waist-high woven panels to keep its contents from falling off. The set-up and the thought of what planetside gravity could do if it failed to work properly set my guts to churning.

I only made a small choking noise as everyone piled inside. When the basket gave a hard jerk and began to move down the dark opening beneath us, I definitely required information. "Where are we going?

"You," Duff said the word emphatically, "are going to talk to the Cheel."

"And the Tabisee?"

"You're their problem, so the Cheel is allowing them to sit in."

Shoff made a soft spitting sound behind me.

Yeah, me neither, lady. "But—" I started.

"Shut up, Zant," Duff ordered. "Someone with the means has to have the motivation to get you off-world and it sure as hell isn't the Frairy."

"A Frairy didn't have any trouble getting us into this situation!"

"Yeah, about that." He moved closer and lowered his voice. "You might want to keep it under wraps. We're not supposed to be helping you Humans."

"Helping us! Helping?" I had to remind myself there was a child present.

"Will you chill out?" he said.

I stared at him. "Where do you get these weird things you say? Do you even know?" I might have been a little hysterical at that point.

He gave me a toothy smirk.

"You're not funny!" I snarled.

"Just be glad you have friends here."

Friends? We had removed our headgear and Shoff and Meeroush were glaring at me balefully, not at all friends, and unlikely as potential allies. Maybe after getting involved in this side trip, they would reconsider following me the next time.

Speaking of allies, I glanced over at Saura.

Her head was lowered, her ears tilted forward. Like someone who had recently survived a med-evac crash.

"Are you okay?" I asked.

"Yes." She did not look at me, but her ears moved, the openings turning outward and the tips pointing forward in our signal, 'preparing for what comes next.'

I knew the other two Tabisee were watching us closely, no doubt trying to read us as we signaled each other a brilliant plan for escape. I looked away, expressionless. Saura was hurting, but not seriously. She would never gloss over her condition with me. We had to trust the other to make an accurate assessment of any situation, including our own physical state. I only hoped she did not deteriorate further. It looked as if we had a long way to go.

In any case, I had two strapping, downside Tabisee to help me get her out, not to mention Duff, five of his men, and little Piika.

The walls of the pipe ended and, except for the faint glow of the basket's walls, we moved into a vast darkness. Cold air flowed up past us as we made our steady, clicking way into the depths. Sometimes the basket changed the angle of descent and passed through a slanted channel in the rock. Those cuts pressed in around us and the clicking sound grew louder. Then the walls would open again, the descent would straighten to vertical, and the volume of the lift's sound would dropped to a steady tap-tap.

After one long, slanted ride a chamber opened up and we continued downward at an angle. The sound of our descent took on a soft echo. We were in a vast chamber kilometers beneath the surface. Recalling the Endar warehouse beneath the spaceport and the lined Tabi passages, I guessed Rhom—the Moneyworld—whatever—was perforated with tunnels and passages that kept the business of life moving inside its hard skin as well as on the surface.

We were descending toward a glow of green light.

Piika whimpered and I realized the child only wore a single layer of play clothes. "Does anyone have something we can wrap her in?" I asked.

The others twitched at the sound of my voice.

Shoff pulled a small pack from a pocket and unfolded it to reveal a thermal blanket. She handed it to the child.

"Thank you," Piika said in a small voice.

Meanwhile, the others went back to staring into the green light below as we clicked down the spiderweb line of black track toward it.

I bit my tongue, determined not to be the first one to ask how much longer our descent would take.

Something bumped my side and I realized Saura had sagged against me. Her shoulder-guard pressed the armor plates covering my ribs. I slipped a hand under her elbow, between us where no one else could see, and took some of her weight. She straightened her spine to stand more alert, but the weight in my hand deepened, along with my concern for her.

"How much longer?" I asked.

The others ignored me, but tiny Piika gave me a perky smile. "Soon."

I realized the light around us had increased and I could see the rest of our jolly company more clearly now. Within seconds, the basket began to brake. I had not realized how fast our descent had become until we were all grasping the metal sides to stay balanced. Gradually the speed slowed and our transport came to a stop with an echoing boom that whispered back at us from all directions. I experimentally bumped the armored back of my hand against the basket and listened for the return echoes. The delay confirmed my suspicions: the place was vast—and dark—outside the dome of un-sourced green light that enveloped us.

One of Duff's men pulled the gate open and I helped Saura step out on a floor as smoothly finished as any surface in the finest Human constructions. This was more than a mere cavern.

"The Cheel will see us now." Piika abruptly took control again as she rearranged the blanket on her shoulders and walked away with the Frairy's bouncing gait.

Keeping a firm hand under Saura's arm, I moved to follow. I could have offered to carry my partner, but I valued my life too much to risk her reaction, especially in front of the two...assassins.

"How much longer?" I asked again.

Piika turned. "Soon." She slowed her pace, giving the rest of us time to catch up.

The pattern of tiles on the floor became more visible as we moved forward. The stones were the size of my palm and fitted in repeating spans of light and dark color. There was no way to tell if they were part of a larger design. The task of laying them must have been gargantuan. But then, the natives had had thousands of years to do it.

Reminded of the prodigious nature of the thing we were about to encounter, I focused my attention on the direction we were moving. In the distance, I saw a glow of brighter, white light. Against it, the floor formed a hard horizon so that it appeared we were walking toward the edge of the world.

Which we were, in a manner of speaking. We finally stopped at the clean, hard edge of a cliff that ran away in a straight line to fade into darkness on both sides of us. The sight before us, however, stole my breath and drove fear into my heart. A hundred meters below the cliff's edge, rolling green hills stretched as far as the eye could see in the dim light of a massive cavern. As I stood there, white shafts of sunlight broke through the ceiling high above, illuminating and slicing across the rolling mounds. Some of the shafts lingered, while others dimmed or chased shadows from clouds above the surface of the planet.

"This is the Cheel?" I asked

"Far beyond the reach of the Endar," Piika said. "The light comes from the glassland. It is cracked and broken and does not sustain life, but the rain and sunlight fall in through the breaks."

"The baked land below the end of the old spaceport launch ramps," Shoff said.

Piika shot her an apprehensive look.

Shoff's ears softened a tiny bit. "We are no friend to the Endar," she said.

Piika nodded carefully.

The awe gripping me tempered with reality: we hadn't come all this distance to stare at a small continent of moss. "We're not going down there, right?"

Duff snorted disdainfully, but Piika smiled. "No one enters the place where the Cheel rests," she said.

Oh. Good. The green stretching off into the distance was a country of its own.

Somewhere above this place clouds shifted and sunlight, in brilliant, blinding shafts poured down through breaks in the cavern ceiling. The beams rippled, the light running across the rolling mounds the way mining platform spotlights searched the surface of an asteroid. I knew it was a sight few people on this world ever saw.

The sight of a lifetime was not why we were here either. Piika turned and walked along the edge of the cliff. After a few minutes, the hard edge curved outward ahead of us, jutting in a projection of stone to hang out over the vastness of the Cheel's space. On scale, it was hardly more than a rough spot on the rim, in size, fifteen meters wide and long, ending in a rounded tip. Its surface was stepped, the first five meters level with the plain we walked on, then a short series of shallow steps led to another flat space, narrower in width. That dropped again, to the last stage. Centered there was a raised, two-meter-wide pool of water. The dark, smooth surface sat flush with its stone rim.

The inside of my nose tickled. "With all the green out there, why is the air so dry?"

"The Cheel hears and speaks through the medium of fluid," Duff said. "That's why most of it dwells here, away from liquid and the sound it conducts."

"The stone cistern above that you emptied?"

"Located too close to a densely populated area. The water amplified the noise."

I stared at the green below us. "Who figured out how to communicate with it?"

"The MoMo. They're communication specialists. Who do you think designed the translation hardware inside that otherwise empty gourd of yours? No one can imitate what they do. They keep tight control over the tech, too, making their deals at the top tier of Whooex members' power pyramid. No deal, no translator. It's what keeps the Endar on the last little bit of a leash. Without translation hardware, they can't communicate with the rest of the Whooex Union or even with some of the technology they've developed. They hate that. If they ever figure out a way around that hitch, they'll declare war on the MoMo, and the rest of us, too."

I thought about the pair who had lured Saura and me into this mess. "They really are telepathic?"

"Yeah."

"Are Frairy?"

"Only if we undergo a complicated surgical procedure the MoMo developed. There are a few people who go into their service, off-world. They can't return to Rhom."

So, Thok had undergone surgery in order to work with His Frilliness.

"Then how does she communicate with the Cheel?" I watched Piika walk to the end of the projection and sit on the rim of the pool. She stared down into the water.

"Children's brains are more pliable and open than an adult's. We all heard the whispers when we were kids Piika's age. Way back before all the other dismal stuff up there that filled our heads." He gestured toward the surface. "Children play games with it, spying on each other. That enables it to select the ones who hear it best to take turns as Speakers. They serve as its mouthpiece for the rest of us. And before you go all Human over it, we don't force them to do it. They can decline and pass the task any time. They'll lose the ability to talk with it in a few years, anyway. It's an important role, and it gives people who need contact with the Cheel access without them having to climb down here—something forbidden under normal circumstances. Sometimes the Cheel will request direct contact with someone."

"Me?"

"Yep."

I thought about that for a moment. The Cheel must be a massive visual network. If it could help me locate the kid, I wanted to talk to it, too.

"You don't let all this go to waste, do you?" I tried to shift the topic to distract my attention away from my racing heart.

"Would you?"

"Not on your life! Humans would use it to the maximum."

"We do, too, where we can. But the Cheel is not everywhere. And it's not foolproof. We're subject to errors sometimes in how we interpret the information it provides. We use its eyes on the street, especially in the lower levels of the city. So don't get any ideas about sliding out of here. We will find you."

Point made: they knew how to work their resources. I reached for the bottle of water I had stowed in a loop of the armor.

Duff put a firm hand on my wrist to stop me. "Uh-uh."

Piika beckoned me to join her beside the pool. She held out a cup in her other hand.

Aw. No. This was not good...

Duff's short fingers tightened on my forearm in a vice-like clamp. He guided me forward down the steps. A couple of his men moved in close behind us as if to block my escape. Like there was any place to escape to.

And, yes, I did consider it. But I wanted to talk to the Cheel.

Duff stepped back up to the second level as Piika walked over and held out the cup. "You must drink the water."

"Why?"

"So the Cheel will have access to your mind."

"You said it wasn't telepathic!" I looked back at Duff accusingly.

"It's not." He shrugged. "There are microscopic bits in the water; they'll seek out certain areas in your brain, allowing the Cheel to understand your answers."

Take part of another living thing into my body—into my brain? "No."

"Stop being such a whiny baby, Zant. They'll fade and wash out during your next sleep cycle."

"How can you be sure of what happens? How do you know it isn't pirating peoples' bodies for physical mobility? It wouldn't admit that, would it?" He might even be aware of it.

"The residents of this world have done this for centuries. Those who communicate regularly with the Cheel need to drink again after a day passes."

"Have you ever done this with a Human before? My biology is different from yours."

"You understand refusing to drink is not an option, right?" Duff said.

I swallowed hard. "Will it affect or change me in any way?"

"It will make you better looking. Sheesh! It hasn't affected any of the rest of us, including any citizens or non-citizens on this ball we've used it on. There's nothing to indicate you're anything special."

"Does that include Tabi?" Shoff asked sharply.

"Oh, because your people don't have a reputation for making trouble here," he shot back at her sarcastically.

I was willing to bet the Endar had not been included in the experience. Or maybe they had, and that's what their hatred of this being stemmed from. "Look. I only want to find the kid before something bad happens to her. I don't need you or the Cheel to help me do that. Just show me the door to the street."

The two gray Tabisee actually laughed.

"Do you realize how large a planetside city can be?" Duff asked.

A city that laid claim to being the hub of Whooex banking and trade? No.

He gave me a hard look and I suddenly knew I wasn't leaving this place if I refused to cooperate. I had peeked behind the magic curtain and there was no stepping away. The Frairy in front of me was the real thing when it came to protecting his world.

"Will I hear voices in my head?"

"Piika will continue to speak for the Cheel."

"Fine." I snatched the cup from Piika and gulped it down.

"A swallow would have been enough," Duff said when I handed the cup back to the Frairy child.

"Really?" It was bad enough to think of the creepy-crawly alien things moving inside my body without unnecessarily overdoing it.

"No." He chuffed amusement.

Bastard. I wanted to reach out and throttle him, but a slow, warm lethargy had begun to spread throughout my limbs.

Piika took my hand and gently guided me to sit on the stone edge of the pool. The water looked dark and green until I realized it was clear, and that moss lined the inside of the bowl. I had to catch myself to keep from sagging forward and plunging face-first into the water.

"Is this normal?" I asked. I wanted to panic, but for some reason I couldn't find the reaction inside of me.

"Yeah." Duff's expression was serious now. "Are you sleepy?"

"No." My thoughts were clear as ever. "Why?"

"We don't want your body to kill the bridge cells before we're done." He glanced over at Piika, who had moved to take a seat again across on the far side. "When you are ready, Speaker." He retreated back up to where his men and the Tabisee stood on the second level, leaving us on the tip of the overhang.

Arm resting on the moss-covered rim, Piika put her little hand into the water. The surface rippled.

The wavelets moved toward her fingers, instead of away from them.

I leaned as far away from the pool as my balance allowed and waited, heart pounding, while I imagined the squiggle of tiny green things in my veins, working their way toward my brain.

CHAPTER 29

Little Girl Not So Lost

"The Cheel wishes to know why you seek the child."

Everything felt normal except for the racing of my heart. "So, it admits the kid is here?"

Piika nodded once. "The Cheel sees her."

I would have turned and glared at the Tabisee assassin-security team behind me in triumph, but staring up their noses seemed anticlimactic. "She doesn't belong here. She's a kid, alone on a world full of dangerous people. I need to get her someplace safe." Plus, I wanted to find out who had attacked her people and me out at Idwal. I didn't see any reason to get this being involved in that.

"You have found your partner. You no longer need the child."

"No!" The statement appalled me. "This is a Human child on a world where Humans are banned. A kid. Alone! Her luck may have held out this long," which was amazing, "but it won't last forever. Someone will get their filthy hands on her! I can't let that happen. I have to find her."

"And what will you do for her?"

"Take her off this world. Find her people or someone to take her in, to feed, protect, and raise her. A family."

"What sort of family? Your first, your second, or your third?"

That was a gut punch.

Three families. I understood the reference to my parents and An-thy, and to Admiral Maxte and his wife, Mei, who had taken me in after the disaster that killed my brother. But the people this thing referred to as my second family were nothing like that. They raided my homeworld of New Bounty, killed my parents, then moved on to destroy the lives of countless children. Memories of our time held as captives by them were the stuff that sent paroxysms of horror through me when the lights dimmed to night cycle in Spacertown. Our time in their grasp was the nightmare that crawled through my brain when I woke from deep sleep.

"You don't have the right to dig through my memories." I found the air to howl in protest. But as I stared at the moss-lined pool, hor-ror and fury tearing at me in equal measure, I was already back there.

***

"He is not your kid." My arms brace the metal frame of our bunkroom door. "Go away!"

The crewwoman's mouth tightens as she looks at me. Her thin face looks tired and sad, but we have more reason to be tired and sad than she does.

We don't need her.

"Okay," she draws a shallow breath. "You are angry and upset. I understand. But your brother needs someone to care for him."

"Not you," I hiss. I push harder against the frame to hide the tremble in my arms. "You are not our Momma."

"No, I'm not. I'm sorry for what happened to your momma. And your dad. I can't help you with that. But your brother is very young. He still needs care."

We all need care—the kind our parents give us. But it can't hap-pen now, because she and the others on this ship killed them. The thought twists up everything inside me and I fight to choke back a sob of fury. "Go away!"

She leans back slightly and her eyes narrow, as if the strength of my anger surprises her. Her head dips in a nod. "I can come in and take him. You know that's true. But it will frighten him and make things worse. He is not well. Let me take him to the ship doctor for care. Will you allow me to do that?"

I look over my shoulder at Anthy. He is a tiny lump wrapped in a blanket on a lower bunk. He is quiet, but Anthy is not a quiet brother. He talks so much he makes me crazy, and he gets into everything. Last night he refused to eat and he whimpered in the darkness. I know I cannot make him feel better, even if I hold him all day and tell him stories.

My heart races with fear.

"Okay." I drop one arm from the doorframe so she can squeeze past.

She moves quickly, going over to the bunk and lifting my little brother. She murmurs to him the way our momma did. I burn with anger because he doesn't protest. I will scold him about it when he is better. I will order him to stay away from her when he comes back.

She carries him past me and out of the bunkroom. The other kids stand by, watching in silence. They are confused about this woman who has entered our area. I glare at them, but they only stare back at me with frightened questions in their eyes.

"He's sick," I snarl at them. "Straighten the blankets on your beds."

When I turn away to hide a sudden blur of tears, I see she has paused outside the door. She nods solemnly at me. "You are a good, brave sister. The doctor will make him well." Then she walks away.

"You tell that doctor to keep his pervy hands off him," I shout after her retreating back. "That means you, too!"

***

A tear ran down my face and dropped into the pool.

Great! Now the damned thing had my DNA to use against me, too. If it hadn't stolen it already. I sucked in a huge gasp of air and forced my body to sit upright again.

You think you failed your brother. A whisper swirled inside my head.

You think you're going to give me therapy? I asked the Cheel bitterly. Locked in our private conversation, I had forgotten everyone else. *Save me from myself? My foster father is a kind man; he and the military both spared no expense on therapy to fix me. None of it helped. Anthy is dead. I didn't save him. I will not fail this child!*

You cannot protect yourself on this world.

Maybe. The Endar would turn my life into hell if they found me. The Earth Alliance's economic agenda would be set back hundreds of years. The Tabi could suffer severe retaliation. But this was not about me, the Tabi, or the EA.

This is a big, dangerous place, I snapped, *full of people who are ready and willing to exploit a child.*

You have experience with this threat. It was a statement of recognition.

I— Fury flashed inside me. *What I experienced is not for sharing with you. I just want to get the kid someplace safe.* The last sentence twisted into a plea.

My anger dissolved away. I saw Piika watching me from across the pool. "I didn't..."

Piika raised her free hand to stop me speaking.

She touched the water and a slow light slid out across the surface.

As it brightened, I realized an image was coming into focus. I caught fleeting impressions of a market similar to the one above us. A face flashed, the front of a stall, bright clothes, fruit. It was as if I was fast-searching images on a computer screen. It reminded me of viewing a piece of 3-D art. I saw the side angle of a face, a mouth front on; the bottom of a basket and the fruit it carried. The flow ran quick and dizzying—an array of flashes that somehow fit into a comprehensible whole. Then everything stilled to focus on a stone wall with a child sitting atop it, munching a piece of fruit.

"That's her!" I leaned forward, catching the edge of the pool with my hands to keep from pitching into it. The visual pieces jerked and settled to a clear image.

"Well, how about that!" Duff murmured from behind me. "You're not crazy after all."

The kid took another bite of fruit and chewed it slowly while she glanced around. She did not appear distressed. At least not nearly as much as I was, seeing her. "Is this real? Is this happening now?"

"It is happening as we see," Piika said.

"How? How are we seeing it?"

"The Cheel," Duff said.

Piika smiled serene agreement.

"Who's taking care of her? Is she free to move around?"

"The child moves freely." It seemed oddly surreal for the tiny Frairy child to refer to another of similar age in such a removed fashion. Then I realized the Cheel must have reverted back to speaking through her.

"Without anyone? For over ninety days? How is she getting food and shelter?"

"She takes what she needs."

Takes? Odd turn of phrase. "Others are sharing with her."

"She takes, but only what she needs."

I frowned. "Is that how it works here? She can take what she needs and move on?"

Duff gave a derisive snort behind me. "Moneyworld," he said.

Yeah, that's what I thought. This place wasn't any different from any other place I had ever seen. So, the kid was stealing her way along and sleeping wherever she found shelter. She was living on the edge of society, where the dangerous and desperate lurked, just waiting for her kind. My concern heightened.

Something intruded over the image and Piika raised a hand to quiet my protest. For a frustrating moment, the image gyrated and lurched, then it cleared in scattered segments until the backs of two people came into view. Two Frairies, a male and female, superimposed over the kid on the wall. They walked, heads bent close in whispers, bodies pressed side to side in the way of young lovers. When they leaned against the wall, the kid gave them a disinterested look. They did not even spare her a glance. The couple talked for a moment, snuggled close, then the boy laughed and broke away from their huddle, rolling his back against the stone and almost pinching the kid's leg against the surface. She silently sidled out of contact and continued eating.

"They treat her as if she's not even there," I said, pushing down anger at their indifference. Of course, they couldn't know she was alone and lost, but, he didn't have to be rude... "If there are no Humans on this world, why do they treat her like she's part of the background scenery? Like she's invisible?"

The two Frairies talked and giggled, their heads bent together for a few more moments, then in large, dark blurs, they pulled away from the wall and moved out of the image. The kid barely spared them a glance.

Saura, Shoff, and Meeroush, along with Duff, had worked their way down beside me. They were leaning forward, intently watching the kid finish her fruit.

"Maybe it's young love. Who knows?" Duff said.

"How far away is she? I'll go out and bring her in." I straightened.

Shoff exchanged a glance with Meeroush and I realized I didn't have a place to claim as 'in'.

Then I could use Duff's network...

"Whoa, Flygirl," Duff exclaimed. "It doesn't matter if the population is ignoring one Human kid. She's not stirring up trouble, which is more than you can say. You are not going out there."

"I can with your help."

Piika smiled. "It would not be prudent at this time."

"Prudent? Prudent for whom?" I demanded. "She's a kid—she is a kid, right?" Piika nodded. "Alone on a strange world. I—we—need to bring her in."

"There is no 'we' in this," Duff said. "You think you need to bring her in. You are wrong. She is not a priority."

"Then make her one!"

"This world has other, bigger concerns. Earth Alliance's arrival for a meet and greet before their membership vote is imminent. So, no."

"You can't leave her out there. I don't care how well she can hide!"

"Why? What's so important about the kid, Zant?" Duff's eyes were suddenly sharp.

There was a lot of impatient shifting of bodies around me as they waited for my response.

They would kill me if I told them she was a telepath.

"Child is telepath," Saura said.

"Saura!" My horrified protest got lost in the gasps and alarmed ear flicks around me.

"Vivi. Is only way we can secure their help."

"You brought a telepath here?" Duff's voice rose. "All those questions... That explains it!"

"No—" I fought to explain. "I didn't know."

Shoff and Meeroush had moved back a pace toward the steps to the plateau. Their ears were pressed back tight to their skulls.

"Take us out of here, now," Shoff snarled. She made a sweeping gesture toward Saura and me. "Feed that to Cheel babies." Her foot was on the first step.

"Wait," Duff said.

On the plateau his men dropped into a crouched, distinctly aggressive posture, prepared to act against the outraged Tabisee if ordered.

"Now!" Shoff demanded.

"Shut up!" Duff bellowed.

The faint echoes of his voice rolled back at us in the silence.

"Yeah, this is a twist," he said. "An unexpected, bad twist. But we won't solve it by falling apart."

"Not falling apart. Not a Tabi problem." The Tabisee security team was already on the second step back up.

"She is searching for something," Piika spoke for the Cheel. "The pattern of her movements reveals that. If the Human interferes," she continued, despite a new round of dismayed reactions, "we cannot discover what she seeks. We must leave her to her own devices."

The kid in the pool continued to eat. When she finished the fruit, she tossed the core and slid off the wall in a blur of movement. I realized that sometime since walking off the Ritto ship she had replaced her white garment with colorful play clothes similar to Piika's. She slung a small bundle over her shoulder, tossed her white hair with a shake of her head, and walked out of the image. The Cheel moved to follow her in a pixilated mass of color shot through with bits of her back that stayed in focus longer than the rest of her.

I tore my eyes away from the image, everything inside of me twisting with horror at what the Cheel suggested. "She's a little kid!"

"Child has survived almost one hundred days on own, Vivi," Saura pointed out. "Perhaps okay few more days, until Cheel discovers what seeks."

"What would a Human child be searching for here?" Duff asked. "It doesn't make sense."

"You think she's a threat?" Of course, it would be Shoff asking that.

"It's worth investigating." And Duff answering.

My heart jerked with panic when I turned back to see a map of T'lek T'la had replaced the image of the kid. A thin red line began at the spaceport and ran into the city. Realizing it had to be the Cheel's record of sightings of the kid, I leaned closer over the pool.

At first, she wandered near the spaceport, the trace erratic. Then she moved into the city. It made sense; she had to go where food, water, and shelter were available. There were occasional short, deviating excursions along the line. Where they occurred, she consistently returned to her former path, moving steadily deeper into T'lek T'la. There was a massive area of the city beyond her current point, but it looked as if she was definitely moving with a destination in mind.

The Tabisee security team had drifted back to the pool edge. "The pattern is not random," Meeroush observed.

"The Cheel agrees with your observation. But it is not telepathic; it does not know where she is going," Piika said.

Everyone turned to glare at me except Saura. She was studying the red line.

"How could she be searching for something when she's never been here before?" I protested.

"You are familiar with this being?" Shoff asked.

"No..."

"Then how can you say where she has been?"

That took me aback. How did I know she had never been here? Because she was a kid. A Human kid. And I knew what a Human kid was capable of doing, having been one. I started to snarl a reply, but Duff interrupted.

"The Cheel has eyes on her. If it says leave her out there, we leave her out there and wait to find out what goes on."

"What are you talking about? The longer she's out there, the greater danger she's in. Bring her in and let an adult—someone with real resources—do the searching for her."

"There's no guarantee we will learn anything from her if we bring her in," he said.

Saura had moved to my side in the press of bodies on the projection. "You are putting too much of past into this," she said softly.

I wanted to argue back, but I knew she was right: I was reacting from my gut feelings. I sighed. "It's only...she wouldn't be here if it weren't for me."

"Would not be alive if not for you. Is surviving. Is well. But cannot ignore child is seeking something. There is much sensitive information on world. Can affect us all. Let people do job."

Again, she was right. But I couldn't help that it went against everything inside of me. "Okay," I said, "But I'm part of this! I talk to her when she's pulled in, and she's coming with us off world."

She tipped her ears in silent agreement. For all that was worth.

"The Cheel will watch, and the Frairy will advise us immediately if there is a change. We are leaving now," Shoff announced.

"Not without Zant and Blue Girl," Duff said.

Shoff swung back toward Duff, her teeth bared. "Best to kill Human now," she said.

"Not your Human to decide destiny," Saura was abruptly in front of her. She stared up at the taller female, her body rigid with fury. I was surprised the armor at her neck didn't bulge with the raised hackles I knew lay beneath it.

"I cannot expect an inferior genetic deviation to understand the intricacies of diplomatic reality, schaa drika," Shoff said dismissively.

Whoa! I recognized 'drika', because Saura frequently used it to describe the people we encountered out on the Rim. It translated into Hume as 'space monkey'. 'Schaa' was new, though. My translator told me it was the Tabi word for 'pampered'.

The red pouf of deathhawk on Saura's head stiffened and bushed out. "Step up, Ground Pounder. We see who understands intricacies of reality."

"You step back."

My partner was two-thirds the size of the Tabisee assassin.

"Saura..." I started.

Her right ear twitched for my silence and claws gleamed through slits in her black gloves.

A few steps away Meeroush watched his partner with overt interest. "Hey," I said to catch his attention.

He looked over at me. "They are evenly matched," he told me calmly.

I wasn't sure if he meant it as a simple observation or to assuage my rising upset at the thought of the two of them going head to head. Whichever, it did not help. "Stop them," I told him.

"Aw right, aw right," Duff actually walked between them, something I was neither brave enough nor stupid enough to do. He extended his arms, flat-handed, toward each of them. "Sort out your problems on your own turf. But you pulled Zant in; she's going home with you."

Meeroush nodded. "We will take them back with us,"

His partner gave him a glare, her ears slanted back, but she didn't argue.

When the Cheel did not add further comment through the Frairy child, Duff shrugged. "It's decided then."

Decided, yes, but no one here was walking away happy.

The group climbed back to the plateau level. For me, it felt as if I had moved one step ahead by proving to the others the kid really did exist, and two steps backward by the revelation she was a telepath, and then sideways with the discovery she was moving across the city with what appeared to be some unknown purpose.

And I had reluctantly ingested a serving of sentient green vegetable.

I just hoped what Duff told me about the water from the Cheel's pool was true.

A hand slipped into mine and Piika smiled up at me. She meant the action to be comforting, I know. I felt sort of rotten wondering how much of it was a child's innocent action and how much was Cheel manipulation.

Meeroush laid claim to my other arm in a hard, black-gloved grasp and Piika's fingers slid away. Before I could react, he had zip-tied my hands in front of me and was wrapping another strip around Saura's unresisting wrists.

"You don't have to do this," I protested. "We can work something out..."

"You put the Tabi Empire at risk," Shoff hissed at me. "You will cooperate."

"She doesn't put you at risk," I flicked my eyes toward Saurubi.

Shoff gave a dismissive sniff and turned away to watch Duff's men lay out a disk similar to the one they had used in the tunnel.

Duff came over to my side.

"Why didn't we use those to transport in," I asked him.

"Nothing transports in to the Cheel. And it controls what transports out."

"People stay down here?" The thought of trying to live in this dead, cold silence sent a deeper chill running through me. "Where do they live?"

"They don't."

"What happens to them?" I had a feeling that if I found myself down here again, I would find out firsthand.

"Compost," he said.

"What's that?"

"Plant food." He grinned, but there was no humor in it. "Lucky you. You're going back with your friends."

"Yeah. About that..."

"The Tabisee are the EA's closest allies. Plus, remember up in the marketplace? They came looking for you."

A few steps away, Shoff made a sound of disgust. "Can't let Endar have her."

Yeah, I held no illusions on that. If the Endar got their boney fingers on me again, they would recover my memories back to my birth. The Tabisee couldn't afford that.

The threat to my partner made me angry. Damn Thok, the MoMo—and me—for getting her into this!

We stood in silence while the Frairies finished assembling the shift ring. When the last piece clicked into place, one of them nodded at Duff.

"Set your destination and scramble it," he told Shoff. "We don't want to know where you take her."

She gave him a dark glare as she stepped inside the ring. Saura followed her.

"The kid—" I tried to reason with them all one last time.

"We'll keep the assassins updated on her status," Duff said.

But would they give me updates? Before I could protest, Meeroush clasped the back of my armor and hauled me into the transport ring with them.

Duff waggled his short little fingers at me as we shifted out of the Cheel's domain.

CHAPTER 30

Fourth Lockup

Pieter bends to look me in the eyes as he straightens my collar.

"This client is an important person," he says. "He wants to be happy. We want him to be happy. When he is happy, he gives the ship money for food. You want your team to eat, right?"

I nod. My fingers are numb, and I can barely move I'm so afraid.

He pats my head lightly and moves on to the girl standing next to me.

I'm supposed to go out on the docks tonight on a new task. I don't know what to expect. I know it's not good. I've heard children from the older teams talk during shower time. What they say sounds nasty. It sounds wrong. But I have no choice. I have been warned; I must cooperate and make this client happy to pay for the food the children in my charge eat. A few weeks ago, a girl down the corridor, Anna, refused something a client requested. When they brought her back to the ship, she was disciplined with the lash and her team got rations of bread and water once a day, for five days. We heard the younger children crying when we passed their door on the way to the toilets. Mandy and Appa looked up at me with fear in their eyes and asked me what the girl had done wrong. I could not explain it to them because I did not know.

I will find out tonight.

I don't want them to feel hunger, but I am so afraid, and I cannot promise them they will have food tomorrow.

I will try my best. I don't want Anthy to be hungry.

***

Shit. I pushed up from my face down position on the cot and glanced around.

I had been out on the Moneyworld less than seventy-two hours and I was looking at my fourth lockup. That had to claim some kind of bragging rights, if I ever got off this ball to talk about it.

This cell was ceramic-barred like the last one and one of a pair taking up the back wall of a plain, white room. A small table and some chairs sat against the far wall outside the bars, next to a low cabinet topped with what I assumed was a food preparation station. All were Tabi/Human scale. A good sign.

I could see Saurubi sleeping in the other cell.

The personal chrono in my head told me six hours had passed since I last checked it down in the Cheel's lair. The torture device my hosts called armor was mercifully gone, leaving me in the natural state of my cobalt blue shipskins. A tray of food and some water containers sat inside my cell. Wincing in pain at my abused muscles, I gathered the bottles and flushed my body with as much liquid as I could drink, trying to wash out the little green Cheel things. Then I ate some flavorless crackers smeared with a pale, bland paste to revive my energy and used the cell's tiny biocenter to clean my exposed skin and the surface of my shipskins thoroughly. After that, I pulled the filters in my left heel, something I had severely neglected over the past few days, and washed the collected debris of skin cells and waste down the recycler. It only occurred to me after the powder vanished that I'd put Human DNA into the city's waste disposal system. Damn.

Surely, in a city of more than fifty million souls, Endar security sensors weren't that sensitive!

Accepting my reasoning, I moved to the bars and stared at Saura's unconscious form. After a minute, I spotted discreet patches on her wrists, ankles, temple, and throat. She'd received medical care. The realization eased some of my fear; it didn't make sense for the Tabisee to patch her up then send her to her death, even if Humans did that all the time.

Settling on my cot, I gazed at the gray cell bars. I should have been plotting a grand escape. Getting out of this cell, snatching Saura, and taking her out into the city of T'lek T'la to help me find the kid, then cleverly hiding us away until the Human trade envoy arrived. I could contact someone in the entourage and get us all smuggled off this world. The kid had survived over ninety days; we could do it too. Afterward, we could find the kid a good home, maybe with my foster parents. Then Saura and I would track down Thok and His Pink Frilliness, demand recompense, get my wetware back, and re-claim the *Hand*.

Four hours later the sound of a tray sliding on the floor woke me. Meeroush had cleared and replaced mine and was moving on to Saura. I watched him walk over to check her vital signs.

"How is she?" I asked. The tray sitting inside her cell door was heavy on fluids.

He straightened. "She'll be up and moving about soon."

"Good." My heart twisted with the thought of losing her, but they had to get her off this world to cover Mathet's story to the High Jerak. She would face consequences for her errant six-year overstay in Human space, but she would be okay.

"Good," I repeated. I should be glad. Glad, yes. Happy, no. I didn't have to be happy. I looked at her outstretched body. "I know you don't think I deserve it, but may I ask one favor?"

His ears tipped with curiosity.

"Before she leaves can I have a minute to talk with her?"

"I can't promise. We have no control over the situation."

"Please ask."

"I'll see." He continued to study me. "How long have you traveled with First Astrogator Cerros Syrhas?"

"We served five years together in Earth Alliance Space Marines and six years as partners on our cargo hauler, the *Thief's Hand*. Now our ship's out on the edge of Union space." I met Meeroush's amber eyes. His ears were perched in interest. "That's where we found the kid. Out there." Found. I nearly died pulling her out of the airlock, then defending us from the ghost ship attackers, but I could not claim I rescued her. The Ritto-ssa had done that. For the betterment or detriment of us all.

"Eleven Human years. It is a long time."

"She's a badass marine." The thought made me smile.

He looked over at me, not understanding.

"Impressive. She's an impressive lady."

"As are all Tabi females," he nodded.

Right on cue, Shoff pushed through the door. She gave Meeroush an impatient glance and thumped two disposable sacks on the counter. He tipped a 'like I was saying' look at me and moved to join her as she pulled packets from the bags. An amazing aroma filled the space.

"You get fast food here?" I exclaimed in disbelief.

"Cannot eat that," Shoff gestured at the tray inside my cell.

Well, yeah, the food was mundane. I pretended their aroma came from my tray as I picked at its contents and waited for them to finish eating. When they started gathering up their debris I took a chance, hoping they were inclined to talk.

"What's going on with the kid? Did you bring her in yet? Can I talk to her?"

Shoff looked at her partner. "We would not hear this one whine from down in the stone cells."

My hairless scalped prickled at the threat. "I have rights, you know." Actually, I probably didn't. "I want to know what's going to happen to us."

Shoff was in my face with a blur of movement, her claw caps hitting the bars right above my grasping hands. "You have caused us enough trouble! Be silent!" Her breath raked my cheek. Her irises were wide and dark with fury. "We only wait for a decision on what to do with you."

She meant how to dispose of me.

Her claw caps were barely five millimeters above the bare skin of my fingers. My knees shook. My mind screamed for me to let go of those bars. Those razor-edged caps might slide down to make a crippling slice across my flesh, but I refused to back down. I was in a weak enough position without ceding respect, too.

She glared. I glared.

Meeroush said something too low for me to understand, and Shoff uncurled her fingers.

Her eyes still locked with mine, she slammed the palms of her hands against the bars.

I flinched. She saw it and her lower lids tightened with satisfaction.

I noticed she had a medical patch under her right eye.

"Idiot Human," she hissed as she dropped her hands and stepped away.

Bitch. My fingers refused to unbend. And, no, I wasn't stupid enough to say it aloud.

"It is undecided." Meeroush pushed the food sacks into a bin while Shoff went to the outer door and stood, arms crossed.

"What's that mean?"

"The ambassador has ordered us to sever all contact with you," Meeroush said after a pause. "We are to dispose of all evidence immediately."

"Me? He wants to dispose of me?" What had Duff said? Compost? I had checked the definition in my chips. I could already feel icy little Cheel roots spreading over the surface of my skin.

CHAPTER 31

No Part In Decision

"It's a suggestion." He shrugged. "It requires higher approval."

"By whom?" If we had to wait for someone back in the Tabi Empire, who required a full briefing, I still had a little time...

"Mathet is considering all options."

Mathet Waa Silvec, captain of an assassin team was considering...? He outranked the Tabisee trade ambassador on this?

Then again, what did I know of Tabi politics and security? I was only a grunt in the trenches, plowing around the universe in guilt-twisted oblivion.

Was. I wasn't anything, anymore. Not without my wetware...

For a moment my mind sort of fogged and I floundered in the emptiness of the Vasty. The *Thief's Hand* was gone. My partner's life was on the line because of my choices. I was putting the economic future of the EA and the Tabi Empire at risk. Hell, I couldn't even save one little kid... Again.

Despair and self-doubt flooded through me. I was useless. I always had been.

Years of therapy, however, had taught me how to shelve that. I required a purpose to move beyond immobilizing despair. Saving the kid was that one thing I could tell myself was not totally lost to me. Before I saved her, however, I had to save myself.

I drew a hard breath. "How long?" I asked.

Meeroush shrugged. "That is under consideration."

"And the kid? She's here by accident."

"The decision will be made at the appropriate level."

"You can't go around eliminating people for no good reason—"

"The future of the Tabi Empire is the only good reason," Shoff snapped. "In war, casualties fall. Not all are guilty or innocent."

"If I could just tell—"

"No tell. No speak. No part in decision except to receive fate."

Again, I was reminded that I could not consider the Tabisee as allies; sheltering me was not worth the consequences of breaking Whooex law. Considering the threat, it was amazing they had let me live this long.

I could let despair take me, or I could start working to keep us all alive.

"Why were you in the Endar warehouse?" I asked.

"You never know what you'll catch," Meeroush said.

"Like a Human escaping a Tabi ship?"

"Told you, that's impossible." He settled back in his chair, facing me. Shoff did not budge from her position beside the door. "Warehouses under dedicated member field areas are considered diplomatic zones. There is no access by other members or locals. We have to supply all our own equipment and maintenance."

"Even your own whizbats?"

He nodded.

Someone had to give in here if I was going to make any progress. I decided to accept their claim as true. "So, why were you really in an Endar warehouse?"

"We were working. That's an automated warehouse. The Endar seldom go there."

"Seldom? I saw two people from up on the flyway. I was just starting to climb down and follow them when you pulled me in. I'm pretty sure one was Endar."

Shoff's ears snapped back in displeasure. The two Tabi exchanged a look. "Missed because of idiot Human," she growled.

That didn't sound good, but it sounded convincing.

Meeroush focused back on me. "Describe the second being."

"Not dressed in leather. I saw legs. And skinny, but not tall." I gestured mid-chest.

Meeroush pushed off the chair and came over to stand in front of my cell. "What else?"

"That's all. They were far down one of the rows, walking together. I needed water and a way out, so I decided to follow them. They turned a corner, out of view, right before you snatched me."

"Would you remember where you saw them?"

As I flew along above endless rows of stored goods, hanging on for dear life? "Probably not."

Shoff muttered something in Tabisee that didn't translate in my software.

Unfortunately, I understood 'maku naku' meant 'halfwit idiot'. For the first six months after Saura and I had been matched as combat buddies I thought that was her affectionate nickname for me.

"If I am to die for this, I should know what it is," I said in Tabi.

Her lip curled in irritation, then she shrugged. "Tell her," she said to Meeroush.

"We suspect that warehouse is an entry point for contraband. We think the Endar are smuggling live cargo."

"Live? Where does it go?"

"To the Grip. Their security compound."

"Is it food? Maybe an animal to butcher?" Who knew what the High Jerak ate?

"We suspect something different."

I waited.

"We suspect they are smuggling beings of a different species."

"As slaves?"

"Possibly."

"Why wouldn't they bring them through legal channels?" Some member species of the Whooex had no problem with slaves and they didn't care what Humans or anyone else thought on the subject.

"They could if the cargo was legal."

"What's not legal here? Beyond a berserker or a war devil. Or a Human."

There was that exchange of looks again.

"Wait." It was ridiculous, but I threw it out there anyway. "Telepaths?"

The tension in the room relaxed noticeably.

"But the law..."

"Bans telepaths, for fear a member will use them to gain trade advantage over other members by gathering insider information. This is different. We think they use them to spy on members of the Consortium and manipulate them."

That was a serious accusation to level against the people in charge of security.

The big guy walked over to the outer door.

"Wait! Can I have a ZEE?" I asked before they could duck out.

A Xeno Expedited Elucidator, or ZEE for short —the MoMo had named the damn things since they owned all the rights to them—was a type of Whooex handheld computer designed for people who didn't have a universal feed implanted in their heads. They were cheap, plentiful—some worlds gave them to their non-chipped inhabitants for free—and immensely useful.

Shoff's eyes narrowed. "Why?"

"Because I don't enjoy sitting here, staring at the walls, waiting for death."

"Use your universal feed."

I sighed. "No legal Human presence, so no auto code for access." And, it went unsaid, if I could access the feed, unregistered, alerts would light up Endar security and trace back to my location. A ZEE would allow me to snoop undetected.

"You don't have access to the feed for this world, but you think you can go out and track someone down in a vast city?" She sniffed in disdain, thumbed her comm unit, and turned her back to me.

Meeroush walked over to lean a shoulder against the bars of the cell. "She likes you," he said in a low voice.

"Yeah, I can tell." I shook my head. They were Tabisee, but they had a whole different mindset than my partner.

"She thinks you are hard to get rid of."

"Tenacious?" I suggested, hoping for a better description.

"No. Hard to get rid of."

"Not for lack of trying."

"Exactly," he agreed.

"Is 'hard to get rid of' bad?"

His eyes slid to his partner across the room. She continued to talk. He shifted his attention back to me. "Tabisee are warriors. We respect dedication to purpose, even if it is misplaced. We may have to kill you, but it is a good attribute."

Okay...

"One of the Frairies in the market referred to you as assassins," I ventured.

His ears twisted annoyance. "Duff is an important ally, but he talks too much. Shoff specializes in technical support. I am the assassin."

I nearly choked in surprise. I had grown to accept I might meet a speedy end at Shoff's hand—which still remained an option—but not from Meeroush.

"Oh," I said.

The amiable assassin shrugged.

Across the room, the technical half expressed strong displeasure with whoever was on the other end of her conversation.

"Why does a trade embassy need assassins? I mean, I'm not naïve, but assassins?"

"We are Tabi security."

"Tabi?" I was confused. "As in 'not' diplomatic?"

"Tabi," he repeated. "Our mission is to protect the interests of the Tabi Empire above all else."

"You can eliminate anyone you think threatens the Empire?"

He looked at me, golden eyes steady. "I just said that." His ears flicked. "Including a troublesome Human."

Yeah, I got it. "Can anyone here do that? Form their own security force?" I could see big problems with that.

"No. It is illegal."

Well, this situation had the potential to be a glorious star spack storm. "Is your ambassador even aware of you?"

"Need to know basis."

I suspected he knew something, but only enough to spare his dignity and preserve his deniability if something went completely sideways. He probably didn't want to know the specifics. "I guess Endar complaints keep him advised on what you're doing."

I thought I saw him smirk

"How often do you kill someone?"

"Very rarely. We are here to protect Tabi interests."

"The way you conducted the raid outside the Ritto warehouse?" There had been over two dozen Tabi personnel involved on the street.

He smiled. "That was a distraction for the Endar."

"And all those Carquetchians?"

"Their arrest records are conveniently lost in the T'lek T'la legal system. We work together for our defense."

"Defense? Against what?"

"The Endar." He looked surprised that he had to tell me.

"I'm not from here," I reminded him.

"The Endar Sat Quar controls Whooex Trade Consortium security. Their jurisdiction is the Trade Compound, which encompasses the Trade Zone and the Diplomatic Zone, where the embassies are located. Their authority does not extend to the city of T'lek T'la unless a Consortium member is involved."

"Tabisee," I said.

He nodded. "We must all work against Endar efforts to intrude their influence into the city. There is very little killing."

Very little killing? On a diplomatic world? "Are the citizens of the city hostile?" My mind flashed to the ragpiles.

He gave a soft snort of amusement. "The citizens are not the problem."

I understood feeling intimidated by the Endar; they sent chills running through me, but something sounded off. "Do the Consortium members all feel threatened by their security?"

He flicked me a look but did not elaborate.

We went back to watching Shoff on the far side of the room. She paused, waited, talked again. Several times her ears slanted back in impatience or irritation.

Finally, she cut the connection, rummaged in a cabinet, took something out, and fiddled with the settings before stalking over to us. Leveling her golden glare on me, she thrust a small handheld device through the bars. "Familiarize yourself with your grave," she snapped.

Yeah, she really liked me.

CHAPTER 32

Xeno Expedited Elucidator Jerk

As the assassin team left on their next mysterious task, I settled on my cot to examine the thing Shoff had handed me. It was a thin rectangle with a 3-D projection port on the flat surface. Its gray-green case had indentations on the sides for varied finger sizes. If it worked with the tech in my head, it was my entryway into this world.

With my heart racing, I pressed a button on the side.

"Pa'tuth," I said in Tabi, commanding it to open. Using EA Standard or Basic might set off security alarms in the dark heart of an Endar facility somewhere.

A series of blue glyphs projected into the air above the device.

"Welcome! I'm your personal tour guide, Totsifee, but you can call me Totsy," a male voice announced brightly from my hand.

I almost dropped the thing.

"If you aim me at any building, image, or object I will tell you its name, specie-origin, and history, depending on how much you want to know."

Son of a bitch! It was one of those handheld data dumpers tourists carried on excursions through a museum or a city. Worse, it carried a context marker that gave it a stinking, cheery personality.

Very funny, Shoff. I'd thought I heard the rumble of her laugh as they'd gone out the door.

Still, for someone who didn't know anything about this world, the tour device was actually a decent start. It contained more information than the EA currently had on the Moneyworld—unless they had succeeded in getting someone to smuggle a 'Totsy' off for them. The image of the EA's most brilliant minds staring at this lumpy-sided, ugly handheld, their faces rapt with anticipation, drew a chuckle from me.

Totsifee had instructed me to aim at things. I didn't need information about the ceramic bars or white walls, so I switched to question and answer mode.

Luckily, my years with Saura had given me a fair vocabulary of Tabi, though I would never be able to replicate some words. "Question" happened to be within my range of vocalization.

Totsifee responded cheerfully, "Ready to begin the adventure when you are." As long as I spoke through the translator in Tabi, it would respond in the same language, and the language software in my brain would translate back to EA standard.

"Can I change your name?" I asked.

"Of course you can! I am at your service for the duration of your use. However, there are a few rules we must go over first." It proceeded to review various violations of usage, advised me it would intercede with suggested revisions if I was in danger of breaching certain ethics or courtesy protocols, would not translate swear words—the Tabi had plenty of those—and would be unable to answer questions infringing on security concerns, but would advise me when those occurred. Then it asked me if I understood and accepted the terms of usage.

"Yes. From now on, respond to the name 'Jerk'." Knowing people are just waiting for an order to kill you can put you in a malicious mood. "Understand?"

"Absolutely! Address me as Jerk any time you wish to interact with me."

First order of business: "Jerk, turn down the cheerfulness level."

"I understand. How may I address you?"

"Ka." The gender-neutral form of address was standard across the Whooex Union. I guessed nearly everyone was capable of expelling a short gust of air that passed the level required by the translators.

"I am ready to serve ka."

Time to go to work.

After the tenth polite response of "sincere apologies, ka, but that information is not available on this device," Jerk switched to a warning 'ding' for questions it considered off limits. After the second 'ding', I decided to keep my exploration within its parameters lest it shut down entirely.

The second 'ding' also stirred the first response from Saurubi I'd heard since I woke. She gave a growl of protest. I stopped, listening for more. Fifteen minutes later, after I started reading the history of Rhom—probably heavily edited by every Whooex member who had a trade embassy on the world—she rolled over and made an angry spitting sound. She would awaken soon.

While I waited I put a few questions to Jerk, located a virtual holo tour that would project into the air around me, and kicked around one of the merchant areas, staring up in awe at towering skyscrapers that housed some of the Whooex's most powerful banks and business conglomerates. It always amazed me how the planetside behemoths managed to remain upright. I was only one hundred and seventy-seven centimeters tall, and the gravity on the Moneyworld was kicking my ass.

After being sufficiently impressed by the architecture, I jumped to a new tour and idly moved up to the gates of the Trade Compound, only to discover Jerk disallowed extending the tour beyond the entrance. I could, however, see past the checkpoint.

Sure enough, no plant life grew within view, though the place had some interesting, twisty kind of mobile art structures scattered about the entry plaza.

I asked Jerk for a map of the city. It happily included the location of embassies in the Whooex Union Trade Consortium Diplomatic Zone. Jerk was full of useful information.

"Whoa," I said,

"Vivi?" Saura sat up on her cot and looked at me.

"Shut down, Jerk." I got up and carried the viewer into the bio-center, set it on the floor, and closed the privacy screen in case it had active spyware that could target on an unauthorized language or any other part of our conversation. Paranoid in the extreme? Not in the least. I knew what I would do if I was in charge of security on this world, and I wasn't anywhere near an expert.

I walked over to the bars. "How you feeling?"

"Muscles are sore."

No surprise after surviving the med-evac crash. "You'll feel better after you get some food and water in you."

She looked at the tray and curled her upper lip in distaste.

Yeah, Tabisee food.

She glanced over at her tiny bio space. "Soon. What has happened?"

"Actually, not much beyond a run through, by me mostly, of all the problems my presence on this world creates for your people." I didn't want to discuss that right now.

She made a sound of agreement. Someone had made her aware of the situation.

"Where did they take you?"

"Attended ambassador. Was not happy."

It turned out Endar security, the Sat Quar, had been trying to reach the Tabisee ambassador for details on her status since the med-evac ship crash. I winced inwardly. In my experience, people in high positions, regardless of species, didn't appreciate being placed in a situation where people in an even higher position were asking them questions they could not answer. They got angry and heads rolled.

The embassy had eventually replied that all individuals involved had been safely recovered, but they were unable to advise on their status. The Endar squad that followed Shoff and Saura, however, were harder to satisfy. Fortunately Shoff had had the foresight to put Saura in a spare suit of armor to mask her blue fur. When the Endar trailed them to the cellar where Meeroush dropped me down the drain and Saura had followed, the Tabisee team reconnected. Two Tabisee in, two Tabisee out. The discrepancy in heights had not come up.

Only then did I notice Saura was wearing her astrogator short gold vest and red shorts.

"Where are your skins?"

Her ears flicked annoyance. "Took."

Damn. The cost of getting back into space was mounting up. "Are your people able to cover for your presence here?" I asked.

"Mathet story is good. Admiral for local Tabi Space Force willing to claim responsibility."

When she got out of here she would go back into the military system for trial, reprimand, and punishment. Then reassignment.

At least they weren't planning to lock her in a stone cell beneath the Moneyworld. Or feed her to the Cheel.

A long silence drew out between us.

"Security not sure what to do with you," she said after a moment.

"Yeah."

We sat in silence again. Then I had to do it.

"Pampered space monkey?" I asked.

She made a spitting sound of disgust. "Stupid ground pounder." I had heard that expression often enough over the last eleven years. "Endured much to become astrogator."

I knew my partner's history well. Her home planet, Uchaf, was the second oldest settled world in the original Tabi star system. It was ancient and populated with old, wealthy families who had long histories and rigidly limited options for the futures of their children. Firstborn or most capable in those high families generally retained the family assets. The second went into government service. The third child pledged to Empire Space Fleet.

The Tabi Empire Space Fleet loved those third-born children from Uchaf.

For Saura, as an astrogator, that dedication meant a great deal of pain in acquiring the augmentations necessary for her job. Coppery wire patterns laced her whole body beneath the dusky blue fur. The enhancements, which directly linked a star astrogator into a ship's navigation system, made the Tabi Space Fleet the envy of all other Whooex members. It enabled Tabi ships to avoid obstacles in folded space, allowing them to explore farther and safer than any other Whooex Star Association. They didn't share the tech, and any discussion with her on the topic was always limited. I sometimes wondered how much the Tabi Empire feared someone taking apart one of those valued members of their fleet to discover their secrets.

Memory of the High Jerak's interest in her at the Ritto warehouse drove a chill through me. The Tabisee had to remove her from this world as soon as possible.

"I always thought you were some kind of space royalty to your people," I teased to distract from my concern.

"Am," she muttered, "to Space Fleet. Not to clumsy, stone-footed dirt wallowers." The irritation seemed to revive her energy. She retrieved her tray and demolished the food and water. Then she disappeared into the biocenter.

When she emerged, she gestured at the ZEE I had retrieved. "What is?"

"An obnoxious tourist device, but it's useful. I want to show you something." I gestured to the bars between us. She came over and settled to the floor with me. "Did you know this?" I tilted Jerk so she could see the display projection.

She looked at the map, perplexed. "No. What does mean?"

"Good question. I think our friends have some questions to answer when they come back."

***

Saura and I sat on our cots, watching our jailers finish their meal. We'd agreed to let them settle in and relax in the hope they'd be more amenable to questions. We had to strike up the exchange soon, however, before they darted off again assassinating, spying on warehouses, or whatever they did outside these walls.

Meeroush laid his eating utensils down and straightened his back, flexing shoulders three times the bulk of mine.

"I have some questions," I said.

Gray ears shifted to attention, and the team exchanged a sidelong look. For a moment, I thought they planned to ignore me, then Shoff looked at me. "Ask ZEE."

"It's a bit out of the ZEE's purview," I said. I had placed the thing back inside the biocenter, out of sight, in case she decided to take it back. "Besides, it might set off a security alert."

They exchanged another look, but by the tilt of Shoff's ears she was...softening is the wrong word. Maybe interested was a better description. Meeroush remained cautiously reserved.

"Hey, you're in control," I reminded them.

She glanced at Saura, then back at me. "What question?"

"Why does the Tabi embassy compound sit outside the Diplomatic Zone?"

CHAPTER 33

No Offset For the Trouble

Meeroush regarded me for a silent moment, then came over to my cell and put a hand through the bars. "Give me the ZEE."

Yeah. I would rather not. If he wanted to take the thing, however, he only had to come into the cell and cuff me aside. I retrieved it and carried it to him.

He handed it to Shoff, who had moved to join us. Saura got up and came to the bars as the other female spoke to the device.

"The Grip," Shoff said.

A 3-D image bloomed above the Jerk's surface, revealing a dazzling blue gem set in a delicate silver lacework.

"I saw it from the spaceport," I exclaimed. "What is it?"

"The Whooex Trade Congress," Meeroush said. "The blue structure is the Saalyu, the Financial Congress of the Whooex Union. The silver bracketing houses the Trade Complex. Better to pay attention to the structure arching over it."

A massive, thin black arch soared above the jewel. My memory flashed to the structure I'd seen above the street during their raid on the Carquetchians. "What is that?"

"We call it the Grip. The Endar call it the Bawo. It's the Whooex Union Trade Consortium Security Facility."

I stared at the structure towering above the Saalyu. "They take their role seriously."

"More than you can imagine."

"I thought you said their role did not extend outside the Zones."

Shoff made a sound of derision. "They are in charge of anything related to security for the Whooex Union Trade Consortium and its supporting areas in the Das."

"Your spaceport is the Das?" I exclaimed. The place was legendary for its immensity. It had looked vast when the two Endar hauled me onto the ship, but I never thought— heck, I'd been in the Das!

Hooray for me, Human tourist on the Moneyworld, jeopardizing the future of the Earth Alliance. The thought pulled me back to reality. I looked at the area around the blue jewel and its ugly accessory. The buildings were towering skyscrapers, closely packed together, similar to the financial districts on Old Earth.

"That is the Trade Zone. Next to it sits The Diplomatic Zone, similarly close-packed with trade embassies representing dozens of worlds in each member star association, along with all their supporting personnel." Shoff's disgust was clear. "Everyone inside them burns with the desire to succeed and gain a financial advantage for themselves, their world, or their star association."

I could almost feel the ambition radiating from the image.

There were Humans who burned with that same fire to get into the midst of this quagmire. "So, why is the Tabi Empire embassy located outside that steaming pile of...life?"

"It's a long story." Shoff's ears dropped into wariness, but Meeroush's turned forward and tilted slightly out.

He really wanted to tell it.

I really wanted him to. "Why?"

"The founding members, Rhom, the Endar Primacy, and Jhampoon Coalition, set up the Trade Consortium Compound with the Trade Zone and the Diplomatic Zone. They located it at the edge of

T'lek T'la, in an isolated area with plenty of room to expand. That was two thousand years ago. As other star regions advanced their technologies and gained admission, both the Consortium and the city grew. Twice the city ceded land for Zone expansion. The third time, the citizens of Rhom protested the confiscation of their property. The city had not prospered as much from the Trade Consortium as they expected. In fact, the influx of non-residents, poverty, and crime was a terrible strain on their system. They rejected the expansion, and the Consortium had to restrict the compounds to their existing size. Everyone built upward.

"Five hundred years ago the Tabi Empire established our embassy on the last available piece of land inside the Diplomatic Zone, and T'lek T'la refused to grant the Trade Consortium any more land for expansion."

"But you're not the newest members," I said.

"No. The Xix and Ritto-ssa were admitted after us. They had to share space in other members' compounds. Apparently everything still went well—until tension escalated between the Proambu and the Endar over Scylla Quadrant." Meeroush sighed. "Then, a little over two hundred years ago, the Endar Primacy expressed an ambition to take charge of Consortium security. Most members, including the Tabi, were leery of giving a single member so much control. It went to a vote. We lost."

"Wait. If most members were reluctant, how did that happen?"

"Some members unexpectedly capitulated at the last moment."

"Did they tell you why?"

"No, but we sensed their unhappiness with their choice. Before anyone could organize an investigation into the vote, the Endar asserted their new authority, demanding approval to build their security structure. Again, despite resistance, the vote went their direction." The big guy's ears dropped in a frown.

"They sacrificed their embassy property for one of the Grip's support struts, but the other property they required was occupied by the Tabi embassy. Our ambassador—a true warrior of diplomacy—snatched the opportunity to request a permit from T'lek T'la to relocate our facility outside the Trade Compound."

"We are Tabisee. We do not create problems," Shoff growled defensively.

Meeroush nodded. "The city recognized that. To the chagrin of the Endar, it granted us permission to seek an appropriate property outside the Diplomatic Zone. At the time, the Xix, who were already running most of the medical facilities in the city, also secured an exemption. The Ritto-ssa, who were sharing space with another member, promptly followed suit. Which also provided an opportunity for the Proambu. They took a more drastic action. They closed their embassy and declared they would conduct their activities from the sovereign territory of their ships in the Das.

"The Endar were furious. They blamed the Tabi Empire for starting the exodus. But our move gave them the property they needed for the base of their security tower, so they clenched their jaws and pretended to fully sanction the moves.

"Of course, there were rumbles of protest and threats from them—how they would deny everyone outside the Diplomatic Zone their protection—which we actually welcomed, but knew would never happen. They warned we were putting our people in danger from the citizens of T'lek T'la. But the threat is not from the citizens of this world.

"Newly admitted star associations were grateful for the embassy space the Xix, Ritto-ssa, and Proambu freed up. Poor fools! We are ashamed to this day that we put new and fragile systems into that situation."

"It was either them or you," I said.

His ears tipped back. "You are not allowed to offer that reasoning for us. It is our burden, for the Tabisee to declare, with the appropriate regret."

"I apologize if I crossed a line."

He nodded. "Accepted." He sighed before continuing. "That is easy for you and me to say. Endar, however, continue to resent the loss of control over four member associations and view the situation as instigated by the Tabi Empire. It is one reason they are openly aggressive toward us. But," his teeth flashed in grim humor, "We do not bow to their will. We are free to support whatever policies we choose, unaffected by their influence."

That seemed an odd thing to say. "You think they wield undue influence inside the Zones?"

"Are you listening? Of course they do! We suspect some sort of blackmail, but no one will say. What fool admits to selling out their people for personal gain or to hide personal weakness? They come, they fall victim, they betray, and they leave. The cycle never ends. The Endar gain some hold on them and they bend to their will. We believe the victims do not know how it happens. They only fall into the trap. No one inside the Zones will speak of it, and we are here, beyond it."

"Nothing destroys the power of secrets like exposure to light," Saura said.

"These are proud people," Shoff said. "We suspect some of their secrets are capable of destroying prominent houses and corporations, and harming the economies of whole Star Associations."

"The deeper you dig your grave," I muttered.

The Tabisee outside the cells gave me a sharp look.

"Nothing." Truisms on how far Humans were willing to go to hide their greed and betrayals were not helpful here.

"The fact we support Human membership on the Moneyworld does not help our situation," Shoff observed.

"Where will the EA embassy locate?"

Meeroush looked at me.

Yeah, that's what I thought. We wouldn't be on the Moneyworld three days before the Endar had some of our representatives under their control.

"But that doesn't make sense. If the Primacy can snare the EA inside its influence, why is it fighting our membership? Wouldn't they want us here, under their chitinous thumb?"

"We suspect the benefits would not offset the trouble you bring," Shoff said.

Yeah, I'd pick that one, too.

"And they claim you are telepathic," she added.

I would swear we weren't, but the kid would be proof positive for that argument.

I could suddenly feel the eyes of the whole Earth Alliance Star Association glaring at me in accusation. I glared back in hypothetical defense.

This conversation filled in a bigger picture on who held jurisdiction over what on this world, and the things I was up against if I got out there to look for the kid. The clock was ticking. I had to persuade the Tabisee to cooperate with me.

"The kid—"

The image of the beautiful blue gem and its ugly counterpart disappeared as Shoff turned Jerk off and passed it back to me. "The Cheel will find the young Human."

My heart squeezed with fear. "What will happen to her?"

"Not Tabi concern." She shrugged. "Our mission is to protect the autonomy of the Empire against Endar influence. We will not jeopardize that for anyone or anything." She glanced at Saura. "Schaa drika will go back to the fleet very soon."

Saura hissed at the larger female, but Shoff ignored her as she looked at me. "Vivi Zant, we hope you are not a problem we will remember."

CHAPTER 34

Zephyr Isles

My stomach roils as the scent of oil and cold metal hits my nose. It's not my first time on the docks. Last night I was ordered to sneak around, listening to the workers. Report back what I learned. Workers know dock rats are thieves and spies for organized crime. The long, quick reach of an adult arm is dangerous. We learn to stay out of their range. You must always know what's behind you. If you are careless, someone could find your dead, mangled body in a container on a far colony world.

Tonight is different. Pieter is coming with me. They expect something more from me tonight.

I am afraid. So afraid. As numb on the inside as the cold of the dock makes me feel on the outside. They have warned me. If I get sick and have to return to the ship, Anthy will not eat. I cannot let him cry from hunger again.

We move on the edge of shadow with silence and purpose, through the chaos and cacophony of ships and station shifting cargo, until the sounds gradually change. They are still loud, overwhelming my senses, but now I hear music and laughter, and the smell changes to things I remember from home: sweat from laboring bodies, cooking, drinking. Mama's perfume. Adults are walking all around me. The lights I see on the buildings between the moving, sometimes stumbling, people are beautiful colors.

A shriek from somewhere nearby causes me to bump into Pieter. The sound switches to laughter and Pieter's hand on my shoulder pulls me closer to his side. It reassures me. Makes me feel protected. Normally I would never want Pieter to touch me or any of the other children in my team, but now I lean closer into him and shiver.

The smell of food from the bars is a stab in my stomach. I'm hungry. The older kids have told me that the client will feed me well. The captain insists on it. Maybe even give me some treats to bring back with me. The older kids talk about the things they eat with a glow on their faces. They do not want to talk about the rest. There is no light in their eyes when they look down and turn their heads. We talk about the food a lot.

We walk for a long time—so long I begin to fear Pieter will lose our way back to the ship. But then he stops at a gap between two buildings. His hand on my shoulder tightens. A voice comes from the darkness beside him. Pieter edges toward the sound, drawing me along. Their voices are low, they speak in a language I do not understand. Pieter is looking at everything as he talks. It is dangerous for adults in this place, too.

He crouches down beside me suddenly, looks into my eyes. "You go now, girl," he says—they always call us 'boy' or 'girl' off the ship. No names. Ever. "You remember your team and be a good girl. I will be here, waiting to take you back to them." His hand grips the back of my forearm and pushes me forward.

I see two men walking toward us. They look official and I freeze, my heart drumming.

Pieter, noting my reaction, starts to stand.

"Earth Alliance Space Fleet." The angry, harsh voice cuts through all the noise. Black-gloved hands have Pieter's shoulder now in the same grip that he held me. People clad in police black are coming from all directions, including the alley. The person who talked to Pieter from the shadows grasps me.

This one thing I know: if the space police butt into our business, the ship will leave us behind. They have made it clear to anyone going out on the docks.

Anthy will be gone.

I shake free of the grip on my arm and dodge beneath the reaching hands, slide between slow-reacting adults, and I run.

I thought Pieter was getting us lost, but we walked straight. There were no turns along the way. I run, zipping between adults, bumping one who cries out in complaint. There are sounds of anger and protest behind me. The police are following.

Suddenly, the bulky, slow forms surrounding me shrink back toward the buildings. The voices fall to whispers. There are shouts outside and inside the buildings. Music crashes to silence. The silence in my ears is terrifying.

An angry cry from behind. It is the police, demanding I stop. A booted foot shoots out from the crowd of people who have drawn to the edge of the street. I dodge it and keep running. Running toward the shadows. I work the shadows. They will not find me there. I need to get back to the ship.

Before it leaves me and Pieter behind...

The shadows fall in around me and I move fast. Faster than the shouts behind me. Their sound switches to confusion, frustration. I keep moving, dodging between containers, working my way to the lights and the oil-stink of the docks.

Something is wrong. The sound of men and machines shifting cargo, the ring of metal striking metal, and the glow of plasma repairs is missing. There are other kids from the ship out tonight. If the police got to one of their handlers first—

Sobbing, I run even faster, not caring now if I am in light or shadow. The docks are quiet, all the movement frozen. Only a few people are standing in clusters. The lights seem brighter. Then I see the berth number for our ship—Pieter made sure I saw it as we walked past. The light on the hatch is flashing red. It is a warning of some type, but I don't know what. I don't care. I run for Anthy and my team.

"Hoa!" An adult steps from the shadows on my right. He carries a weapon in one hand. He reaches for me with the other. Behind me, there is sudden screaming. I recognize it from the lash. It is one of the older girls.

The policeman's hand catches my collar. I try to twist away, but his grip makes it hard for me to breathe. I kick at his shin and strike hard armor with the bottom of my foot. It hurts badly. I don't care. I swing my right arm back, over my shoulder and hit the arm gripping me. The grip is not as tight as a crewmember's would be. I knock it away, duck, and keep moving.

Two more police are coming toward me, one from each side. Between them, I can see the stationside hatch to the ship. It has changed. Now it is gray and has the berth number, huge and red, on it: the airlock is sealed.

The ship is leaving without me.

I scream as the police come together, catching me up. They pull me backward, then down. Between their shoulders, I see the lights around the hatch go from red to white and I know.

Anthy is gone.

There are more cries, children's voices swiftly stifled behind me, but I can also hear the voices on the comms of the police who have wrestled me to the dock. There is anger and urgency in their tones.

"...a mining tug on final approach," the anxious voice says.

"I gave orders to shut down all insystem activity," the policeman on my left barks back. He gets to his feet, dragging me with him, then thrusts me at the other officer, who holds me tight.

"It came from the outer system, ser. We couldn't stop it without tipping our hand," the comm says back.

"Well stop it now! That ship isn't paying attention to what's moving out there. It's focused on escaping!"

"Anthy!" I scream as if he can hear me across the vacuum. "Anthy!"

The man lifts a hand in a silencing motion. He is listening intently to a swarm of voices suddenly filling the air from his comm.

The station system begins to boom an announcement ordering residents to return to their living quarters immediately.

"Someone lay a shot across their bow. Make that pilot stop!"

There is a jumble of replies back on his comm. The one I hear is: "They are not responding."

Now it is like slow motion as everything rolls on around me. I see the officer's face in the light. He is angry and frustrated. Our ship will not listen. They will not answer, and the shuttle is moving across their flight path. My heart twists with hope; maybe they will stop.

But I know they won't.

An adult somewhere nearer the outer dock is raging at the top of his lungs. He is cursing Earth Alliance Space Fleet. He says they will get everyone killed.

The officer looks at the policeman who grips me. "Order the stationmaster to close all port shields immediately," he says. He returns to talking on his comm.

The police holds me with one hand and makes his call on the comm with the other. The stationmaster confirms the station shields are lowering over debris-sensitive areas. They don't want the station taking damage from wreckage...

Shields. I look up at the small plasglass panels high above, that let sunlight into the dock during day cycle. Protective shutters are beginning to slide over them, but I can still see out.

I can see the ship. Our ship. The one Anthy is on. I want to be there with him.

Then I see the tug. It is not some tiny lifeboat. It is a great, hulking chunk of metal, and it is moving across the bow of the ship.

It is moving too slow.

The ship plows into it, catching the front corner, causing the tug to swing on its axis. It burrows along the ship's side, its momentum fueled by its weight, and a long, ugly gash opens onto space. Atmosphere and fluids flow out of the tear in a slow fog peppered with specks of debris. I know some of those tiny specks are bodies.

I am screaming now, fighting to go out there. I want to be with my brother. Anthy needs me. The policeman has me by the arm, wrestling to hold me. Other people rush forward to help him.

The shields roll down as a brilliant flash engulfs the ship. I am on my knees, wailing.

I cannot save Anthy.

I am not enough.

***

A slap stung my cheek.

I drew a breath, choked on a sob, and opened my eyes.

"Get up," Meeroush said. "You're coming with us."

CHAPTER 35

Stray DNA

A quick look about told me it was the middle of the sleep cycle for the Moneyworld. Shadowed walls. Black consoles. The only light source in the room appeared to emanate from scattered workstations. The place was too small for an official security operations base inside an embassy but it housed some serious tech. The four black-clad Tabisee working at the various stations did not even react to our entry.

Mathet stood in the open center of the space, in front of a huge, gray-lit wallscreen. With arms crossed and head bowed, he looked like some pensive god of war.

He looked up, eyes locking on me. "Tell me what you know about this, Human."

A slow shift in the light of the screen behind him caught my eye, and I realized it wasn't actually dark; it was gradients of gray. Small particles moved in the darkness surrounding a larger mass that his shoulders had previously blocked. The tiny bits sparkled in a slowly expanding cloud.

Sudden dread flashed through me. "What is that?"

"The *Obega*," he snarled. "It exploded."

Shoff, Meeroush, and Saura stared at the image in stunned silence.

Shit. "I don't understand." I took a step forward to see more clearly. "Why are you asking me? You said it was impossible for the Endar to put me on your ship—"

"You were never on the *Obega*!" Mathet slammed a hand against a nearby console, causing us all to flinch. He glared at me. "Yet our ship is mysteriously destroyed." Thin light burned over hard Tabisee features. He was keeping his fury tightly contained. "What game is the EA playing, Human?"

"None! I swear! What happened? From the beginning, please."

"The *Obega* broke fold at Vasheesh Point to make the course adjustment necessary to continue to the Tabi Empire. When an Endar security vessel approached, hailing it for what they claim was a routine boarding inspection, our vessel exploded."

I recognized the word 'Point' as a Whooex term for a station similar to the EA's Black Rock, only much larger. The first Points out from the Moneyworld were staffed with Endar because of their role as Trade Consortium security. Others were staffed by their local Star Associations.

What to say in the face of such a disaster? "Were people hurt...?"

"It was automated."

That matched what I knew about the ship. I stared at the screen, watching the cloud of debris expand into gray space. Light from the local star glimmered off the pieces of tumbling wreckage, making them twinkle. Amazing how disaster could look so beautiful. The image reminded me of a fireworks display I had seen on a world somewhere. Only these didn't darken. They kept glittering, a cloud of space confetti celebrating the worst day possible for Tabisee and Humans.

"How are we seeing this?"

"A real-time feed from an Endar Talon investigating the incident."

"What caused the explosion?"

"You tell me. I want to know your mission. Now!" He took a step toward me, capped claws bared.

"I swear—" I stammered, Meeroush's hand holding me firmly in place.

A shrill tone pierced the tension.

"Ser, incoming urgent from Consortium Security," a tech announced.

Mathet spat a curse. "Background mask," he snapped as he turned to the screen. He raised a hand and held it motionless while the air between him and the rest of us shimmered and darkened.

The deepspace image disappeared as the High Jerak, his blood-red eyes matching his satin collar, loomed on the screen.

"Captain Waa Silvec." His gaze swept the room. I cringed, though I knew the Tabi mask blocked us from his sight. The red eyes returned to Mathet. "I'm sure Ambassador Ressu has made you aware of current events. Allow me to express my sincere sympathy on the loss of your ship, the *Obega*. We, the Endar Sat Quar, want to assure the Tabisee people we will do everything in our power to find the underlying cause of this tragic incident. However, we have discovered something which seriously complicates your situation."

My stomach lurched with an instinctive sense of menace as he folded his long multi-jointed fingers to rest like some horrible spider on the surface before him. The narrow slash of mouth bowed tautly upward on the ends. "We understand how the Tabi hierarch of security works here. Your division must assess the threat level and sanction any action your ambassador takes." The strip of mouth straightened. "So, we come to you first with our concern."

I imagined claws grating on hard surfaces as everyone waited for the High Jerak to get to the point of his contact.

He paused, straining nerves further, then leaned in, as if to make the encounter more intimate. "Our debris scans of the unfortunate *Obega* have picked up trace elements of Human DNA."

"That is impossible," Mathet stated without a twitch.

"Impossible, indeed. I believe your declaration of ignorance. But what are we to think? We find it difficult to understand why Humans would infiltrate this world at a time when the Consortium is willing to consider their acceptance for membership. They obviously do not consider the repercussions of their actions on their allies in their reckless drive for...whatever they seek."

Mathet did not move or speak.

"Such catastrophic betrayal must be a shock to you. We do not expect you to accept it, unsubstantiated. I have forwarded a file to your embassy, marked for your eyes only. It contains our ship's scans, with locations of the detections in the debris. We do not want you to think we misinterpreted the evidence, and we certainly do not expect you to proceed in your next steps without careful consideration.

"The Tabi Empire is a respected member of the Whooex Trade Consortium, with a reputation for integrity. If you say you are unaware of illegal Human activity on this world, we believe you. I am sure the other members will rally around you in this time of terrible betrayal. It is difficult for the Primacy to understand why the Tabi Empire would choose to ally with such an irresponsible, primitive culture. The association is not to your benefit. Or so it would appear," he added.

"Our choices appear to be in question," Mathet's voice sounded rock hard and emotionless.

"They do, don't they," Seok feigned sympathy. Failed. "It pains me to think we could have prevented this senseless loss had the Sat Quar been more involved in your security. Tabi are good, trusting people. It is regrettable someone would place your Empire in such a position."

I had to admire Mathet and his crew; they remained rigidly nonreacting as they stared at the cold, threatening face. I, on the other hand, trembled with cold fear.

Seok leaned back. "Until our investigation is completed, Whooex Union Trade Consortium Security will consider the Tabi Empire the innocent victim of subversion. If no implicating connections are uncovered, we shall declare this a failed attempt at espionage by the Earth Alliance and close the file. You may go about your Empire's business knowing we are doing everything in our power to protect the interests of our fellow members. If there are further developments, be assured, you will be the first to know." The screen abruptly returned to its view of deepspace disaster, made even more significant now by the High Jerak's threat.

"Do we have the file?" Mathet snapped as the mask lifted.

"We do, ser. No spyware detected. Preparing to move over to a secure work file. Scanning. Again, no tags detected. Transferring through our filters. Done. Sending to lab for comparison to on-file data, request tagged immediate."

Before I could draw a breath the tech sang out, "the DNA is a match to hers, ser."

Mother Universe, I wished things worked that fast in the EA!

As Mathet swung around, looking like a god of war again, I had second thoughts on that.

"Tell me," he said in the same low, controlled voice he had used with the High Jerak, "how your DNA is in the debris of a Tabisee freighter at Vasheesh Point?"

"He ordered me to be put on that ship..." I sensed he would not be any more receptive to my explanation of escaping a Tabi ship into an Endar warehouse now than before.

"Two hundred years we have evaded their treachery. Two hundred years we managed to stay free of their influence! Now it is all undone!"

"There must be something—" I stammered.

"There is nothing! They can claim we smuggled a Human spy off world and programmed the *Obega* to self-destruct if it encountered a boarding threat. We have no defense against DNA evidence!" He scowled as if he wanted to shred everything in sight. "Their scan can only lead to one of two conclusions. Either Humans are working behind the backs of the Tabisee and betraying our alliance with them; or Tabisee are conspiring with Humans against the laws of the Whooex Trade Consortium."

"But—"

"The High Jerak laid down an ultimatum," Mathet continued over my protest, "We must reject Human admission to the Whooex Trade Consortium. If we do not, they will release the scans and accuse us of colluding with the EA."

"But you didn't bring me here! The Rittos and Zeeks know that."

"As do the Endar. It does not matter! The Ritto-ssa and Xix will come under similar pressure."

After what I just witnessed, I didn't care if the EA was rejected for membership on this twisted hellhole. It wouldn't hurt anything but our pride. But I did not want to be the cause of the Tabi Empire falling into the Primacy's web of manipulation. "There must be something I can do to help."

"We do not want your help! The Tabi Empire will make a decision after careful consideration."

"But I can go before the Consortium and explain what happened." I would be forever damned with Humans, but it could save the other star associations from the Endar's threat.

"Further entangling us and other members in the Primacy's conspiracy accusations? Do you think anyone will believe you?"

CHAPTER 36

Glittering Dust

I stared at the sparkling cloud of debris on the screen behind Mathet, knowing it was the last bit of space I'd ever see. It was so disastrously beautiful.

And not quite right...

"What makes the debris glitter like that?" I asked.

"Vivi," Saura's tone warned caution.

"No. Wait. If your ship hulls are light-absorbing black, why does the debris shine so bright?"

A tech lifted her head, ears flicking attention.

"The *Obega* is—was—a light-shifter," Shoff snapped. "Their hulls are highly reflective, allowing them to utilize any available light for their drive systems."

Shiny? "No," I said slowly. "The *Obega*'s hull was black. Death black. Light absorbing black." My heart began to race.

They all stared at me.

"Tabi hulls are reflective." Shoff repeated. "Endar ships are black."

"That could explain why we found her in an Endar warehouse," Meeroush observed.

Mathet scowled. "Check the Endar ships that lifted from the Das the same day as *Obega*," he told Shoff.

"Did not check already?" Saura demanded, her wiry muscles starting to coil with anger.

The Saurubi I knew was firing to life.

Mathet glared.

My partner's ears lowered in fury.

Meanwhile, Shoff worked her personal display, her eyes narrowing as her fingers flicked the air. I clasped my hands to hide their sudden shaking while we waited for her results.

"The *Faulpaxit* left the same day as the *Obega*, returning to the Primacy world Caul," she announced. "It is also a fully automated ship."

"Caul is central world of Endar Empire," Saura said to me. "Is known as Hive."

Shit! "What does that mean?" I suspected, but I really wanted someone else to say it, to make it real.

"Base on the evidence, it could mean Seok put you on an Endar ship to take you to the heart of his power," Meeroush replied.

"Then he knows I was never on the *Obega*! This is a setup! The Endar can't have my DNA. We can expose them! Tell everyone the truth. The Ritto-ssa can confirm how I got here. The Xix can back our story."

"Make no mistake, the Sat Quar has your DNA," Mathet said sharply. "All this means is you escaped their ship and remain here on Rhom. Once he discovers that, he will order the Sat Quar to sweep out into the city in search of you. They will hit us first." He turned his attention to the techs. "Advise our contacts. We have...?"

"The Endar Point, Cromitch Pa, is farther out than Vasheesh Point. The *Faulpaxit* is due to arrive there in twelve hours planetary time," one said.

"Twelve hours. Notify the others. Emphasize discretion. The Sat Quar is not yet aware she escaped, but they are watching us all."

"But his claim is impossible! The Endar never touched my flesh, and the things they used to prepare me for the SAC were on the other ship. Their ship..."

Then it hit me. "My arm. They could confiscate tissue from the hospital. That's where the DNA came from! They found a way to smuggle it onto the *Obega*!"

"Possible plant on ship in courier pouch," Saura spoke up.

"The hospital can confirm if they took my DNA." I felt a surge of triumph. "That's our proof—"

"Proof of what?" Mathet's voice rose a level in volume. "Stupid Human! The spotlight is not on the Endar. It is on you and anyone who has come in contact with you. The Ritto-ssa brought you here, the Xix assisted you, and we sheltered and aided you, as have the citizens of the city.

"The Endar acted lawfully in removing you. Whether to a Tabi ship or their own, whether they filed a report or not, whether they are lying now, it does not matter.

"We can protect our economies by giving in to their demands, or we can deny the evidence and face expulsion from the Trade Consortium. Whole world economies will be destroyed. That is our concern!"

"The Endar threaten blackmail and they win," I said bitterly.

Mathet's eyes flashed fury. "Perhaps for you this is some game." His claws slid out, catching the edge of the counter. The metal surface dimpled under the tips. "We successfully evaded their traps for two hundred years. That is one of the reasons they hate us. Now, because of you, they triumph. They will wield their power to humiliate us at every opportunity. Every vote; every trade decision; every move we make, we will do as they instruct us. It is more than a win for them. The Tabi Empire will never be free again. And now you bury us even deeper with this Human telepath you brought with you! If you suffer an eternity in the Pit of Ballith it will not be enough."

My brain had stopped listening to him at the word telepath.

The kid! How could I have forgotten about the kid? "But they don't know she's here! If we can find her and get her off this world—"

"Fool! You don't seem to understand what you've done!" Mathet snarled. Metal shrieked as he ripped his hand away from the console. "You have destroyed the Tabi Empire's economic independence! It doesn't matter what you say or do. We can reject the EA's membership to buy a little time, but it won't save us. We must decide if we will acquiesce to Endar demands and forever be under their control, or if we will refuse and lose our place in the Trade Consortium."

Not only was I depriving the EA of a place on the Moneyworld and full membership in the Whooex Union; I was costing us our most valuable ally. The Tabi Empire would sever all ties with the EA, isolating us. The fallout beyond that was too overwhelming to imagine.

"Vivi not cause this," Saura said. "*Thief's Hand* was in Proambu space when ghost ship attacked—"

"First Astrogator Syrhas, you will remain silent unless addressed." Mathet ordered without sparing her a glance.

Blue fur puffed with indignation.

"Your orders, ser?" Meeroush asked.

"Take Captain Zant to the Cheel. It is the only way to remove all trace of her existence. The order extends to the child, as well."

"You can't kill an innocent child!" I cried.

"I can do anything I deem necessary to protect billions of other children."

Of course he could. He commanded a team of assassins with the sole mission of protecting the interests of the Tabi Empire.

His attention locked on Saurubi. "First Astrogator Saurubi Cerros Syrhas."

"Ser."

"This issue is sealed and never to be spoken of again under any circumstances. That is the stipulation for your return to rank and position in Tabi Space Fleet per order of Tabi High Command. It is not negotiable. Any perceived violation will bring you the death sentence and the loss of all holdings and title for your family. Do you understand?"

"Yes, ser." She stood at attention, her eyes riveted forward, but her whole body quivered with rage.

"You are ordered off this world immediately, and you will never return here, under any circumstance."

"Yes, ser."

"This is Tabi Empire business," the captain said to Meeroush. "It is not for the citizens of this world to take up at their discretion. Leave nothing to chance."

He meant I should be dead before they turned me over to the Cheel, to prevent anyone with other ideas countermanding his order.

"Yes, ser." Meeroush's grasp on my upper arm tightened.

"Vivi..." Saura looked over at me.

"It's been an honor to serve with you, First Astrogator Saurubi Cerros Syrhas." I nodded curtly.

There was a lot more I would like to have said. Drinks and reminiscing would have been nice.

Beneath Saura's yowl of rage and despair, I heard a discreet musical tone.

CHAPTER 37

What You Can't See

Everyone froze as a life-size hologram of a Frairy appeared in the space between Mathet and the rest of us. It wore a baseball cap, a lime-color lace turtleneck, white foustanella, and beaded sandals.

"What?" Mathet snarled.

"Sheesh! Who pissed in your water bowl?" Duff asked.

"We have no time for this." The captain cast a glare at one of the techs behind him. She poised a hand over the board in front of her.

"Make time!" The Frairy barked, his tone marking the two of them as equals. "This is critical."

Scowling, Mathet lifted his hand to stay the tech's action. "What is it?"

"We need Zant."

"No." The hand started to drop in a gesture for the tech to cut contact.

"Shit! You haven't killed her yet have you?"

"Doesn't matter." The hand stopped, poised. Ears twitched impatiently.

"We have a big problem. We need her."

"Why?"

"Because we can't see the kid."

Mathet's raised arm drifted downward. "What are you talking about? The Cheel sees where it is."

"It does. It sees her. But no one else can. We even had a team with hands on. By the time backup arrived to assist them, they were standing around, looking confused, and couldn't remember why they were there. She wiped their memories."

My mouth dropped open while ears around me slanted forward and out in disbelief.

The Frairy's 3-D image twisted to look at me. "Oh, hey, Flygirl. Glad you're still alive." He turned back to Mathet. "We need her. She may be the only one who can help us bring in this kid. "

"Explain," Mathet snapped at the Frairy.

"Coming through."

"No—"

Before Mathet finished his refusal, Duff materialized in place.

"No," the captain repeated, this time directing the word over his shoulder at two of the techs as they surged toward the Frairy, weapons in hand.

Duff shoved a small mechanism into a baggy pocket and looked around the room again. "You all look appropriately on edge. Good. We need that."

"Are they allowed to do that?" I asked Meeroush, my stunned brain trying to sort out what was happening.

Instead of answering my question, Meeroush snapped a narrow band around my right wrist and another onto his. A wireless hand-cuff. I wasn't going anywhere without him now.

"Well played." The Frairy nodded at him. "It doesn't solve the problem, though."

"Explain," Mathet demanded again.

"The Speakers constantly monitored the kid in the Cheel's Eye, as we agreed. For a day, she drifted aimlessly. Yesterday something changed. She started moving straight across the city, toward the Zones. She even took some public transport. Now she's on the outer perimeter of the Compound. If she goes in, the Cheel loses eyes on. A short time ago, we decided to pull her in before that happened.

"It should have been easy. We were monitoring the whole thing through the Cheel's Eye and talking to our people on the ground. But, when the recovery team moved in to retrieve her, they didn't see a darned thing. Nothing! The Speakers had to give them instructions on how to get their hands on her. She fought them, but things were going okay; we had her. Then all of a sudden, they straightened, dropping their hands, and she took off. We watched it happen! By the time a backup team arrived, the others were wandering around, wondering why they were there. They didn't remember anything about the encounter! Meanwhile, courtesy of the Cheel, we watched her running away!"

"Mindwipe? That's not possible," I said.

Duff looked at me. "Invisible and mindwipe. Should be impossible. Apparently isn't. We have footage." He lifted his hands to expand a personal screen in the air for the rest of us.

A dimly lit area next to the wall of a building bloomed. The kid sat on a stoop peeling a piece of fruit.

But if she was invisible... "How are we seeing this?" I asked.

"The Cheel presence," Duff said without looking away from the image.

I remembered the questions I put to Piika after her declaration that the Cheel was one yet many parts. She said the parts all saw as one. The true impact of her answer sent a jolt of shock through my brain now. Every little blade I had walked past had been seeing me.

I had not appreciated what an amazing aid the plant was until now. The realization forced me to view Duff in a new and different light. Official or unofficial? Covert ops or organized crime? He was something far more than a security-minded citizen.

Mathet's order for his techs to notify the others of the Tabi situation suddenly seemed a bit strange. What the heck were these people up to?

The kid on the viewer looked up, an expression of concern passing over her angelic features as several Frairies moved into view. They walked cautiously, arms out, as if they were herding fish.

Trying to catch something they couldn't see.

She scrambled to her feet, fear touching her face. I had seen that before, out at Idwal. It stung me.

She took a step toward the wall on her left, and the Frairy on that side lurched toward it, too. The others shuffled forward to close off her escape from the other direction.

The kid frowned, perplexed, as if this was the first time she had encountered this problem. She made a swiping motion with her right hand.

The Frairies on that side did not react to the movement.

Smart kid. She was figuring it out from their lumbering approach. She knew they weren't seeing her, even if she didn't understand how they were aware of her presence.

My mind flashed back to the Cheel pool and the Frairy boy—at my outrage when he leaned carelessly against the wall, nearly pinning her leg. He hadn't even known she was there!

As I watched the Frairy team sidle forward, trying to corral the kid, it hit me: the Cheel had not realized there was a problem with the kid up to this point, either. Since its many eyes viewed her, it had not imagined other beings on its world could not.

Two of the Frairy team got their hands on her. My heart twisted with pain at the terror on her little face as she fought to free herself. Other Frairies reached in, snatching at her.

Then her expression went hard. Startlingly, coldly hard.

The five Frairies suddenly straightened. They dropped their hands away from her and looked around in confusion. She dived between the closest would-be captor and the wall and ran. The image shifted, blurred. Her feet running on pavement edged with green clumps of plants flickered in and out of our vision.

The image on Duff's screen returned to focus on the Frairies as another team moved in to help them.

I exhaled a long, silent breath.

"They don't remember any of that. Crazy, hunh?" Duff glanced at me. He didn't sound amused. He looked back at Mathet. "So we thought maybe we should dig a little deeper. Find out what the people who brought her here had on her. The way maybe someone else should have done."

Mathet's lips drew back to expose long incisors. "The Ritto-ssa gave us the location of our missing navigator. They did mention any Human child."

"Yeah? Well, guess what? The Ritto-ssa didn't have a clue what we were talking about, either. No report of a kid rescued from space outside Idwal Station. We persisted, so they checked with their fleet office. Turns out the ship had all kinds of skewed numbers on their life support records. Not a lot, but a little beyond the expected usage of air, water, and food consumption after they added in Zant and the SAC. They went back and drew security footage from the ship's files. Wanna see what they found?"

See what the Rittos had from my time on their ship? Hell yes! I bit back my response.

Mathet was slower to respond. His eyes moved from Saurubi to me before he nodded. Duff pulled a narrow metallic strip from another pocket and held it out.

"Whose?" Mathet asked warily.

Duff cocked an impatient eyebrow. "Ritto. It's safe, but if it makes you feel better, run a check."

Shoff took the chip to a console where she and the tech conferred. The tech ran a handheld device over the chip.

"It reads clean, ser," Shoff said.

"We can view it on something external to our system." The tech held up a small, slotted device.

"Shoff." The Captain gestured to the console beside him.

She set the device on the indicated spot, slid in the strip, and passed her hand over it. A screen blossomed in the air. It showed a view of two intersecting passageways typical of a large, foldspace ship.

"This is from a monitored junction outside the medical facility on the *Baccquey*, the Ritto-ssa ship that brought them in," Duff said.

"Vivi!" Saura exclaimed.

The Tabisee in the room shifted uneasily, their expressions concerned.

"What?" I exclaimed. "I didn't see anything!"

Shoff's ears slanted with impatience. "Humans. Your eyes are too slow." She made an adjustment to the viewer.

I gasped as a small figure, dressed in white, crept around the corner from a side passage. "That's her. That's the kid!"

The figure moved carefully, checking every direction before continuing forward out of monitor range. Shortly afterward, it passed back the way it had come. Time stamps on the footage showed the record had been edited to collapse the time gap as she—the tiny form had to be the kid—passed through the intersection several more times. After the fourth time, her caution disappeared and she walked boldly, as if no one would question her presence. Sure enough, in the last pass, she encountered a Ritto going the opposite direction. It ignored her.

"Wait!" I exclaimed. "The crewman didn't acknowledge her. Were they used to seeing her by then?"

"That crewman has no memory of the encounter," Duff said.

"She walked right past them!"

"No memory. You said the kid hung out in the medical bay with the Ritto-ssa med crew?"

"Yes. She put her hand on the cover and smiled at me while they monitored readouts on the critical recovery unit. They even moved her out of their way!"

"None of the crew remember seeing her."

"Is Ritto visual perception different than ours?" I asked cautiously. I didn't recall any special notes on it in basic species training.

"They have the same visual physiology as Humans, Frairies, or Tabisee. Maybe a faster eye-brain exchange rate than some." Shoff gave me a meaningful glare.

"She can alter memory and perception..." I stared at the video log, my mind wrestling with the obvious conclusion. "But not a recording device."

"She may not be aware the devices exist. Yet. When she does find out..." Duff shrugged.

"And the Cheel? Will she be able to blank it?"

"Too many eyes from too many places, we think. Plus, the eyes have no mental presence of their own. The big problem with the Cheel is that its sight does not extend inside the Trade Compound. She gets in there, we lose eyes. Literally."

What must the brain of the Cheel be like, to coordinate the billions of images it received from all over its world every second?

The image on Duff's device looped back and the kid walked past the Ritto crewmember again. "Where the hell is she from?" I said aloud.

Everyone except Saurubi glared at me.

"That is a matter of considerable concern to us all," Duff said.

"Look, I agree, there's the obvious possibility she's Human, but we are not telepathic. I swear! Has anyone ever heard of a species, anywhere, who can block and erase the memory of its existence from the minds of the beings around it?" Like the Cheel, it was an awesome concept. And an equally terrifying one. The implications—beyond us trying to find her—were troubling on a massive scale. "Can any telepathic species, including the MoMo, do that? Block perception or alter memory?"

"None," Duff said. "That we are aware of," he added.

Yeah, kind of like, how would you know?

"You Humans are always working to change everything you get your hands on!" Mathet snarled as Shoff shut down the viewer. "What have you done?"

CHAPTER 38

The Only One

"Nothing! I don't know," I conceded after taking a breath. "I just contracted to run out a quarantine by taking our cargo to Idwal and picking up a new load. We didn't know what the new cargo was."

The others flinched at the mention of our destination.

"You knew where that was, right?" Duff said. "The problems out there?"

"We shove cargo forward; we don't have to like the destination." I said sourly.

"What quarantine?" Mathet broke in.

"Mandragala Station received a report of slagmander contamination at our cargo's source world, Galray."

"We are aware of that history. What was your cargo?"

"Metal ingots. Picked up at one of their orbital smelting facilities."

"You know—" he began.

"Yes. But the station put us on a forty-two-day quarantine anyway. Accepting the job was our only way to save the *Thief's Hand* from repossession." Why was I doing this?

Because a little kid was still out there in danger.

"What," Mathet asked me coldly, "were you supposed to do at Idwal?"

"Pick up new cargo. The contractor refused to give us the details until we got there." I quickly explained the disastrous incident. "That's how the Ritto-ssa got involved. They pulled the kid and me from the Vasty and Saura from our ship. You know the rest."

"Who attacked you?"

"I don't know. I have never seen a ship profile like it."

"And the contracted destination for the new cargo?"

"Saura says it was Jian Jian," I said. "It's—"

"An EA military science facility," Mathet finished for me.

"That's not an unreasonable destination," I muttered.

"Who contracted you?" He continued to press.

"The cargo owner. Not who we originally signed with."

Everyone waited. I sighed. "There was this MoMo and Frairy..."

All the gray ears tipped in disbelief and the Frairy's twitched.

Mathet closed his eyes and drew a long, slow breath. "You Humans are such fools," he said.

Yeah, in retrospect, maybe. I didn't have enough energy left to defend against his statement. "But we wanted to keep our ship."

Mathet looked at Duff. "What do you know about this?"

"Nothing. The MoMo do their own thing." He scowled at me. "Flygirl did mention contact with a MoMo earlier, but I didn't pay much attention since we had Endar security invading our poker game."

"I don't understand," I said loudly to draw their attention back to the present issue. "If the kid can affect Ritto and Frairy memory, why not mine?"

"Maybe she trusts you because you look similar to her," Duff suggested.

He appeared remarkably calm, considering the situation. In contrast, the furry ears around me were twitching with tension. If mine could have twitched, they would have, too.

"Maybe. Or maybe she can't erase my memory because Humans aren't telepathic!"

"Then what is she?" Shoff asked. Leave it to her to find the core issue.

"I don't know. I didn't recognize the shape of their shuttle, either. But we have to bring her in before the Endar can lay their claws on her!" I said.

"What, so Humans can claim her skills?" Duff demanded.

"No!" His insinuation infuriated me, even though his suspicion was justified. "I don't want anyone to claim her. She's a kid. She should be returned to her people." And their world isolated from Whooex contact.

"Agreed." Saura gave the others a sweeping glare. She understood why I wanted to secure the kid's safety. "But, Vivi, how?"

"Tabisee can move around this place freely. I'll go back out in the torture suit and find her." I could survive a few pinches, bruises, and blisters to save a little kid.

"Even Tabisee have limitations on our activities set upon us by the Sat Quar inside the Zone," Mathet said.

Damn the Endar! As I opened my mouth to protest, a shadow glided across the live feed on the screen behind him and my heart gave a twist of shock. "What was that?" I gasped.

Mathet's ears flicked irritation. "We will not play this game again."

"No! Seriously! Can you replay that last bit?" Mother Universe, please let them have some type of recording system on the feed! I looked at Shoff. "In slow motion? Please."

It appeared the female half of the assassin team had learned that if I turned white and started to shake it might be worth investigating. She looked at Mathet. He grudgingly made a gesture for one of the techs to replay the image.

I watched the shadow darken the lower edge of the screen again. Starlight rippled out and back in along its wake.

"What is that?" I croaked.

"An Endar ship. Skate Class," Shoff replied.

My heart tried to leap out of my chest. "Do you have an image of one?"

"Yes." She made it sound like a stupid question. Again, Mathet nodded.

Her fingers danced in the air between us. A black ship, its lines broken with a profile of sharp spines, formed in 3-D detail on her personal display screen.

Space rippled with the passage of those jagged edges inside my head.

"Vivi? Okay?" Saura pushed at my shoulder.

"No, Saura, not okay," I said. Meeroush gripped my arm as I sagged. "The ghost—it was Endar. They fired on the shuttle at Idwal."

"Not Endar territory," she said in a carefully correcting tone.

"No. But close to! You said."

"Yes." She stared at the screen behind Mathet. "You certain? Grave situation if right. Or wrong."

"I'm certain." The long, skinny, black-clad spacers...

"Why would Endar attack Humans outside Primacy space?" Mathet demanded.

"They didn't. I told you. They jumped into Idwal's grav well and attacked a shuttle. A shuttle that I didn't recognize. They killed everyone except the kid, because the explosion threw her into the airlock and I pulled her inside the ring." My stomach churned at the memory. I looked at Saura. "Did you see anything?"

"Only ship's movement on *Hand's* screens."

"It's the same profile. The same death black hull." The same ripple of starlight in its wake.

"You're saying the Endar destroyed the shuttle and then tried to get the kid?" Duff said.

"Yes," I said slowly. "When they realized she was alive they tried to breach the ring. My guess is the Ritto-ssa ship, responding to the station's distress call, forced them to decide killing her was preferable to letting her fall into other hands." I had only been peripheral damage, along with the facility.

What had been the Endar reaction when that Ritto ship arrived on the Moneyworld, carrying an Idwal survivor? My shipskins were working overtime to control the sweat that drenched me. "The High Jerak questioned me about what I saw at Idwal, but I didn't tell him anything, and he couldn't pressure me in front of the Xix attendant."

"If Endar stalked ship to Idwal and committed act of war to prevent contact, they know something of child," Saura said.

My partner had just hit on a cold truth.

"He ordered you put on a ship to the Endar Primacy," Meeroush said.

"And told me it was Tabi so I would go quietly."

"Even as he put DNA from your medical detritus aboard our ship, to force our submission to their future demands." The tips of Mathet's claws dug into the surface beside him again.

Seok, the clever bastard, killing two birds with one stone. I didn't dare say that out loud or I'd have to explain it.

"They're making a move to entrap the last of the independent votes," Duff said.

"They destroyed a Tabi ship," Mathet growled.

"That too," Duff agreed. "But the big issue right now is what Seok will do when he discovers Zant is not on their ship. He'll turn attention to us and the city. The Sat Quar will try to shut down T'lek T'la."

"They will demand access to all embassies and restrict our activity."

And what activity was that?

"All because of one Human."

"No." It was not all because of one Human. I'd had the help of a renegade Frairy and a MoMo, but it didn't seem the time to point that out. "We have an invisible telepath out there. The Endar know something about her. If they find her first, she'll disappear and we'll never know what they're up to." It hurt to think of the kid as a political object. "They could load the Trade Zone up with spies like her. No one would be outside their influence." I visualized a swarm of tiny, invisible blond angels spreading out like a disease across the Whooex Union.

"You can't kill her or me," I said abruptly. "I'm the only one who can bring her in without creating a big scene and she's the only one who can tell us what the Endar are up to."

"We must move now while have chance," Saura said.

"Major Syrhas," Mathet scowled at her. "This is Planetary Force jurisdiction. Do not presume to tell us what to do!"

"Ambassador on the verge of capitulating to High Jerak's demands," she reminded him sharply.

"We cannot—will not—gamble the future of our people on a bumbling Human idiot." Mathet looked over at his assassin team. "Go with the Frairy squad and eliminate this threat. Others will take care of these two."

"What? No!" I yelled. I had to give him a reason not to kill the kid beyond her being a child. "What if she's not the only one?" I stammered.

That went over well.

"She cannot pass our mechanical security," Shoff said.

"Not now. But you can't anticipate what the Endar will figure out in the future. Then it could be too late."

"There is no guarantee you will succeed in finding her and bringing her in."

"No. But the outcome is guaranteed if I don't: you'll all be hopping around like little puppets on strings, mouthing Endar script."

Ears flattened and eyes blazed.

"Okay, puppets was a bad choice of words," I conceded. "But you'll have to do whatever they tell you. You won't have a choice. This is your one chance to turn their manipulation around on them. Find out what's going on, call their bluff, and force them to back down on their blackmail."

"We can make all the other members aware of the threat this child represents," Mathet declared.

"Then you should do it right now. Because as soon as the High Jerak discovers that you've seen her, he'll shut you down and no one will ever know what happened to you. He'll create a situation—anything! Who's going to argue with him? You'll be dead and everyone will be under Endar control."

Mathet stared at me.

I counted to twenty.

"I know why the Primacy hates you," he said at last. "Humans bring nothing but trouble."

"Does that mean you'll let me help?"

"Do we have a choice?"

It seemed wise to treat that as a rhetorical question.

CHAPTER 39

Going In Facedown

"Well, you'd better decide something quick," Duff announced. "She's arrived outside the security gates to the Trade Compound."

Piika and her little friends were still on the job, helping keep tabs on her with the Cheel.

"What's she doing?"

"Looking around. Sizing things up."

"At least she didn't run straight up to Endar security," I said. "Can you make another attempt to catch her?"

"Sat Quar have the area under heavy surveillance. If we create a commotion it will all be over."

"Tranquilizer dart?" Shoff suggested.

Meeroush's ears dipped slightly forward. "If she is actively maintaining this cloaking skill, it might fail when she is rendered unconscious."

Duff went silent, listening to something beyond the Tabisee chamber. After a moment, he swore softly and turned his back to the rest of us.

The ears around me strained to hear. All I could do was frown.

When he turned back, he shook his head. "We had a team moving up on her, but she slipped into a group of tourists as they went inside the Zone."

"And the Endar reaction?" I asked.

"The guards didn't twitch, but you can be damned sure they have other mechanical monitoring systems that did. As long as she stays inside the crowd they may not notice her."

"If Vivi only one can see child, she must follow inside Zone," Saura told them. "I go with to protect."

A wave of gratitude rushed through me. My partner would never abandon me.

"No." Mathet snapped. "We will not put a Tabi Astrogator at risk."

Saura gave him a glare. "But are willing to eliminate astrogator?"

"If concern for Tabi security makes it necessary." He glared back.

That exchange could go on for a while. "So, how do we do this?" I asked. "Can you port me in?"

"No one ports in or out of the Trade Compound. The transfer system inside is totally independent of any other system on this world and is administered solely by Whooex Consortium Security," Duff said.

"The Endar Sat Quar."

"None other than."

"So, how do you usually do this?" I was sure they ran black-ops inside the place.

"For this, someone has to smuggle you in."

"Smuggle? Are you kidding me?" The thought of smugglers running contraband in one of the most secure places in the Whooex Union seemed ridiculous.

Duff shrugged. "Everybody wants something, and it isn't always legal."

I always thought Frairies were obnoxious but harmless beings. My mind flashed to cigar-smoking, wisecracking Thok and how he'd gotten me and Saura tangled up in this. I needed to slap an "avoid at all costs" sticker on my mental file for all Frairies.

"How long will it take?" Endar security could have the kid in their grasp at any moment.

"We'll get you in."

"How?" No way was I blindly stepping into a plan put together by this bunch. They all had too much to lose, and I didn't amount to star spack in their overall concerns.

Duff cocked his head at Mathet.

"No," Mathet said.

"The clock is ticking, and they are the only ones with sure access," the Frairy said. "I can set things up. We'll pick her up inside."

"And if they try to cut themselves in or go independent on us? No. It's too risky."

"We know their movements. The city monitors them."

"And they know that. They're as slippery as bartok."

"They are our best option." Duff smiled widely.

"Who are you talking about?" I understood they were considering having someone smuggle me into the Zone, but 'slippery' was not a description that lent a sense of security to a plan.

"Ragpiles," Duff said.

"The ones who wanted to eat us and sell our hides? No!"

Mathet gestured me to silence. "They collaborate with the Endar," he continued to argue with Duff.

"Of course they do. They'll do anything for money. That's what makes them useful. They take her in, we use her to locate the kid, and we smuggle them back out."

"How certain are you we can pull this off?" The Tabisee captain asked.

"Mostly."

***

"Half now, half on delivery." The Frairy's voice sounded muffled outside the opaque wall of my container.

I stifled a grunt of discomfort. Making the ragpiles curious enough to lift the lid of the white cylinder was not a strategic move in an already bad plan.

"Not much jing," one of the ragpiles grumbled.

"It's bartok," the Frairy snapped. "We just want it delivered to the embassy kitchen while it's fresh."

"Endar hate bartok," the ragpile said.

"Exactly. They hold it up in inspection until it spoils. There's an important dinner at the K'buug embassy tonight and bartok is on the menu."

"Humans come to eat?"

"Other stuff goes on in the Zone besides trade crap. Deliver it on time or you own a capsule full of dead fish."

"Take now."

"Good. There's a twenty percent bonus waiting if you get it there in the next hour so the kitchen can start cleaning them."

The ragpile grunted something in acknowledgment.

The cylinder tilted forward forty-five degrees, sending the fluid that filled all but the top six inches gushing over my facemask and into my ears. Panic threatened to overwhelm me. I could breathe fine, but the experience of water pooling over my face unsettled me. Liquid is not a space thing.

I felt squiggles of movement as several of the plump, half-meter long, eel-like bartok moved out from between my body and the container wall. Duff had insisted on putting some of the creatures in with me, claiming their tendency to cluster together would explain the dense clump of my body if someone scanned the container. The shapes of real eels, with their thick, writhing bodies, would add to the effect. He said they didn't bite or secrete poison. I remained unconvinced.

"Should deliver to wrong dock," one of the ragpiles said to muffled chuckles after the Frairies left.

A dull thud and a yelp of pain sounded outside.

"Not get paid," another of the other rags said angrily. "Is lot jing! Now move."

I heard a sniffle, then the cylinder tilted further down to horizontal. The eels along my sides squirmed violently past my body as it settled. The movement of the cylinder, however, did not stop. It continued over on its other end, leaving me upside down. The eels squirmed around my legs in the new 'up', but the space was too tight for me to turn. Great. My mask remained in place, but it felt as if fluid would pour in at any second and drown me.

I settled downward, my neck bending under the weight of my body. With my arms pinioned to my sides, unable to relieve the pressure, I fought panic.

"Says other end up," a voice observed.

"Just stink fish. Not work to turn for that. Get in."

The cylinder rocked precariously, and I realized we must now be in some type of boat.

"Endar on extra alert with arrival of Human-things. Do this now before security gets tighter."

"Filthy stink fish."

There were grunts of agreement all around, then silence filled with more rocking and the splashing of water. I dug down into my Marine training to put myself in a brain-numbed state to block my discomfort.

A series of thuds and thumps outside my narrow confines jerked me back to awareness. Pain shot through my neck and spine as the cylinder moved, tilted, and slammed forward to a horizontal position.

The eels had settled around my body during the lull of our passage. The lucky ones squiggled up my sides. The unlucky ones knotted and twisted beneath the weight of my chest and thighs.

The container began to roll.

Shit! I knew what had to happen next. I was still trying to straighten the crick in my neck as the container dropped, slammed another surface, and rolled a few times before coming to a stop. The bartok erupted in a churn of muscular activity. I figured they were pretty much at the edge of their tolerance at this point, the same as me.

"Help lift on cart," a voice rumbled.

"You do."

"Help." The word was an order. I heard another thump and a whimper of pain.

"Use grav lifters," the whimperer muttered sulkily.

"You got grav lifters?" Rumbler exclaimed. "You waste of—"

Seconds later, I heard the solid thud of something connecting with both ends of the container. Panic flashed in me as the force of gravity abandoned the cylinder.

In space, where you know it can happen unexpectedly, because grav systems will occasionally glitch, it's okay. The possibility of grav-ity failure is always in the back of your brain. When you're planet-side, however, you're not prepared for gravity to simply disappear. My stomach lurched with nausea. If I puked in my mask, this whole thing was over.

The wrestling eels went limp.

Gravity returned seconds later and I sucked in a gasp of air to calm my churning insides. The cylinder went into an upright posi-tion again. I pushed my feet against the bottom of the tube and felt the muscular bodies of bartok roll away.

A faint purple streamer of color rolled across the water in front of my eyes.

"Bartok?" There was a note of concern in the rumbler's voice. Ap-parently, someone could read a marking posted on the outside of the cylinder.

"Tried to tell," the whimperer protested.

"Lie!" This time I heard several thumps, accompanied by yelps.

"Problem?" Another voice joined the exchange. Even beyond the muting quality of the container wall, the tone of the boss man was apparent.

Protests and explanations erupted, flowing so fast my translator could not follow them.

The growl of fury the exchange elicited, however, was clear. "If is ruined you pay loss."

There was a stream of whining from two sources now.

"Open."

Open? Aw, no!

Dim light suddenly flooded in around me.

There were gasps as the top curve of my bare head, sticking above the water, caused a stir of consternation. A hand clasped me by the base of my skull and dragged me upward. I managed to grasp the lip of the cylinder and straighten my knees so my feet flattened against the bottom.

A stunned silence hung over us all as I stared into the sheet-covered faces of the three ragpiles.

There was no way I could take on the being whose hand gripped the back of my neck. Its bulk blocked the entirety of my forward view.

"Ah, ah,ah...?" the original whimperer made nervous sounds on my left.

The one standing between them reached out and yanked off my mask. "What is?" he hissed. His rags were amazingly clean in comparison to the grubby ragpiles that bracketed him.

I stared at the three of them, my lower body trapped inside the container and my mind blank.

Red light suddenly lit up the shadows and illuminated the rough stone walls around us. Shrieks and the sound of crashing boxes shattered the silence. The two beings beside me collapsed as a crimson blast struck them. Another glow of red silhouetted the hulk in front of me. I watched the life go out of his eyes as the big guy's hand released my neck.

He teetered and then fell forward, carrying the cylinder and me with him.

CHAPTER 40

Death at the Door

I hit the surface of the dock hard, purple water and lifeless bartoks gushing out of the container with me. There was a splashing sound as some of the contents hit water beyond my head. Without thinking, I slithered out of the tube and followed, headfirst, off the dock.

The cold water was a shock after the warm contents of the cylinder, but I managed to control my gasp reflex as I flailed for something to catch on to. The fingertips of one hand scraped slime-covered rock. I lunged toward it, thrusting my fingers into the shallow crevices of the wharf, and pushed upward to keep my face clear of the water. The lid from the container bobbed, top down, an arm's length to my left. For a second I thought about trying to shelter under it, but I lacked the swim skills to stay afloat. The light source for the chamber was somewhere high above and off to one side, throwing the water directly beneath the stone lip of the wharf into dark shadows, so I cringed close to the rough surface and waited.

A few more flashes of silent, deadly red played over the arched stone ceiling as the attackers finished their murderous task. Seeing the chamber's surfaces and dimensions in the flickers, I realized the place was another ancient stone cistern similar to the one we'd passed through on our way to the Cheel. My toes curled at the thought of how deep the water lay beneath my feet.

The lifeless body of a bartok sailed off the dock to plop into the water a meter out to my left.

"Filthy rot," a scratchy voice said above me.

"Ser?" My translator said the word inside my head, but my ears picked up the creaking, chittering sound in the echoes of the vast chamber.

Endar.

"Leave it all," the being standing over my head ordered. "Let it remind the skulking vermin the Endar Primacy controls what happens here."

A thin, intense beam of light sliced the container cover in half. The clicking above me sounded extremely satisfied as the pieces bobbed on the surface of the water. "We go."

I slid beneath the water and waited, fingers clawed into the cracks until I thought they had enough time to leave. I re-emerged to silence. After waiting another couple of minutes, I worked along the wall to a small jetty and pulled myself up. Eight mounds of lifeless cloth, mixed with dead eels, smashed crates and equipment littered the stone surface.

Red meant the Endar weapons were set to kill, making it pointless to check for survivors. I sighed as I looked around. This place was probably another maze of tunnels. How the hell was I supposed to find the way out with my escort dead?

I should go the opposite direction of the Endar. Unfortunately, I had no idea which way that was.

Realizing the Endar must have picked up the ragpiles' activity on some type of monitoring equipment, I crawled across the surface to the mounds beside the overturned bartok cylinder. Every moment I lingered increased the possibility of someone returning to find me, but if I planned to wander these tunnels as innocuously as possible, I needed something to cover the cobalt blue of my shipskins.

Tazers do not break the skin, so there was no blood on the rag-piles' clothes, and the cleanest ones would make the best disguise. I tugged and pulled, wrestling with the Frairy boss man's body while I vowed to buy a more discreet color of shipskins when I got back to Human space. Gray or nude—or something.

I salvaged several loose garments to envelop my body from head to foot, including a voluminous hood. Flicking that over my head, I stood up and shook the long sleeves down to cover my hands. I nodded once at the biggest ragpile in appreciation for blocking my presence at the start of the raid and saving my life.

Then, skin prickling with the thought of hidden monitors drawing another murderous Endar response, I scurried over to the opening in the wall farthest from the dock and peered cautiously out into a passage that stretched unbroken in both directions. The smooth gray floor looked surprisingly clean, with no dust to indicate which direction the Endar had come or gone. Everything was quiet except for the soft lap of the water behind me. I swore under my breath and rolled back against the wall inside the chamber and steeled my nerves.

I still had a schedule to maintain. None of the people waiting to pull me out of a barrel of purple-blooded fish, except Saura, put my survival at the top of their priority list. I only hoped that if I didn't make the rendezvous, bringing the kid in safely remained their primary focus.

Feeling like a moving target, I took a left out into the hall and followed it to a T-intersection.

The wall in front of me was smooth, finished construction, while the cistern chamber and tunnel walls up to this point were natural stone. Recalling the immense structures I'd seen on Jerk, I was willing to bet I was inside the Zone, staring at the foundation wall of one of those immense buildings. The nice, clean, well-lit hallway also meant someone actually used this area.

Endar? A chill ran over me as I took another left and followed it up to a heavy security door that firmly blocked the passage.

Well, crap. The door had an official look, which seemed a reasonable precaution, considering the ragpiles had access to this area. I doubted anyone would give them an entry code. Which meant I took a wrong turn when I exited the cistern. Cursing under my breath, I turned to retrace my steps.

Two Endar security guards were walking up the passageway, their eyes riveted on me.

I crumpled with my back against the door. Burrowing into the rags, I waited, my only hope that they mistook me for a skinny ragpile and killed me before they discovered I was Human. A cowardly way out, yes, but better than what would happen if they took me alive. I didn't want to think about how my response under torture would add to this mess I had created.

As the chirring, creaking sound of their conversation approached, words began to run through my translation software.

"By the ... fire!" one exclaimed. "What ... are doing here?"

"It ... ill-used," the second one agreed. "Robes ... dirty."

My cringing reaction was genuine when bony claws closed on my arm.

Shiny black-lacquered nails glinted millimeters from my eyes as one caught the edge of my hood and flipped it back off my head.

I know my eyes were glassy with terror as I stared up, expecting an eruption of strange curses or shrills of triumph.

Instead, I met stunned silence.

"By great apocalypse!" the one gripping my arm finally exclaimed. "What happened to scalp growth?"

"How this happen? Who do this?" The exchange sounded heavy with rising concern and urgency.

For a supposedly non-existent language pack in my head, my chips were doing a strangely proficient job of interpreting Arpi since my arrival on this world.

The Endar who held my arm pulled me to my feet with surprising gentleness. "Are you injured, Minder?" he asked as he leaned over me.

What? I had expected them to bash my head against the wall, but they were only concerned with finding me in that location and in that condition.

The shudder that ran over me, standing so close to them, only added to an effect they seemed to accept without question. "Someone has failed their task," one hissed.

"Careless," the other one agreed. He placed the hood back over my head.

"Bad time," the first one creaked. "Who is in charge of Minder division?"

"Walglike."

There was a long moment of silence.

"No report of missing Minders, but concern over some intrusion at entry post..."

"Such carelessness can greatly damage a clan," the Endar gripping my arm said.

"But good for clan who makes the fix," the other countered.

"High Jerak Seok will elevate Clan Veragtelike."

I heard a soft clatter of chitin surfaces and wondered how high in status Clan Veragtelike would soar if I didn't escape these two.

"Do not put out security alert at this time. Could be viewed as distraction. Call Captain. Let her decide." The guard tried to position me to face the door.

How was it these beings, who hated Humans so passionately, were reacting so counter to what they should? My mind spun with disbelief as long fingers reached past me to key a code into the pad on the door.

I felt sure the Endar held control of the space beyond. If I entered, chances were high I would not come back out. Worse, the Endar would discover everything I, and the others, had done.

I turned, trying to push past them, to run back down the corridor, my thought being they would consider dragging a dead, escaping whatever-they-thought-I-was before the High Jerak adequate enough to elevate their clan over the of risk of losing me completely. Again, cowardly, but I knew dead, for me, was preferable to what I faced once they figured out who I was.

It was like pushing against some tall, deep-rooted planetside growth. The Endar did not yield.

A hand gently pulled me about and guided me through the door.

CHAPTER 41

The Strategic, Fastest Route

The Endar hustled me along a passage similar to the one we'd just left, except both walls were finished material now. My heart leaped painfully when they pulled me into a notch in the wall. If it was a Consortium teleportation station, I was done for.

I waited for it to scream an alert as it keyed on my Human DNA.

Instead, it turned out to be a high-speed lift that enclosed us in a field of thin blue light and whisked us upward.

"Cannot access minder aerie from here," the second guard said after a moment of silence.

"All Sat Quar are moving to positions," the one clutching my arm said. "Must move by strategic fastest route. We accessed lowest, so must go up central shaft to Minder base." It felt eerie hearing their conversation carried out nearly a half-meter above my head.

"We will report late to posts. There is no honor in late."

"This is priority. It will elevate clan," came the reply.

While the two fretted over what appeared to be a delay in getting to their assigned positions, I fought my way through stunned confusion. It was obvious these guards had mistaken me for someone else. Was it possible the Endar had Human clones inside the Grip?

Could they have actually cloned me from the genetic material in my lost arm?

Would the Xix Nation let them do that? Maybe they weren't given a choice. The hard noose of the Endar Primacy would be tightening on their neck in the same way it was closing on the Tabi Empire.

It was impossible for the Endar to have cloned me; reason pulled me back from the dark edge of horror. It took longer than a few days to get a clone moving and functionally responding at the level these two seemed to expect. Then again, maybe that was why they didn't seem to expect much of a reply to their questions.

The thought made me lightheaded. I moved a foot to brace myself and got tangled on my trailing hem. The Endar on my right caught my shoulder and lightly supported me. If he had known who I was, the claws that held my flesh would have sunken deep into me. Instead, he maintained my balance as our upward movement came to a stop.

The hood hid the fear that locked my expression, but it also blocked my view of the area around me. All I could see was a narrow bit of the floor in front of my feet. The sight, when we stepped off the lift, was enough to take the last bit of my shallow breath away.

It was beautiful.

Of course, everything was black. It also had smoky, semi-transparent tracks shot through, with veins of gold and dense black swirls that twined through its depths. It looked as if we walked over a solid surface at least two meters deep. An occasional glimmer of light glided through its depths.

I wondered if we were in the lower level of the Saalyu, but the color of the décor was all wrong for that piercing blue exterior, and, considering the animated way one of the guards was now talking on his comm unit, I was pretty sure I knew where we were.

Inside the Grip.

These Endar seemed to think I was a prize to elevate their clan. The sense of urgency I got from them also indicated they thought something had gone very wrong somewhere else. For that matter, so did I. But, if I held my silence and listened, I could pick up some useful information.

Sharing it, once they discovered my true nature, would be a different matter.

Every step became an effort to move without tripping over my robes as my escort whisked me along. We came to a two-meter square of shining black slab. There was no sound except the creak of leather as they positioned us all on it. It took a long moment for me to realize we had begun to rise upward again in the darkness.

It was difficult to judge how far or fast we moved without a sense of motion. I locked my eyes forward on a spot of light across from us that I thought was stationary. It swirled down and away, and I realized the plate we stood on was spiraling up and around the sides of an immense, dark tube.

Lights in the darkness over deceptive distances are not unsettling for a spacer. We see them every day. I fastened my eyes on the next light above us with no idea whether it was a massive, illuminated opening or a tiny fixture. It swirled by and fell away fast, forcing me to find and lock on another one. I did it over thirty times before one fell into view and did not drop downward. Our upward motion slowed and the light grew larger as we moved sideways toward it. By the time we stopped, the square of illumination was over ten meters high and wide, and my knees felt rubbery with the realization of how high and fast we had risen.

We stepped through a curtain of light into a broad, black-walled but brightly-lit hallway.

"Humans have arrived at Pashmikt." My chips identified the name of the space station above Rohm. "They are passing through security," one of the Endar said.

"Vermin," the other responded. "This event will not be for their success."

I kept my face buried in the shadows of my hood to hide my scowl.

"They are doomed to failure." The first one made a rattling sound I guessed was a laugh. "They will go back to their dismal hole in the universe in humiliation to await their demise."

Rejection hadn't brought our demise on our first or second bid for membership, why should they think it would work this time? Assholes. They were gloating over Human demise while carefully whisking one through the halls of their security stronghold.

Clearly, they did not think I was Human. As obvious as that seemed, it hit me so hard I almost stopped walking. If they didn't think I was Human and I wasn't a clone, what did they think I was?

Memory of the kid hiding behind me as we stood in the shadows of the public ring at Idwal, flashed in my mind. She knew who those lanky figures outside that airlock were. She feared them. Now she was running into the Zone toward them. Why? I tried to disconnect from what I knew about the situation and think from her point of view. What had changed? Things had gone wrong and she ended up stranded and alone on this world. If the Endar were the one thing she was familiar with, perhaps they had begun to look like a refuge.

The memory of how hard I fought to get back on the doomed pirate ship before it fled the Zephyr Isles flashed in my mind. I hadn't cared about anything except getting back to Anthy.

If it was the only life she knew...

But why had it taken so long for her to make her move?

What would a kid on an unfamiliar world do?

Hell, I was on an unfamiliar world right now. What had I done?

Unsuccessfully tried to lay low until I got a sense of the place.

Even though Endar controlled the port, other distractions, like the immensity of the place, might have overwhelmed a small child, making her miss their presence there. And Duff said they didn't have an actual, official presence in the city, which would make it difficult for her to find them there. She had lurked in the outer city, staying hidden from everyone for months. Then she suddenly ran in a straight line for the Zones, toward the Endar.

Maybe she was simply tired of being on her own, tired of running and hiding. I had not sought out the Tabisee, but a part of me felt relief when they snagged me. They were a familiar thing in an unfamiliar world.

But she had not made contact with the Endar at the entrance to the Zones. She had chosen to sneak inside. What if she was looking for someone? What if something snagged her attention—confirmed a presence she wanted to connect with strongly enough to brave the Endar and their security.

Now I had discovered the Endar were immensely concerned, but not surprised, to see a Humanoid wandering the passages below their security structure, all while they gloated over Human's demise. Numb with confusion, chilled and sweating with apprehension, I trudged along in the company of two Endar who, I was sure, would gut me if they discovered what I truly was.

I had to escape, to find Saura, Duff, and the others. Tell them what I had learned. But at the moment, the chances for escape weren't looking good.

Endar Left was not taking whatever communication he was receiving very well. He hissed and spat, demanding "someone arrive to take it off their hands." That "their assignment was not to escort soft ones."

I think most beings can feel a tug of empathy for another species dealing with bureaucracy; it seems like we all pull from the same employment pool there. Meanwhile Endar Right renewed his grip on my upper arm. The longer the one-sided conversation continued, the tighter his grasp became, until, even with my shipskins hardening to disperse the pressure, it was all I could do to bite back a protest.

The kid's unprotected arm would have fared much worse.

Our pace had slowed during the exchange. Endar Left ended his communication and spat a few untranslatable words in obvious fury. "We will take to threading floor."

That led to a brisk, silent walk.

Finally, we stopped before a light-rimmed triangle in the wall. One of the Endar passed a hand over a panel beside the door and we passed into a narrower corridor.

"Ordered to positions," Endar Left said. "Late arrival will dishonor clan."

"Soon. Explain situation again. We must return the Minder to Threading Central M'Faiya. Honor to clan is assured." Despite the confidence in their reward, the two picked up the pace until I was jogging to keep up. I had to lift the robes clear of my feet to avoid tripping over them, making an occasional flash of cobalt footwear inevitable. Luckily, my escort was preoccupied and we did not meet anyone coming toward us as we rushed along.

They pulled me to a stop before another sheet of light doorway. It was the first opening we had come across in the smooth span of wall. Endar Right's fingers stroked a meter-long vertical plate beside the entrance. I heard a rasp of Arpi from some remote source. My captor made one sharp noise back. It did not sound friendly or respectful.

Then we stepped through into a corridor full of light and mild floral scent. Both my escorts made a noise that sounded of disgust, but something inside of me unknotted. This did not feel like exclusively Endar space.

The corridor widened ahead of us. The wall on the left continued on, but the one on the right ended. My escort picked up their pace even faster.

As we swept past the right corner, a huge space opened before us and my mind blanked with shock.

CHAPTER 42

Thousands of Lights

The room was massive and brightly lit. The ceiling high above—why did everything here have to be on such immense scale around here?—was a honeycomb of thin, angular partitions that glowed with a golden tone. The partitions looked huge, slightly irregular in pattern, and translucent. Beneath them, in the space above the activity on the glistening white floor, thousands of tiny lights filled the air. Most were pale yellow, but scattered among them were others that burned a more intense white. Many, mostly in the highest reaches, were varying shades of darker yellows and golds. A few were brown, dull, but still visible. The lights did not blaze, yet I could see them individually if I focused. Toward the center of the room, pale threads formed links like spiderwebs between the bright ones. It gave those areas a glow, as if I gazed into a galaxy swept clean of all dark debris.

The sight was stunning, but that was not what caused my heart to stand still.

In rising, tiered circles beneath the lights lay glistening white, oblong boxes similar to suspended animation chambers. They tilted upward on one end, making their contents visible from the outer edge of the room where we stood. Inside the ones closest to me, sleeping on pillowy, golden interiors were what appeared to be pale, blond Humans.

I stopped walking.

My escort gently nudged me forward.

As I moved along the edge of the room, my attention remained locked on those SAC-like chambers. I watched as two Endar in crisp white coats, accompanied by a white-robed Human, walked to a chamber on the second tier. One of the Endar adjusted some settings along the chamber's side, and the Human inside it sat up. The attendants removed sensor pads from its head, then assisted as it climbed out of the SAC. They guided the Human accompanying them in to replace it. As an attendant led the newly removed being away, the other proceeded to reattach sensors to the replacement.

My mind flashed to the conversation with the Tabi security team, when I asked why they were in the Endar spaceport warehouse. How they were monitoring it for smuggled cargo...

I sensed a sudden change in the atmosphere of the room. Instinct made me tuck my head deeper inside the cowl of my robe.

Curiosity made me peer back out.

Atop the three circles of the mechanical mountain sat what appeared to be a workspace surrounded by floating virtual screens. A Human stood its center. Despite the distance, I knew he was staring right at me. I couldn't see his expression, but his posture said he was not happy with my presence.

Of course. I was a non-telepath and beyond their influence. Maybe that was a good thing. Or not. I couldn't tell him to resume whatever he was doing and ignore me.

Up there in his tech nest, he probably was not used to others 'telling' him to do anything, anyway.

The figure ducked down among the screens.

Meanwhile, we'd come to a stop, and my escort was having a contentious discussion with a leather-clad peer who must have represented security for the area. I pulled my focus back in time to see a new Endar in a white coat approaching from deeper in the room. Its coat stretched tautly over layers of black leather. They were nowhere near as thick as the High Jerak's.

He waddled briskly up to us.

"M'Faiya," my escorts acknowledged it. My translator didn't interpret the word, but it came through with a tone of respect, confirming he held some rank.

As expected, the new Endar officiously demanded my escorts' credentials and the reason for their intrusion into the middle of a critical operation.

"We found one of your charges wandering in the lower tunnels, M'Faiya." Endar Left pulled the hood off my head.

Intense red eyes flicked over my bald head and locked on my face. "Contract and pod number," the lab-coat-over-leather Endar demanded.

I had no answer for him.

"Is it damaged, M'Faiya?" Endar Right asked. "We discovered it outside our walls, cringing in fear against an entrance in the base tunnels. It appears ill-used."

"We found no report filed on a missing Minder, so we brought it to you," the other half of my escort added. I wondered if that was how smugness sounded in Arpi.

"Do you insinuate my division is ineffective or incompetent in some way?" The leather-layered Endar made a hissing sound. Two more Endar guards sauntered over from the space along the wall to stand behind the M'Faiya. They squared off as if they were ready to physically engage with my escort.

Two groups confronting each other for honor and prestige: I guess every species has them.

It seemed a good time for a soft Human to get out of the way and let them sort things out. Before I could move, however, the M'Faiya put his hand on my bare pate, the razor edges of black claws settling dangerously close to my eyes and ears. It could have easily plucked my head from my body. Instead, it tilted my face up to stare into it.

"Scan this creature," he snapped.

Not good.

A lesser lab-coated Endar carrying a small device came across from the lowest row of white chambers. With the scanner poised, he lifted my left arm and flicked up the sleeve of my ragpile robe.

Seven Endar stared at my cobalt blue shipskins.

The fingers on my skull tightened. "Scan it!"

"There is nothing, M'Faiya," the Endar holding the scanner over my wrist announced.

"A spy," the M'Faiya hissed. "Alert High Jerak Seok." He released my head and turned to my escorts. "You did not check this thing to confirm what you had?"

"It is forbidden to touch the Minders beyond rendering basic assistance," Endar Left protested, the anticipated disgrace of a rival clan crumbling around him. "We could not know!"

"This is not Minder-wear," the M'Faiya plucked at the shoulder of my robes.

"Perhaps the coverings are part of the assault perpetrated on this Minder..."

"It is not a Minder!" The M'Faiya caught my upper arm with hard fingers. Before I could flinch, it ran the foreclaw of its other hand slowly down my bicep.

The robe shredded, but my shipskins hardened to dissipate the pressure from the sharp tip. They remained intact but the pain nearly took me to my knees.

"This is Human clothing worn by their spacerpeople, you incompetent dung-dwellers. You should have called for a handler who knew what to look for in a Minder. You bring this enemy spawn into the heart of our operation and interrupt me at this critical time! There will be severe repercussions."

The M'Faiya released me and I clutched my forearm with my other hand. The shipskins had protected me from a flayed muscle, but the resulting bruise would be wide and bone-deep. I panted, trying to focus on anything that would distract me from the pain while they continued to argue.

My desperate eyes found a doorway in the wall a short distance past the opening through which we had entered. I stared at it, knowing what I'd just experienced was a mere prelude to what the High Jerak planned for me. There sure as hell was no hope of him changing his mind and parading me before the Saalyu now. I had seen too much.

An Endar security guard walked through the door, a white-robed child tagging along behind him.

Holy shit!

My tiny angel stopped in mid-step. Her escort paused and said something, but she ignored him as she stood, rooted in place, an expression of uncertainty rolling across her features as her eyes swept the room.

The process of changing out Humans in the chambers, which had continued while the Endar surrounding me argued, came to a stop. The three Humans scattered across the levels turned to stare at the kid.

Their Endar handlers, unaware of her arrival, chittered at them impatiently.

The kid's eyes had moved over to me. They widened. Narrowed. She looked back at the others and frowned.

The three blond people suddenly lost interest in her arrival and returned their attention to their Endar attendants. At the same moment, the guard who had entered with the kid looked around the space in what I interpreted as confusion, then backed slowly out the doorway and left.

The kid had erased memories again. I saw her do it. She knew I saw her, yet, she didn't erase me.

Mother Universe! While she was erasing memories, why not include the seven Endar surrounding me? Idiot kid!

I jerked my chin in a gesture for her to leave.

Endar Right's attention snapped to me. "What are you doing?" he demanded.

I shook my head, feeling pretty confident that, even though she was in plain sight across the room, he could not see her.

By now, I was fairly certain the Endar were not real telepaths. They had driven the MoMo off their homeworld because the jellyfish had the skill—a skill which presented a threat to merchants, bankers, and negotiators who wanted to do business on the Moneyworld. The MoMo would have fought the eviction and won if the Endar shared the skill.

So why in hell would the Primacy risk using telepaths who might manipulate their minds? No sane species would do that.

The image of the hostile, glaring figure at the top of the tech pyramid flashed in my memory. Were the people in those white robes slaves, accomplices, or the true manipulators here?

"The High Jerak orders the prisoner and its escort to his private interrogation chamber. He wishes you to continue with your own work," the security officer behind the M'Faiya told him.

The M'Faiya waved a hand in dismissal. "Reports. I want reports on all of this from you."

More black uniforms had emerged to dominate the area around us. One moved up on my right, cutting off my view of the kid.

At least for now, she was able to move about, erasing memories. For me, it looked as if my time was up.

Endar Right and Left vibrated as the new guards enclosed us in a wall of security black and herded them, with me in the center, back into the maze of silent corridors and spiraling lifts.

CHAPTER 43

Experimental Subject

The High Jerak's private interrogation chamber looked unpleasantly similar to any well-equipped laboratory with its mechanical testers, glowing specimen containers, and cluttered work stations.

It was not the sort of place I wanted to be, especially with him standing at its center.

A hard shove sent me stumbling inside.

Seok's hand snapped out, catching me by the throat. His long fingers wrapped almost twice around my neck as he lifted me off my feet to stare into my face. "The Vivi Zant Human." His grip tightened until I felt my heart punching beats inside my chest. My fingers pried at his boney hand as the pressure in my head mounted.

Yeah, I should have let him kill me right there, but in moments of mortality, the will to live usually overrides everything the brain reasons.

"It is good you are here." Though his face was nearly against mine, I did not feel his breath on my skin. "I suspected something was afoot when the ship signaled an error in the life-containment area. We could only wait until the *Faulpaxit* dropped out of fold-space to investigate. That is yet several hours away. This is better. I have many questions and it will take time for the Hive to wrest you away from me." He released me and I fell limply to the cold white floor.

I curled there, staring at the bases of strange, menacing equipment as I struggled for breath.

Behind me, I heard a rattle of armor against chitinous limbs as Seok transferred his attention to the guards who had brought me inside the Grip.

"You are a disgrace to the Empire," he told them. "The fool who nominated you for the Sat Quar will know the cold darkness of the Endtime before this day closes. Your living families, back three generations, are sentenced to public death by the flyss."

I can confirm firsthand Endar guards do emit a bad odor when a merciless commanding officer sentences them to terrible fates. Choking on the sulfurous scent, I tried to squirm away.

Something hit the floor in front of my knees. For a moment, I thought the High Jerak's foot was blocking my retreat. Then I saw it.

Emitting a most un-Marine-like squeak of horror, I scrambled away from the guard's head, oozing yellow liquid, as it rolled against my shins. The eyes blinked once—I swear they made a clicking sound—then stayed open. At the same time, there was another sharp-scissor snip above me. Something heavy and liquid struck the side of my thigh and I heard another dull thud behind me.

I froze, too terrified to move. And saw the kid, huddled against the wall in front of me.

She looked at me, eyes wide with terror, and lifted a small, trembling hand, palm outward, as if pleading for me to stay silent about her presence.

She crossed a massive city, walked into this stinking hellhole, performed her hoodoo on the demons who occupied it, then followed me into a hopeless situation and appealed for my silence?

Well, hell. I stared back at her, helpless to protect either of us from what would come.

"Two of you. Remove the trash. The other two, get this cringing insect up." The High Jerak stepped back, blocking my view of the kid.

Talons pulled me up and held me so the balls of my feet barely touched the floor.

This was the nightmare scenario the Tabisee had warned me about. The Endar were going to rip my brain apart and know everything and everyone I had interacted with, here or anywhere in my past.

"Where is the child you stole from us at the Proambu facility?" Seok asked. "Her body was not in the debris."

He didn't see her, three meters behind him, against the wall.

"I didn't steal anything from you," I rasped. "I rescued a survivor from a ship your people destroyed."

His hand flashed forward, and I shivered at the light touch on the muscle at the back of my neck. He leaned in close. Whispered. "I know the child did not wipe your mind. You could not have answered my question just now if she had."

Yet he didn't see her right here in the room with us...

He straightened away from me. "Do not test the Endar Primacy's resolve in this matter. Where is the child?"

When I remained silent the claw slowly pressed into the flesh above the collar of my skins. "Where?"

I might have whimpered a little. Maybe my feet thrashed once.

Now that he had moved closer to me, the kid was back in my visual range. She cringed, her eyes locked on me. I tried to pull my reaction together and compose my features, but I didn't do too well.

Her little features hardened with resolve as she tensed to step away from the wall.

"No!" I gasped.

The High Jerak thought it was my answer to him, but the kid settled back, her expression tight and frightened. She couldn't touch my brain, but it appeared she understood the context: she shouldn't reveal herself to these bastards.

Warm blood trickled as the claw pressed deeper.

"You have no right to lay claim on any Human!" I gasped.

The pressure lightened, as if my torturer was surprised at my response. He withdrew his hand and took a step backward. Stared at me.

For a moment, silence and private pain reigned.

"Lirilune is not Human," he said.

"Liri—?" My brain stumbled on his words.

"The child. Lirilune. She is not Human," he repeated.

"So you altered her genetic codes. It doesn't mean—"

"The Makima are not Human."

Makima? "But..."

"But they look Human? Indeed they do. It is possible you once shared a common origin. No more. They are not Human; we are sure of that." He cocked his head in what I took as a mocking gesture, inviting me to pursue the statement.

It wasn't necessary. I got his drift: they had experimented on our two genetic materials to compare them. "You kidnap—"

"No! You kidnap! Zam Fiella is a world inside the Endar Star Association. Its residents claim the protection of the Primacy. The Ritto-ssa ship logs do not record her rescue. Where is she?"

I opened my mouth to say something, then closed it, my brain churning with all the things that had slapped it since leaving Mandragala Station. This situation went beyond a damaged ore processor and a few murdered people.

Seok watched me, waiting.

"I'm guessing their world is in a star system close to the Proambu processing facility," I finally managed. "That's why you're contesting Proambu claim on that adjacent area of space. You don't want them anywhere near a world full of telepaths—especially with the Primacy in charge of security here on the Moneyworld."

"Humans have such an annoying ability to connect random bits of information and arrive at correct conclusions."

"Anyone could figure that one out," I said, goading him.

I must have hit a sensitive spot beneath all the leather because he twitched. "But no one else will, because they will never know the Makima world exists," he said. My translation software actually blinked a yellow hostility-level warning in my left eye—something it hadn't even done during my interactions with Mathet or Shoff. "No other species besides Humans goes blundering through the galaxy, invading other peoples' star associations, digging into things that don't concern them."

No one else except the MoMo...

Well, Sonnofabitch! I must have a sign nine meters wide on my back declaring 'the universe's biggest patsy.' His Frilliness and that bastard Thok had reeled me in like an asteroid in a tractor beam—probably manufactured the whole quarantine situation. And I had helped them along by getting into a fight with Dallas Ellerby, which sidelined me long enough to prevent us rejecting their offer.

I was an idiot.

Being an idiot was not illegal. It was just extremely painful when you realized it.

"I did not invade your territory," I told him.

"You were there to assist in a criminal act against the Primacy. Your complicity forced us to destroy valuable Primacy assets. And now you are here, on a world where your species is specifically banned, interfering in things that do not concern you. Humans! You disgusting vermin insert yourselves into everyone's business. Always interfering. Tampering. Always trying to change things."

That was true. Sorta. I even understood how some of those things annoyed them. But, if the Endar Primacy had a problem with us, there were avenues to address it. As far as any criminal acts were concerned, my being here on the Moneyworld was accidental. Their actions at Idwal were a direct result of cold, murderous calculation.

The large white room with its reclining rows of fair-haired people flashed in my mind. The guards had called me a Minder...

"You're using telepaths to spy on other members of the Consortium!"

My translation device didn't tell me if the hollow sound he made was a laugh or a hoot of scorn. "They are not only telepaths; they also have the marvelous ability to perceive another being's thoughts, undetected. They are the perfect tool, naïve and living on a world so isolated they only know what we tell them. Yes, we use them to target individuals with potential influence in the Consortium. They sweep the Zones, looking for despicable, devious thoughts and behaviors—which further reinforces what we tell them about the people they monitor. The filthy, devious things people do here! The Minders glean information and channel it back to the room you saw, where someone evaluates its usefulness. It takes many Makima to cover the number of potential candidates inside the Consortium. They are simple, disposable conduits sucking up information for the vast complex system behind them."

I glanced over at the kid. She was staring at the High Jerak, her expression a mixture of horror and pain, and, I realized, as a citizen of a world inside the Endar Primacy, she probably understood Arpi.

She had just heard some terrible things.

She was young and didn't deserve this pain. Unfortunately, the universe is a harsh place, and the young are often caught on reality's front line.

"The Earth Alliance is arriving onworld at any moment," I raised my voice to draw her attention. I had no idea if she was equipped with translation hardware for any other languages, but I thought if I could get Seok to say something and she understood it, she had a chance of getting out to safety before he discovered she stood right beneath his flat gray nostrils. "They'll arrive at the Saalyu soon. I demand to speak to someone from their delegation."

I gave her an intense glare, willing her to understand: if she could find the Human delegation, she could get help.

"You think the Primacy will let you go after what you've seen and heard? We have a better use for you. You will spend the rest of your limited days knowing Humans will never have diplomatic status here."

"Because you'll blackmail the other members to vote against them!" I blurted. I had to keep his attention focused on me.

He took a step forward, his right hand coming up, fingers clawed as if to slash at me. "That is why Humans will never be part of the Whooex Trade Consortium," he hissed. "It is why we have resisted your membership from the beginning. We don't need your endless, infernal interference! We don't need your—how do you say it—your 'white knight' to ride in."

Especially considering what they were doing.

"Besides," he continued. "It is the members' own weaknesses that trap them." The layers of leather creaked as he dropped his hand. "We do not force them into their bent, deviant, unscrupulous behavior. It becomes their choice to preserve the lie."

"You're breaking Whooex Union laws you're supposed to protect."

"We are protecting the Primacy against the weakness and decay surrounding it!"

"Why? Why should the Primacy care what the other members do?"

"The weak and the corrupt cannot rule effectively. Their depravities make them vulnerable. We will carve the decay from the Whooex Union of Stars and make it strong."

It looked to me as if the Primacy had a few depravities of their own. "You think you can control the Whooex Union? Well, don't hold your breath." I didn't know if the phrase held any relevance to him. "No one will accept it!"

"They will accept whatever we tell them once Human influence is gone and we finish crushing the few foolishly hopeful, errant strays. We should have destroyed Humans ages ago, when you were isolated to one miserable planet and no one else knew you existed. The names of those who failed to put the Endar Primacy first in their duty are no longer a part of our glorious history. You are an inconvenience that will soon be remedied."

"You can't go to war with another Union member!"

"Not openly," he agreed. "That is why I cultivated Lirilune. She is the jewel of my personal project. Her abilities go far beyond other Makima. The ones in the monitoring center, the Minders, search among the influential minds inside the Trade Zone day and night, looking for transgressors. They submit those potential targets to the Threadmaster . He can see the links between Whooex members and potential effects. He generates possible lines of attack, which enable us to secure the member's cooperation. "

All those thousands of lights out there; they must represent every influential Whooex citizen inside the Consortium. All with a Makima spy peeking into their brain, evaluating their thoughts and activities, and submitting them up the chain of blackmail. The brighter ones inside the nebulous clouds of webs must be the targets of the Threadmaster.

The image of the blonde being staring down at me from the perch high above flashed in my mind.

But the Endar didn't have control over all the Trade Consortium members. "Their range is limited," I said, "Otherwise, you'd have control over the Tabisee and the others."

"You think you are so clever, Captain Zant. Yet, you, single-handedly, have brought down your allies. The Tabisee are under our influence; they simply have not accepted it yet. The same with the Ritto-ssa and the Xix. The security of their economies is what matters most to them. They will all reject the Earth Alliance bid for membership in the Whooex Trade Consortium because they must maintain their own trade status here. You Humans, of all species, understand that best. What do you call this place? The Moneyworld? Crude but appropriate.

"I, for one, would allow your membership here. Your species is weak-minded and ambitious. What would be more efficient than observing and countering your actions in order to keep you under control? That is not the Primacy's current strategy, however. They want you isolated and destroyed.

"Which is my own fait accompli! You see, I am the one who heard the whispers about the phantom child, who could block perception and hide from the sight of other Makima. I found her. I saw the potential and envisioned the plan to create an army of her kind."

Create? My mind stuttered. Even Humans had learned better than to— "You're trying to clone her?"

"Trying? No. We have cloned her."

Horror twisted inside me. Now I knew why he'd shown up in the Xix hospital and tried to shanghai me: he wanted his original subject back and he thought I knew where she was.

But—did he realize she could block Endar awareness too?

The High Jerak continued. "Our labs are working furiously to create more children with her skills—Makima who can move about, unseen, anywhere—who can alter and erase memory. We will use them to infiltrate the highest levels of the Earth Alliance government, reaching into the most secured places to influence minds. Under Endar direction, our phantom children will move out across your worlds, inserting themselves into places of power, using their skills to precipitate wars and catastrophic events, and erasing memory of our influence. We will destroy your civilization from the inside, moving you back to the barbaric state in which you belong. Humans will fall below acceptable membership levels of technology and the Whooex Union, which, by then, will be under the control of the Primacy, will eject you. We will rule everything and Humans will disappear from history and from memory."

CHAPTER 44

Purple Pain

"The other Union members won't let that happen!" I sputtered at him.

"Of course they will. Who will tell them what we are doing? Not you. They will think Earth Alliance's decline is the natural progression of your irrational, primitive nature. Humanity is merely an insignificant dust speck on a plan that has been in process for hundreds of years. Your DNA merely allowed it to take a swift step forward. You are correct: our Minders cannot monitor members outside the Zones. Their reach does not extend far enough. Your illegal presence has enabled us to remedy the problem and rein in the last of the resistant members. We have something much more substantial than petty conspiracies or tampering with economics to use against them. Their collaboration with a Human on this world could destroy them. It was what we needed, and you, Vivi Zant, gave it to us. Now all of them except the Proambu—who are cowards and who do not act against aggression—will do what we tell them to do." His thin lips split to reveal sharp gray teeth in what I guessed represented the Endar version of a triumphant smile. "Soon you and the pitiful faction helping you will be swept up and disposed of, and no one else will ever know any of this. They will only see the results."

All I could think about was protecting the tiny circle that had formed around me on this world. "There isn't anyone else—"

"Don't waste your oxygen on a lie. You are a spy, and you have collaborators on this world!"

"That's ridiculous! You know how I came to this world."

"I also know, now, how you escaped down the loading umbilical into our warehouse system and eluded our detection equipment while making contact with certain individuals on this world."

"I stumbled in the dark and followed some vermin out."

"Vermin, yes, but not the kind you wish me to believe. You Humans think you are so clever. You inspire others to dare think the same way." He flexed a gray hand, gesturing to the city beyond his walls. "While we speak, your allies are inciting riots around the Das to distract us. They underestimate our response to social unrest on this critical day. I have declared a state of martial law over the entire city and port. We have the means to enforce it and we will deal ruthlessly with anyone found in violation. No one is allowed to embarrass the Primacy!"

Had Duff really called up the city for protests, to create a distraction and stretch Endar resources after I missed my connection with the others? If so, it was a noble effort, but it was also a waste of resources. He and the others could not rescue the kid and me inside the Grip.

Judging from the gleam of anticipation in the High Jerak's eyes, the citizens of this city were about to encounter a ruthless retaliation from the Sat Quar.

He continued. "Colonel Mathet Waa Silvec and his ridiculous dark ops team will meet with an accident this day. Unfortunate. Your little astrogator accomplice is quite a treasure. We have always wanted to take one apart and find out how it works. Regrettably, her abduction is too risky at this time. The Tabi value them highly, and, since our hold on their officials is not yet firmly established, her disappearance could stir resistance." He shrugged. "We will find another one in the future. This one must die today, along with anyone else on this world that has come in contact with you."

Saura... I couldn't force a sound through the tightness in my throat.

"You and your blight are ending, Captain Zant. The downfall of the Earth Alliance has begun even as they arrive here. Now," he leaned in, putting his face close to mine again, "I want my original back. Where is the child?"

I stared straight into his red eyes. Not because I was any kind of bold—I was a quivering mass of terror—but because I was afraid I would look at the kid and he would realize she was in the room with us. I suddenly, desperately, wished we did have some connection. I mentally screamed for her to get out. To go find Saura and warn her... "I don't know."

Seok straightened and turned away. For a moment, I thought he saw Lirilune, but then I realized he was speaking with someone beyond the room. His tone was too low for me to hear what he said. He started to turn back, twitched, listened, and began to talk again. This time he raised his voice and spoke in the sharp way he had addressed his guards and me. "It is not his concern! Tell him to focus on his task!"

With an abrupt movement of dismissal, he returned his attention to me. "We have a little time before I must put you on a ship to one of our science facilities."

"You can't kidnap a citizen of the Whooex Union!" I stammered.

"Who is going to stop us? No one will file a report on a missing Human who was never here."

He was right; the Tabisee would never acknowledge my existence, and I would not implicate them—at least, not until I arrived at his so-called science facility and underwent questioning.

"I could forgo the pleasure of working with you except for one thing," he continued. "I want the Makima child you pulled from the airlock on Idwal!"

"I don't know what you're talking about."

"Then, much to my pleasure, it is necessary to encourage your co-operation."

My time advantage evaporated. "I demand proper representation..."

"Strip it!" he ordered.

For a moment his words confused me, then his intention sunk in. "Aw, no!" I exclaimed. "Don't—"

Too late. One of the Endar guards caught something beneath the collar at the back of my shipskins and gave a hard tug. The material tightened on my neck, cutting off my air.

"Don't," I gasped. "There's an easier way—" I tried to pull an arm free of Endar claws. If they insisted on removing my skins, there was a place on the left cuff that would relax the fabric for removal. They didn't have to damage—

The material abruptly gave way against the edge of the Endar tool like a razor cutting silk, splitting down the back and exposing my skin to the air.

Outrage seized me. First the "*Hand*", then my wetware, my away-suit, and now my shipskins—all of the things that were almost im-possible for me to replace. The bill for this job kept adding up, and that didn't include the devastating loss of my partner.

The guards shucked the skins off me like they were peeling a Sol banana, leaving me standing in my skivvies.

"You owe me for those," I snarled at the High Jerak's back.

He was bent over a counter full of containers, searching through them. "Put it in restraints," he ordered over his leather-bound shoul-der. "Pad the cuffs well. We do not want it to tear off an extremity."

The guards clasped my bare shoulders and dragged me to a contraption previously obscured by a row of lab equipment. It looked similar to a ship's launch couch, with all the pads, straps and belts, except the fasteners weren't made for the occupant to release them. One guard held me while the other inserted thick gel strips into the cuffs and headrest. Despite my struggles, the two easily held me down and fastened my head, wrists, and ankles into the restraints while the High Jerak removed the cover of a small jar with long, knobby fingers. He brushed a fingertip lightly across the material it contained.

It came away with a thin smear of brilliant purple on the gray tip.

He walked over, the finger extended. "Do you know what this is?"

I flexed my wrists and ankles against the restraints. The soft grip could hold something far stronger than a Human. A puny spacer sure wasn't going to break loose. "No."

He moved his hand, lifting the finger closer to my face so I could see the purple stain. It looked slightly luminescent.

Glowing, luminescent purple could not be good for me. I twisted in the restraints.

"This is ndu. A perfectly harmless sounding name, yes? For Endar, that's what it is—a perfectly harmless life form. It is my favorite organism, exclusive to my homeworld. A bit of color from home. My people are immune to its effect." He waggled the finger to hold my attention. "The rest of you...are not so fortunate."

He leaned in close and I caught a whiff of scent like cold, sweating metal. Was it the Endar smell of anticipation at another creature's pain? If so, it was not something I wanted to get familiar with. "It only takes a tiny brush on the surface of the skin. The ndu organism locks onto the nerves and feeds on their electrical impulses. You will feel a certain numbing effect. That is not its charm, however. It secretes the waste it generates from feeding back into the nerve tissue beyond its attachment point. I'm told the byproduct creates a pain that feels like the burning heart of a star. The more stress you feel, the more the ndu can feed. And excrete. A dangerous, deadly cycle." He raised the finger and looked at the smear. "I do not know. Some creatures are prone to such exaggeration."

A trickle of my sweat found the corner of my eye. No matter what you have heard, everyone breaks under torture. Some EA special agents have a chip inside their head that can cut off the pain center of the brain if agony reaches a certain level. It can even kill them under certain circumstances to protect what's in their head. But not a low-level grunt like me. My tech only dulled a level of pain to get me through a bad day—such as losing a hand to a plasma blast. I wouldn't withstand torture for long. But I wasn't giving anything up. Not here, not yet, at least.

"Humans can't think through intense pain."

"Few creatures can." He shifted his hand, and I realized he held another small jar in the crook of another finger. "This will neutralize the toxin the ndu secretes and prevent you from going into shock. It works quickly—once it is applied. Save yourself some pain, Captain Zant; tell me where the child is."

"And deprive you of the hunt? No." Was I insane, taunting an Endar while it held torture powder over me?

He stood still for a moment, studying me, then he cricked his head in an odd, jerky motion. "She is here, on this world."

Damn me for a fool! It had to be a lucky guess on his part, but the twitch of my facial muscles must have reinforced his observation.

"Helpful," he said, "but I think we can narrow it down more." He paused expectantly.

The cricket track from the Xix hospital recovery room would have sounded loud in this silence.

The High Jerak nodded. "This is good. I was hoping for some tiresome Human bravado." The bony finger descended—not for the surface of my arm, but for the bare skin on the back of my right hand. I pulled against the restraints, trying to break them, to no avail. I felt a light brush midway along the back, over the tendon of my middle finger.

My heart thundered in my ears. Three. Four. Five.

Maybe the ndu didn't work on Humans.

I felt a sudden tickle of itch in the area of the purple smudge and the screaming began.

CHAPTER 45

Lesson

The end of the pain was like a knife chop. Clarity slammed my brain while my body, struggling to curl into a fetal position, tore against the restraints.

I sobbed. Tears and snot smeared my face. My skin was filthy with sweat and piss, and the room stank.

Off to my right was a smear of black and white. I blinked, trying to clear my vision and it resolved into the High Jerak. He was holding the kid in front of him, one of his long, boney hands gripping her shoulder.

I think I wailed in despair.

"She surrendered to me as soon as she witnessed your pain," he said. "But we shared a few additional moments so she could understand the situation. It is simple. If she is difficult, you will suffer. Everything goes so much better when everyone understands how things work."

A few moments? My arms and legs felt as if someone had tried to wrench them out of their sockets. A shudder ran over me.

Bastard! "Now you know I had nothing to do with taking her family—" I rasped.

The High Jerak cricked his head in that odd, jerky gesture again. "Captain Zant, this was not an interrogation. It was a lesson. There will be other times for questions." He straightened. "Enough with these distractions. Remove this filth and throw it in the silo. I will devote more time to it after we repulse this newest encroachment of its stinking kind into our territory."

The guards undid the restraints and hauled me to my feet.

I had totally failed. The Endar had the kid, along with a whole room—a whole world—of her telepathic people. The EA's bid to join the Whooex Trade Union would be the first step in its downfall and the Whooex Union of Stars would crumble under Endar manipulation. Awash in misery, I sagged between the guards.

"There is one last thing."

I looked up through blurred vision. The High Jerak held Liri, but now he had a claw poised at her throat, ready to pierce it.

Liri quaked in terror.

"No! Don't hurt her," I sobbed.

The display was not meant for me, however. "Block this Human and erase all its memories of you, back past your first encounter with it," he ordered her.

This was it. If she had selectively left my memory intact because I rescued her, I was about to lose it all. I would not remember why I was on this world—or why the Endar were torturing me. I stared at her, waiting for the moment when she disappeared from my sight and mind.

The kid closed her eyes and screwed up her face with effort.

I watched her, my heart thudding with fear and regret.

She opened one eye a crack and looked at me. The dismay that washed over her face told me what I suspected: she could not influence my mind.

Too late, I realized, for the sake of Humankind, I should've simply looked away and pretended to be confused, but the shock of confirming she really couldn't affect me had dulled my response.

"Do not play with your life! Block her and erase her memories," the High Jerak repeated. His claw pressed her neck and a bead of blood welled.

"No!" My cry was barely a whisper from my raw throat.

The child scrunched up her face in a massive effort.

My attempt to blank my expression was too slow.

"I said erase it!" Seok snarled. His fingers twitched as if, regardless of her value, he would lose control in his fury and tear her throat out.

"She can't block me," I choked out.

"That is impossible!" he hissed.

Adrenalin born of fear for the kid's life gave me the strength to get my feet under me. I stood between the guards, not daring to breathe, terrified his gleaming lacquer claw would plunge and rip her neck.

Instead, he gave a piercing shriek of rage and flung her at me. "You have ruined her!"

A small kid striking a spacer body at any speed is not a pleasant feeling. I slid from the guards' grip and we both went to the floor. I did manage to keep her head from smacking the surface with my ribs, however.

"How can this be?" the High Jerak raged. "She can mindwipe any species we tested!"

The Endar guards rattled, but they made no attempt to answer him or to pick us up.

Gasping for air, I struggled to my feet and pulled the kid up to stand with me. She wrapped her arms around my waist and held on tight.

He paused in his rant to glare at Liri. "We will review what has happened here. If you have deceived me, your people will suffer. Do you understand?"

I felt the movement of her head bumping my lower ribs as she nodded frantically. Her whole body trembled.

He shifted his attention to me. "Human filth! The ndu is only the beginning of your pain. We will take you apart cell by cell to find the reason she cannot affect you. If what happened here is real we will erect a memorial to honor your role in exposing a flaw in our plan."

He turned, reached into a drawer, and pulled something from it. When he turned back, he had a small triangular metal device suspended on a metal circlet sitting in the middle of his forehead. "Senior, approach," he spat.

One of the guards stepped toward him. The High Jerak dropped something into his hand. "Put these on, both of you. It will enable you to see the Minder and block any attempt to influence your brain."

Well, that answered that question...

The guard slipped a similar circlet on his head and carried the other back to his companion.

"You will not remove those under any circumstance unless I order it. As of this moment, your duties are reassigned. You report solely to me. I do not need to remind you of the level of security that entails." He paused, then stepped forward to stand in front of us. Bending, he lifted a hand as if to caress Liri's small face. A claw plunged and sliced her flesh from her cheekbone to her jaw.

She jerked with shock, but made no sound as blood welled.

I made up for her silence with a whimper of outrage.

The Endar leader ignored us both as he straightened to look at his guards. "Observe the mark. You are ordered to kill this Minder if you see it anywhere outside the silo unless I have ordered you to bring it to me."

He looked at the kid as the guards peeled her off me. "You know what this is." He gestured at the triangle with his bloody nail. "You cannot blind them to your presence now. You will remain silent and do as you are told. If you attempt to block Endar sight or memory again, you will die. Do you understand me?"

He turned away, not waiting for her response. "I have pressing matters to attend. Take them away. One of you will stay on guard outside the silo at all times. The other will return here for further instructions. Speak to no one in between."

As their spindly fingers grasped our arms, I wondered if he actually intended to reassign the guards' duties, or if they were also facing death for what they had witnessed here.

The door behind us slid open and a white-robed figure swept into the room.

One of the guards stretched his free arm to block its forward momentum.

"What happens here?" the being demanded as it came to a stop.

The High Jerak spun back, the shading on his face going dark gray. "I said not your concern! Return to your station," he snapped.

Some things are so unexpected that they can jerk you back from the edge of utter collapse. This being—he had to be Makima—had spoken in Union Basic! The other surprise was his physical appearance. He was beautiful, with Liri's lovely features matured to a fine elegance. On second look, however, the warmth and animation that lit up the kid were missing.

The Makima certainly didn't act as if he considered himself subservient to anyone in the room. He drew his body straight, putting him maybe five centimeters short of my height, and set his shoulders back. He looked at the kid. I sensed there was a flash of information exchanged between them.

"This is Phantom Child," he said, glaring at Seok. "Never asked to remove from Zam Fiella. Why is here? Explain child's state!"

The High Jerak gestured at me. "This being did," he lied.

I managed to summon a choking sound of denial.

The Makima's brown eyes swept over me again. They narrowed in curiosity. "Look, see wild animal." His fine features wrinkled with distaste.

Yeah, I stank so bad I was aware of it, even beyond the shock that was trying to shut my system down.

"I see before," he continued. "Not Makima. What are you?"

"Human," I said.

"Is animal, Threadmaster," the High Jerak spoke over me.

The Makima looked at him.

"I said return to station!" Seok snapped.

Unbridled contempt swept the Makima's face, turning it cold and malicious.

I closed my eyes, expecting the Endar to lunge forward and snip off his head right there, but the High Jerak did not react.

Did he even recognize the expression on the face of this being he called Threadmaster, who he obviously deemed a minion?

"And what of child?" the man persisted.

"Child damaged. Primacy must evaluate," the High Jerak said. "Will tell you all in future."

But the Makima male had dismissed Seok from his attention, turning to the kid. He looked at her without sympathy or consolation.

"You speak aloud!" The High Jerak ordered.

"Remember Sameirat," the Threadmaster said to her in a low voice.

She swallowed hard and gave a single nod.

"Enough with the gibberish!" The High Jerak tone rose. "Return to your station immediately!"

The cold, speculative look the Threadmaster gave me as he turned and swept out of the High Jerak's chamber sent a stab of fear straight into the seething mass that roiled inside me.

That kind of beauty was a dangerous thing. Would Humans recognize that it was not to be touched?

I stared down at the purple stain on the back of my hand and shivered.

CHAPTER 46

The Silo

The guard shoved the kid through the nondescript double doors in the empty white hallway beneath the Grip. She came back out clinging to his arm, terror etching her features. He hissed and shook her off, snatched the hood of her robe and tossed her back inside.

I opened my mouth to protest and sucked in a mouthful of the cold, putrid air that rolled out the door. I bent nearly double, gagging as an Endar hand caught the back of my neck and pushed me in after her.

Lirilune met me on the other side, throwing her arms around my waist and burying her head against the bare skin of my side. I put a sympathetic arm across her shoulders, but I reserved the other one to cover my own nose and mouth.

The guards pitched my shipskins in behind me and slammed the door, leaving us in the reeking cold.

"Shit," I muttered. "Shit, shit." What the hell was this place? As my watering eyes adjusted to the thin light, I looked around.

We stood on a landing perched high on a wall beneath an arched stone ceiling with a huge hole at its center. The platform extended out in a two-meter square and connected to a ramp that curved down to the floor along the circular wall.

I'd seen a similar place on this world, but from a different angle. Beyond the rail that edged the platform, the walls looked like the chamber where Duff had rescued Saura and me from the first bunch of ragpiles. Even the lighting emanating from the stone looked the same. The eerie, moaning howl was missing, however. The place was as silent as death. Which matched the smell.

This was Seok's silo. It surprised me that I remembered anything after the pain he put me through with the ndu.

The first thing I had to do was look around and assess our situation, but my internal feeds were blinking red, an insistent alert in my left eye that I could not ignore. They read an ambient temperature of fifteen centigrade from the sensors implanted in the surface of my skin. A horizontal scroll running beneath the feed warned me that, based on my current physical state, I was at risk of hypothermia and advised I should find suitable clothing or shelter as soon as possible.

Shit.

I quickly queried survival time limits for a near-naked Human body from my chips. The answer came back with four to six functional hours for a skinny spacer with low body fat, and seven hours or a core body temperature drop to twenty-eight centigrade before complete, irrecoverable shutdown. Possibly less. It advised me to seek warm clothing and shelter immediately.

Yeah.

I wondered if the High Jerak was aware of the limitations of the Human body or if he was only interested in salvaging my brain.

My dying would seriously curtail his fun.

I grasped Liri's shoulders and set her back a step away from me. Saw the blood smearing her face and robe from the slash on her cheek. The bastard! I had something to fix the wound, but right now it was not life threatening and therefore not a top priority.

"You talk Union Basic?" I asked her. For me, the mongrel patois spoken in Rim-space between star associations, was the lingo of docks and dives—not something a kid on a remote, isolated planet would learn.

She nodded.

"Stay here," I told her. I needed to recon the place and assess our prospects for escape.

She latched back onto me, small fingers digging into the skin of my sides. I patted the backs of her hands, then peeled her off me. "Stay here."

I had no idea if she understood, but she relaxed her resistance. I raised both hands in front of me, palms outward in a Human gesture. "Stay."

Her face muscles twitched silent protest, but she retreated to cringe against the wall.

"Good. Sit." I motioned downward. "Now, stay."

Despite the fear in her eyes, she settled to the floor.

I didn't have to strain over the rail of the platform to see the gaping pit centered in the circle of the floor below. The light from the walls cast its edges into shadow, but I could see white and grey shapes piled at its center. Add in the smell and it didn't require any imagination to know what lay there.

I didn't want to go down for a closer look, but my pesky training told me the Earth Alliance and the Whooex Union required every detail of what happened here and, when I got out, I had better have my facts straight. Too optimistic? No. It was the beginning of a plan. The place was cold, we were under-clothed, and I had no idea how long we would be stuck here. I doubted our captors were concerned with supplying us food or water. Our escape fell on me.

And, yeah, the last part might be a bit overly optimistic, but I needed something to keep me going.

First priority, however, was taking care of myself.

I snatched up the tattered remains of my shipskins. Technically they were ruined, but wearing them, even damaged, would extend my effective operational time by a few extra minutes. Turning my back to the kid, I pulled off my skivvies and used them to clean up as best I could, then I tugged the bottom half of my skins over my feet and wore the top as an open-back shirt. With their integrity destroyed, they sagged on my body, but they were still a damned sight warmer than bare flesh.

Should I have given them to the kid? No. She had her long-sleeved robe. I had no idea what features it possessed to protect her from the cold. And second, we had less than six hours to escape this place. Although I had a pretty good idea of the High Jerak's plan for me—or my brain—I didn't know what he intended for the kid he called his 'ruined' prototype. I sensed it wasn't good. How can you let a telepath who has seen her family murdered and overheard your secret plans live? Her survival hinged on me getting us out. If I failed, she died.

I would not let that happen again.

I glanced behind me at the kid, sitting with her back against the wall, her knees huddled against her chest to conserve body heat.

"You wait. Me come back." I tried to give her a reassuring smile as I started down the ramp. I'm sure it came off more like a grimace.

A thick layer of fine white dust lay over everything, but long, thin Endar footprints had packed a path into the surface. I walked inside their impressions to avoid stirring the powder as I descended. I wanted to avoid breathing it as much as possible, though the hazy quality of the air told me I was already taking in lungfuls of the stuff, along with any dangerous organisms it carried.

I was shivering before I got to the floor.

It appeared the Frairy and Cheel were not the only people carving out pieces of Rohm's old infrastructure for their own private use. Like the previous chamber, this one had six arched entryways. Unlike the first one, however, white mortar blocked these openings. From what I'd seen from the platform, something blocked the bottom of the pit in the center, too.

At floor level, the dust over the pit looked denser than the air around me, giving it the effect of a pale, glowing column. That meant fans in the opening above were quietly pulling up the air and scrubbing away the odor and any poisonous gases from decay before venting it, while the dust from the rot fell back into the chamber.

The opening offered a possible way out. Unfortunately, the height put it beyond our reach.

There had to be vents somewhere else in this place to feed that airflow, however.

I followed the worn trail across the floor and stared down into the pit. After the High Jerak's torture I didn't think I could feel a stronger reaction, but my stomach twisted in horror at the sight. So many bodies! Hundreds of skeletal remains lay in the shadows below the lip. Dried skin stretched over skulls agape with gleaming white teeth. Withered, dry, pale hair snagged in tangled white rags filthy with death stains. The most recent body still had gray flesh desiccating beneath its white robes. It was the size of an adult Human.

Makima, I corrected.

Some peoples did not make a big deal of burying their dead. I got that. Environment, circumstance, and belief varied from world to world as much as the planets in our galaxy varied, but most sentient beings had some ritual for the parting of life from their own kind. Considering the positions of the bodies on the top of this pile, their limbs splayed where they landed, I did not believe this was a respectful observation of life or death.

Did the elegant creature the High Jerak called the Threadmaster know the end destination of his people?

My mind churned with horror and outrage. From the looks of things, the Endar Primacy had gotten by with this crime for what—a hundred years? More? They took Lirilune's people from their world, used them illegally, then dumped their bodies in this 'death silo' to hide the crime.

I wondered what the people back on her homeworld thought: that a little golden colony existed, where their people retired in luxury? That little palaces dotted the back of their Endar masters' properties? After more than a hundred years, when none of their people returned home, did they wonder?

An image flashed in my mind and I choked back a sob. Were there pits full of baby skeletons from failed Endar cloning experiments back on their world?

Makima leaders couldn't be that stupid. They had to suspect something.

Perhaps they couldn't, or wouldn't stop it. Maybe they didn't care. Then again, all their leaders might be tall, chitinous creatures. A single world, on the outer edge of the Orion Arm, probably not technically sophisticated, up against the Endar Primacy. Their sole source of information and tech might be the Endar. It was a chilling thought.

And, yeah, maybe I was being a little too kind to them.

If it was true, however, the High Jerak had a huge problem. After ninety days wandering the Moneyworld, seeing things, seeing people, having experiences a sheltered telepath inside Endar control did not have, Liri knew things. He couldn't allow her to spread that knowledge.

He thought I should die, too, eventually, after he was done with me. He probably thought the same for her. So, if we wanted to live, we had to go to war.

It would get dirty. I asked myself if it was better to drag Liri through the nastiness, subjecting her to what must be done, or, keeping in mind she was a child, try to protect her sensitivities. There had never been anyone to protect mine, and, despite the terrible things I had experienced, I survived and turned out okay—mostly. I had to give her the same chance.

The fire in the thought fizzled when it met reality. The clock was ticking fast on our survival in this cold air and the return of the guards.

Duff may have created a distraction to pull Endar attention away from us. Saura and the others might be diligently searching. Inside the Grip, no one could get us out except us, and, even if I got back out the door above and overcame the guard, at least two more Endar wore circlets to protect against Liri's hoodoo. And I wouldn't be able to find a way out through the maze. The place was far too alien.

That left us two other possible exits...

Fighting revulsion, I stared into the pit and wondered how far down the bodies went. Duff said the holes were very deep, making me believe something blocked this one. The Endar would want to keep their filthy graveyard hidden from the tunnel-wandering populace.

I took a step back, away from the pit and bumped something.

Images of feral, carnivorous creatures flashed in my brain. "Shit!" I exclaimed, leaping sideways.

I spun around.

Liri was standing there. Tears coursed down her face, streaking through dried blood.

"I told you to stay up there!" I shouted. "I told you..." Hell, why was I yelling at her? None of this was her fault. "I didn't want you to see this," I finished sadly.

I extended a hand and she took it.

This was a mess. A Whooex Union shattering mess. There was one thing I could do: get us out of here and stop the Endar.

CHAPTER 47

Lirilune

I figured if the Endar monitored anywhere in this place, it would be the entrance on the platform, my logic being: why would anyone need to keep an eye on a pit full of dead bodies?

I had something up my sleeve, literally. So I needed to relocate somewhere else.

First, however, I had to make a decision. Should I trust the kid? Even if the High Jerak scared the hell out of her, it did not mean she would choose me over him in a high-pressure situation. She had run to the Grip, to a room full of her people, despite the Endar presence. Besides, Seok had threatened to kill whatever was left of her family if she tried to escape. Even if she appreciated what I had done, pulling her from the airlock and all, when things came to a head, she might go with what she knew over a stranger. She might tell the Endar everything she saw or knew.

If I left her on the platform, they could snatch her back while I wasn't looking despite what the High Jerak had said. I would never be able to live with that. Besides, I hoped she had something to contribute to our escape.

"Come." I led the kid along another path in the dust, to an area beneath the ramp.

As we walked, the events since I emerged from a tub of purple-blooded fish crashed in on my brain. Aside from a room full of the kid's people and an Endar plot to destroy the EA, the next shocking thing was that I understood Arpi. In the passages above, with survival being my first concern, it had been a passing flutter of surprise. Now the realization fired suspicion and confusion.

Since the Corp enhanced my original civilian language package when I joined up, and they claimed not to have an Arpi package—the reason being the Primacy denied our right to access—I had to suspect Thok and His Frilliness provided my sudden skill. They had, after all, supplied Saura with enough Proambu for us to arrive and find our way around Idwal.

I still had to wonder why they thought I needed an Arpi package. It was obvious they had manipulated Saurubi and me, but I found it hard to believe the clown duo intended us to end up on the Moneyworld. I was also sure they hadn't expected the Endar to interfere with us or to kill Lirilune's family, so they weren't as smart as they thought with their messed up plan. People had died. A kid was in danger.

Whole Star Associations were under threat...

I muttered a curse. If they were passing out translation upgrades, a Makima one would have saved me a lot of time and trouble.

Oh, wait, the Makima were telepaths. Guess they couldn't help me with that one. I cursed the clown duo under my breath again.

The kid and I settled where the base of the ramp met the floor, the cover overhead giving us the advantage of three points of protection. The location could become a dangerous trap if something came out of the pit after us, but the tracks in the dust showed limited movement to the ramp and along the second path. All the prints were the distinct, narrow pattern of Endar feet.

We discovered two long metal poles with large hooks on the ends lying against the wall, which explained the second path. Dark debris caked the curved ends. I moved them farther along the wall, and we settled in the dust. I showed Liri how to scoop the stuff into a pile to sit in—the powder was warmer than the bare stone surface—and cleared a spot on the floor in front of me.

First, to introduce ourselves. I pointed at myself, "Vivi Zant." I pointed at her. "Lirilune."

She nodded when I said her name.

"Lirilune. Liri?"

She nodded more enthusiastically at the second option.

'Liri' was okay for me, too. "Good. We talk more. First check, see things can use. Fix hurt face." No need to go into how dangerous our situation was right now. It was more important to assess the resources we had available to aid our escape.

Of course, we had the files stored inside my head, my training, and my experience—all of which had not been much help up to this point. Lucky for us, I had things stored in the cuffs and a heel of my shipskins that might be more useful.

It had been a while since I inventoried my survival backup kit, but I knew I was short a number of useful things. Saura warned me every time we put into port that I should replenish them, but the supplies, in their particular packaging, which reduced their weight and size, were expensive. The excuse that we were short on creds the last time we put into Mandragala Station stung sharply now.

My shipskin had taken so much damage it was technically dead. My fingers felt like thick stumps from the cold as I struggled to force the small compartment in the left sleeve open.

Finally, I succeed in pulling the little, color-coded wrappers out. "Okay," I said as I spread them on the dust-cleared area.

"This filter clean water." I held up the thin wrapper for Liri to see. No need to get complicated on how it worked. She listened attentively as I ran through the rest of the stash. I displayed two packets that held expandable camo-film bags, several packets of sealant, four oxy/air tabs, three sleep tabs, a disinfectant pack, two nanite patches, a med seal, and three stimulant tabs. Among the missing, not-replaced items were two micro-explosives and calorie tablets.

I swallowed one of the stim tabs and slapped the nanite patches on my wounds to start repairing the torn flesh on my wrists and ankles. Had I known less about Liri I might have given her a stim, but the fact she was not Human made that risky. Besides, with no food and water available, the stimulant would burn through calories and put a body on the dangerous edge of exhaustion faster.

There were things I did have that would help her, however.

"Liri come." I tore open the disinfectant pack and motioned her closer. The swab wasn't wet enough to clean all the blood off her skin, but it took care of the wound. The slice was four centimeters long and a centimeter deep. Without medical help, it would leave a scar, but I didn't dare use a nanite pack on her for the same reason I didn't give her a stim: just because we appeared similar did not mean that we were. Instead, I covered the cut with the med seal—the edges of the wound had already closed—and hoped for the best. At least it would keep the dust out.

She slid back into her spot, curled up her knees, and watched as I turned my attention to the heel of my shipskins, to the foot opposite the cleaning mechanism. If I wondered why I was making this effort, all I needed to do was look at those big brown eyes. Anthy's eyes had watched me in the same way down in the cold, dim hold of the ship during the many times we crouched in fear and misery. It wasn't so different here, except I was old enough to know the consequences of my failures, from Anthy's death, to missing the connection with Saura, Duff, Shoff, and Meeroush.

I had failed so many times over the past thirty years...

I exchanged my regret for anger—it being a warmer emotion—and turned my attention to the items stashed in the compartment of the heel, continuing my chatter with the kid as I worked.

"This fifty meters of monofilament." I held up a tiny spool with hair-fine wrap, which wasn't much use without my wetware. I needed codes to plump the wire to a larger, selectable diameter. The packet included four fingertip covers for handling the filament, and—"Crap!"—the tool to break it into lengths was missing. There were two programmable chips, also useless without wetware. I laid them aside without comment.

"This best stuff." I showed her the first of my personal favorites, a gray curl of chameleon material. "This change into cup." With an expandable cellular structure, the gray one morphed into a container that, used with the now-precious filter, cleaned urine or dirty water to make it potable. A great piece of survival equipment, but not the kind of thing I wanted to explain to a little kid.

I didn't show the blue chameleon curl to her. It straightened and expanded into a combat knife that sported a hundred and sixty-millimeter blade with a rippling blue molecular edge, or, with pressure applied in the right place, converted into a tool with a malleable tip that would mold and harden into any shape until pressed again to soften the tip or return to a curl.

I could kill an Endar guard with the blade; its seething edge would make the necessary cut, even against a dense carapace, in a microsecond. Doing that wouldn't be a wise act, however. If I got out of here, there were many things the Endar could rightly accuse me of doing, but none of them currently rose to the level of murder. That crime didn't go over well in any society, especially if you killed its version of a police officer. Earth Alliance might find that difficult to ignore or defend. And I wanted to avoid unnecessary violence in front of the kid.

I would not hesitate to use it if pushed, though.

I laid the thin tubes aside with the rest of the items and shook out the last bits of treasure: a peel-and-slap seal and a small packet that contained a dark ring. Again, things that did not generate an urge for discussion.

I picked up the packet containing the ring and shook out the tiny, powerful laser into my palm. When I slid it on my right ring finger and pried up the tiny optical resonator from the surface, the inside of the band tightened against my skin, securing it in position. Good. No accidental severing of digits today. The thing keyed on the software in my head and the network of sensors the Marines had implanted in my body, instead of my lost wetware. It had three large power blasts, or a dozen small ones, or it could serve as a flashlight, depending on the command I sent to it. If it worked against whatever material the Endar had used to fill the tunnel openings, it might prove our ticket out.

All the while Liri watched me in silence.

Yes, if I had made use of these items back on Idwal, we might not be in this situation now. But everything had been securely stored in my shipskins, beneath the awaysuit I wore. Accessing them would have required stripping out of my protection in the middle of an alien environment while under the pressure of attack. My training went against that, and for a sensible reason: after my injury I might never have gotten back into my awaysuit. The Endar would have blown the section, and we would be dead. Besides, I'd been sure my glove could break the plasma stream.

Another of the many mistakes I had made up to this point.

The Endar, however, had made a few mistakes too. I still couldn't believe they had left me in possession of my shipskins. The EA never would have done that without closely inspecting them first. Their carelessness marked their naiveté of Humans. Or their disdain. Either way was a good thing for the kid and me.

They would take my skins at some point, however, so I had to use or find another place to hide the items I'd retrieved. Opening one of the packets containing a film bag, I dropped everything inside except the ring and a pack of sealant, which I used to glue the bag into my left armpit. The location was awkward, but the contents were thin, and the camo-film took on the color of my skin, making it difficult to detect.

I sealed back the compartments of my shipskins.

The kid was a resource, too. I just had no idea how to use a telepath to our advantage. Calling for help from the Makima inside the Grip seemed unwise; the Threadmaster had not impressed me as overly concerned with Liri's condition or what became of her.

I would have to be very careful to make her understand what I wanted her to do if I figured out a way to use her skill. Meanwhile, there was no point in stirring her up. I had so many questions, some of them critical, but if we didn't get out of this place, none of the answers mattered.

Liri was staring at me, her expression solemn. She squinched her face.

I waited in case we experienced some kind of breakthrough.

Nope.

She rose and proceeded to explore my head, her small fingers feather-light on my bare scalp.

Her mystification at my lack of telepathic reception struck me as odd since the Endar did not appear to be telepathic, either. Maybe it was because the Makima and Humans looked so similar that it perplexed her, or the fact I didn't require a mechanical device to counter her little mind tricks. Or maybe her time in hiding on the Money-world left her with the impression everyone was susceptible to her influence.

Which might be unpleasantly close to the truth. The Endar were certainly using her people to great effect pushing their agenda forward here in the Trade Compound.

The baffling part for me was the High Jerak's conviction she could manipulate Human brains. It sounded as if his whole plan was built around that premise. So why couldn't she influence mine? An error in his calculations? That was strange for something he claimed so many years in the making. I was not the first Human the Endar had gotten their chitinous claws on.

I did not intend to stay and help them solve the mystery.

CHAPTER 48

Dust Flow

It was time to find a way out.

I considered the kid. Was it better to keep her moving to stay warm, or to let her huddle? My files told me smaller bodies burned more energy to generate internal heat.

I decided conservation was the best choice for her.

"Me look," I told her. "You stay. Keep warm."

I circled the perimeter of the silo, examining each arch in turn. The wall was made of the same roughly cut blocks I'd seen before and the white material filling the arches was consistently smooth and unmarred. More than likely it was deeper than my laser would cut before running out of charge. I tried the knife blade, set to micro-edge. It left a thin, shallow groove. We'd be dead from cold before it cut through.

The third arch from the ramp showed signs of mortar decay along its left side. The stone was darker there, suggesting damp was breaking down the mortar. There was a chance I could work that stone out of the stack, but the ones above would not topple with the arch blocked.

Completing the circuit revealed nothing with better potential.

I walked to the deathpit. It was about seven meters across. The bodies were stacked higher in the center, and tapered lower toward the rim. By the stretched and distorted positions of the remains, it appeared the Endar pitched them in, then leveled them out, which explained the poles with the grimy hooks we'd found earlier.

Going to the wall, I picked one up and carried it back to the edge of the pit. Along the rim the bones and rags lay around fifty centimeters below the floor level.

The hole in the previous chamber, where Duff recaptured Saura and me, had howled with airflow. This one was silent. The dust inside rose thickly upward, however. That meant air was flowing into this place from somewhere below. With no visible vents in the walls, a screen set in the bottom or sides of the pit remained the most likely scenario.

I raised the pole vertically and dropped it down the side of the hole, planning to see how far it would go. The moment my hands cleared the stone lip they plunged into an icy current of slow-rising air.

Cursing, I released the pole and stepped back.

The air was definitely pulling from somewhere inside the pit. I looked up. Heavy, ragged crusts of accumulated dust flapped at the edge of the hole above.

I had already eliminated that direction as a means of escape. Even if we climbed up there, which we couldn't, we would have to cope with passing through the mechanicals that drew the air out of the chamber. It would take too long. We would never survive the temperature of the air rising inside the pit.

Clenching my teeth, I grasped the pole and resumed my effort to work it down the side. The thing stopped where the base of the attached hook fell level with the lip of the hole. Either it was catching on a rim down there, or I had found the bottom. I pulled and tugged until I worked the pole out at an angle to clear any lip and tried to move it downward again. My chips told me it stopped at the same depth.

Interesting, but not much help.

My arms and hands felt frozen. I withdrew the pole, taking a step to the side and tilting it the last meter to get my hands clear of the updraft. The tip raked up, lifting bones and fabric farther along the side as it came free.

A cloud of dust surged up in front of me like a ghostly spirit. I swore and stumbled backward, causing the shaft to jam farther out into the remains. It sent a bigger cloud swirling toward the opening above. Jerking the pole clear, I vented my frustration while I rubbed my numbed hands together.

Something along the edge of the pit, where the pole stirred the dust, caught my eye. Shivering, I returned to the edge and crouched to have a closer look.

The stone pattern an arm's length below the rim was different from the stonework above it. The layer of dust on the bones in front of it was also noticeably lighter. I picked up the pole and, standing further along the edge to keep my hands out of the updraft, went to work with the hooked end, raking away the debris piled in front of the space. Before long, I uncovered an approximately sixty-centimeter wide rectangular opening. I worked down to reveal a forty-centimeter depth.

Moving around the pit, I searched for other areas where the dust was lighter. I found four more places, spaced at intervals coordinating with the arches, but the spot furthest from the ramp was curiously missing that detail. I focused there, stirring up a storm of dust so heavy I had to wait for it to settle before I could see the vent in the wall.

No air stirred the debris piled in front of it.

Was it intentionally obstructed by the Endar, or by something else?

The thought of a Makima, thrown in this place while still alive and attempting an unsuccessful escape out the opening sent chills running over me despite the sweat I had worked up while moving the bones.

Sweating in this situation was bad, but I couldn't stop work now. Something blocked that vent.

I took the pole and, moving around the perimeter so I could hit the opening at an angle. Rammed the end in. It struck something solid.

Hands shaking with desperation, I slammed harder, trying to break the clog. A few gray chips flipped out. I kept ramming. When I stopped to catch my breath, I saw a thin stream of dust rippling upward in a tight swirl.

I had broken through.

Time to move over and attack the situation head-on. I pulled out the blue tube and converted it to a chisel-form as I walked over to stand above the vent. The thought of reaching back into the cold, streaming air of the pit made me mentally cringe. I took up the pole and used the hooked end to pull some cloth, along with an assortment of bones that clung to it, from the pit. Ripping the dusty fabric into strips, I wrapped it around my hands to give them some insulation.

"Thanks," I muttered to the bones before shoving them back over the edge.

Oh, shit! My mind shrieked as I thrust my arms back into the cold of the pit.

The opening was too far down. I pulled back, huffing to fight the cold. If I wanted to get to the vent, I needed to extend my reach. Cursing a steady stream of obscenities, I wrapped more cloth around my head, leaving an opening for my eyes and nostrils. Then I got down on my belly and put my ribs on the rim. Plunging my head and arms into the freezing air, I reached down.

Gray, semi-transparent bits flew out as I hacked with the chisel, creating little poufs as they struck the dust. The blockage was not made of the same material as the white stuff in the arches, and, since it only clogged the opening, it seemed reasonable to think something other than the Endar had put it there.

Within a few moments, warm air rushed over my fingers.

The air streamed out into the pit, sending powder swirling upward.

I sat up, pulled my head and arms out of the cold, and stared at the column of dust. My heart and my brain raced. If the air was warm, we could crawl out through it—provided the vent did not narrow to a bottleneck or form some other odd configuration.

Was I willing to risk it? I looked over at the kid huddled beneath the ramp.

If that were Saura, she'd be the first one in the hole, all the while carping about how slow I moved. This, however, was different. The High Jerak had threatened Liri's people. She might be afraid of what would happen to them if she came with me. I knew firsthand how that worked: Fear for Anthy and the other children's safety had kept me under the control of the slavers for years.

People who did that sort of thing to little kids should be kicked into an event horizon.

I could not let that fear doom her, too.

If the other vents were warm, there would be no reason for me to continue clearing this one. Not to mention the fact something had already laid a claim on it. I traversed the circumference, braving the plunge into the current on each of the other five openings.

They all blew freezing air.

So, we had to confront whatever created the obstruction in the sixth vent if we wanted to escape this silo of death.

Trying to squelch images of a writhing battle with some slithery monster, I walked back, swung my legs over the edge, and cautiously put my weight on the bones piled in front of the opening. They slipped and compressed, but held firm.

Keeping my body tilted over the floor in case they suddenly gave way beneath me, I stood.

Solid.

Squatting, I converted the chisel to the knife with the micro-edge activated. It sliced through the remaining blockage as if cutting soft cheese, which further encouraged me to believe the stuff was organic in nature, put there by something other than the Endar. When I got it half-cleared, I set the laser ring to illuminate and peered inside. Other than the chipped debris in the opening, it was the same stone construction as most everything else in this place. Three meters forward, the channel slanted slightly downward.

The flow of warm air felt like heaven on my face.

The vent was large enough to crawl through and I was willing to accept 'somewhere else' over 'here', so I hurriedly finished clearing the opening.

As I got to my feet and straightened, I almost bumped my head on the kid's shins. She was standing at the edge of the pit, her little face drawn with stress.

I scrambled out. "Is okay. Me find way go out." I pulled my camo bag free, grabbed one of the two remaining stim tabs, and dropped it on my tongue.

Liri's eyes strayed to the pit. Cruel as it seemed, its ghoulish contents were my best argument for her to follow me into the vent. She would need every bit of motivation she could summon to get out of this place.

I gave her another moment then snapped my fingers to draw her attention back. "Must go now," I said. "Air is warm," I added, throwing in a bonus as I climbed back down into the freezing air of the pit.

An uneasy feeling suddenly ran over me. Something was wrong.

It was the stim tab taking effect, I reasoned as I squatted down in front of the opening.

Wrong.

There was no air coming from the vent. It was blocked again.

CHAPTER 49

Zam Fiella

The clog appeared to be made of the same material I had chipped out earlier, only this time, when I reached a cautious finger to push against the surface, it flexed.

Did I want to take on the occupant of this vent? Nope. But there was no other way out of this place.

Muttering curses under my steaming breath, I cut the clog out again. Then I climbed back out of the pit and, grasping Liri's hand, pulled her a few steps along the circumference of the rim, to crouch and to watch the opening. I did not convert the knife back to a harmless tube.

We waited in silence, staring at shadows inside of shadows.

Within moments there was a shift of movement inside the vent. A short, thick shape reached out of the opening to probe around.

I had trimmed out the fresh blob in one piece and laid it aside on the bones. The tendril found it, swelled on the end to increase contact, and began to tug it back. It looked as if it planned to use it to reseal the opening.

I leaped up, ran to the space above the vent, and reached down with both hands to catch the end of the sticky slab before it disappeared inside the hole.

A wave of energy shot through it, rattling my body from head to toe.

With a yelp of pain, I released it and collapsed onto my side.

A pinkish semitransparent glob slowly raised above the rim in front of my face.

A Brktar!

The bastard had paralyzed me!

More important, however, the Brktar at Duff's poker game had responded to Union Basic.

"Help us," I gasped. "Local 100866. Duff. The Cheel. Tell we need help."

The blob vanished downward.

Did it understand? Down in the tunnel, the Brktar seemed to understand what I said. Or was I violating the first rule in interspecies communication by superimposing Human responses onto an alien species?

This was bad. Even through my numbed flesh I felt the floor sapping what little body heat I had left. I twisted and thrashed, fighting to regain control of my muscles.

Liri came over and pulled my legs straight. Then she lifted my head and pushed me upright by the shoulders to a sitting position.

Squatting in front of me, she peered cheerfully into my face. "Okay, Vivi Zant?" She giggled.

She talked? After all this time, the kid talked? And she thought this was funny?

For a moment, I was dumbstruck. Then I realized, in all this mess she deserved some reason to laugh and I probably did look ridiculous, caked in white powder and flopping on the floor.

"Yes," I gasped. Thank the Goddess my toes were tingling and I could wiggle them again. While I waited to repossess my body, I decided I might as well use the time productively. "How why you speak Basic?"

Her smile faded as she lifted a hand to tap her temple. "Endar not hear." Her word for them sounded more like Endiel. Her hand fluttered down in a gesture toward her throat. "We no talk Endiel words. We talk Basic words."

Vocalizing actual Endar sound was impossible for a Human throat, too. "They teach you?"

She nodded.

"Me no telepath." The last word was not part of Basic. "Me no hear you," I corrected.

"No telepath," she repeated. "You no hear talk inside head."

I thought Saura might strongly agree with that on a certain level.

"Yes." I wondered why she had never spoken before, then realized, of all the times I'd seen her, there was only one other place where we'd actually had a chance to exchange words. "Why no speak on Id-wal Station?" And, yeah, it was an insensitive question, considering everything that went down out there, but I needed as much infor-mation as I could grab while I had the chance.

She took a moment to respond.

Names of places remain a problem in Union Basic. Not everyone calls them the same thing.

Liri's expression tightened to sadness. "Mother and fa-ther—Endiel kill. Me was fear."

I shivered, then realized feeling and motion were returning to the rest of my body.

There were a few more things I wanted to know. "How old are you?"

"Nine turns." She held up nine fingers.

"Do you know where here is?"

Her frown reappeared.

"No," I corrected hastily, "not here." I made a small circle with my hand. "Here." I flopped an arm in a broader gesture. "Where see me with Endiel. Where more Makima is."

That brought an anxious reaction. She shook her head. "Here look same Endiel place, Zam Fiella, but big! Makima here listen... Do hurt them?"

"Makima or people Makima listen to?"

"Makima."

"Not know."

"Steyl hurt you."

Seok? "Him not like Human."

Her hand touched the patch on her face. "Not like me here."

Here? "You know him?"

"Steyl Seok rule labs on Zam Fiella. Many babies there. Steyl say me special. Father say must return me home. Is big angry. People help mother, father, me run away. Endiel follow, kill ship."

I wondered if I knew anyone who had backed that play. Right now, it didn't matter. "Sad happen."

She nodded solemnly.

"How are you special?" As in, was there anything else I should know?

She smiled shyly. "You know."

"Tell."

"Make people not see me. Make people do and forget why. No others can do." Her expression clouded. "Steyl Seok say make others to learn do. He say make new children same me."

The High Jerak said his labs were working to produce clones of Liri with her skills. Would her loss set his vile program back? I didn't think so. He had behaved as if he were ready to destroy her—like he already had what he needed from her.

"Ones Liri make forget," I asked, "can remember later?"

She looked frightened.

"Is okay," I reassured her. I was pretty sure I knew the answer but it never hurt to confirm. "Can tell."

"No. Not remember."

"Never?"

"Never no more. Thing Steyl wears. Thing he give guards. You have?" She asked.

"No. Why? Want erase me?"

She considered me with a solemn expression. "No. Want know if bad person. Vivi Zant not bad?"

"No try be bad. Sometimes fail." I sighed. This kid had been through bad things beyond losing her family. I tapped my forehead with a forefinger. "Endiel thing protect from erase?"

"Yes. Steyl Seok think shield stop all things can do," she added.

Was that a smirk?

A chill crept down my spine. "Can do things shield no stop?"

She looked at me with a guarded expression. "Think learn more things when grow."

Well, by the Holy Plinth, why not, considering everything else?

The last of the tingling sensation was leaving my muscles. I rubbed my hands together. They felt like clubs. "You know here situation bad, yes? Cold kill if we no go."

"Yes." Her eyes went to the pit.

"Can you telepath person outside here? Me friends help." I had no idea how to convey Saura or Duff to her as a target.

Fear flitted in her eyes. "Threadmaster—" her word sounded different to my ears from the one the High Jerak used; more like Uranta. The variations told me her people actually did have a spoken language of their own. "Him hear me. Momma say Urantas not good."

Ah, yes, the Threadmaster—only she had added an 's' for plural. Urantas. I wondered how many levels of deepening uneasiness I had the capacity to feel. "How?"

"Urantas have much power. Can pull minds together, make work as one. Endiel take them away Zam Fiella. They make plans."

"How many Threadmasters here?"

"One."

"Liri afraid of Endar and Threadmaster, why come here?"

"Feel my people. Walk many days before feel."

Yeah, she had done that. The High Jerak said the Minders' range was limited, which was the only thing keeping the renegade embassies outside the Zone free of his influence. "You know Endar here?"

"People tell, yes."

"People?"

"My people here."

"Tell you Steyl here?"

"No. Maybe not know. Steyl rule Zam Fiella." Her face twitched with sadness and fear.

"Thing in hole," I gestured toward the vent below us. "I ask help us."

"Understand. I no blank mind."

A stab of panic drove through my body. With no threat to me, I had not realized how dangerous the kid could be to the people around me! "No blank people's mind! Only when me tell! Please."

She nodded.

"And the Brktar? Liri tell help?" I ventured hopefully.

"No. Gone fast," she said.

Well, that was a big opportunity lost.

CHAPTER 50

Plants in the Darkness

I had no idea how far the Brktar would travel to carry my message—if it even understood Basic. If it was a kid playing in the tunnels the way kids did on stations and ships, I may have scared it out of its mind.

At least it hadn't closed the opening again.

While I finished recovering, we used the hooks to fish more fabric from the deathpit. Most of it was old and fragile, crumbling in our hands. Liri finally found a piece that held up under the knife well enough for me to slit it into strips. Together with the rags I had previously salvaged, we wrapped our hands and knees. The tunnel floor was smooth, but a prolonged crawl would require as much cushioning as we could find.

By the time we finished we were both shivering, a sign our bodies were fast depleting the resources we needed to fight the effects of the cold. My chips warned me that when the shivering stopped, we would be in a state of peril.

I really didn't want to tangle with a defensive Brktar again, but if they used the tunnel it had to lead somewhere outside this place. It would be difficult to talk once we started crawling, so I told Liri to touch my leg frequently to stay in contact and to tug my foot if she had a problem. If we had something major to discuss, she would have to squeeze up beside me. "Know I want help you," I said.

She nodded.

"Trust?" I had never asked my little brother for trust; he had given it unconditionally.

Again, the nod.

I could not fail this child.

Climbing down into the pit, I motioned her to the edge. "We go."

She stiffened as I lifted her into the bone-chilling cold.

"Inside warmer," I promised as my breath steamed.

Her expression said she wasn't thrilled with the plan, but she followed me in. I set the laser ring to a beam of light and we began to crawl.

Two meters in, I realized I had made a major tactical error. The air flowing from the duct had felt blissfully warm on my skin compared to the pit. That quickly changed when it blew steadily into my face. Windchill factor, my chips whispered. Great. I hadn't wrapped the rags around my head this time for fear of the dust getting in my eyes. Now the draft was seeping away the last of my body heat.

Still, my bulk protected Liri from its effect. I clenched my teeth and kept going.

It didn't take long for boney spacer flesh to feel the physical effects of contact with the floor of the vent. I paused, muttering curses at gravity, planets, and people in general, and rolled on my side to check the kid. "You okay?"

Telepathy might not be such a bad thing in some situations.

She squirmed over to where I could see her in the light of the ring. "Okay, Vivi Zant." She sounded positive.

"Good." I rolled back and continued onward.

The slant in the tunnel I had seen earlier lay ahead. I pulled myself to the edge and peered down. The incline was doable at twenty degrees, but my light didn't reach the bottom.

It would be hell trying to back up this thing.

As a spacer, I was used to moving through tight access shafts inside ships. Even stations didn't waste room on ship people. Some of them kept debarkation tubes down to one-person belt tows so small in diameter that planet-born and heavier first-gen crew had difficulty using them. The restricted space didn't bother me. Not knowing how long we would have to crawl or what lay at the other end, however, did.

By the time we reached the bottom of the incline, which ended up being roughly ten meters in length, I had begun to question my judgment. Another ten along a flat stretch led to twinges of claustrophobia. I tried hard not to think about the mass of world sitting above me—like a couple hundred meters of planetary crust, and teaming streets, and massive buildings...

"You do good?" I asked Liri again.

There was a moment of silence. "Knees hurt."

Yeah, mine too. "Will be out soon." I hoped that was not a lie.

At least the crawl worked my system to keep me warmer. It was also exhausting the last of my energy reserves. I took the last stim tab and moved on.

We passed several side vents branching off at different angles. I would pause at the openings, sucking air to calm my instincts of a pending, horrible death. As we moved along, some of the side tunnels looked different. They were round and smooth-sided. The clog in the vent had kept the powdery white dust of the pit out of this maze, but in the glow of my ring I could see faint trails cutting through a light accumulation of debris inside those tubes. Something dragged up and down this system often enough to wipe a wide strip down the center. Meanwhile, down to pulling along on my belly, I was doing a terrific job of sweeping up the rest, right to the edges.

Somewhere along the way, we moved out of the rushing air current into a gentler flow.

Ahead of us, my light revealed a clump of material at the base of a wall. I paused, my heart hammering. If that was fur, it might herald a problem.

I crawled cautiously into the cross section of vents to investigate.

The clump was a little tuft of green moss.

Well, sonnofabitch!

I sidled up as close to it as I could and shined the light on my face. "Hey," I said softly. "See me? I need you to get a message to that Frairy bastard, Duff. We have big problems. Tell him to meet us wherever this duct comes out."

Then I pinched off a small clump and stuffed it under my sleeve. Duff said the stuff would grow wherever it was dropped, which meant it didn't die right after being uprooted. Maybe the Cheel could use it as a tracking device, to target our location and send someone to help.

Maybe the stuff was Cheel. Maybe not. I didn't linger over it, and I sure didn't plan to tell the kid about it.

Kids don't need to know everything.

***

Even if my shipskins had been intact, my knees would not have taken much more wear. I was hungry and thirsty, dirty, stinky, and my wrists and ankles leaked blood where I'd torn at the restraints in the High Jerak's torture chamber. Not to mention I needed to piss. The filter and cup could alleviate my thirst, except I couldn't reach them in the tight confines of the tunnel.

I figured if the kid saw the process it would put her off the water. But desperate thirst had a way of getting people past that. We just hadn't reached that stage yet.

I paused to give my body a break, half-rolling onto my side. Liri squirmed up even with my legs and flashed me a brave smile. Then she laid her head down on her extended arm to rest.

Yeah. Crawling was exhausting. I decided to snatch a few moments of R and R, too.

The moment I rested my head, it filled with swirling thoughts. I wondered what was happening outside, where Saura was, if she was still onworld, and if the EA had already left the Moneyworld with a new rejection slip in hand. Which, considering what I knew now, would be a good thing. Of course, they wouldn't agree. Would it even matter if I got out of this maze and explained it to them?

Probably not. We Humans make our moves and pay our dues.

Funny, that. It sounded like a rhyme a little kid made up. I had to get Liri out of here so she could make up her own new, better rhymes.

I suddenly realized that my face felt warm. The air current had stopped flowing over me. When I positioned the light of the ring forward, it reflected off a shiny, bulging surface that filled the vent ahead of us.

"Oh. Hey, hi," I said. Shit!

Liri shifted against my knees and scurried back to hide at my feet. She put a hand on my heel.

"We no threat," I said to the Brktar clogging the tunnel. My voice sounded thick and muffled in the space. "Need help. Want out. Cheel," I added as an afterthought.

The Brktar extended a bit of its body along the floor toward me. Remembering the nasty shock from the rim of the pit, I watched warily.

"Need help," I repeated.

It emitted a low, melodic tone and tapped the pod on the floor three times.

Liri shook my foot. "Wants you touch, Vivi Zant," she said.

"Don't erase it! Is it friendly?"

"Don't know. Is three," she replied.

Three? Three Brktar? We couldn't move forward with three Brktar blocking our way.

The Brktar repeated the action and sound.

"Help, Please. Want out." I said to the glistening surface.

It repeated the tap.

I slowly reached out and touched the extended pod.

Electricity shot through me, rattling my teeth. Lirilune, with her hand on my foot, got the worst of it.

Paralyzed and unable to speak, I felt the smooth fluid-filled sack of the Brktar glide over and around me. My body rolled and I realized the flexible wrap completely encased me, with my face pressing into its surface.

Air! My brain screamed as darkness closed in.

Pick a Different Day

"She doesn't look too good," Duff said.

Saurubi hissed him to silence as Meeroush and Shoff caught at my shoulders and rolled me onto my back.

I opened my eyes to find the four of them staring down at me.

"Tell the EA to stop everything," I gasped. "We don't want membership!"

"And you think they'll listen to us?" Duff growled.

No, but they had to listen to me. "Liri—we have to help her—" No matter how many times I had rehearsed the explanation in the tunnel, my brain, left on automatic, put the conspiracy to destroy the EA and seize control of the Whooex Union second to the kid's safety.

I pushed up and looked about groggily. Duff, Saurubi, two Brktar, Meeroush, and Shoff. No kid.

Panic kicked my alertness up a few notches. "Where is she?"

"Who?"

"The kid," I gasped. "She was behind me! Where is she?" The open mouth of a tunnel yawned beyond my feet. I tried to squirm toward it.

Saura squatted beside me and put a hand on my arm to stop me. "Vivi. All good. Take breath and relax." She wrinkled her nose and lifted her hand away. "Stink like death."

A shudder ran over me. "Saura, you have no idea."

The assassin team had moved past us. They pulled a fluid sack from the vent and rolled it out on the floor.

Liri lay encased in it. She appeared to be sleeping peacefully.

"It's okay! She won't do anything to you," I told the Tabisee. Meeroush cast me an indifferent look. Shoff ignored me.

The Brktar split and flowed away, settling her gently to the surface as it reformed into a familiar blob. It hooted at the other two.

The three of them carried on a musical conversation while the rest of us stared at the kid.

She jerked to a sitting position, her eyes wild.

Ears dropped and bodies tensed as everyone froze warily.

Oh, yeah. Mind erase! "Lirilune!"

Her eyes found me. With white powder clinging to her flesh and caked in her hair and clothes she hardly looked sane. I didn't want to think about how strange I must appear.

"Is okay," I told her. "Friends."

After a moment, the expression in her eyes pulled back to reality. "Vivi Zant," she said placing her hand on my foot.

"Is okay," I told the others. "Liri no harm you. She speak Basic."

It took a moment for the others' translation software to kick over to Basic.

They did not look convinced.

"That's great, really great," Duff exclaimed. "Now can the assassins get these two on their feet so we can get the hell out of here?"

Saura moved to help Liri stand.

"How did you find us?" I asked the other two Tabisee, who were carefully minimizing contact with my tattered shipskins as they dragged me up to stand on wobbly legs.

"The Cheel you passed in the tunnel helped the Brktar locate you," Shoff said. "You nearly scared the little one to death with that ugly face of yours."

My knees tried to buckle when they released me. "A minute," I pleaded. "Do you have food and water?"

Shoff came up with two small, flat bags from a pocket in her vest.

With a nod of thanks, I took them and passed one to Liri. "Hold tight," I instructed her, holding mine up for her to see what I did. It took everything I had to rip the end off the shaped nozzle. The compressed fluid unpacked, pushing the bag to a quarter liter cylinder. I squirted the contents into my mouth.

The kid managed her own drink just fine.

"We did not plan for this situation," Meeroush said as he passed me two food packets. They were a popular cherry-flavored energy bar often found on the Outer Rim. I hesitated, wondering if it was safe to feed one to Liri, then remembered that she'd pilfered her way across T'lek T'la in the last ninety-something days, eating whatever she got her hands on.

She gobbled it down.

Food and water helped, but I needed something more in order to get out of here. "Saura, give me a stim."

"Shipskins confiscated." She was wearing Tabi armor again. Her ears tipped irritation at the Tabisee security team. "Give." She stretched out a hand and waggled her fingers at them imperiously.

"They are for Tabisee. It could be bad for her," Meeroush warned.

"Of course, bad," she spat irritably. "Not as bad as dying in cold tunnel! Vivi will handle pain."

I probably questioned my handling of the pain as much as Meeroush did, but I couldn't acknowledge it. "I won't last without it," I told him. That was the truth.

With a doubtful tip, he passed a thin packet to her.

Saura punctured it with a claw and unwrapped the tiny wafer.

"It's fine," I said. No need to explain how we had confirmed we could use each other's stims during a long night of drinking back on Pele' Station. There was a lot of pain and elevated heart rates involved, but we had survived.

I dropped the tab on my tongue. Same bitter as hell taste.

I did a slow thirty-count with the others hovering watchfully. A tingle spread along the nerves of my extremities, then adrenalin slammed in, causing me to suck a deep breath. My eyes widened, my head cleared and the weakness fell away. The trembling in my limbs shifted from exhaustion to contained energy.

"Okay." I exhaled and pulled up straight. "What's the plan?" I already felt a twitch in my fingers and toes as those muscles constricted. Things were going to start hurting very quickly.

"We walk. Fast," Duff said. "The Brktar carried you a long way, but we're still underneath the Trade Zone. We can't port out until we're outside the Compound perimeter."

"We should hurry." I shivered.

Meeroush shucked out of his jacket and dropped it over my shoulders. He turned to Liri. "Carry?

"No. Thank you." She smiled up at him boldly, but she slid her hand into Saura's.

As I gratefully tugged the black security leather closer, a movement beside Duff caught my attention.

"Piika?" I exclaimed in shock. One kid in danger was one too many. "Duff, what the hell is she doing here?"

He shrugged. "We need her."

"This is no task for a kid! You have no right to put her in such danger!"

Piika peered at me from beneath her jacket hood and smiled serenely. "It is for whomever the task falls, Vivi Zant. The circumstances and person are not always ideal."

That pretty much summed up the whole situation for me, too. Not ideal. Yet here I was. I had not chosen to be a part of this. But she had. Guess that made her the better person.

Saura suddenly caught at my right arm. "What is?" She had the good sense not to touch the purple smudge on the back of my hand as she turned it for a closer look.

I saw uneasiness shift ears as the two other Tabisee exchanged glances. They knew.

So did Duff.

Shoff silently tugged Saurubi's hand away from my arm.

"You should know," I said, "Seok tortured me. I don't know who or what I gave up."

"You spilled your guts." Duff shrugged. "Now can we please get moving?" He shifted his attention to the stone wall to his left. "Thanks for your help, folks."

It took me a moment to see the three blobs huddled along the side of the viaduct, their transparency camouflaged them so well. "Is one of them Local 100866?"

"He couldn't make it. This is some of his top crew."

"Thank you much," I told them solemnly in Basic. I mentally reserved my thanks for the two electrocutions they'd issued to me.

"Is good," they chirped in unison. They slid over to the vent and dropped low to slither inside.

I wished our way out of this place was as simple as theirs.

"What is happening outside?" I asked as sudden heat ran through my limbs. The stim was taking effect.

"Civil unrest," Duff answered without looking back. "We're keeping them distracted, but it won't last. The Sat Quar has the Earth Alliance diplomatic envoy confined to the transport ship at the Das until everything settles down. We must get you two out of here and stashed somewhere."

To begin a new round of negotiations for our lives.

The muscles in my fingers snapped rigidly straight for a painful moment.

"Why is all this down here still open?" I asked to shift my attention away from my discomfort. It did seem like gross negligence on the part of Endar security to ignore these subterranean passages.

"These tunnels may be vastly old but they are still in use. The first one hundred meters depth beneath the Zones falls under Whooex jurisdiction," the Frairy explained. "Endar have full authority to isolate that area. But not to damage the infrastructure. We're well below that depth."

"The Brktar carried us down?"

"This is their terrain. They specialize in moving light freight between the Das and other points through their network of tunnels."

"Discretely?" I asked. For a spacer, the word was synonymous with smuggling contraband.

Duff chuffed.

This world was a hub of illegal activity! "So, the round tunnels..."

"The tubes. They belong exclusively to the Brktar. They burn them, and any monitoring devices the Endar try to plant in them, with their excretions."

My skin suddenly itched.

Talk of the Brktar shady activity reminded me of a more serious topic. I looked at the Tabisee security team. "The live cargo you thought they were smuggling? It's Liri's people. The Endar have hundreds of them inside the Grip. Apparently they can't do everything she can, but the Endar use them to telepathically mine other members' thoughts and actions for information the Primacy can use for blackmail and manipulation. Luckily, the Makima—her people—have a limited range that can't reach members outside the Trade Compound. They planted my DNA and destroyed the *Obega* to force the rest of you under their influence."

Shoff gave a spitting curse and the two assassins leaned their heads close to talk.

"Can't we port out?" I squeaked as the muscles in my calves tightened.

"Just because the Endar don't have jurisdiction down here doesn't mean they don't monitor it," Duff said. "If we port now, they can run a trace to our destination."

"There is movement in one of the lateral passages behind us," Shoff announced abruptly.

"Endar?" Duff asked.

"The Cheel sees them," Piika spoke up. "There are seven—" She broke off, with an outraged gasp.

"What?" Duff asked.

"They are destroying the Cheel colonies." The grim expression on her little face was intimidating. She squared her shoulders. "It does not matter. There is always more Cheel to see."

I was sure the loss of a few clumps of growth was tragic to her, but the idea of spying plants everywhere was kinda creepy. On the other hand, the green stuff had saved the kid and me.

I thought about pulling out the clump I had stashed under my cuff and dropping it here, but that seemed a betrayal of intent. It deserved a sunny spot.

If we got out of here.

"The Sat Quar does not have jurisdiction over city levels," Meeroush objected.

"When the riots ignited, they declared martial law, claiming a threat to the Consortium," Duff told him. "Their current authority covers the whole city and the Das. We should have thought that through a bit better. We'll know next time."

The assassins sniffed in amusement.

I didn't find it funny. "So, what do we do?" Being recaptured was not on my agenda.

"How close are they?" Duff asked Piika.

"At our original entry point."

He swore. "We'll have to find another passage out."

"Tabi are not herded." Two pairs of gray ears were set hard against that option. From the way the fur on their ruffs puffed, I guessed they were prepared to fight their way through any blockade.

"Pick different day to be heroes," Saura told them sharply.

The larger Tabisee looked at her, their ears twisting edgily, and I held my breath.

"Is strategic," Saura said.

"Acceptable," Shoff agreed.

Three sets of furry ears dropped to situational awareness. Three pairs of amber eyes locked on Duff.

"Now that you have your family differences sorted, let's pick up the pace," he said.

All three made a spitting sound of dismissal. I exhaled a silent sigh of relief.

Saura clutched Lirilune's hand and followed Shoff. Meeroush pushed Duff, Piika, and me after them as he brought up the rear.

I waited for red fire to light the walls behind our backs.

"They are expanding out into other passages to cut us off," Meeroush told Duff.

"We have to go to plan B." Duff panted.

"What's plan B?" I asked.

No one replied as we continued at a light jog, which was slower than the others wanted but the best I could manage. Little shots of pain dinged the muscles in my calves every time my feet struck the floor.

I was not going to last much longer at this, or any other, pace.

"What's plan B?" I asked Duff again.

"We have to use the Zone system to port up. But, first, we have to go farther in so we can come up on a street."

"Seven beings rising into Zone without gate clearance will set off security alerts," Shoff warned.

"Gee, thanks," Duff snapped. "Just be ready to grab Zant and the telepath and run for cover. We meet up at the Rhomian embassy."

"The kid," I said. "Liri can erase the minds of any observers."

"She has done it before," Meeroush agreed.

"I'm dealing with a bunch of geniuses," Duff growled. "Her trick doesn't work on Zant. So, who else is immune? No. There are too many uncontrolled variables."

Shoff froze. Her ears made several lateral twitches, then slowly laid back. She was not happy.

"The sensors we dropped along the way are going dark," Meeroush told us as we slowed and looked at her.

"They're extending a tech-eclipse," Duff exclaimed. "We won't be able to port out if their blackout zone reaches us."

"We must use the Zone system now," Shoff was moving forward again.

Duff swore. "Do you know where we are?"

"It is a public place. There will be witnesses. We can use them to argue our defense."

"No!" The Frairy exclaimed furiously.

"Where is it?" I asked between gasps.

"The Saalyu," Duff snapped. "There's no way I'm porting us there."

The assassins' expressions said differently.

The Saalyu

Shoff warned us the port would take us to the highest horizontal level of the Saalyu above our current position. If there were any walls or physical barriers between us, we might emerge in a different hall, room, or even level from the others.

Miraculously, we came out together inside what looked like a luxury entertainment suite in an athletics arena. It was fronted with a huge viewing screen and furnished with four long couches that had strange, wavy surfaces. Everything that was not floor to ceiling gray-tinted screen or rich, brown wood trim was covered in a lush burgundy fabric.

Meeroush still gripped my arm, but his attention was focused on Duff and Shoff as the pair fumbled with some type of device. No one was running, and the Frairy was vehemently swearing over "black market junk." I took a moment to catch my breath, straighten kinked fingers, and stare at the vast space outside the chamber window behind us. Somehow, the screen warped the perspective on the area beyond it so that anywhere I looked snapped into clear view. I could see we were so high above an arena floor that it was dizzying. The glass-fronted levels in the circle around us continued upward, rising to a serene blue ceiling filigreed with silver trim. If I turned my eyes in any one direction that area jumped into clear focus so I could see lights and movement in alcoves across the space, or activity on the floor below. Piika and Liri were pasted against the surface, staring down. Saura was two meters across the thick carpet from me, her body tensed in a crouch that I recognized.

She was prepared for a fight.

Whatever Duff and Shoff were struggling with, they were too slow getting it activated. One moment they were kneeling on the floor across from each other, working frantically on some multilegged electronic tube, the next they were flying backward, bowled over by the sudden importation of two Endar guards.

Saura, however, was ready.

She leaped, swarming over the Endar like blue lightning dancing across a black surface. I was pleased to see she even used a few EA Marine combat moves as she went for their headgear.

"Don't—" Meeroush barely got the word out before one of them crumpled to the floor, pinning Duff under layers of dark leather. Blood the color of yellow-green bile flowed across the beautiful design of the carpet. The other guard managed to get off a single shot. The red blast hit the elaborate wood trim that framed the window of the chamber. I didn't know whether it was the ricochet from the shot or Saurubi that caused the Endar to collapse backward against an ornate door.

"—kill them," the Tabisee male finished, which seemed ironic since the red blast from our attacker's weapons showed they were set to kill us.

I was afraid my partner only heard the last part of his statement as she stood up, her claws dripping yellow ichor.

"Not dead," she stated flatly as she flicked her wrist to clean the stuff off. "Will just require extra work to function normal again."

Her fellow Tabisee nodded at her with what I interpreted as a newfound respect.

She put a foot on the first victim and shoved it off Duff.

"Great, just great!" He came up yelling. "Can we all get together and move out of here now? There are at least five more of these murderous bastards out there looking for us."

Meeroush released my arm and moved to clear the second Endar away from the door.

"We saw the other five," Piika announced calmly. "They are way far below, in the big flat area at the center."

Liri was still looking out into the vast space of the Saalyu. She reached back to fumble at my sleeve. "Vivi Zant!"

Duff scooped up Piika and carried her to the door.

"You stay down and keep silent." I heard him tell her.

Someone had wrestled the door open and the others were leaving, but the kid was still pressed to the window.

"Liri, we have to go."

She turned to look up at me.

I had seen enough terrified young faces in my youth to recognize one here. Shit! "What?"

"Makima up there," she jabbed a small finger upward. "Makima!"

An elaborate, highly wrought, gleaming structure hung from the blue span of ceiling in the center of the Saalyu. The sight of a mass that large, suspended in gravity made my skin creep. "Inside that thing?" I asked her. Even from here it looked big enough to house the population of a small station.

"No! Those. Fly things!"

It took a moment for me to see the metal spheres moving in the heights. The balls were mere specks compared to the chandelier.

"Sat Quar security drones?" Shoff was suddenly beside us. "They are exclusive to the Saalyu. We go now!"

Liri had located her people inside a massive city; she would recognize them here.

A sickened anger crept over me. The Makima I'd seen appeared to be adults. Did the Endar keep children here, too?

"What size are they?" I asked Shoff.

"This." She indicated a space of about fifty centimeters. "Too small for a Frairy child to fit inside." She grasped my shoulder and pulled on me.

She was right; not big enough for a small child.

"Other telepath life on Zam Fiella?" I asked Liri as I caught her hand and dragged her away from the window.

"No!" She shook her head. "Makima. They come."

A glance back confirmed that at least a dozen of the dots were zipping toward our location. Shoff was right: they were too small to fit a child inside.

But their size was enough to house a brain and support mechanicals. I thought I would puke in horrified realization. "Liri! We must go now!"

Shoff thrust us out of the chamber and closed the door.

I stumbled off a step and over a raised strip with a gently curving trough down its middle that projected from the center of the hallway.

"Bipeds on the left side." She heaved me back on the broad, flat border along the wall. "This is a Jhampoon Coalition level."

One of the original three founders of the Whooex Union—and something to help redirect my horrified thoughts. "I've never seen one," I babbled as I ran.

Liri was a reluctant weight trailing on my arm. I knew she wanted answers for what she had mentally touched outside that screen, but my suspicion of what they might be made my whole body cringe. I didn't want to address it with her. I didn't know how. Right now, we had to get away before those spheres found us.

"Lirilune! Not now, please," I snapped raggedly.

We ran through empty corridors until Meeroush threw open a door and we charged into a small room full of cleaning gadgets and supplies.

No one asked how he knew the location of this particular supply closet as we flooded in to collapse on the floor or lean against the shelves, catching our breath.

"Can we port out of here?" I rasped. I was fighting to straighten my knees from a muscle-locked bend.

Meeroush passed over another stim pack. Saura ripped it open, and I swallowed the tab.

"Not using a Zone port," Duff said. "We're lucky we got through the last one. We should have been shunted directly to a security point."

"Endar allowed the port," Shoff told him. "They did not want it to register on the Saalyu's official record."

"Oh," he said.

Yeah, oh. No record, no questions. It meant if intruder alarms were going off, they were not sounding a general alert. Only Endar security knew about us.

We couldn't stay here.

"Maybe we should get out into the public areas," I said between gritted teeth as my calf muscles knotted.

"Past secret now," Saura agreed. "More witnesses see, better chance to live."

The others exchanged looks.

"True. There will be many beings in public areas," Meeroush observed. There was a rustle of activity as the others prepared to get back to their feet.

"Vivi Zant!" Liri was pulling at my sleeve again.

My fingers had locked in clenched fists. I shoved them to my sides. "Can we talk about what you saw later?" I asked through a haze of pain.

"Yes," she nodded briskly. "But Steyl is here. Makima brought."

Mother Universe! Five Endar following us, and one had to be the High Jerak.

"What?" Duff demanded.

"Seok is here. She can erase an Endar mind, but he has a mechanism to counter her effects. It's some type of triangle-shaped thing they wear on a circlet on their foreheads."

"All of them?"

"I don't know how many he has."

"I have enough," a purring voice announced in Tabi as the door flung open and the High Jerak stepped into the storage room.

CHAPTER 53

When the Universe Comes Together

"Disarm them," he ordered the four guards behind him. Only he and one of the guards wore the circlets, so maybe they were in short supply.

"No make forget," I warned Liri as she cringed beside me.

As two of the Sat Quar pushed into the space around us, light glinted on metal in the air behind Seok. One of the spheroids hovered at his shoulder.

Liri moaned and pressed into my side even harder.

The High Jerak looked at her. Glanced at the globe. "Return to your post," he ordered.

It zipped away as another of the guards stepped forward.

Long ebony fingers shoved Liri aside and slid over my skin. Meeroush's jacket and the camouflaged pack stashed in my armpit joined the pile of weapons collected from the Tabisee and Duff.

"Tabi property," Shoff—the one with the most confiscated items—snarled.

"You'll get them back," Seok replied. "It only depends on whether you carry them out or they're found on your dead bodies." The distorted sounds of the Tabi language from the translator made my insides twitch. I could only imagine it how it affected the Tabisee.

One of the guards was focused on Duff. I heard a sudden squeak of outrage and a clatter as the Endar pulled a wiggling, fighting Piika from a box of supplies on the shelf behind the Frairy and dangled her in the air.

The High Jerak's reaction was startling. He jerked a step back, the layers of leather making a whuff of sound as he bumped the face of the door. "What is that creature doing here?" He screamed in Arpi fury. "Search the vile thing!"

When the guard pulled back the Frairy child's jacket hood, several clumps of green tumbled to the floor. She squealed in outrage as a second guard switched the setting on his tazer and blasted the Cheel bits to ashes.

Which reminded me of the blades I had tucked under my cuff.

Eyes to her ears.

I pried the fingers of one hand straight with the bent claws of the other. This was not sunlight, I thought apologetically as I fumbled the plant out from beneath my sleeve. While everyone focused on an outraged Piika, I awkwardly pressed the roots onto the floor in the shadows beside me, taking care to give the blades a clear line of sight to the whole spectacle.

The guard finished peeling Piika's clothes away, then threw the child at Duff.

Duff caught her and shoved her behind him. "You should be very careful what you do here," he warned the High Jerak calmly.

Seok's face flooded darker gray. "City Councilor Duffpa Bah-prexnopha. Do you threaten us?"

Piika gave a plaintive wail as the guard finished burning her clothes and her Cheel blades to ashes.

Saura's hand flashed a message at me against the armor on her thigh. "Prepare. Neutralize threat."

Liri still pressed hard against me, but she was calmer now that the drone was gone. I wished again that I had a mental link with her as my heart raced. The Endar could burn us to a cinder right here and no one would ever know. But if they wrested her away from us, everything was lost for sure. "Good go," I signed Saura. There was no doubt in my mind that my partner could handle whatever she planned to do.

"Do you threaten us?" Duff fired back at the High Jerak. "We are citizens of this world and member species of the Whooex Union of Stars."

"You are aiding a Human spy," Seok snarled.

"Human!" Duff exclaimed. He stared over at me in outrage. "You lying piece of excrement! You said you're the same species as that telepathic kid!"

The remark caught Seok off guard.

It was the best opening we could hope for.

Saura's thigh muscles uncoiled like springs as she threw herself at the High Jerak. Her claws clipped the metal ring and whisked it off the guard's head as she sailed past.

"Erase guards now!" I fired at Liri. "Not erase Steyl!"

The guard slashed at Saura, its ebony nails scoring furrows in her breastplate as it knocked her away. She twisted lithely under the fingers that snatched after the circlet and hit the floor on her feet, the ring and pendant in her hand. She flung it toward the shelves at the back of the space.

"Do!" I told Liri again.

I had no idea how far back she wiped their memories, but when those red, beady eyes started looking around in confusion, I knew she had succeeded.

The High Jerak gave a shriek of outrage and lunged for Saura, his hands clawed.

"No!" I shouted.

Shoff kicked out a foot, striking the nearest guard, knocking him sideways into Seok. The High Jerak's shoulder slammed the wall.

The guards reacted by surging to enclose him in a protective circle, blocking any retaliatory action he could make against the Tabisee. He emitted another furious shriek and the guards turned outward, toward the rest of us, their bodies lowered aggressively to block him even more tightly.

If he recovered enough to give them an order, we were dead.

"Tell go corridor and wait. Now!" I told Liri.

Instantaneously, the four straightened, dropped their weapons, and made an orderly retreat past the High Jerak to the hallway.

"Make deep sleep, no wake for Steyl orders," she said.

Brilliant. Hopefully it didn't result in brain damage. I shifted my attention back to Seok.

The High Jerak regained his composure. He smoothed his leather. "Clever, Captain Zant. You obviously exert strong influence over my archetype. Again, you help me refine my plan." The icy calm he exhibited in his torture chamber had descended over him again. "If you think my resources are limited to six soldiers, you are a fool. I have an army at my command. None of you will leave this place alive, so your small success is short-lived."

"Just shut up and listen." I had no idea what to say beyond that.

Duff and the Tabisee were on their feet now. Furry ears twisted as the assassins chose strike points on the tall being that stood in the doorway threatening us.

Killing the Endar in charge of security while he appeared to be performing his job would send us all to prison worlds, no matter what our defense.

"No one has to die," I said firmly. "We simply have to come to an agreement." Reeking and dressed in tatters, I hardly seemed the one to initiate some type of deal here, but no one else seemed to have the inclination to settle this—or the information that I had.

"The Primacy will never negotiate with filthy Humans," he snarled.

I shrugged. "We can take it before the Consortium—"

"Vivi," Saura said uneasily.

"Be careful what you do here," Duff muttered from his place farthest to my right around the wall of shelves.

"Just wait. I think you'll all agree on this once you hear it." As I told them about Seok's plans to clone Liri and use her skills to devastate the EA and seize control of the Whooex Union the scowls around me deepened to deadly glares. There were even a couple of rumbling growls.

Through it all the High Jerak seethed, his fingers twitching with rage.

There was a long silence when I came to the end.

"Hunh," Duff said at last.

"That is all a lie," Seok declared.

"You've seen what the kid can do," I reminded the others.

"You have no proof of anything," he said. "You will all die here and none of this will ever come to light."

He was right—if the next bit failed.

I feared it was mostly a bluff. I had to make him believe it. "You are wrong. Everyone will find out. This whole incident is on record." My stomach churned for making tiny Piika a target of this monster's unpredictable rage, but she, as well as the rest of us, were doomed if I failed to convince him.

The Frairy child moved a step out away from Duff and puffed out her little chest as she glared up at the Endar.

"The Cheel!" he spat in fury. "She only lets it hear. Its eyes are scorched to ashes."

"Oh, the Cheel has seen everything." I gestured to the ragged clumps of blades I had placed beside me. They'd had a clear view of everything that had played out here over the last few minutes. It wasn't a complete record, but he didn't know that.

The Cheel strands looked limp and withered.

It only takes one to see, I reminded myself.

Liri shifted in sudden interest and uneasiness flickered inside me. She hadn't known about the Cheel. If she was faking this whole situation, everything was over.

Her little fingers clench my arm and she pressed closer against my side.

"You can't erase this evidence," I told Seok. "It is out there, and everyone will be able to see and hear the Primacy's treachery. Your people will face humiliation and expulsion from the Consortium. Unless we work out a deal."

A wave of unpleasant odor wafted through the storage room, affirmation that Seok recognized when he was trapped. Duff, the two girls, and I coughed, but the Tabisee did not twitch a muscle as they stared at him.

"There is nothing I can do for you," he snapped.

"I think there's a lot you can do for us," I corrected him. "I think you carry a great deal of influence in the Primacy. You are head of the division running the research on the Makima. Maybe even the head of the whole project. And your clan is highly ranked." I saw him twitch. "This will be a major personal failure if the Primacy is embarrassed by your actions."

"What do you want?" he snarled.

"A change in your plans. Return all the Makima citizens the Endar Primacy holds in its control to their homeworld of Zam Fiella, and cede control of that area of space, including all citizens and their planet, to the Proambu. Do it and back out quietly. You can possibly play it as the end of your harassment campaign on your neighbor. No one else need know anything about it except a map-keeper in a dark little closet somewhere in obscurity." And his people at the highest levels, of course. "Just turn your back and walk away."

"And let Humans claim the Makima's skills? No!"

"No. You are right." The thought of some devious bastard in the EA gaining control of the Makima made the non-existent hair on my head stand on end. "No one should have access to their skill. Zam Fiella and all its citizens must be quarantined." I was familiar with that concept by now. "The Proambu can see to it. In exchange, your nasty little blackmail operation on this world stays hidden and in place—but without the Minders and Threadmasters. Your betrayal and your illicit information will remain unexposed." There was a lot of shifting and murmuring going on around me now. I rushed on before anyone could interrupt. "The representatives you control by blackmail can go on folding to your demands until they figure out you can't hurt them and they call your bluff. The ones you don't control right now: the Tabi, Xix, Ritto-ssa, Frairy, the Proambu, and anyone else that has slipped your net, will go on about their business, unthreatened by the Primacy. If you pursue your threat against the Tabisee over my DNA on the *Obega*, you will force them to reveal your activities. If you think you can use me to block EA member-ship in the Trade Consortium, go for it. Just be aware, you will bear the consequences if you void this agreement. In exchange,"—I had to raise my voice over the rising sounds of protest—"we agree not to reveal anything related to this situation, including what is discussed in this chamber today. That will include the Cheel—"

"I will not let you destroy centuries of work—" The High Jerak stopped, as if realizing his words only further implicated the Primacy in the things I had revealed.

"Agree and save face," I told him. "The alternative is the exposure of your illegal use of telepaths on the Moneyworld, your blackmail schemes, and your betrayal of trust and position. You will go down in Endar history as the one who got the Primacy ejected from the Whooex Trade Consortium.

"And don't think we can't verify the return of the citizens you hold in your possession," I added. "We have ways." After all, someone had gotten Liri and her family off that closely guarded planet in the first place.

If the MoMo wanted to take on a project this big, they should expect to follow through on it.

"Did I forget anything?" I asked the others.

"Human filth!"

Ignoring the High Jerak's outburst, Duff grinned cockily. The Tabisee continued to glare stonily at the Endar.

"I think we can make a deal," the Frairy said.

Three sets of ears tipped in cautious agreement.

Duff looked at Seok. "The number of people who are currently aware of what Zant has revealed is small. We can keep it that way. But don't get any ideas about killing off the people who are standing here. In fact, you better pray they all stay healthy. I can assure you there is a witness to this incident who has no problem exposing your treachery if any one of us gets a stubbed toe."

His skin darkening with rage and his leather layers rustling with contained fury, the High Jerak snarled.

"So," Duff reiterated. "The Endar Primacy will return all Makima citizens it holds in its custody to their homeworld, then cede the world and the surrounding space to the Proambu, for them to quarantine. To take effect immediately. In exchange, you secure our silence and the ability to carry on with your illegal activity on the Moneyworld, sans your telepathic spies, for as long as you can pull off your con. You'll leave the rest of us alone, and, of course, you will not want to mention the existence of any wayward Human who inadvertently arrived on this world, which means Captain Zant's presence will not go on record in any way and you will allow her to leave unmolested. The Tabi will ensure her partner and the child—"

"No!" The High Jerak shrieked.

"—and the child," Duff continued when Seok did not expand on his objection, "are removed from the Moneyworld immediately to save you any further concern on that issue. The vote on Earth Alliance admission to the Whooex Trade Consortium on the Moneyworld will remain active, and you agree to honor it, whatever the result."

"Humans will never gain admission to the Trade Consortium!" he hissed.

"I don't care," I told him. It was the one thing in their plan that would actually succeed, and that was fine with me. Whether Humans wanted to believe it or not, we were not ready for this place.

The High Jerak went still as stone.

I waited, not daring to breathe. The thought of destroying the Earth Alliance's financial future was bad enough, but humiliating the Primacy on such a massive scale was extremely dangerous. It might inflame their hatred of Humans to overt aggression and outright war. I sure didn't want to go down in history as the woman who destroyed the EA and the Whooex Union.

I had given him a face-saving, if painful, way out, but no one could ever be sure how another being would react under duress—

"For the integrity of the Endar Primacy, I accept this agreement," the High Jerak grated. "By my honor, the terms are recorded and will stand uncontested."

How the hell high up in Primacy leadership did he rank to make that sort of declaration? But, in his chamber he had spoken of the plans to take over the Whooex Union with authority, as if he was one of the architects, and he hadn't tried to argue the details now.

I was under no illusions. He only considered his plans temporarily delayed.

His red eyes locked on me. "Know this Captain Zant: you will feel the cost of obstructing the Primacy's destiny."

Yeah, I suspected that would not disappear off the Endar agenda.

They would have a hard time finding me without even the most basic wetware in my body.

I nodded. "No problem." My whole body gave a throb of pain as the second stim gave up its last bits of energy. I sucked in a deep breath and stiffened, refusing to show weakness in front of him.

So, was this it? Was it all over except for the secret negotiations and the messy clean up? Now everyone—maybe even the High Jerak—could go back to their lives. Except me, Saura, and Liri. We were the blasted space debris that the massive hull of the Whooex Union serenely passed through. Overdramatic? Maybe. But the thought hurt. A lot.

"Liri, wake the guards," I told the kid. Maybe Seok would spare their lives, but I doubted it.

He turned to look at his escort as they stiffened to attention. "Arrange transport for these people to the Tabi embassy immediately.

"Just take us to the Rhomian embassy," Duff said. "We'll manage it from there.

CHAPTER 54

The Fallout

I shivered in the cold wind that blew, unchecked, across the vast expanse of the Das. In my shipskins I would never have noticed it, but they were gone. I had to get used to the plain pants, shirt, and boots that represented my future.

Several Ritto approached from the base of the ship ramp to surround me with their large, ghostly-pale bodies. I wondered if they meant their action to shield me from the wind or to protect me from a tiny, poison dart seeking warm flesh out in the isolation of the port—possibly the High Jerak's parting gift to me.

Would my death even matter?

Saura was back in the hands of the Tabi Empire Universe Force, to whatever fate she faced. She refused to discuss it during the few moments of parting time her people allowed us. Mathet wanted us off world quickly, in case Seok had some crazy second thoughts and decided to storm the Tabi embassy for revenge. I understood. Besides, it made the ordeal of saying goodbye easier. It was an abbreviated exchange of words; if I hugged her, she would have stabbed me with a claw for exhibiting weakness.

The assassins and I exchanged a formal nod. But as he was turning away, Meeroush winked and grinned. Shoff gave a sniff of irritation when she saw him, but I swear, her ears softened a little bit.

The kid was a different thing. Under other circumstances, we could have been family. But not where I was headed. Life as a scrub, scrounging and begging on a station dock or space platform was nothing to offer a child. Just being there would put her in danger.

The Tabi ambassador graciously extended the custody of the Tabi Empire over Liri, temporarily guaranteeing her safety from the Endar or other curious seekers. The kid had grown close to my ex-partner in the few hours they shared, and the Tabi were letting her travel to their first jump point with Saura. At least Liri would know someone for a while, but they made it clear: devoting a star navigator to her care was not an option.

They weren't the most affectionate species around, but they would find Liri a good home and family. It could not be Makima, but it was a chance at some kind of life. She promised she would keep her telepathy in check, to be good, and we both cried at parting.

I had ensured that for her. Not perfect, but it was more than I could ever do for Anthy.

Mother Universe, my throat felt tight!

My own destination was the EA Outer Rim and the first Human settlement where the Ritto could safely set me off. The Tabi Empire had supplied me with some Whooex cred. It wasn't enough to get back the things I'd lost, but it would take me a little further into EA space without having to beg for food and a bed for a while.

Eyes on the future, Zant. I locked on the ship hull, not wanting to look around the Das. I was leaving so much behind on the Moneyworld.

Why did doing the right thing feel so wrong?

The hatch to the Ritto-ssa ship looked like a section of their hull was melting around the opening. I hadn't noticed that the day I arrived here: my eyes had only been for the little kid skipping off the ship behind me.

There was some kind of disturbance at the base of the gangplank. A Ritto was grappling with—Liri? Blood roared in my ears until I realized the figure was taller than the kid, then everything snapped cold and still inside me.

The Threadmaster? Shit! What had we done to contain his specific threat of mind control? I began to run.

He was spitting and fighting, but the Ritto had him securely restrained as I skidded to a stop. No, no, my brain screamed. I didn't want to deal with this!

"Must help me," he cried. "Want claim sanctuary. Sanctuary! Is word?"

"How did you get here?" Did he already have control of the Ritto-ssa crew around me? How could I tell?

"Ported." He glanced about nervously as he tried to edge toward me. "Need you protect."

But the Endar controlled the Das and its teleports... "I can no protect." Not where I was going. I tried to walk past him.

"Humans must help me!"

"Why?" I just wanted to leave this world.

"Because me help you."

Help? Shit! "How?"

"Fix vote so Humans come here," he said.

That stopped me cold. "What?"

"Fix vote so Humans come here," he repeated. "Change Steyl order before Minders go home, tell members vote Humans yes."

A Ritto caught my arm as my knees tried to fold beneath me.

I clenched my teeth to keep from screaming in rage and frustration. I was so done with all this! Duff, the MoMo—someone else had to deal with it.

"Must go," the Ritto beside me said in its low, whispery voice.

How did I know if this ship and crew were even bound for the EA now?

"Must help me! Two people cannot go back Zam Fiella. Two people see, know Humans exist. Cannot return home. Cannot stay. Endiel will kill!"

It made terrible sense. Things had happened so fast. We had considered the effects of returning Liri's knowledge of things outside Zam Fiella back onto that world. How had we missed this serpent in the larger equation?

I couldn't abandon this dangerous being here. His action—if really meant to help us—was a major setback for the High Jerak, who was already in a rage over what he had agreed to in order to protect the Primacy from humiliation. And now, thanks to this viper, there would be a bright, sparkly EA delegation—ignorant of the Makima threat—which he could snug up to if he remained here.

My instincts screamed in protest. This was someone else's problem!

I could leave him, to disastrous effect, or take him with me and have some control over the slimy bastard, up to and including the option to slit his throat.

But I could never take him into the EA...

I forced a smile while my mind churned with confusion. "Then the Earth Alliance owes you our appreciation." Mother Universe, those words tasted bitter!

In that heartbeat of a second, I saw his eyes narrow and I knew: he hadn't acted for Human benefit. He was simply not accustomed to dealing with someone who could read his body language and expressions. He would remedy that quickly enough.

A Ritto touched his shoulder and he collapsed to the rough surface.

"Dangerous creature distresses you," the Ritto whispered. "What want do?"

Don't do it! It's over! My mind screamed in protest. I looked at the beings around me.

They were asking me.

"Can you put him in a SAC and bring him along?" I wanted to shout: say no! Tell me no and leave him here!

The Ritto made a gesture toward the hatch, which I took as assent, and I trudged on without looking back.

I was abandoning Lirilune, and trading Saurubi for a treacherous Makima asshole who wanted to destroy Humans.

There was no justice in the universe.

CHAPTER 55

The High Cost of Living

I came out of deep sleep without a whimper of nightmare.

Asleep. Awake. Just like that. No flashing dark.

I stared at the curved glass cover of the SAC, not sure how I felt about that. There was no furry blue face on the other side to reassure me things were okay. I didn't know if I wanted 'okay' if it meant losing those vivid memories of Anthy.

The SAC lid slid aside and I sat up.

I stared at the Frairy, dressed in a beautiful turquoise and gold saree, accessorized by pink paisley rubber boots, red ascot, and a bowler hat.

"Hey, Flygirl! Welcome back to life."

Thok.

"No," I said. I had prepared for hopeless devastation. This was worse. "Where am I and why are you here?"

"Zant. Listen—"

"No! You destroyed my life. I should kill you!" The last exclamation left my throat feeling a little raw. I paused to look around the large, shadowed dome. Nothing but support beams and piles of boxes. Not a place I'd ever been before. "Help!" I yelled as loud as my throat allowed.

"That's rude. This is His Frilliness' residence," Thok said patiently. "There's no one else here."

One of His Frilliness' under-ruffles rippled as he floated silently behind the Frairy in the dim light.

"Help!"

"Trust me, no one can hear you. If you listen, we can work this ou—"

"You can't hold me against my will. I demand you release me!"

"Look, we can fix this."

"Fix the loss of Saura? My wetware? The loss of my shipskins, awaysuit, the *Thief's Hand*? The kid? No! Help!"

"Okay," he sighed. "Not gonna fix things quite the way you want, but we can—"

"I demand to speak with an EA representative. Help!"

He shot me with a tranq dart.

***

I came to on the metal decking. Someone had extricated my body from the SAC, leaving me on my side with the container supporting my back.

"Don't make me shoot you again," Thok warned from where he stood several meters away. His Frilliness still floated behind him.

Compounding the ache in my head with another tranq dart seemed a bad idea. I pushed myself up to a sitting position. "What do you want?"

"You have some grievances. We understand." He raised his hands to stop my objection. "We'll address them. First, let me explain something. It's complicated, okay? So just shut up and listen.

"Ninety Sol-years before the Earth Alliance was invited into the Whooex Union of Stars, His Frilliness spotted what he thought was a Human in the company of an Endar in the street on a Mu Juad world—they get along, the Mu Juad and Endar—if you didn't know."

Of course they would. I stayed silent.

"Your people were off limit to Whooex member contact at the time, so it was a major concern. However, it was difficult to investigate the incident, the Primacy being as closed and unfriendly to certain original members as they are. Around that same time, the Proambu and their worldbuilding project got too close to Primacy space on the outer arm and stirred up the Endar, who were on the brink of declaring war for no apparent reason."

I knew the reason.

"It just happened the Proambu were on the verge of revising their model of worldbuilding. Spurred by Endar hostility, they shifted their attention away from that area of space and moved on with their projects. Later, when Human membership in the Whooex Union came up, the Endar were so violently opposed to it that the idea of them collaborating with Humans seemed outrageous and the earlier incident fell in priority and remained uninvestigated.

"If the Primacy had let things subside with the Proambu, everything would have faded to obscurity. But they didn't. They kept up their aggressive stance and drew attention to that region of space. His Frilliness felt compelled to investigate and found Zam Fiella, a world occupied by what appeared to be a Human colony, just inside the edge of the Primacy, in an area of space the Earth Alliance did not have the ability to reach at that time.

"Had the Endar illegally snatched a Human population to seed a world? We—well, the MoMo—wanted to explore the genetic link between the two peoples, but it was not a top priority and stirring up an overly aggressive old enemy seemed ill advised. His Frilliness decided to monitor the situation from time to time.

"When the Endar presence on the world suddenly and sharply increased, His Frilliness took a renewed interest. Discovering the Makima were telepathic, he made discreet contact with them. The general population are gentle souls, but there are a few individuals in leadership positions that fit right in with the Endar Primacy's attitude of superiority and control. Those people, along with members of the general population, began to disappear to some unknown off-world destination. It was obvious the Primacy was up to something. Then came our little girl, Lirilune, and High Jerak Seok's arrival on Zam Fiella. Laboratories sprang up and suddenly there were nurseries of beautiful babies, all with the same sweet little face. Meanwhile, Seok was keeping Lirilune under his tight control. It was time to investigate Primacy activity. Our Makima contacts on Zam Fiella agreed."

The Frairy's expression darkened. "Clearly, with their particular talents, these people's existence was not something the Endar wanted exposed and we needed to explore the link between Makima and Humans. Getting Lirilune's family off world was a real bitch. The Makima had limited space travel in the past. We had to dredge up one of their junk ships and quietly restore it to space-worthiness. It could never have made a journey beyond Idwal, however. That's why we arranged for you and catgirl to pick up three people, Lirilune's family, and take them to the Jian Jian Research Facility."

My mind flashed to our third cabin, packed from deck to ceiling with foodstuffs.

"Yeah, you get it." He looked smug as he straightened his ascot. "They were going to participate in a multi-species study into their genetics. It was their choice," he added when I narrowed my eyes. "No mad scientists like in your Old Earth videos.

"You and Catgirl were our best option to facilitate this. You had skills and compassion, but we knew there was no way you would agree to do it, so we arranged things so you had no choice. We had to put a hard squeeze on your buddy, Scriver, if that makes you feel better.

"Anyway, I don't need to tell you how things went badly. Luckily, Ritto-ssa and Proambu trade together and we had arranged for a

Ritto-ssa ship in the area for backup, just in case. The Endar wouldn't dare challenge them in Proambu space."

And Lirilune's family had paid the cost, I thought angrily. "You knew there was a risk people might die?"

"There was a certain level of danger, yes, but our Makima contacts were willing to accept it. You Humans, of all species, understand risk-taking."

"The Endar killed Lirilune's family! They tried to kill me. The Primacy nearly took control of the Trade Consortium because of your manipulation! And now, because of your stupid, ill-conceived activities, the kid can't go back to her world, the Makima have an army of mind-manipulating clones, and the Tabisee have taken Saura!"

"Zant. This will all work out—"

"Work out?" I surged forward and managed to get a firm grip on the red ascot. I twisted it, burying my knuckles into the flesh of his throat, against his windpipe.

"Stop," he choked, trying to push my hand away.

"Save your air," I snarled, twisting harder.

Something brushed my arm.

All the muscles in my body went numb and I collapsed, the hand caught in the Frairy's neckcloth the only thing saving me from head trauma.

Damned cloudhead!

"Sheesh!" Thok disengaged my fingers and lowered me to my side again. "We knew they were telepaths. We knew the Endar had a lab on Zam Fiella and were experimenting with the cloning process. But no one warned us of Lirilune's special abilities." He had the consideration to sit down on the floor nearby so I could see him. "Were we played by the Makima? Maybe."

I struggled to form words, but my muscles refused to respond. Shit! So many questions and no way to ask them!

"Oh," he mocked my frustration. "You don't understand why the EA and the MoMo are intensely interested in a seemingly estranged Human colony out on the edge of nowhere. Well, Flygirl, it didn't take long for us to figure out that they're not Human.

"Now, here's the really curious thing; they haven't been on that world for as long as they claim, though they've made it look that way. We think the Endar just don't know enough about Human civilization to detect the anomaly."

That was enough to stop all my efforts at freeing my locked jaws. Now I was listening intently.

"Yeah, they come from somewhere else. We think probably across the void from the next galactic arm. And maybe they're not lost. Maybe they're an exploratory probe. There is only one reason a civilization sends out an exploratory probe, right? To assess the potential for expansion. Is that good or bad? I don't know. You heard the Primacy's plan. You're a bright girl." He patted my head and the lock on my muscles released. "What do you think?"

I sucked a gasp of air and sat up. "They're willing to let the Primacy do their dirty work to conquer the Whooex Union," I said.

"There's hope for you yet."

Memory suddenly pushed through my hostility and anger. "The Threadmaster! Where is he?"

"We placed him in the care of the Proambu."

"Why? He's my one bit of proof the EA is under serious threat!"

"Do you think the EA is up to handling him?"

After everything I'd just heard? "No." My heart rate was beginning to level off.

"Neither do we—think we can handle him, that is. We put someone in charge of him who can."

"The Proambu? How?"

"For one thing, the instrument of their sentience is different than the rest of us, making it unlikely he can manipulate them. And they have no interest in achieving more power. "

"What did they do with him?"

He grinned. "He's got a world all his own."

The grin broadened at my blank expression. "You are aware of what the Proambu do, right?"

"Disassemble and reassemble planets into ringworlds. They wouldn't give him a whole ring."

"Actually, I did mention they moved on from that. Their Dyson model is a bit different now." He waited for me to mentally catch up with him. "They found an easier way to do things, which is why they left Idwal Platform in place instead of moving it. It's easier for them to shift an entire planet to a stable star and place it inside its habitable zone, than to move the material and reassemble everything. It takes a lot less time, and if they want a different type of world, they just set the planet's revolution a different distance from the star. Your Threadmaster friend has a whole world all to himself."

I opened my mouth. Shut it.

"They recognize a threat when they see one," he said.

"What about Zam Fiella? The clones? And Liri said there were more Threadmasters."

"Most of the Threadmasters were returned, though we suspect the Endar held a few back, along with some telepaths. We'll have to address that eventually. The clones were too young to take off world. Our contacts among the Makima have agreed to care for them. And to keep them under observation. Meanwhile, Zam Fiella is isolated from outside contact and the Proambu are prepared to enforce it. You can appreciate that, can't you?"

Quarantine? Hell yes! "But the Makima—"

"Jeez, Zant, stop being such a crusader! They'll be fine, and the rest of us will be even better. Now get up, because we have a lot of work to do."

"We?"

"You, me, His Frilliness—"

No. Not we.

"—First Astrogator Cerros Syrhas..."

"Saurubi?" I froze, one knee still on the floor.

He shrugged. "The Tabi have always had an eye on the future. Which brings us to you. The outcome of this gig ended pretty well considering how badly you botched it."

I made a choking sound, which he ignored.

"We need a Human who knows the straight on things, and you are reasonably competent. It's easier than finding, recruiting, and convincing another one of your people that the universe is a big, bad place."

"You could have tried doing that with me from the start!"

"We weren't completely sure of everything back then. Besides, you wouldn't have signed on. It took a threat to the kid to get you fully engaged."

That was true: I might never have stepped up if Lirilune hadn't been under threat. It had offered me a chance to achieve a tiny bit of absolution for Anthy's death...

My face burned with shame. Was I that selfish, that I had only acted out of an altruistic sense of guilt over my little brother's death?

The anger at the MoMo and Thok drained away.

"Relax, Zant, you made some decent decisions." He offered me a hand up. "Nothing blew up in your face."

I still resented the whole situation, but the "we" had me hooked and he knew it. Ignoring his hand, I climbed to my feet. "What about Saura?" I asked.

"The Tabi military and their political structure, along with certain other members of the Union, are currently getting an update on the situation. Need-to-know, of course. Select individuals in the EA are also aware."

"Saura," I repeated.

"Tabi-sanctioned part of the team. On her way here now."

"What team? We lost our ship. We lost our shipskins, our away suits, my wetware..."

"First, that tin can ship of yours was never lost. It was only waiting for your return. And your gear is an easy replacement."

"My wetware—"

"Give me your left arm," he said.

"Why?" I had only recently gotten it back, and I didn't feel like putting it at risk again. "The Xix didn't—"

"Give it!"

I reluctantly extended the arm.

His short fingers flicked lightly over the surface of my exposed skin.

"The Xix didn't..." I began again. My wrist and forearm tingled and grew warmer. "What are you—?"

Pain shot along my nerves, up to my shoulder and neck. A blast of light inside my brain blanked my vision and sent me staggering back a step. I stood there, stunned, my left forearm burning like fire. I looked down to see an unfamiliar pattern beneath my skin. Unfamiliar in configuration, but marked with Human symbols that I recognized.

There were more contact points than there should have been. More than EA military wetware.

"That could have been done better," I observed weakly.

Thok grunted. "Sheesh! Stop whining."

"Why's it look different?"

"The Xix misunderstood and installed the newest version of Whooex wetware instead of your old junk. The EA doesn't have this tech yet, which means you have to be discreet. Certain individuals objected, but it's too late now."

"It works the same as the original EA version?"

"Better. It gives you added access to certain things. We'll discuss that later."

"I had this the whole time?" My anger started to boil up.

"The High Jerak interrupted things at the hospital before the Xix could activate it. Which turned out to be a good thing, since you gettin' cocky on Rhom coulda' got you killed."

I needed a moment to stop and consider everything.

He waited.

"Why can't the kid mindspeak me?"

"Because your language hardware occupies those necessary receptors in your brain. Telepathy can't get in. It's that way for all Human hardware implants. The MoMo recognized you people were trouble enough without that skill a long time ago."

"But the High Jerak..."

"Thought Lirilune was the prototype for the Primacy's destruction of Humans? He based that on early experiments, on some remote colonists they snatched before Humans became Whooex members. He was wrong. For a successful Human invasion, that is. He can use the Makima to manipulate other members and to isolate the EA, though."

"We're not telepathic."

"Given the right situation everyone is. Hence the precautionary hardware. Catgirl heard the kid out at Idwal."

Saura had told me that. "This is all great and everything—though I'm still pissed and I sure as hell don't intend to thank you since you got us into this—but no one does anything for free. What do you want?"

He smirked. "We need someone to work with us. Occasionally," he added when I opened my mouth to protest. "We're not demanding exclusivity. And you'll work through a contact in the EA. I can't swear you'll never see us again, though, no matter what you'd prefer." He started to walk toward an exit port.

I stayed firmly in place. "And if I say no?"

He stopped. "We'll deactivate some features in your wetware. You can have your stuff, your ship—the title's clear in gratitude for your service—and a sincere thank you. We'll find First Astrogator Cerros Syrhas a new partner inside our organization."

My eyes flicked over him. No bandages covering wounds from pulling this stunt on her? Maybe he had healed in the time it took to get my SAC from the Ritto-ssa. Or her orders had officially come down from the top.

"She's already in? The Tabi are good with this?"

"They were good with things when they loaned her to the Earth Alliance Space Marines. They didn't complain when she developed an affinity for a Human idiot and decided to stick around."

That explained a few things. "And the kid?"

He cleared his throat. "That's another issue."

My heart jerked up into my throat. "She's happy? She's got people who want her and love her?"

"She could have better."

"What do you mean?" Apprehension rushed through me.

"She's not just some kid we can drop into a family. Someone will eventually notice something odd and come sniffing around. We have to put her in the care of people who can be trusted with knowing what she is. Someone whose brain she can't influence, and who stays on the move."

"You mean us?"

"No one else is volunteering."

For me, it sounded great, but how would Saura react?

The door slid open behind him and she strode in, dressed in cobalt blue shipskins, her dusky fur puffed out below the cuffs, and above the collar, giving her the appearance of a skinny, half-drowned cat.

She looked ridiculous and wonderful.

"Idiot!" she snapped. "Tired of waiting! Make decision!"

I already had. "One last thing." I turned to Duff. "Why work with us? Why Humans?

"Because you moralistic, preachy, nosey, interfering, curious, bold idiots are always running around, trying to make things better."

Like the Ritto said: shouting at the universe.

Okay. "And the Tabi?"

"Because those sons of bitches don't mess around. They know how to keep a focus on the big picture and get the job done."

That sounded right. I smiled at Saura. "I'm in. Where's Liri?"

"Locked in third cabin considering new ship rules. Now move! Must do training on wetware before we can leave!" She turned and swept back out the door.

"By the way," I said to Thok before following her. "What is this organization of yours called?'

"The MoMo call it the Curious Fifty-two, for their numbers."

Fifty-two interfering Oulunsk, or MoMos? Could the Whooex Union survive that?

I had to ask one more thing. "What does MoMo translate to?"

He grinned. "Something like, One who Sets the Universe Right."

"They think they're Gods?"

"Nah. They just like to level the playing field."

I nodded thoughtfully. "Yeah."

Maybe we could help them.

End

ACKNOWLEDGEMENTS

My writing journey began a long time ago and, though there were times when I could not devote time to the process, it was always present at the edge of my mind, like puzzle pieces turning to fit the whole. There are people that kept me moving forward along the way, from my high school friend, Brenda Kirk, to Joan Summers, to the members of our local writing critique group, past and present, the SKY Writers. I would not have been so bold as to believe I could do this without your inspiration, especially those of you who published before me. And then there's Sam, my loving husband who was always there to support me with anything I needed to get the job done.

I sincerely thank you all.

Bobbie Falin lives in Bowling Green, KY with four friendly stray cats who stop by for breakfast and dinner every day. She began to write novels on cocktail napkins as a waitress while earning a BA in art education from Western KY University. Now she spends her time writing science fiction and fantasy. She reads voraciously, dabbles in 3D art, gardens and collects beautiful images of all sorts on Pinterest. If there was a space program to explore the stars, she'd be first in line.